THE CRIMSON FATHERS

THE CRIMSON FATHERS

A DEIPARIAN SAGA NOVEL

J. TODD KINGREA

Livonia, Michigan

THE CRIMSON FATHERS
Copyright © 2022 J. Todd Kingrea

All rights reserved. No part of this publication may be reproduced, distributed, or transmitted in any form or by any means, including photocopying, recording, or other electronic or mechanical methods, without the prior written permission of the publisher, except in the case of brief quotations embodied in critical reviews and certain other noncommercial uses permitted by copyright law. For permission requests, please write to the publisher.

This book is a work of fiction. The characters, incidents, and dialogue are drawn from the author's imagination and are not to be construed as real. Any resemblance to actual events or persons, living or dead, is entirely coincidental.

Published by BHC Press

Library of Congress Control Number: 2021944529

ISBN Numbers:
978-1-64397-319-7 (Hardcover)
978-1-64397-320-3 (Softcover)
978-1-64397-321-0 (Ebook)

For information, write:
BHC Press
885 Penniman #5505
Plymouth, MI 48170

Visit the publisher:
www.bhcpress.com

To my dear childhood friend, Joaquin Bowen.
I miss you and can only imagine what we would've done
with a story like this during our *Dungeons & Dragons*
sessions back in the early 1980s!
Thank you for so many wonderful memories.
Rest in peace, my friend.

And to my grandparents, Howard & Eleanor Hunter—
you always encouraged and supported me in everything I tried.
I still feel your loss.
I love you.

THE CRIMSON FATHERS

1
SOUTHWEST

SATURDAY, AUGUST 1, 999 AE

Malachi Thorne squinted into the broiling white anger of the sun, set against a multihued blue sky devoid of clouds.

"Last chance, Thorne," the man below him said. "You come peaceful, I let you live. If not, I kill you."

Thorne turned his head and looked down. He was more than ten feet off the ground. The muscular arms of Thorne's captor held aloft his six-foot-three frame as easily as a normal man might raise a shovel over his head. Massive hands supported his shoulders and lower spine. He felt like a turtle flipped on its back.

"Piss off," he grunted through bloody lips.

The man below him snorted and lumbered forward to build momentum. With a snarl of exertion, he hurled Thorne through the air. He collided with the weak and ruined wall of what had once been a small house. As Thorne crashed through it, he carried termite-riddled timber, dust and plaster chips with him. What remained of the wall creaked and shuddered.

The giant appeared in what was left of the doorway.

The wall groaned again. Bits of the ceiling rained down. The remnants of the wall swayed with a deep grinding noise and crashed down on Thorne. The ceiling shed more wood and plaster before caving in. Thorne lay beneath the pile of debris, coughing dust from his lungs.

The giant wiped sweat from his face. At least seven feet tall with shoulders the length of a barrel, his arms were still too long for his body, giving him a simian aspect. He wore dark breeches and sandals but no shirt, only a leather vest. Coarse, wiry hair covered him. It curled on his arms, sprouted from his chest, carpeted his shoulders. The majority of his face lay buried beneath wild, uncut hair and a beard the size of a badger. He carried a coil of rope.

Thorne groaned. Every part of him ached.

"Let's go, Witchfinder. Up," the man said. He waited with arms crossed.

Thorne pushed aside the rotted timbers and detritus and wiped dirt from his eyes. He sat up. His long black hair hung in sweaty strands around his shoulders. He wiped blood and dust from his mustache and goatee. Minor cuts oozed blood, and bruises darkened on his arms. His tunic was ripped in several places, as were his breeches. Sitting amid the debris, he looked like a pauper after a windstorm.

"Who are you?" Thorne asked as he spat blood.

"They call me Mathan the Bear. Claiming the bounty on you," the giant rumbled beneath a mustache two fingers wide.

"What?" Thorne shook his head and sent fragments of wood flying from his hair. "Bounty? What bounty?"

Mathan had not moved. He stood several feet away, eyeing his prey with caution. "Five hundred silver coins for you alive. Two hundred and fifty for you dead."

Thorne glanced around. What remained of the room was empty except for the debris in which he sat. His fingers felt around under the pile for anything he could use as a weapon. They found the handle of his dagger, which had been knocked out of his boot when he went through the wall.

He let his head and shoulders droop. Through the strands of his hair, he saw Mathan uncoiling the rope. "Who issued the bounty?" He tried to make his voice sound weak. It was not difficult.

"Witchfinder Imperator Zadicus Rann."

Thorne sneered. His cheeks flushed with rage. It was an instinctual reaction when he heard that name. He gripped the dagger beneath the debris.

"Stand up. Slowly," Mathan commanded.

Thorne struggled to his knees, then to his feet. He kept his right hand at his side, the dagger pointed away from the bounty hunter. Rann's smug face swam before his eyes. One way or another, he was going to kill Rann. Not because of the bounty—although that infuriated him as well—but because of what had happened to his mentor, Valerian Merrick.

A month and a half ago, Thorne had watched, helpless, as Zadicus Rann disemboweled Merrick. He had done it merely to torment Thorne. Rann had almost succeeded in executing Thorne and his friends, but they had been rescued by Teska Vaun and other members of the witch cult, the Enodia Communion.

Mathan stepped forward. "Don't move. I can break your spine with one punch."

Thorne crouched like a whipped dog.

"Hands behind your—"

Thorne dove into a forward roll and came up in a crouch beside the giant. Mathan stopped, surprised at the unexpected move.

Thorne sliced the giant's left leg just behind the ankle. The dagger slipped through the flesh and severed the tendon. Mathan's bellow of pain came with the blood.

The bounty hunter swung at Thorne, but he rolled out of range.

The Bear tried to pivot, forgetting his left foot was useless. Blood pooled in the dirt and dust. He almost collapsed as he fumbled his own dagger free.

Thorne advanced on him from behind. Raising his foot, he smashed his heel down onto the exposed tendon. Mathan screamed like all the souls in all Twelve Hells. He toppled forward. Only a wall prevented him from falling to the floor. Tears streamed down his pale cheeks. He tried to speak, but the words dissolved in another bellow of pain. He braced himself against the wall and brandished his dagger.

"I'm just…the first of many." His features twisted with hate. "Your days are numbered, Witchfinder." With a ferocious war cry, he lunged at his opponent.

Thorne guessed that the Bear intended to gut him or at least pin him to the floor.

Mathan did not get the chance to do either.

Thorne leapt forward and wrapped his arms around Mathan's right leg. Once again, Thorne's blade sliced through sandal, flesh and tendon.

Even with Thorne around his leg, the giant's momentum carried them outside. Mathan hit the brittle yellow grass like a crippled horse. He screamed in agony, and his writhing kicked up clouds of dust.

Thorne rolled away and paused to catch his breath.

"Oh shit, oh fuck," Mathan said, gasping. "Damn you to hells! Oh shit, oh shit." He managed to sit up and stared at his feet. They lay at odd angles against his legs.

"How many more?" Thorne asked. He stood over the bounty hunter but well out of range of those apelike arms.

"Wh-What?" Mathan glared at Thorne through narrow, watery eyes. "Fuck you!"

"How many more bounty hunters?" Thorne knelt at Mathan's feet. Their eyes locked.

"How. Many." He grabbed a foot and twisted. "More?"

Mathan's shriek startled a nest of birds in a nearby cottonwood tree. Sweat stood out on his pallid cheeks. His breath came in hitching gasps.

"T-T-Two. Maybe th-three." His head rolled to one side, and he fell back on the ground.

After several minutes—and making sure that the Bear was unconscious—Thorne knelt beside the body. He thought about Rann and the bounty. The fury built within him once more. One day soon, his nemesis would pay for everything he had done. Picturing Rann's smug face, Thorne slit Mathan's throat. He wiped the dagger on the bounty hunter's vest. Being killed while unconscious was a better death than the one he would have been dealt by the Bear.

Thorne stood on weak legs and looked around, suddenly aware of how exposed he felt. The ramshackle houses—mostly just crumbling walls and desiccated wood—stood in rows along the street. A su-burb, the place had once been called. Now it was just the decaying evidence of a long-lost world. Thorne retrieved his sword from where Mathan had clubbed it from his grip.

He walked down the street, sword in hand. Weeds and saplings reached through the ash-colored hardtop. He kept to the center, scanning both sides of the street for any sign of movement.

He had wandered into this su-burb by accident. He had been walking and thinking when Mathan jumped him. Thorne cursed himself again for his lack of vigilance. It had nearly cost him his life. He was lucky. But you could not survive in this strange land by luck alone. He knew he needed to reclaim the attentiveness and discipline that had made him a feared Witchfinder Imperator. That seemed like a lifetime ago. But it had only been two months.

Malachi Thorne, Teska Vaun and Thurl Cabbott had left the village of Saintgen, south of Last Chapel, the day after they had buried Valerian Merrick. They traveled south along the Black River. To the west lurked the Devouring Lands, a waste teeming with mystery and death. No one knew how big the Devouring Lands were, just as Thorne had no idea what route to take to get to the land of the Tex'ahns.

Thorne intended to visit the Tex'ahns and learn more about the concept of freedom—an idea that Merrick had paid for with his life. If he was to take up Merrick's mantle, he felt he could only do so by spending time among the people who had influenced his mentor.

Teska came with him, not only because their relationship kept them together, but because she had a special task of her own. The Enodia Communion had sent her west to discover and train more Nahoru'brexia—a new kind of witch with unique abilities. However, she knew from Maiden Mallumo, the Witch of Darkness, that this quest had not been well received by many of the older members of the Communion. They resented the younger ones with their individual supernatural gifts. No one knew where these manifestations came from, although many speculated they originated with Hecate herself. Why the younger witches had these abilities, while the older ones did not, was cause for simmering animosity and jealousy.

Cabbott came along for their protection, not to mention his life was just as forfeit in their homeland of Deiparia as Thorne and Teska's.

They had followed the river until it emptied into the Arkan Sea just north of Baymouth. Turning southwest, they skirted the edge of the Devouring Lands. The terrain varied little from that of their homeland. They climbed hills and crossed meadows and vast fields that once likely produced fine crops but were now shaggy with trees and undergrowth. They navigated through forests of ancient spruce, pine, post oak and mimosa with their pale pink blossoms. Everywhere, they saw the remains of the world that used to be.

Ruined, skeletal dwellings and buildings—once part of the pre-Cataclysm world—were everywhere. Walls lay where they had fallen centuries ago, blanketed with kuzda vines, the invasive but useful plant that seemed all but indestructible. The pale gray roads—buckled, crumbling and overtaken by weeds—often contained the wasted metallic shells of peculiar conveyances. None of the three had ever seen anything like them. They appeared to have had four spots to attach wheels, but there was no place to hook a team of horses. Doors often stood open, showing rotted benches within. On the front, beneath a flat square sheet of metal, sat a mechanical contraption of blocks and pipes that defied explanation.

They had occasional encounters with wild dogs—but mercifully no hellhounds—and saw countless human skeletons along the roads and inside the buildings. Game was plentiful, and they often had squirrel, rabbit and deer. Water, too, was luckily not an issue, but the wicked summer heat of Deiparia, smothering and relentless, ruled these lands.

At night, they had talked of Merrick's crusade for freedom and what Malachi hoped to find and learn in the Tex'ahn lands. They spoke of the Church of the Deiparous and the emergence of the Fifth Order, as well as the invisible God that Merrick claimed the Tex'ahn's followed. They had kept watch each night, unsure of what dangers lurked around them. Yet they had encountered no other living humans since leaving the shoreline of the Arkan Sea. They were cognizant that each day took them farther beyond the boundaries of Deiparia, deeper into the unknown.

Malachi and Teska's relationship grew over the weeks they traveled together. Teska had feared that Thorne would turn out to be like all her other lovers, abusing her for personal gain. But he was considerate and kind in a way she could never have imagined when he was a Witchfinder Imperator. It was as if his excommunication had released him from unseen burdens, like a beetle leaving behind the husk of its old self. A whole new man was emerging before her eyes.

But their affection for one another did not blind them to the changes in Thurl Cabbott. Once Thorne's constable and trusted friend, the sixty year old had grown quiet and withdrawn. He slept little, often sitting watch the whole night so that Thorne and Teska could rest. Thurl no longer joked with Malachi like he once did, and on occasion they had caught him staring at them with a peculiar gleam in his eyes. When they asked him about these things, he shook his head, saying his near-death experience in Last Chapel had affected him more deeply than he first thought.

"Concentrate," Teska Vaun said to the young woman across the table from her.

Amelia Sloan closed her eyes and wrinkled her petite nose.

"Repeat the phrase."

"Sestre Tuga, venas sercanta vin'ahd,

Motika pagnanha malaman'ahd,

Matronis, Matka, Maag'deh, venas sercanta vin'ahd."

"Nice," Teska whispered. "Keep at it. You've got the hang of it." She stood, stretched and walked to the window. She eased open one of the shutters and looked out at nothing.

Amelia's simple three-room house hunched in the middle of a dusty plain, in an area that had once been called Richland Hills, although Teska could not understand why. There were no hills to be seen. Anywhere. The land was as flat as a sword blade, the horizon broken only by a few buildings that refused to collapse. The cabin was a half-day's ride west of Dallastown, and the closest village was a windswept speck called Hirst seven miles away in a sea of prairie grass. Besides a barn and the fallow fields nearby, the hardscrabble ground receded into the hint of mountain ridges far to the west.

Teska was frustrated. After three weeks, Amelia was the only witch she had found. She turned around, leaned against the wall and watched the woman.

Amelia Sloan was twenty-five—three years older than Teska—and a few inches taller but thinner in the shoulders. Freckles dotted the bridge of her nose, cheeks and forearms. She wore her blonde hair loose down her back, the sides swept behind her head and tied in place. She wore a simple blue dress and dusty black button-up shoes. She continued to intone the invitation, her voice like gossamer.

Teska waited another minute. "Anything?"

Amelia opened her eyes—azure irises flecked with teal—and slowly shook her head. "Maybe you've got the wrong person?"

"Nah," Teska said. "You're Nahoru'brexia."

"What's that mean again?" Her voice had a pleasant drawl.

Teska returned to her chair. "It means that you and I—and others like us—are a special breed of brexia. Witches. The Three-Who-Are-One believe we are the future of the Enodia Communion."

"But why me?"

Teska shrugged. "Hells, why any of us? Who knows? It's just something we're born with. I've told you about my gift. Every Nahoru'brexia has one. Yours, you say—"

"I can see in the dark. Just like it was daytime." She smiled, and her face lit up.

Teska knew how good it felt to be able to tell someone who understood. She saw the relief on Amelia's face.

Amelia leaned forward, elbows on the table. "So if I'm Nahoru'brexia, why can't I, you know, contact *them*?" She whispered the last word and glanced around the room.

"It takes time," Teska said with more confidence than she felt. She was still new to all of this, too. She had only learned about the Nahoru'brexia a little over a month ago. And then her education had been interrupted when the Fifth Order took Last Chapel. She felt as if she knew as little about all of it as she did about bricklaying. Yet here she was in the middle of nowhere, trying to convince this woman she was qualified to teach her.

How did I get myself into this shit?

But she knew all too well. She just did not want to think about it. Even after all this time, she could still smell the musky stench of the serpents that had cocooned and constricted her at the Maiden's command.

"Would you like something to drink?" Amelia asked as she stood up.

Teska nodded. Her curly red hair bounced. "Yeah, that'd be good."

Amelia walked to the other side of the room that served as the kitchen. "I have water, of course. I can make some tea. I'm afraid I don't have any alcohol."

"Tea's good."

While Amelia worked, Teska looked around the room. The cabin had a high ceiling with a loft over the bedroom. There was only one door inside, which led to the bedroom. Three windows, two at the front and one near the fireplace in the back, were shuttered against the heat and blowing dust. Everything smelled of pine, wood smoke and dried meat.

"So you say you and your husband settled here," Teska said.

"That's right. Alec believed he could farm this land. He was determined." She stopped for a moment and looked through the back window. "He had it in his head that he was going to grow wheat and cotton here. He tried, sure enough. But it wasn't meant to be. Soil's too bad."

"How long you been here?"

Her voice was softer and despondent. "Alec built us this house two years ago. We moved out here then."

"If you don't mind me asking, what happened to him?" Teska had an idea. She had been around enough men to know how often they ran out.

"He passed away. At the end of April."

That was not what Teska had expected. Her apology sounded thin even to her own ears.

Amelia offered a wistful smile. "Thank you."

"How long were you married?"

"Five years."

For a moment neither spoke. Amelia continued to make tea.

"I, uh—I've had some shitty luck with men. Never have found what you found."

Now it was Amelia's turn to apologize.

Teska brushed it aside. "It's all right. There's a guy now…"

Amelia turned around with two wooden cups in hand. "What's he like?" she asked, expectation in her voice. She sat a cup on the table in front of Teska and took a drink from her own. Her eyes shone with excitement.

"He's, ah… Well, we've only been together for a little while."

"Do you love him?" Amelia asked over the rim of her cup.

Teska smiled, the dimples in her cheeks deepening. She blushed. "Yeah. Yeah, I do."

Amelia had not stopped smiling. "And does he feel the same about you?"

Teska nodded, her blush intensifying.

"How wonderful for you!" Amelia took another drink and set the cup down, her blue eyes reflecting the light. "Teska, you enjoy every moment. Cherish every little thing. Because it's the little things that matter most. If you love him and he loves you, don't you let nothing keep the two of you apart."

Teska raised her cup and took a drink. The tea was sweet and cold.

She was still getting used to this Tex'ahn beverage called sweet tea. When they first arrived in this barren and windswept land, they had been given cups of the stuff. After her first sip, Teska had spit it back in the cup. "This shit's cold as a well digger's ass," she had exclaimed. Their hosts had been perplexed. Thorne, Teska and Cabbott had explained that they were accustomed to hot tea and did not have sweet tea back in Deiparia.

The Tex'ahns made it from kuzda leaves since there was plenty of it to go around, and they drank it all the time. They made it by pouring hot water into a pitcher of cold water with sugar and stirring it together. Teska had asked why the hot water was needed. Why not just put the sugar in the cold water? "Because a cup of cold water with grit floatin' in the bottom ain't sweet tea," she had been told. "You *taste* the sugar. You don't *see* it." The tea had the slightly bitter aftertaste that was common with kuzda leaves, but Teska had to admit it was refreshing in this scorching, humid climate.

"Sweet tea's a staple around here," Amelia said. "It's been around forever. Our history-tellers say it goes back way before Judgment Day."

Teska frowned. "Judgment Day?"

"When God judged the Earth."

Teska shook her head.

"The moon falling. All the natural disasters. The radiation."

Merrick had told them about the radiation. Before he was murdered.

"Oh, you mean the Great Cataclysm."

"Is that what your people call it?" Amelia asked.

Teska nodded and pushed a strand of hair behind her ear. "Why'd you say that God judged the earth?"

Amelia refilled their cups and told her the story.

Thurl Cabbott was losing his mind. He could think of no other explanation.

He sat outside the livery on a wooden boardwalk that ran along the front of the main buildings in Dallastown. People passed by on errands of one sort or another. The street, still identified as Shady Grove by a twisted and faded sign at one intersection, served as Dallastown's main thoroughfare. The original city a few miles east had been all but obliterated by a lunar fragment during the Great Cataclysm. A crater marked the spot, and nothing grew within a half mile of it. The soil was a putrid greenish gray and no one ventured there.

Cabbott stared at a man leading a horse down the street, a rickety wagon squeaking along behind. The longer he stared, the clearer he could see. It felt like staring through a tunnel.

His vision had been like this since Last Chapel. Sometimes he could see well; other times, like now, he had to concentrate and focus in order to make out details. It was as if he were seeing through someone else's eyes that he couldn't control.

Losing my mind, he thought.

That must also be the reason he had memories that were not his own. At least he assumed they were memories. In his mind's eye, they were never clear, like trying to see through fog. For weeks, he had been unable to identify a single thing in any of them. Recently there seemed to be more of them.

On top of that, he had gaps of missing time he could not account for. It happened most often during the day. He was unable to remember where he had been or what he was doing. He was grateful that Thorne and Teska did not seem to notice. He said nothing about it, of course. He did not want them to think that he was insane.

The elderly often lost their grip on reality—talking to loved ones who were no longer there, seeing things that no one else could see, forgetting simple things. Was that what was happening to him? Was he becoming old and senile? He sometimes wondered if maybe it would have been better if he had died in Last Chapel. Because he did not like whatever was going on.

His body felt heavy. He needed to sleep. That happened more frequently now, too. Not wanting to fight it, he leaned back in the chair and closed his eyes. Immediately the darkness enfolded him.

Thurl Cabbott sat on the boardwalk, watching people come and go with keen interest and a peculiar glint in his eyes.

2
NORTHEAST

SUNDAY, AUGUST 2, 999 AE

"I've got to find Cassidy and Cassandra. We must keep going." Dario Darien looked at the two men in the cell with him. He ran a trembling hand through his wooly gray hair. "We've got to go on to the Citadel."

Tycho Hawkes sat down beside Darien and laid a hand on the old man's shoulder. "Hey, we'll find them. Don't get worked up. It's not good for your heart."

"We're close. I know it." Darien paused, licked his lips and said in an almost inaudible voice, "We *have* to be. It's been so long."

"Maybe you oughta get some rest," Solomon Warner suggested. While Darien's skin was the color of a caramel apple, Warner's was like the night sky. He was short and solid with broad arms. A strip of cloth was wrapped around his bald head and obscured his left eye. He had lost it while attempting to arrest Teska Vaun a few years ago. The story behind the injury, and Hawkes's nickname for him—"Jester"—went back to that day. He used the cloth to hide the empty socket.

Hawkes nodded and patted Darien's shoulder. "That's a good idea. Why don't you try to rest now?"

The old man mumbled under his breath but lay down on the mildew-speckled straw pallet. Within moments, his breathing slowed. He snored softly.

Hawkes returned to his pallet beside Warner. He sat cross-legged and sighed.

"He's gettin' worse," Warner said as he rubbed the stubble on his chin. "And he's right. We gotta keep lookin'."

"Hells, I know that," Hawkes said louder than he intended. Darien snorted and rolled over, his back toward them. Hawkes lowered his voice. "You got any ideas on how to get us out of this?" He gestured at the bars.

The trio occupied one of eight cells that made up that wing of the Kithanink jail. Each cell contained three or four men. Mumbled conversations floated through the stuffy air that reeked of body odor and human waste.

Warner shook his head. "No. But they gotta let us out soon, right? I mean, they can't hold us forever. It's been two days already. Why ain't we been able to see a Witchfinder? Or even a lawyer?"

"I'd guess it has something to do with the Fifth Order. They're pretty much in charge of everything now," Hawkes said.

The existence of the Fifth Order was now common knowledge. The Church had released a statement that the Four Orders would henceforth answer to the Fifth rather than to the Heiromonarch. Congregants were assured that little would change in their daily lives. It had been a quiet, smooth and, most importantly, bloodless transition of power. The majority could have cared less since new jobs were being offered. But it soon became apparent that something dark and monstrous had taken over the realm.

Darien, Hawkes and Warner had been arrested on Friday, on the road to the Citadel of the Crimson Fathers, just north of Three Waters. They had been crammed into a foul-smelling wagon with several other captives and brought to the jail. Formal charges had yet to be filed—an obvious oversight to anyone well versed in Deiparian law.

Dario Darien had nearly twenty years' experience as a clerk in the Cartulian Order, the arm of the Church of the Deiparous responsible for record keeping, historical documents and the general day-to-day governance of the realm. Hawkes and Warner had served as deputies in the Paracletian Order, the Church's legal branch. That is, until they had been labeled heretics and traitors along with their mentor, Thurl Cabbott, and the man they were assigned to protect, Malachi Thorne. Darien had once known just about everything regarding the law. Before his trauma.

In a frantic effort to uncover the truth about his brother-in-law's death, Darien had made a pact with a witch. Her magic helped him, but it came at a staggering price. Forty years had been added to his life. He was now eighty—actually eighty-one since his birthday was two weeks ago. His health and mental acuity deteriorated more with each passing day. Even so, he held on with stubborn determination, driven by the need to find his niece and nephew.

Warner stood up and stretched. He put his face to the bars of the cell door. "Hey, Tyn!" he called. "Tyn!"

A form moved in the second cell opposite theirs. A bleary, narrow face peered back through the bars. "What?"

"You all heard anythin'?"

Tyn's cell had the only window, set high in the wall. It was on the side of the building where the jailers often sat on the porch, talking.

"Nuh-uh," Tyn muttered.

"That was helpful," Hawkes said.

Warner cursed. He hung his head and gripped the bars. He faced Hawkes and said, "You think if we told 'em we're members of the Order—"

"*Were* members of the Order," Hawkes said. "And no, I don't think that would help. At all. If we want to rescue those kids, we've got to keep our heads down. I'm sure the Fifth Order would just love to find out they've got three wanted fugitives already in their custody."

Warner paced, a frown creasing his features. He huffed and plopped down on his pallet, staring into the far corner with a forlorn expression.

After a few moments, punctuated with an occasional cough or curse, the main door to the holding area opened. Two deputies entered. They walked to the last cell on the right.

"You three. Out."

One of the deputies unlocked the door while the other held his short sword ready. As each prisoner stepped out, their hands and feet were manacled. A set of hinged metal jaws was locked around each waist, and the chain from it connected to the metal jaws on the prisoner in front and behind. Everyone watched the prisoners and deputies shuffle past. The door clanged shut.

"Psst!" A prisoner in the next cell motioned for Hawkes and Warner. "What's going on?" he whispered, his breath like rotten cabbage.

"Dunno, Blake," Warner replied.

A man behind Blake raised his head. "I've got an idea." His voice was low but authoritative.

Hawkes and Warner looked at him with suspicion. Blake had been arrested and brought in with them. But the other man had only arrived last night. He stood, straightened his shoulders and walked over to stand beside Blake, who crouched on the floor.

"Who're you?" Hawkes demanded. He frowned at Blake's cellmate.

"Pardon my lack of manners. I'm unaccustomed to being"—he glanced around the cell—"on this side of things. My name is Matthias Hart. I'm a Witchfinder from Three Waters." He looked down at his boots. "At least I was until yesterday."

"What happened?" Warner asked as he stared up into the man's hooded eyes.

Hart was silent long enough that Warner was on the verge of repeating the question. The Witchfinder let out a long sigh. "Three Waters has fallen."

Blake looked up at his cellmate. "Fallen?"

"Like Last Chapel fell," Hart replied. "To the Crusaders and the Fifth Order."

Hawkes said nothing but studied the man. Hart was older than he and Warner, probably somewhere in his mid-thirties. He was of average build, but there was no mistaking the confident authority of a Witchfinder. His hair was brown and full. It hung over his forehead and down to his eyebrows. A thin, perfectly trimmed mustache drew attention to a nose that had obviously been broken before.

"What? How?" Warner asked.

Hart sat down on top of a wooden bucket. "The way they've been infiltrating all over the place. The Fifth Order comes in and takes control on orders from the Crimson Fathers. In Last Chapel, they initiated a curfew, monitored all traffic in and out and began to round people up."

"Round 'em up for what?" Warner leaned closer to the bars that separated the cells.

"Nearly everybody is being interrogated by the Crusaders. Those who comply with the orders they're given get to go about their lives as normal. Those who don't are sent to compliance camps." He nodded toward the main door of the holding area. "I figure that's where those three are headed."

Darien, Hawkes and Warner had heard about the compliance camps in their travels over the past few weeks. The Fifth Order built them to "reeducate" people about the new regime. There were countless rumors as to why and how this was done. When Darien, Hawkes and Warner first heard the rumors, they ignored them. Surely the Church would not sanction such a thing? Incarcerating its own congregants for some vague purpose? No, it had to be an obfuscation or misunderstanding, they thought.

However, they had quickly learned the truth. The Church *was* constructing such places. Congregants were being "temporarily relocated for educational purposes."

"From what we've gleaned in our travels," Hawkes said, shifting his weight from one leg to the other, "there's no real distinction made between who's taken. Is that right?"

Hart nodded. "Men and women both occupy compliance camps. The only thing you won't find in them are children."

Warner shot Hawkes a worried look. "What're they doin' to the kids?" Dread stirred in his stomach. He looked back at Hart.

The Witchfinder shrugged. "No one's really sure. The Crusaders take children—on orders from the Crimson Fathers—and sequester them somewhere. It's happening all over." He hesitated, bit his lip and looked away. "They've got my three daughters," he said. "I haven't seen them in two weeks. I overheard your friend." He nodded toward Darien. "Sounds like he's looking for children, too."

"We think they got his niece and nephew at the Citadel," Warner said. "We been followin' them all the way from Last Chapel."

Hart shook his head. "You won't get near the Citadel. It's too heavily guarded."

Hawkes folded his arms and scrutinized the Witchfinder once more. Hart wore the standard uniform of his rank in the Paracletian Order: black shirt and breeches, matching boots. His rank insignia, cloak and capotain hat were gone.

Hawkes ran his tongue along his upper teeth. "Why're *you* here?"

Hart looked through the bars. There was a spark in his eyes. "I asked too many questions about my daughters. I wanted to know why my wife had disappeared." His voice softened. "And I refused to arrest and jail people who hadn't broken no law. At least no legitimate law. I-I don't know what's happening anymore." He hung his head, hair tumbling forward. When he looked up, there were tears in his eyes. "Is the new millennium truly going to be the end of everything? *Is the world coming to an end?*"

Hawkes unfolded his arms. Growing up in a traveling fair with his family, he had learned to read people well. Body language revealed whether they were excited or distracted or bored with a performance. Facial tics and expressions often let him know which jokes and routines would work best. Honesty, kindness and trustworthiness could be discerned by observation, as could their opposites. He believed that Hart was genuine and telling the truth. Hawkes stepped over to the bars between their cells and rested his forehead against them. He was still getting used to his head feeling lighter since he kept his once long red hair cut short to alter his appearance. He sighed.

"Matthias, there's something you need to know. It's going to be hard for you to hear. It was for me and Solomon."

Warner clasped his arm. "What're you doin'?" he whispered through his teeth.

"It's okay, Sol," Hawkes replied. "We've got to trust somebody eventually. And I think he's a good place to start."

"Say what?" Warner's one good eye widened.

Hawkes pulled his arm away. "They've already got us, Sol. Sooner or later they'll figure out who we are. And if we're going to get out of here"—he looked at Hart, who nodded—"then we're going to need help."

Warner was skeptical, but he said nothing else. Technically, Hawkes was his immediate superior even though they both held the rank of deputy. Or they had, not long ago. And Hawkes was right. They needed to escape as soon as possible.

Hawkes turned back to Hart. "Like I said, what I'm about to tell you will seem like madness. But just hear me out."

Hart nodded again.

"It's the truth. I give you my word as a—" He hesitated and glanced around the holding area. He looked as if he were searching for a safe place on a ledge he was not sure would hold his weight. He sighed. "I give you my word as a Paracletian Deputy." He said it so quietly that Hart had to lean against the bars to hear it.

The Witchfinder did not react. Hawkes figured the man had already ascertained that they were more than common laborers or merchants.

Sitting on the limp straw on the floor, Blake pulled his knees up to his chest. He looked like a child ready to hear a fairy tale. A third man in their cell rolled over on the straw and faced them so he could also listen. Hawkes and Warner sat down.

"It's about the Church," Hawkes began.

For two hours, Hawkes and Warner told their story: of pursuing Traugott and discovering his true identity, of the ideas about freedom that Valerian Merrick brought back with him from the Tex'ahn lands, of Jairus Gray's death, the kidnapping of Cassidy and Cassandra and the emergence of the Crusaders. They told Hart about Malachi, Zadicus Rann and the fall of Last Chapel. Then they told him about the manipulative purpose behind the rank pins worn by every Church official.

They stopped while jailors emptied three more cells.

Hart had interrupted several times to ask questions or express disbelief. However, the more they talked, the harder his face became. When they had finished, he was as immobile and grim as a cathedral gargoyle. He spent a third hour telling them what had been happening in Three Waters. All of their experiences fit together in a way that bespoke patient planning and sinister intent by the Fifth Order.

Hart's eyes blazed with barely controlled fury. "What do we do?"

"Honestly," Warner said, "after we rescue the kids and return 'em to their mother in Talnat, I don't guess we've really thought much about what happens then."

Hawkes said, "We're going to find Malachi. See what he's learned from the Tex'ahns. Regroup and come up with a plan of some sort." He sounded less confident the more he talked.

"The Fifth Order has to be stopped," Hart declared.

"No argument from us."

"Me neither," Blake said with a grin. "Hells, the Church is bad, but them bastards is worse."

The third man in their cell rose to his feet, walked to the bars and stood between Blake and Hart. "Count me in." His voice rumbled from beneath a brushy mustache that tapered to pointed ends. A single eyebrow ran across his forehead, and underneath were large moss-colored eyes. His skin was black, and recent cuts and bruises covered his head, neck and arms. "Name's Erik Landrew." He shoved a calloused hand and muscled arm between the bars, and Hawkes grasped his forearm in greeting.

"What'd they get you for?" Warner asked, clasping the man's arm next.

"I'm an armorer by trade. From Three Waters. They rounded up all of us in the city. Told us that from now on we'd be making stuff for the Fifth Order—for those damned Crusaders."

"And you didn't go along," Hawkes said, more a statement than question.

Landrew snorted. "I told them to go fuck themselves."

Warner checked on Darien, who was so still it seemed as if he had stopped breathing. Hawkes turned and kicked two rats away from the cell's water bucket. Both disappeared down holes in the floor.

"Let's try to get some rest," Hart said. "We'll talk more later."

Hawkes lay on his pallet, staring at the stone ceiling, hands behind his head. His group had left Last Chapel in pursuit of Cassidy and Cassandra. They knew the children were being taken to the Citadel of the Crimson Fathers, at the headlands of the Great Appian Mountains. They had tried to go as fast as they could in order to cut into the Crusaders' lead. Some days, they had made good time. Others, they had struggled to get in ten or twelve miles due to Darien's health.

Hawkes was thankful that for much of their trip they had managed to stay connected to several large caravans. This had given them protection, as well as the opportunity to blend in and remain inconspicuous. It had also helped when Crusaders stopped the caravans to ask for paperwork and search cargo at checkpoints. If they had been traveling as a small group, the Crusaders would have nabbed them long ago. The caravans had moved northeast along stretches of highway left unbroken by the Great Cataclysm. They had overnighted in the open countryside and whatever towns they came across.

The land had been flat for the first part of their trip but gradually developed into rolling hills and low mountains. The closer they came to Three Waters, the taller the hills became. The forests grew thicker and wilder, the ground rockier. The massive granite peaks of the Great Appian Mountains, snowcapped and majestic, formed a treacherous barrier to the east.

They kept to themselves, interacting with other travelers only when necessary. They were still wanted fugitives. Heretics, according to Church decree. Rewards had been offered for their capture. So they lived under assumed names, changed their appearances as much as possible and passed themselves off as pilgrims taking the old man to one last shrine in the north.

At every stop, they sought information on the children by eavesdropping around tavern tables and campfires. In doing so, they had discovered something chilling. It was not just Cassidy and Cassandra. Their quarry was collecting children as they went along, adding them to their own growing caravan. And there were dozens of them across the realm.

It was being referred to as the "Children's Pilgrimage." The Church was inviting children to Three Waters for special instruction from high-ranking Church officials. Each child would receive a personal blessing from the Church. Their involvement promised fortune and favor to their families. These children were excused from chores and schooling and set off on an adventure like none they had ever known before. Hamlets and towns were left with only infants and those past the age of fifteen. It meant more work for those left behind, but it was too good of an opportunity to pass up for poor families in need of Church benevolence.

There had been no shortage of talk in the villages about the new jobs the Church was creating. Many formerly unemployed men had found work as laborers and builders on the compliance camps that were being constructed everywhere. The Church paid well for their services, and the realm's economy flourished. A great many people were benefiting from the Fifth Order's new plans.

It was said that the compliance camps were only for dissidents, heretics, witches and traitors to Deiparia and the Church. But people had begun to disappear—not all at once but slowly, over a period of time. It was said to be those who disagreed with the Fifth Order—like Matthias Hart—and those who refused to give in to new demands—like Erik Landrew. It was men and women the Church viewed as troublesome, who could be disciplined into obedient behavior. But rumors persisted that the camps also included the powerful, who could be humbled, and the wealthy, since their properties and lands would be confiscated by the Church. And of course, those who were viewed as expendable—urchins, paupers, the idle and the mad—because few cared what happened to them anyway.

The first compliance camp had opened on July 15th, a mere two weeks after Last Chapel had fallen to Zadicus Rann and the Crusaders. The Saxonburgh compliance camp northwest of Three Waters began operating on July 22nd. Camps were scheduled to open near all the major cities of the realm.

As Hawkes stared at the dismal gray ceiling, he worried about his three sisters. They were all married with families of their own. But how had all these changes affected them? Did they still live in the same places? Were his nieces and nephews being carted off on the Pilgrimage like Cassidy and Cassandra? And what about his Papa? Were any of them still alive? These thoughts made him weak. He was glad he was lying down.

"Hey, Sol," he said in a low voice.

"Yeah?"

"What do you think's happened to your family? Your brother and sister, your mother?"

Warner shook his head. "I told you before, I try not to think about it."

"But you're curious, though?"

"Hells, of course I am! But I can't do nothin' about it, can I? It don't do me no good to dwell on it. Don't do you no good, either."

Hawkes sighed. The thoughts would not stop swirling through his mind. His stomach tightened.

Suddenly, the holding area door flew open.

"All right, you shiftless turds! Everyone up!" The Kithanink constable strolled in, bow-legged, thumbs hooked in the leather belt around his waist, most of which disappeared beneath the overhanging belly. Several deputies with weapons ready followed him like goslings behind their mother. Two remained by the door.

"Move it!" he bellowed, clanging the flat of his sword against the bars of the cells. "Line up inside. One out at a time. You know the drill."

While Darien, Hawkes and Warner were shackled to one another, Hawkes asked, "Where're we going?"

The constable grinned, teeth yellowed from smoking too many tabáks. "You're being transferred. It's the Saxonburgh compliance camp for you sorry bastards."

3
CONNECTIONS

TUESDAY, AUGUST 25, 999 AE

"Try it again," the man standing behind Thorne said.

Thorne fitted another arrow against the bowstring.

"Breathe," he instructed. "In rhythm with your actions."

Thorne drew the arrow back to the side of his face and pointed the metal head at the remains of a slatted wood fence.

"Don't hold your breath."

The bowstring sung its reverberating note. The arrow buried itself in the sandy ground several feet to the right of the post, joining seven of its brethren. The earth looked like a pincushion.

"That's it. I'm done!" Thorne said, tossing the longbow aside. "Give me a crossbow any time." He eyed the weapon that hung from his horse's saddle.

Without a word, the smaller man retrieved the bow, notched an arrow, drew and released. The shaft embedded itself in the center of the slat.

"Show off," Thorne said.

Tua'Ahtaki's long, narrow mouth eased upward in a grin. "You rely too much on the mechanical. You cannot have a connection with gears and a crank."

"I don't want a connection. A crossbow is point and shoot. Simple. Easy. Effective." He shaded his eyes from the burning sun and stared at the western horizon, vast and ready to swallow the unwary. Teska and Cabbott should have been back by now.

"As is the bow," Tua said. "But when the mechanics break down, your weapon is useless. No warrior should have a weapon he cannot mend with his own hands." He slung the quiver across his back and went to retrieve the arrows.

Thorne had met Tua only last week. The Nermernuh, as Tua's tribe was called, had volunteered to take Thorne to what remained of the town Road's End—once known as Fort Worth—west of Dallastown. Thorne had wanted to examine more ancient documents that were kept in some of the remaining buildings. Tua had kept him from falling victim to sand traps, carghella snake dens and bandits that frequented the area.

Road's End was the last outpost of human civilization according to Tua. Beyond it, vast rolling plains—broken only by an occasional stand of scrub oak or limestone buttes—had reasserted their dominion over humanity's roads, burying them beneath grama grass as high as a horse's belly. Only a handful of pre-Cataclysm buildings remained upright since vicious tornadoes had scoured the plains for more than a millennium.

Tua of the Nermernuh tribe, which he sometimes also referred to as Co'manche, was a tracker, guide, handyman and history-teller. He stood nearly a foot shorter than Thorne, his skin ruddy and weathered. Both had long black hair. Thorne wore his in a ponytail, while Tua's hung in two long braids halfway down his chest. Gray was more evident in Tua's as he neared his half-century mark. His face was round, with pronounced cheekbones and chin, and dark, heavy-lidded eyes that missed little. Sharp creases lined the edges of his eyes and mouth. He returned to Thorne's side.

"They're late," Tua said as he placed the bow and quiver on his silky dun mustang. Tua wore tan leggings held up with a leather belt, a blousy white tunic and short cowhide boots. He hoisted himself into the saddle with practiced ease.

"I know." Thorne scanned the horizon again. "Do you think—?"

"There they are." Tua pointed past the fence. "A storm's following them."

Thorne narrowed his eyes. "I don't see a damn thing." He climbed into his saddle, but the added height did not help. Maybe there was the slightest hint of dark clouds on the horizon.

They waited and watched. A few minutes later, Thorne was able to discern the small shape of a wagon. Jagged forks of lightning danced among the clouds that boiled along behind it.

While Tua watched, Thorne opened the large metal door at the rear of the cavernous DIY Mega-Emporium building. The northern half of it had collapsed ages before, but the southern part still stood. Across the interior, scorch marks and brittle blackened sticks showed where others had spent the night or sat out a storm.

Thorne stood with hands on his hips as Tua brought both horses inside. A few minutes later, the wagon rolled in amid a plume of wind-swept dust.

The horses, lathered from the exertion and heat, hung their heads, tongues lolling out. Tua dismounted and began to unhook them from the wagon tongue. He spoke to them in a low, soothing voice.

The wagon was similar to those Thorne knew back home—the boxy, wooden sort used by traveling thespians and carnival fairs. It had a window on each side and a door on the back. Thurl Cabbott climbed down from the driver's bench.

"Good to see you, Malachi," he said, although his features registered minimal emotion.

Thorne stuck his arm out to his friend, but Cabbott ignored the customary greeting. He busied himself with lowering the steps at the back of the wagon.

Thorne withdrew his hand. "Was the trip successful?"

"Seems so." Cabbott rapped on the weather-beaten door and walked off among the floor-to-ceiling shelves scattered haphazardly throughout the interior of the building.

The wagon door opened. Teska Vaun stepped out smiling, her dimples pronounced. She jumped the last two steps and flung herself into Thorne's arms. She was an inch shorter than Tua, the top of her head coming only to Thorne's chest. He looked down into her hazel eyes and felt his heart thunder like a stampede. She stood on her tiptoes, laced her fingers behind his neck and kissed him.

He held her waist and returned the kiss. She smelled of old wood and danger and wide-open spaces, and he wanted to disappear with her and never return. He felt her breasts against him. His tongue probed the softness of her lips.

She giggled and leaned back. "Take it easy, old man. Wouldn't want you to get too worked up now, would we?" She offered a coquettish grin. "At least not yet." She planted another quick kiss on his mouth and wiggled from his grasp.

Teska was twenty-two, a dozen years his junior, but that was common enough in Deiparia. The unusual thing had been a Witchfinder Imperator of the Paracletian Order falling in love with a witch.

"I want you to meet somebody," Teska said. She turned to the wagon, her fiery curls bouncing around her shoulders. "Amelia Sloan, this is Malachi Thorne."

Amelia stood in the doorway, smiling. "It's certainly a pleasure to meet you, Master Thorne," she said as she descended the rickety steps and curtsied. "Teska's told me so much about you."

"I'll bet she has." He grinned at Amelia. "It's my honor to meet you. And please, no 'Master.' We're all equal here."

Thunder boomed outside as rain began to hammer the roof high above them. Water poured through broken skylights. Sheltered among the ruins of the northern wall, Cabbott sat and stared at the downpour.

"Yeah," Teska said, slipping her arm through Thorne's as he watched his friend. "I think he's getting worse."

"What happened?"

She closed the wagon door. "Just the usual. He's silent more often than not. Just sits around, watching stuff."

"What stuff?" Thorne asked.

Teska hesitated. "Me, mostly." She caught the flicker in Thorne's green eyes. "No, not like *that*. It's like he's studying me, like he's never seen me before. Kinda creepy sometimes." Her voice dropped. "And he flew into another rage."

Thorne raised his eyebrows.

Teska nodded. "Two days ago, he started in on that bounty hunter again. Mathan. He yelled and cursed like a eunuch in a whorehouse on half-price night. He kept on about how he had to protect you—that nothing like that could ever happen again. He said, 'It's my responsibility, and there'll be no more bounty hunters, do you understand?' It went on like that for twenty minutes at least. And I'd swear by the Heiromonarch's balls that at times he was talking to someone else."

Thorne sighed and put his arm around her shoulder. "Maybe he is, Tes. Maybe whatever Mallory did for him back in Last Chapel…well, maybe it didn't quite work right for him? Or maybe only some of it worked? Hells, I don't know."

"You have brought one back, I see," Tua said to Teska. He nodded at Amelia.

Thorne walked toward Cabbott, and the others followed.

"She's a good one," Teska said.

Amelia blushed. "I ain't nobody. Just a settler's wife is all."

"Stop being so bloody modest," Teska told her. "You've got the gift. You've successfully made contact with the Three-Who-Are-One."

Amelia glanced around as if enemies were hiding in the shadows. "Th-They frighten me."

"Welcome to the club, Sister. They're supposed to. They're not to be trifled with, that's for sure. But be obedient and faithful, and you'll have a share in their power."

"Who is this Three-In-One?" Tua asked. Teska and Amelia walked on either side and told him about the Matriarch, the Mother, and the Maiden—the Three Witches who rule the Enodia Communion.

Cabbott watched them as they approached. If Thorne had to put a word to the way his friend looked at them, he would have said *warily*.

Teska sat down cross-legged on the floor. Thorne joined her. Tua sat with his legs straight out in front of him, his back against one of the rusted shelves. Amelia occupied the edge of a large chunk of the fallen wall.

Thorne studied his friend. Physically, Cabbott looked okay. His thinning brown hair, his beard and mustache, all showed the same speckling of gray. Perhaps the lines on his face were a bit more pronounced. That was probably due to all the traveling they had done. And the weather. And the stress. But he could not account for the eyes.

Cabbott's blue eyes had taken on a paler hue, and Thorne swore they were sometimes streaked with yellow. The lines around the edges seemed sharper and somehow hateful. Cabbott caught Thorne staring at him. He smiled. But it seemed forced—expected—and Thorne felt no warmth or familiarity in it.

Cabbott was still his friend. Yet the distance between them grew. Normally a long journey brought travelers together and bonded them. But not Cabbott. Thorne was convinced it had to be some side effect of Mallory's magic. It had changed Cabbott somehow. The day that Zadicus Rann had attempted to execute them in Last Chapel, a fierce battle had broken out. Cabbott had been mortally wounded, and they were unable to flee the city. So Teska had volunteered the aid of another young Nahoru'brexia she knew—going against the wishes of the Maiden in the process. Somehow Mallory's special gift of healing had brought Cabbott back from the brink of death. But he was not the same. Thorne felt guilty for his friend getting into such a dangerous situation in the first place.

"Malachi," Amelia said with her sweet drawl, "Teska tells me that you've been learning about our way of life."

He looked away from Thurl and smiled at her. "Yes. I first learned about your existence from my mentor, Valerian Merrick. He spent several years here, in a place called Magnolia City. He taught me a lot about freedom, and that's something that our people desperately need. I wanted—needed—to find out more."

"Some of us in Dallastown know his name," Tua said. "We never met him. But traders from Magnolia City spoke of the strange man they pulled from the sea."

Thorne told them about his relationship with Merrick and about how Merrick had returned to Deiparia as Traugott, a freedom fighter who tried to rally the people against the Church. He shared about the secret meetings they had attended with Merrick to discuss and learn about freedom.

Thorne noticed Cabbott sit up straighter and pay more attention. He hung on every word as if hearing them for the first time, though Cabbott had been with them during that journey and knew everything they had talked about. Thorne chalked it up to another of the peculiarities in Cabbott's behavior. He concluded by telling them about Merrick's death at the hands of Rann. His face tightened in anger.

Amelia changed the subject. "Well, I don't know much about freedom like you're talking about. We don't have anything near like what Teska's told me you have back home."

Tua nodded. "We are a loose confederation of communities. Tribes, you might say. Each live by their own set of rules and laws."

"So who is in charge?" Everyone looked at Cabbott when he asked the question.

"Each community has its own elders—its own set of leaders," Tua replied. "Each has a mayor—"

"What's a may-or?" Teska asked.

"A man who oversees a village or town," Tua replied. "He can select people to help him with various tasks. He speaks on behalf of the community. In the ancient ways of my people, he would've been called a 'chief.'"

"Like a Primar in Deiparia," Thorne said to Teska, who nodded. He reached over and held her hand.

"So people are free to do…whatever they want?" Teska asked.

Amelia chuckled. "Well, within reason, of course. We have people who enforce our laws. And we have a system to punish those who break the law."

"Since being here, I've had the chance to read and study some of your old manuscripts—books that predate the Great Cataclysm." Thorne leaned forward but still held Teska's hand. "According to some of them, you are part of something called a 'constitutional republic,' meaning you give authority to people to act on your behalf."

Both Tex'ahns nodded.

"You *vote* for these people. And they do what you tell them?"

"Essentially," Tua answered. "But the actual practice is much more complex than that. It was the way things worked before Judgment Day. And afterward, those who survived kept it going."

Teska squeezed Thorne's hand. "So it's like Deiparia was when it first started," she said. She looked at Tua and Amelia. "We had something like that after the Great Cataclysm. All the surviving groups of people nearly tore one another apart for food, water, shelter. One tribe, Deiparia, became the dominant one by helping others and providing those resources."

"Not long after that," Thorne picked up, "the congregants of Deiparia signed an agreement, which we call the Concordat. People surrendered some of their personal freedoms in exchange for the Deiparian rulers to reestablish a working society once more."

Tua nodded. "Yes, yes, we have some here who are saying much the same thing. They want a single unified leadership." He looked through a hole in the wall at the pouring rain. "Many oppose the idea. But not as many as before."

"Be careful," Thorne said, his voice tight. "We're learning that giving up freedom for total authoritative control leads to some unintended—and unwanted—consequences. It has its benefits. But they aren't worth the ultimate cost."

Cabbott's eyes locked on Tua as he cut through the discussion. "So each of your 'tribes,' as you put it, have their own leadership. What about military strength?"

"Well, each area takes care of itself. We can raise a militia when needed. But we haven't needed to in many years. The petty squabbles between our settlements have long passed. Now the only squabbles are over trade!" He chuckled.

"And how long does it take to assemble a militia?"

"Thurl, what're you—" Thorne said.

"Not long," Tua answered, not taking his eyes off Cabbott. "Maybe a day. Sometimes two." He searched Cabbott's stone face. "Why does this interest you?"

Cabbott said nothing and averted his gaze. Teska squeezed Thorne's hand and shot him a see-what-I-mean look.

Amelia was oblivious to the tension creeping around the fire. "So in Deiparia you have one group that's in charge of everything." It was not a question for anyone, just a statement of acknowledgement. "And Teska has told me that you worship your church?" She scowled in confusion.

"The Church of the Deiparous," Thorne said. "It's comprised of four Orders—well, five now. Each one oversees different aspects of our society. The Paracletian Order, which Thurl and I used to belong to, is responsible for all law enforcement and judicial proceedings. The Kyrian Order handles all worship and liturgy. The Abthanian Order is for education, and the Cartulian Order does most everything else—from taxes and record keeping to municipal improvements and the treasury. We—" He caught himself. "*They* worship the Church as God."

"But not you?" Tua asked, gesturing between Thorne, Teska and Cabbott.

Thorne shook his head. "We discovered that the Church is involved in some… questionable activities."

"They're a corrupt bunch of bureaucratic ass kissers who only want to get richer and stay in power," Teska spat.

Cabbott almost growled his reply. "The Church is God. It has been and always will be. It is the visible expression of beneficence, grace and order. The Heiromonarch is the Avatar of all existence, the supreme leader of the Church. Deiparians worship the Church—or they are executed as heretics." His eyes blazed as they locked onto Thorne's. "Or traitors." He stood up and walked away toward the loading bay door. He leaned against the frame and stared into the driving rain.

"What the hells?" Thorne said.

Teska pushed a curl behind her ear. "That's what I was telling you earlier. He just goes off on a tirade every so often."

Thorne stared at his friend. Something unsettling scratched at the back of his mind, but he was distracted when Teska spoke.

"Amelia told me about who you worship," she said to Tua. "You call him 'God.' And he's invisible."

Tua shifted positions on the floor. "Well, as far as beliefs go, I don't really worship God. I have more of a spiritual connection to the world around us."

"Merrick told us that you could worship whoever you wanted," Thorne said, "and no one had the authority to say you couldn't."

"I worship God, I guess you could say," Amelia said. "He's invisible, but he's here with us."

Thorne and Teska exchanged perplexed glances.

"But how—" Thorne began.

"I don't know"—she held up a hand—"but the Bible—"

"What's that?" he interrupted again.

"It's their holy book," Teska said. "Kind of like our Testament. Here's what Amelia told me." She looked at the young woman. "Let me know if I screw any of this up."

"The God of the Tex'ahns," she said, "is talked about in their holy book—this Bible. It's got two parts called the Old Testament and the New Testament." She glanced at Amelia for confirmation, who smiled and nodded. "There's a lot of stuff in them about their God and people, and about how they're supposed to live. Anyway, the New Testament talks about a man named Jesus. He's God's son. The Tex'ahns worship their God with services and songs and prayers, just like we do. And they believe that this Jesus was supposed to come back when the Great Cataclysm happened—"

"Judgment Day," Amelia interjected.

"—but he didn't. So they're still waiting for him."

Thorne shook his head. "I don't understand a bloody bit of this."

"I don't really, either," Teska said. "Amelia just told me about it a couple of weeks ago, and I still can't get my head around it."

Thorne turned to Tua. "But you don't believe this?"

"Not all of it, no. I can agree with the idea of a higher power. Someone must have created everything. It is too intricate, too incredible, to be random. There must be a guiding hand and creative mind behind it all. But the stories of God and Jesus and the church—"

"What church?" Thorne asked.

Amelia smiled. "The church is a group of people who believe in and worship God and Jesus. We're taught to love others and do good to them, to pray and to gather together for worship."

"Like the tribe of Deiparia," Thorne mused. "They gave aid and comfort, order and hope, to people." He was silent for a moment as he gathered his thoughts.

"That's why the Deiparian tribe grew. They helped people. Gave them work. Purpose. Tried to bring order out of the chaos of the Great Cataclysm. I wonder…" he paused again. "Did our forefathers—before the moon fell to Earth—did they have this holy book, too? This Bible? Could it be that they worshiped this 'God' as well?"

"Do you not have books or writings where you come from?" Tua asked, the disbelief registering in his voice.

"Oh, we do," Thorne said. "But many such writings are restricted. Access to them is only for extremely high-ranking Churchmen." He remembered how Gemmas Earl had once told him that he could be the youngest Heiromonarch in history. And he remembered his own tempting thought of earning more standing in the Church to gain access to all the knowledge that the Cartulian Order kept hidden away. But to follow such a path would make him no better than Zadicus Rann.

Thorne dug into the pocket of his tunic and pulled out a scrap of parchment. Tua, Amelia and Teska watched as he carefully unfolded it. "I copied this from a piece of a book I found at Road's End. It didn't make much sense to me at the time. But now, after hearing all this…" He read from the parchment:

> "Our fathers' God, to thee,
> Author of liberty, to thee we sing;
> Long may our land be bright
> With freedom's holy light;
> Protect us by thy might, great God, our King."

Silence filled the cavernous building, save for the drumming of rain on the roof.

Thorne tucked the paper away. "On our journey to Last Chapel to find Dario's niece and nephew, Val and I visited a number of villages. He wanted to meet with other freedom fighters. He talked to them and encouraged them and offered them guidance. He always ended their times together by quoting from an ancient document called the Declaration of Independence. Part of it said, 'We hold these truths to be self-evident, that all men are created equal, that they are endowed by their Creator with certain unalienable Rights, that among these are Life, Liberty and the pursuit of Happiness.'

"If the Tex'ahn's God is the author of liberty, as this says"—he patted the pocket of his tunic—"and if all men are created equal and given specific rights by their Creator—which I'm assuming means this 'God'—then…"

"What, Malachi?" Teska asked.

"Then freedom isn't just something Val or even the Tex'ahns came up with. It's something bigger. From God. God wants people to be free. Being subservient to the Church of the Deiparous, or the Heiromonarch, or the damned Fifth Order, isn't how it's supposed to be." His eyes flamed with possibility and potential. He looked at Teska. "If the Deiparian tribe once believed in this God, and God wants people to be free to make their own decisions and live their own lives, then the Church has corrupted something that was originally intended for good."

Tua stood up and stretched. "No. It's more than that. Your Church hasn't just corrupted what was once good. It has taken the place of the good. That's why you are told that your Church is God. The ideals of freedom and choice have been replaced."

"So Merrick was right all along," Teska said.

"Yes," Thorne replied. "But he didn't have any idea of the scope of it all. It's not just about telling people that they can be free, or even helping them to be free. It's about bringing down all that is false so the good can be rediscovered."

Cabbott struggled to see the rain. The world beyond the DIY Mega-Emporium was a fuzzy ball of gray light and bleary lines. The harder he tried, the more his head hurt. He cursed silently. It made no sense. He could barely see his hand in front of his face.

And yet he had heard every word spoken from the other side of the building as clearly as if he were standing among them.

Let them try, he thought.

They could no more bring down the Church than he could command the rain to stop. He paused, closed his eyes and tried to focus his mind. Something important lay just beyond its reach. For the moment. Just a little longer and he felt he *could* make the rain stop. The thought thrilled and terrified him at the same time. What was happening to him?

Thurl Cabbott felt as if a massive door had slammed shut over him, trapping him in a stygian darkness that quivered and pulsated. He cried out but had no voice.

"The rain is letting up," Cabbott shouted across the room. "We need to get back to Dallastown before nightfall." He set about hooking the horses to the wagon.

4
QUESTIONS

SUNDAY, SEPTEMBER 13, 999 AE

The days grew shorter. Another month and the snows would come. Thorne had intended to winter in Dallastown. He needed more time with the documents he had discovered and the people who lived in this democratic manner. Questions still abounded about the Tex'ahn form of governance, as well as their God and his holy book. He yearned to visit Magnolia City to see if he could find any of the people that Merrick had known.

None of that's going to happen now, he thought as he led his small entourage along crumbling highway pavement littered with debris and weeds. *If it wasn't for the damned Maiden…*

A few days after the DIY Mega-Emporium, Teska had a vision. The Maiden had instructed her to return to Deiparia. The Enodia Communion needed all brexia, which Thorne found odd because the Communion had withdrawn. They had gone underground to conserve their power. He had attempted to dissuade Teska from acting on the vision, a choice that resulted in their first argument.

"I can't leave yet," he had said. "There's still so much—"

"Then stay if you want!" she fired back. "I've got to go."

Thorne shook his head. "I won't let you make that journey all by yourself!"

"You won't *let me*? It's my fucking life, I can do whatever I want!" She hesitated. "You want me to disobey the Maiden?" Her laugh had been like hoarfrost on stone. "Let's just say I've had a taste of what would lay in store for me if I did—and I want no part of it."

"But she can't just expect you to drop everything."

"She can and she does! You don't get it. I'm in this thing now, for better or worse, and I can't just back out when it's inconvenient for you. So I'm leaving tomorrow."

Bad weather had prevented that from happening. A tornado sliced across the plains, and for two days everyone had hunkered in the strongest buildings. Thorne and Teska made up, but the night before her departure, emotions erupted once again.

Thorne reluctantly announced that they would all head back to Deiparia. If she must go, he wanted to make sure she had his protection.

"I've told you before, Malachi, I don't need protection. I've managed quite well on my own."

"I'm not questioning your ability to take care of yourself."

"Then why the sudden change of heart? A few days ago, you were bleating like a lost lamb about not being finished here."

He worked hard to control his temper, but his words came out clipped and sharp. "I'm *not* finished here! There's still so much more I need to learn. But I won't let you go alone. It's out of the question." He paused. "I love you. And I don't want to risk losing you. I-I don't think I could survive if I lost you."

Things calmed down after that. On Tuesday, September 1st, Thorne, Teska and Cabbott left Dallastown, heading south. Tua'Ahtaki rode with them on his small mustang, and Amelia Sloan drove their wagonload of provisions. It took them two days to navigate the Central Range, a spine of mountains that effectively split the land in half from east to west. They had spent a few days in Shrev Town, along the coast of the Arkan Sea.

Teska found another Nahoru'brexia. She had grown accustomed to the feeling that came upon her when one was near. It was not discernment so much as attraction. Maybe it was magic calling to magic? Maybe Maiden Mallumo had done something to her to make her sensitive to the presence of Nahoru'brexia? Whatever it was, all Teska knew was that it worked. She had explained about the Communion, but the woman would not leave her family to join them. The small group continued northeast.

That was five days ago.

They rode across shaggy fields covered by towering trees already shedding their brittle leaves. The roads were littered with more metal shells. "They were once called auto-mobiles. Or cars, for short," Tua, the history-teller, shared. Thorne could not understand why "car" was the shortened form of auto-mobile.

They passed through pre-Cataclysm towns but saw no other human beings. Everything was overgrown with kuzda vines, and moss often engulfed entire buildings. The roads lay gray and broken, but only occasionally did they have to leave them due to damage or impediment.

The angry Tex'ahn weather had not followed them, and since leaving Shrev Town, the journey had been pleasant and uneventful. Now they rode along the remains of Highway 63 toward a village once called Cornersville, where they intended to spend the night.

Thorne rode in front on a black stallion he had named Nightwalker, whose coat bore reddish-brown highlights. Teska sat astride a dappled mare while Amelia kept pace beside her on the wagon pulled by two chestnut geldings she had named Jacob and Esau. Tua followed on his mustang, the smallest but swiftest of the animals. Cabbott brought up the rear on a sorrel saddle horse.

"What's the Communion want us for?" Amelia asked Teska over the creaking of the wagon wheels.

Teska shrugged. "The Maiden didn't say. My guess would be they need more power. Magic is like water during a drought. There's only so much of it to go around. Whoever holds the most calls the shots."

"And right now, this Fifth Order has it all?"

Teska nodded. "Nearly all of it. The Communion lost most of theirs when I—" She cleared her throat. "A member of the Fifth Order sacrificed himself to cast a spell. They were able to take the majority of the Communion's power for themselves."

"What do you think they intend to do with it?" Amelia asked.

Teska's face darkened, and she stared off into the distance. "They're taking over Deiparia. They've got some plan to rule everything in their own way. According to the Three-Who-Are-One, the Crimson Fathers have an iron grip on just about everyone and everything. And they're plotting something even the Three cannot foresee. Something big."

For the next few miles, Amelia said nothing else but wore a worried expression.

Teska spurred her horse and caught up to Thorne. "Hi."

He smiled.

"I wanted you to know—in case I haven't said it—thank you for coming with me. I know you wanted to stay." She reached over and grasped his hand. The sun rippled over her curls.

Thorne smiled again and squeezed her hand. "Your safety is more important to me than anything."

"You learned a lot while we were there. I think you're ready."

He looked at her sideways. "Ready for what?"

"To pick up where Merrick left off. That's what this whole trip was about."

Thorne snorted. "I'm nowhere near ready. I don't know enough about—"

"We've been over all that." She squeezed his hand back. "You know more about freedom, and what it means, and how it works, than anyone else in Deiparia. And what you don't know, you'll figure out. I'm sure Merrick's friends will be happy to help you."

"I hope so," Thorne said, admiring the perfect symmetry of her face. He never tired of looking at her. "Has the Maiden told you where to go once we're back?"

"Attagon."

Thorne raised his eyebrows. "Really? Why?"

She shrugged. "I don't know."

They rode another hundred yards before Thorne spoke again. "Since we're heading toward Attagon, I'd like to see if we can locate Rich and the other freedom fighters."

"That sounds like a good idea," Teska said.

Thorne frowned. "It won't interfere with the Maiden's command, will it? I don't want to get you in trouble."

"No, not as long as we're in Attagon by November 12th for the Feast of Michael the Second."

"There's something I've been wanting to ask," Thorne said. "The magic—how does it work? I mean, what's involved in doing it?"

Teska acknowledged the question but remained silent. Thorne gave her time to formulate her reply.

"Everything around us"—she gestured toward a forest of thick hickories and oaks—"has an innate energy. A life force. A soul, if you want to think of it that way.

"Magic is the process of tapping into that energy and using it. But it's not a limitless energy. When a brexia accesses the life energy of nature, or another person, that energy is depleted. It can be replenished, but it takes time. And the larger and more complex the spell, the more energy is required.

"You told me about the Carnifex that chased you and Thurl, and the demon that attacked you in Colobos. In both of those cases, it required several brexia to get everything ready and cast those spells. They not only drew on the natural world around them, but from other brexia as well. Do you remember Mallory after she helped Thurl?"

How could I forget? Thorne thought. He nearly lost one of his oldest, closest friends because of Zadicus Rann. "She was as wrung out as a goodwife's cleaning rag."

Teska nodded. "Mallory used her Nahoru'brexia gift of healing to help Thurl. And it drained her energy to an extremely low level. The concept is the same whether it's our gifts or a spell. Using magic leaves us weakened. You've seen how tired I am after using my gift. That's why I can't do it as much as I used to. And that's why whoever has the most magic—the largest reservoir of energy—can control nearly everything."

Thorne watched a flock of birds take flight from the nearby trees. "So in the case of the Crimson Fathers and the Fifth Order, they have the Communion's magical energy, and they've got it—what? Stored up somewhere?"

"Probably. I'm not sure how magical energies are kept."

"So the Communion needs to take back their energy."

"That's the idea."

Thorne was silent for a moment. The sun eased toward the west. Behind them Cabbott coughed, and Amelia hummed to herself.

"What if the Crimson Fathers use all the magic before the Communion can reclaim it?" Thorne asked.

Teska said nothing but shook her head.

"And what would they use that much magic for?"

Only twice before had Thorne seen Teska's face darken as it did now. The first was when they blundered into a town crawling with Vulanti'nacha, the flying spiders that had annihilated the village of Honvale. The second was when the Maldormo appeared in Last Chapel's main square. Maiden Mallumo had sent her silent, monstrous servants, also known as the "Dark Forlorn," who attacked anything that moved. It was a look that foreshadowed uncertainty and fear.

About an hour before dusk, they arrived in what was once Cornersville. A single road labeled AR-11 cut through an intersection surrounded by brambles, trees and thick weeds. The foundations of four structures were nearly hidden among the browning grass. A single-story building remained loosely intact. The rear had collapsed, leaving only piles of mossy rubble. The front half was covered by a roof with gaping holes. One door, held by a rusty hinge, drooped between the two vacant front windows. A metal awning had partially collapsed. On a pole above it hung a cracked, discolored sign that read:

GR C RY

Thorne looked around in confused disappointment. "Well, I had imagined this place would be a bit *larger*."

"It's this or the outdoors again," Teska said.

Cabbott steered the wagon through the back of the building and underneath the sagging roof. After unhooking the team from the wagon, Thorne and Amelia picketed all the horses in a field across the road that had the last vestiges of summer grass. Teska searched the grounds for firewood.

Tua explored the front of the building, finding peculiar pre-Cataclysm objects. There was a series of several long, narrow, flat surfaces, like unrolled bolts of cloth, each ending at small kiosks. The remains of what might have once been bags of some kind littered the area. Tua picked one up and it fell apart in his hand. He shrugged and turned to discover a few metal cans, dented and covered in dust, and broken shelves like a merchant would use.

The sun disappeared behind the untamed, forested hills to the west, changing the striated blue sky into a kaleidoscope of pink, orange and yellow that slowly dimmed to dusky purple.

Amelia kindled a fire, cooked the last of their venison and made fresh cornbread. From the beginning, they had been thrilled to have her along. She could create wonderful meals from the simplest of ingredients. And she was as curious about Deiparia as Thorne was about the cause of freedom.

Tua smoked a thin pipe as he sat beside the fire, enjoying the evening. Cabbott leaned against the front wagon wheel. There was little conversation during dinner, aside from requests for seconds. Afterward, Amelia and Tua cleaned up, and once again everyone sat around the fire. As the stars came out, Thorne and Teska watered the animals before bringing them inside the building and tying them around the wagon.

"What does your name mean?" Thorne asked Tua.

He blew a thin stream of charcoal-colored smoke into the air. "It means 'cricket.'"

Amelia giggled. "Why did your parents name you that?"

"My parents didn't. Well, not completely. Ancient Co'manche custom held that the tribe should name each child born to them. I was very small and quite loud, so I was told," he said. "And the tribe called me Tua'Ahtaki."

Teska took Thorne's hand. "How many people are in your tribe?"

Another stream of smoke dissipated in the night air. Tua sighed. "As far as I know, I am the last now. But it was not always so. Long ages past—many generations even before the Judgment Day—the number of my people had dwindled. But at one time, before the rails of iron carriages began to scar the land, we were as numerous as the wildflower. However"—he paused—"that was a different world."

The subject turned to freedom. Thorne told them more about what he had learned from the ancient records and documents he found in Dallastown and Road's End, as well as a few smaller towns he had explored. They talked for another hour as the fire burned low. Teska lay her head on Thorne's shoulder.

The memory of a dream washed over him, its vividness as startling as a dash of cold water. He remembered sitting with a redheaded woman as the world collapsed around them. Her head rested on him the way Teska's did now. He remembered images of a burning horizon and clouds with tendrils that touched the earth.

Despite the suffocating doom of the place, he knew he would keep her safe. Or he would die trying.

"Your heart's beating faster," she said as she felt the pulse in his wrist. "Anything wrong?"

"Not at all," he replied with a contented smile.

Tua cleaned his pipe and put it away. He adjusted his saddlebag several times before laying back and using it for a pillow. He stared at the stars through the holes in the ceiling. Amelia, Teska and Cabbott spread their bedrolls around the fire. Thorne took first watch.

I wonder where Dario and Tycho and Sol are right now, Thorne wondered as he sat at the front of the building. From this vantage point, he could see through the windows, as well as through the exposed back. He hoped his friends were okay. He longed to see them.

How was he going to carry Merrick's mantle when he got back to Deiparia? If he jumped in and started off like his mentor, then he would be treated in the same way. The Church would hound him relentlessly.

Just like how I used to treat heretics and traitors.

No, there had to be another way. He had to figure out how to spread the message in a way that would reach more people. Maybe Rich DuBose and Murnau Carden and some of their companions would have some ideas.

DuBose and Carden had been two of Merrick's closest associates—some might even say disciples. While Thorne's initial encounter with the two freedom fighters had gone somewhat crooked, they had all rallied around Merrick. It was Rich and Murnau who had devised their secret entrance into Nashton when the Church was looking for them.

The Church.

It had only been a few months, but it felt like a lifetime ago that Thorne had broken faith with the Church. They had labeled him and his men traitors and heretics and nearly executed them. With the Fifth Order now in control, were they still so highly sought after? Of course they were. Mathan the Bear proved that.

Thorne shivered as he remembered the zeal he once possessed as a Witchfinder Imperator and how he had fulfilled his duty with unrelenting determination. How many people like him—like Thurl and Tycho and Solomon—did he run to the ground? How many innocent people did he imprison or sentence to death as witches, as members of the Communion? And all of it for nothing.

Thorne remained conflicted about the Maiden and the Communion. He still bore resentment and prejudice against them, as the Church had taught him. They deliberately stood outside the Church's beneficence and rule, forging their own pagan path. They were dangerous. Unpredictable. They were the enemy.

But they had also saved his life in Last Chapel. Not only had the Maiden sent her little pets, but several of the witches fought alongside him that day. And Mallory had helped Thurl. So were they truly evil?

One of the horses neighed and twitched its tail. Insects chirped in the tall grasses outside. The air through the window carried the faint promise of colder weather.

Thorne got up. He placed several branches on the glowing coals of the fire and blew on them. Flames rose to embrace the fresh wood like long-separated lovers.

"*NO!* Nooooooo!" Cabbott's cry ripped through the night.

Thorne spun around.

Cabbott sat up in his bedroll, eyes bulging. "Malachi! Don't trust—" A fit of gurgling and hacking choked out the rest of the words.

Thorne ran to his friend. Cabbott fell back, limbs stiffening. His eyes rolled back, and his body arched like Tua's longbow.

"Thurl! Thurl! It's me. Wake up!"

The constable spasmed as if being lashed, moaning through gritted teeth.

"What's happening?" Amelia hollered, already on her feet. Teska joined her. Tua sat still, watching.

Cabbott bucked and trembled as Thorne held him down.

"What's wrong with him?" Teska shouted as she knelt across from Thorne. She helped to hold Cabbott still.

"No idea." Thorne said between breaths. He was drenched in sweat. "He just started screaming."

Cabbott's head snapped forward so hard that Thorne and Teska flinched when they heard something in his neck crack. Cabbott's eyes, lucid but strained, pleaded with Thorne. "Malachi." He gasped. "Malachi, I've tried—please believe me." Tears ran from the corners of his eyes.

"Tried what, Thurl? Tried what?"

Cabbott looked at Teska. "Be…careful…" He coughed. A tiny trickle of blood leaked from the corner of his mouth. "You can't—you *mustn't*—trust—" His neck arched back, and a brittle groan escaped his lips. The convulsions passed. His body began to relax. Cabbott looked at Thorne. "Strong. Almost made it…" His eyelids fluttered shut.

Thorne released his friend, his own hands slick with sweat. He looked at Teska, who was not as pale as he felt himself to be.

"What the hells was that?" she asked.

"Malachi? Is everything all right?" The voice spooked Thorne and Teska.

Cabbott was awake, eyes clear and searching. "You both look rough."

"What was that all about?" Teska said with more hostility than she intended. Cabbott did not seem to notice.

"Are you okay? How do you feel?" Thorne asked.

Cabbott raised a hand, motioning for a moment and some space. He sat up, rubbing his neck. Tua and Amelia watched in silence.

"I am sorry," Cabbott said. "I did not mean to disturb everyone's sleep."

"Thurl, what happened?" Thorne asked, more demanding this time.

Cabbott glanced down at his jumbled bedroll. He shook his head as he looked at Thorne. "Just a bad dream, I suppose." He walked to the water barrel on the side of the wagon, removed the lid and ladled himself a deep drink. "I guess bad nightmares come with old age, eh?" He replaced the ladle and lid and returned to his bedroll. He smoothed it out and lay down, hands clasped over his chest.

Tua, Amelia, Thorne and Teska looked at each other, dumbfounded.

"That must've been some nightmare," Tua said.

Teska shook her head. "That wasn't any fucking dream. Or nightmare." She paused and looked at the confused faces around her. "That was a warning."

"A warning? For what?" Amelia asked.

Teska's brow furrowed as she crossed her arms. Her mouth was a crevice cut in stone. "Someone is hiding something," she said. "According to Thurl, one of us can't be trusted."

5
SAXONBURGH

THURSDAY, SEPTEMBER 17, 999 AE

Darien, Hawkes and Warner had arrived at the Saxonburgh compliance camp on Monday, August 3rd. There had been a total of eighteen prisoners at the time. Their transport from Kithanink added another twenty-two. Today marked their forty-sixth day of internment, and the camp's population had swelled to 179.

The purpose of the camp was to reeducate congregants to the Fifth Order's rule. The facility occupied the buildings and grounds of what had once been a school. It was laid out in a square with stone walls twenty feet high. Wooden watchtowers in each corner rose fifteen feet higher. A fifth watchtower stood beside the main gate, and a sixth sat in the middle of the camp. The surrounding land had been cleared of foliage, ruins and debris on every side, creating an open perimeter two hundred yards from the nearest tree line or pre-Cataclysm building. While there was only one entrance—the two wooden doors that formed the front gate—prisoners had quickly learned there were two exits. Complete subservience to the Fifth Order. Or death.

Everyday life remained the same for everyday people. People stilled worked, ate, raised families and worshiped. But the Fifth Order demanded absolute fealty. Those who balked or asked too many questions ended up in the camps. To ensure conformity of thinking and total allegiance, prisoners had to stop their labor and attend mandatory reeducation sessions twice per day. In each session, they heard speeches and propaganda about the Fifth Order, its vision for the realm, and the necessity of dutiful obedience.

Prisoners who acquiesced were allowed to return to their lives, although they were kept under observation to ensure that they did not lapse back into old thinking or practices. The prisoners who resisted reeducation or fought back—as well as those the Church deemed subversive—remained in the camp.

In the beginning, it had been said that Saxonburgh only housed criminals, and some inmates did fit that category. It had not taken long, however, for the Church and the Fifth Order to begin sending resisters, freethinkers and heretics as well. From there, it was an easy step to incarcerate anyone the new regime considered problematic. Men and women, old or young. Educators and artisans. Excommunicated Church officials. The wealthy and paupers. Intellectuals and the illiterate. All found themselves under suspicion and surveillance and became prime candidates for reeducation.

At first, there had been defiance from those who refused to capitulate. A group of two dozen men had once attempted to overpower the guards and escape from Saxonburgh. Their efforts were met with swift and ruthless retaliation. Eight of the men were executed on the spot. The others were confined to cells, starved and beaten.

New arrivals quickly learned that refusing an order meant abuse and torture. Anyone caught with contraband was stripped of their rations and branded with a symbol on the back of their hand. Attacking a Churchman warranted extended torture. It was not the Fifth Order's goal to kill prisoners. They needed them for labor, inside and outside the camp, and for subservience when they returned to their homes. Execution was sanctioned for escape attempts, but not before three random prisoners were killed in slow and agonizing ways while the escapee was forced to watch. No one wanted that on their conscience.

One of the most effective punishments was withholding food. Starvation became commonplace. The earliest prisoners were now hollow-eyed scarecrows. They moved and worked slower and received more beatings as a result. Scraps of food became black market commodities. When bored, guards sometimes took several famished prisoners, chained them together and tossed them a loaf of bread or wedge of cheese. The rest of the camp was often made to watch.

Saxonburgh was subdivided into three areas. The main gate opened directly into Camp One, which measured approximately seventy square yards. New arrivals marched single file into an open area. To their left were the former school buildings, now repurposed as offices, barracks and a kitchen for the Fifth Order and Churchmen. A livery, latrines and a private well stood near the western perimeter.

To the right of the open area was a single-story stone building that served as a processing center for new arrivals. Upon entering, a prisoner's personal information was carefully recorded. Each received a number, which the guards used instead of names. Dario Darien was Twenty-Three, Tycho Hawkes was Twenty-Four and Solomon Warner Twenty-Five. Blake was Thirty, Matthias Hart Thirty-One and Erik Landrew Thirty-Three.

From there, the frightened and confused prisoners were herded into the next room, where they received a bedroll, hygiene bucket, camp garments and a barracks assignment. Before exiting, prisoners had their heads shaved. The Fifth Order said it kept lice to a minimum. It actually made escapees easier to recognize and served as yet another humiliation.

Camp One was surrounded to the south and west by stone walls. The northern and eastern boundaries were marked by ten-foot-high barbed wire fences—barbed wire being a recent discovery by the Fifth Order. Rolls of it were being made by hand in Saxonburgh and sent out to other camps.

A gate in the northern fence opened into Camp Two, the primary reeducation and work area. It was approximately 150 yards long from east to west, and seventy yards wide north to south.

To the left were masonry and carpentry workshops, as well as a general repair shop. Materials were stored in a separate building behind them near the western wall. Two fenced-in work yards—one north of the shops, the other to the south—were busy from dawn to dusk as prisoners busted and carried rocks, crafted doors and furniture, shaped stones for the walls, and fixed weapons, wagon wheels, saddles and anything else that broke. A small infirmary was located near the northern wall.

Camp Two's main feature was the compliance center and chapel. The single-story buildings were connected by an enclosed hallway. The compliance center was a long, empty hall with a raised platform at one end. Prisoners sat on the floor during the sessions. Below them was the torture chamber referred to simply as "Downstairs." Chapel was mandatory on Worship Day.

Just north of these buildings was a long row of jail cells.

Separating Camp Two from Camp Three was a sandy staging area used for roll call and public punishment. Camp Three consisted of prisoner facilities. There were six barracks—three for men, three for women. Each was made to accommodate thirty people. Prisoners also had their own mess hall, kitchen and latrines. A growing cemetery rested between the first barracks and the northern wall.

The camp commandant was Witchfinder Supreme Basil Gries, who openly embraced the Fifth Order and carried out their policies with spiteful zeal. His pointed head and ears had earned him the secret nickname "Elf." Always at his side was a German Shepherd named Lump. Twenty deputies, twelve Crusaders, two Witchfinders and two constables served under him.

Inmates handled all the daily tasks in camp. Laborers toiled at whatever jobs they had been assigned. When Erik Landrew's vocation of armorer was discovered, he had been forced to work almost exclusively for the Crusaders. Men and women worked side by side but were forbidden to speak. Because of their youth, Hawkes, twenty-six, and Warner, twenty-four, performed hard labor. Since their arrival, they had felled trees to make fence posts, gates and buildings. They dug the prisoners' well, hauled stones to fortify the wall and unloaded crates of supplies and barrels of ale that came from Three Waters. Not that they got any ale. It all went to Gries and his men, as did all of the best food.

Breakfast consisted of oatmeal and bread with watery tea to wash it down. Lunch was normally potatoes or carrots in a thin broth, bread and a bit of cheese. Leftovers often reappeared at dinner. Prisoners got little meat. As a result, they lost muscle mass. Hair and nails became brittle. With each passing day, it became harder to fulfill work quotas, and beatings increased as a result.

Dario Darien, on the other hand, had miraculously landed a clerical job in the processing building. The day they arrived, the prisoners had been lined up and ordered to stand in the brutal heat for two hours. Eventually, a Crusader had appeared, purple cape flowing behind him. A Witchfinder and two deputies accompanied him.

"Blacksmiths, grooms—step forward!" the Crusader had bellowed.

Two did. The Crusader ordered them to the side.

"Masons, carpenters!"

Four had moved out of line and were grouped together.

The Crusader continued, calling for tailors, repairmen, tanners, wainwrights and just about every other known occupation. When he called for general laborers, Hawkes had signaled Warner with a tiny nod. They and Matthias Hart stepped forward.

"Who can read and write?"

Darien had been one of several to raise his hand.

They had all been questioned about their skill and abilities, then ordered to follow the Witchfinder. Hawkes and Warner had watched the group disappear into the processing building. Though a small measure of good fortune remained: they all shared the same barracks.

During meals, men sat together at one end of the mess hall, women at the other. A Crusader stood by the main doors. Another walked the perimeter of the room while a third strolled among the tables, listening for dissent or complaint. A Witchfinder named Frazier Clement also policed the tables. All wore the new regulation rank pin: an inverted triangle underneath a regular triangle, with red stone insets in the points to delineate rank.

What conversations took place were brief and, by necessity, hushed. Darien and two other inmates had developed a series of hand signals that allowed for additional communication.

"Anybody heard anythin' new today?" Warner muttered as he ate the last morsel of sausage. It had been two days since their last thumb-sized piece of meat. Warner savored the bite, chewing slowly to make it last as long as possible.

"Nashton fell yesterday," Matthias Hart said. He held a heel of black bread in his fingers.

"No shit, another one already?" Hawkes asked. "It was Baymouth just two weeks ago."

The main door opened, and Dario Darien shuffled in. Like all prisoners, he wore a loose-fitting gray tunic and matching breeches. He had no socks, but at least his boots weren't full of holes. A black letter C was sewn on the left side of his tunic. He got his soup bowl and went through the serving line. Hawkes slid over so the old man could sit between him and Warner, but Darien went around the table. He sat beside a scrawny man named Garvan Kirk.

"How're you feeling today, Dario?" Hawkes whispered when the old man was situated.

"About the same," he said. "Maybe a little better." He offered a feeble smile, and his voice sounded as weak as he looked. Bags lay deep and dark under his eyes. White stubble peppered his chin. The skin of his face and hands was wrinkled like a dried-up apple.

"You look better," Warner lied, trying to raise the old man's spirits. Darien's health had been poor when they arrived, and the harsh conditions in camp weighed heavily on him. Warner knew Darien could not survive the long winter without thicker clothes and extra blankets. But from what he had experienced so far, Warner had no reason to hope that such consideration would be given.

Darien reached into his pocket, eyes flitting around the room. Confident he was not being watched, he placed a closed fist on the bench beside Kirk.

Tears gathered in Kirk's eyes. He patted Darien's hand like a child comforting an ailing grandfather. Darien withdrew his hand. Kirk made a fist and shoved it into his pocket.

"Y-You didna have ta do that," Kirk whispered. His lower lip trembled.

"You need it," Darien said to his plate. "You take it."

"What'd you get him?" Hawkes asked.

Darien crunched his crust of bread. Crumbs fell on his chin. "Some ham left over from *their* breakfast." He said nothing else as Witchfinder Clement strode behind them.

The one ray of hope in this bleak misery was Darien's job. He was assigned to a recordkeeping role because of his extensive clerical skills. It took him longer to write things these days, due to the palsy that often afflicted his hands. But his mind remained sharp, for the most part.

There were benefits to working in the processing building. Darien received slightly better treatment. The C on his tunic reminded the guards that he was a clerk, and therefore a more valuable prisoner—something they needed to remember when dispensing punishment. Darien could sometimes take leftover food from the officers' table to supplement his own rations, which was where the ham had come from. He did not have to work outside. And most importantly, from his desk he could keep tabs on just about everything in the camp. The Fifth Order saw no harm in letting an old man handle the paperwork. They assumed he would likely die soon anyway, and this way none of them had to do the job. Plus, he was quite good at it.

While some prisoners trafficked in contraband, such as stolen food or tabáks, Darien's currency was information. Everything coming into or going out of the camp passed through the processing center. He saw the work orders and supply lists and special requisitions. He recorded every prisoner who arrived. He knew when the guards were scheduled to rotate in and out, the latest gossip from the Fifth Order and news of the outside world. The only thing he never got to see were the private messages sent by Appian redvalk. The camp kept one of the massive messenger birds in a cage. A prisoner named Fairchilde had been a 'valkmaster before being arrested and was put in charge of sending and receiving messages. Unfortunately, he never saw the content of them, either.

With Witchfinder Clement now strolling the aisles in the women's section, Darien lowered his voice and spoke just over the top of his bread.

"More prisoners will be arriving early next week. Sixteen more."

Hart shook his head. "We're running out of space. The barracks are already at capacity. How many more are they going to try and cram in?"

But they knew the answer. The Fifth Order would continue to bring in more prisoners. Soon they would be stacked like cordwood in the bunks of every barracks. The number of latrines was already insufficient.

"What about the children?" Hart asked, his voice hard, his blue eyes like ice.

Darien sat back. His shoulders slumped as a desperate longing filled his eyes. For a moment, he simply stared at the far wall. A tear dripped from his eyelid and landed on the back of his hand. When he spoke, his voice was so soft the others had to lean closer.

"I've…heard things. There's a connection between the Crusaders and the children."

Erik Landrew looked around the room without moving his head. "What sort of connection?"

"I don't know. But that's supposedly why all the children are being taken. They're being used for something."

"Is that why there ain't no children in these camps?" Warner asked.

Darien nodded. "They're kept in other places."

"Like the Citadel," Hart growled. "So the Children's Pilgrimage was just a way to get kids away from their families."

"Their families supposedly receive"—Darien cleared his throat—"special dispensations from the Church." He looked at Warner and then at Hawkes, his voice breaking. "We've got to save Cassidy and Cassandra."

"I know," Hawkes said. "And we will."

The Crusader by the door bellowed the command that signaled dinner was over. Standing in single file, the prisoners shuffled toward the door, leaving their cups and bowls. Those on kitchen detail would clean up.

As they stepped outside, a northern wind whipped their thin garments. Hawkes and Warner did their best to shield Darien with their bodies. The only light came from torches set at intervals along the walls and near the entrances to each building. They guttered in the wind.

Prisoners were allowed a little free time before lights out. Many waited in line for the latrines. Others huddled around fires, sneaking tabáks and talking about what had happened to their world. The camp roster included a few musicians, and the guards sometimes let them play in the evenings. Instruments, just like weapons, were kept locked away in the officers' building.

Darien, Hawkes, Warner, Hart and Landrew stood against the side of barracks Number Four, out of the wind. They had stuck together since their arrival, although Hart and Landrew slept in different barracks. Unfortunately, the benefits of Darien's job did not extend to more comfortable lodgings. His hard slab bunk lay between Hawkes and Warner's.

They had all made connections with other prisoners through work details, in the latrines and during the evenings. No matter where people came from, what family they belonged to or what station they held in life, all were the same now. Everyone suffered, without exception. They shared despair, anger and fear. A few of the older men were already giving up hope, shuffling around the camp like lonely ghosts. They went about their tasks, saying little, their spirits all but broken.

At the end of the second week in camp, a man and woman had attempted to escape. They hid in a wagon filled with stones and dirt. On the way out, the wagon had lurched, causing the rocks to shift. The woman cried out when one mashed her leg, and the guards apprehended them. They were forced to watch three older female prisoners have their throats slit before being hanged at the staging area. Since then, no one else had tried to escape.

There had been three suicides since they had arrived. But even that caused more suffering for those who remained. After the first suicide, prisoners had been forced to stand outside, naked, in the pouring rain for hours. After the second, random prisoners were tortured by having the soles of their feet whipped with ropes. A third suicide attempt had failed. After three weeks, the woman still remained locked in one of the camp cells.

Erik Landrew pulled a crinkled tabák from the pocket of his tunic. He went to a nearby fire, squatted down to talk with someone, and used a brand to light it. He returned with a stream of silver smoke following him. He did not care if tabáks were illegal. To hells with the Fifth Order.

"Look," Hawkes said, voice low, "if we're going to do something, it better be soon. We've already been here too long."

Hart agreed. "I want to find my wife and daughters."

"It's gonna be tough," Landrew said, pulling hard on the tabák. "We all know what happened last time."

Everyone fell silent. The only sound was the crackling of flames and the wind moaning around the eaves of the barracks.

Hawkes wrapped his arms around his thinning torso. "It's only been a few weeks. I don't think the Fifth Order will be expecting another attempt so soon."

"We need to act—" Darien said before breaking into a coughing fit. He caught his breath and added, "—while the weather's still on our side."

"All right then, enough talk," Hart declared. Like all Witchfinders, he was a man of action. "It's time to put something in motion. We've been looking for a way out, an idea we can pull off. Dario, can you keep us posted on what's going on in camp?"

The old man nodded.

"Erik, you're in the workshop most of the time. Can you trust anyone in there?"

He pinched out the tabák and slipped the remainder back in his pocket. "Don't trust nobody. Not except you all."

Hart scratched his head. His hair had recently been shaved again, and his scalp itched. He hoped it was not lice. "Sure, I know. But can you think of anyone who might support us when the time comes?"

The bulky black man listed three names. The group agreed on two.

"Talk to them when you can. Discreetly." Hart looked around the circle of shadowy faces. "Don't tell anyone what we're doing. Not yet. Just gauge their interest in the general idea. And no names. If someone gets caught, we don't want anyone else compromised. Tycho, can you and Warner do the same in your work groups?"

"No problem," Warner said.

"Tycho, from what I've seen most everyone likes you. You're outgoing, trustworthy and you don't seem to mind being the center of attention."

"Whew, ain't that the damn truth," Warner said.

Hawkes punched him in the shoulder. "That's what comes from growing up in a traveling carnival."

Hart continued. "Will you be our central point of contact? Every piece of information and every detail will run through you. You don't have to do everything or make every decision, just make sure that what needs to be done gets done."

"Absolutely."

"We need to consider *everyone* in camp," Darien said. "There are people in the infirmary. And the women. Whatever we attempt will affect everyone. If the time comes—*when* it comes—we have to give everyone the same opportunity to escape."

"He's right," Landrew replied. "Anybody left behind after the escape'll be punished, if not killed outright. It's not fair to them. So whatever we come up with, we let everyone know when the time is right. Choice'll be up to them. Can't make people go if they don't want to."

Warner smiled, his teeth beaming in the darkness. "Malachi would say that's what we're fighting for. The right to make our own decisions."

Hart smiled. "Then we're agreed. We'll look for options. We'll find out who we can trust when the time is right. Tycho will be our contact. Dario will keep us informed from behind his desk. I guess if there's anything else, we can take it as it comes."

A bell, deep and mournful, clanged over the camp like a dirge.

The men all clasped forearms before Hart and Landrew walked off to their barracks. All the men in barracks Number One made their way inside. Shuffling feet accompanied mumbled conversations and the creaking of wooden bunks. Ten minutes later, the bell sounded again.

In the blackness, Tycho Hawkes and Solomon Warner listened to Darien's raspy breathing as he slept. They had a plan now. Not much of one, but it was a start.

6
HOMECOMING

TUESDAY, SEPTEMBER 22, 999 AE

"Welcome to Deiparia," Thorne said to Tua and Amelia with false enthusiasm. They stepped off the ferry on the eastern shore of the Black River, just north of where it emptied into the Arkan Sea. They waited as the ferry returned to the western bank to shuttle Cabbott and their wagon across.

Thorne rubbed his eyes. Fatigue ate at him like a locust on a leaf. He wanted to lie down and sleep for days. But there was too much to do, too much at stake. He adjusted the bastard sword sheathed across his back and watched the ferry glide across the water.

Teska came over to him. "You're still pissed, I see."

"I'm fine." He avoided eye contact.

"Look, you may not like it, but it's the truth."

He spun around to face her. "You're just so damn sure, aren't you?"

Her hazel eyes darkened, and she stuck her chin out. "You don't have anything better! And it makes sense!"

"That Tua is some sort of…what? A spy? A plant by the Fifth Order? A shape shifter?" Thorne barked a humorless laugh. "I know him."

"We don't really know *anything* about him! Who knew where you were going when Mathan attacked you?" She gave him no chance to reply. "Tua."

Thorne shook his head and closed his eyes. Another headache was building behind his temples. He looked at the ferry. "I'd trust him with my life."

"Then you're just as likely to wake up with your damn throat slit!"

"And what about Amelia?" he asked the river.

"*Amelia?* Oh, for fuck's sake, Malachi! She's a farmer's wife. She's about as dangerous as one of her skillets of cornbread."

Thorne gave no reply. He hated when they did this. It clouded his judgment and tore at his guts. He preferred things neat and orderly, and it seemed this relationship was becoming more chaotic by the day. At least it had been more chaotic since Thurl's nightmare. Or prophecy. Or whatever it was.

Their most daunting obstacle during the last leg of the trip had been each another. Teska was adamant that Cabbott's nocturnal ramblings had been a warning that someone in their group was not who he—*or she*, Thorne reminded her—appeared to be.

Since their departure from the empty mercantile nine days ago, it had rained for five of them—the chillier, heavier rain that presaged winter. Two of those nights, they had no fire since there was no dry wood to be found. While water was abundant, their food supply was nearly gone. The past two days had been hardtack and wild carrots. The travel had not been overly strenuous, but the tension among them was as thick as cold porridge.

Cabbott still claimed no remembrance of his nightmare. "Whatever I said," he had declared, "was just gibberish. The ramblings of dreams, nothing more." After that, he refused to speak of it again. He continued to remain distant from the group, working on a map and journal of their journey to the Tex'ahn lands. "As far as I know, we're the first Deiparians to go there and come back."

"Other than Merrick," Thorne had replied.

"Yes. Other than *him*."

Tua and Amelia did not know Cabbott as well as the others. The uncertainty about what lay ahead made them anxious. Once, Tua had announced that he would be returning to his home, but Thorne convinced him to stay. That angered Teska. When she suggested that Cabbott was also worth watching, Thorne became enraged. He ranted about all that had happened to his friend and how his new demeanor was the Communion's fault.

For two days, the lovers had been sharp as razors and cold as January toward each other. Yesterday, they'd reached a fragile détente with a brief, passionless kiss and a hug.

He looked at her as she watched the ferry. The lines on her brow had deepened over the past few months, and she smiled less than as she used to. His heart ached for her to be happy again. He hated being a source of bitterness for her. He realized he had grown more selfish and demanding. He loved her and would do anything to keep her. But her words about his friends cut him, and he retaliated with his old Witchfinder Imperator arrogance. Of course, that never helped.

He reached out and stroked her ponytail with thick, calloused fingers.

She shot him a defiant look, but it softened as she searched his face. He knew he could be inflexible and infuriating. But he still could not stop trying to protect her. Yes, she had made it on her own just fine before they met. But everything was different now. She was no longer just a thief on the run from the Church. She was Nahoru'brexia. She had a position of importance in the Enodia Communion. The Church would love nothing more than to have her put to death.

She dropped her gaze to Thorne's mud-caked boots.

Teska Vaun was the best thing that had ever happened to him. He did not want to push her away. He stroked her cheek with his thumb. She looked up at his tentative smile, the kind that wonders if it will remain alone.

She could not help herself. She kissed him and felt her own smile return.

Amelia and Cabbott sat on the driver's bench as the wagon rattled along the road. Thorne, Teska and Tua rode ahead. The closer they came to Baymouth, the heavier the traffic became. Farmers hauled their final harvests of corn, pumpkins, wheat, apples and potatoes to market. Pigs, fattened throughout the summer, were ready to be sold to sustain families through the snow and ice. Textile merchants hawked new cloaks and robes. Wine criers encouraged patrons to stock up while they had the chance. And wagonloads of barley, smelling of summer's end, were headed to stables and silos. Flimsy white clouds that looked ready to disintegrate somehow clung to the pale, blue-streaked sky.

Another few miles down the road and traffic halted. Animals milled around as herdsmen tried to keep them together. Merchants cursed, and travelers exchanged news and gossip. Pilgrims and families and even some Churchmen blocked the road ahead. Children scampered and played. Merchants groused about the delay. Thorne questioned several travelers about the holdup, but no one knew the cause of it. After a thirty-minute wait, the traffic began to flow again. They continued south without incident for the remainder of the day.

"There," Thorne said, pointing to a small dirt road off to the left. "Head down that way. We'll stay the night since we're not going to make it to Baymouth before nightfall." Small campfires off the side of the road showed that others had reached the same conclusion.

About fifty yards down the side road, Cabbott and Amelia pulled off and stopped in a partial clearing. Thorne and Tua picketed the animals near a rough patch of grass. As Cabbott and Amelia slid from the driver's bench, Teska unfolded the rear steps and opened the back door.

Something thumped inside the wagon.

Amelia walked toward the back. "Teska, did you fall or—"

A burly man with a trimmed beard and heavily scarred face held a dagger to Teska's throat as he forced her down the steps.

She strained to pull away from the man's grip on her arm. "Let go of me, you bastard!"

Two more men emerged from the wagon. The first was of medium build with stringy hair and baggy eyes. He carried a dagger and a length of rope. Behind him was a broad-shouldered man. He had a tanned, oval face and a lazy eye beneath a shock of black hair. He held a loaded crossbow.

Thorne, Tua and Cabbott arrived behind Amelia, who wrung her hands.

"Let her go!" Thorne demanded, defaulting to his authoritative Witchfinder Imperator voice. "Who the hells are you? What is this?"

The man who held Teska grinned, a front tooth missing, and forced the blade harder against her skin. Her curse dissolved into a gasp.

"Got you, you son of a bitch!" he cried in triumph. "Now hand over those weapons."

Defiance burned in Thorne's green eyes, but he saw the anger and fear on Teska's face. This man would kill her without thinking twice. Thorne removed the sheathed sword from his back.

"Slow-like," the man with the crossbow said. He leveled it at Thorne's heart. "Take it nice 'n' easy. You two fuckers, too." He pointed at Cabbott and Tua.

"Move away from each other," the leader demanded. "Lay facedown on the ground. You too, bitch!" he bellowed at Amelia, who crumpled like a broken doll.

"I'm gonna kill you," Teska snarled.

Thorne handed his sword to the Crossbow Man. He threw it on the other side of the wagon. Thorne knelt, eyes flicking back and forth, assessing his options. Tua surrendered his weapons. They were also tossed out of reach. Cabbott remained standing, fists clenched.

Baggy Eyes stepped in front of Teska, uncoiling the rope. Her glare held all the fury of the Twelve Hells. She shifted her weight slightly, just enough to press the heel of her right boot into the ground. Neither man noticed the soft click that accompanied it.

"Boys," the scarred brute said, "we're gonna be rich! Damned stroke of luck, that jam-up on the road."

"Hopped in easy as you please," Baggy Eyes agreed. He smirked at Thorne.

"More bounty hunters," Thorne spat as he laid facedown on the ground.

"Franco Lynch," the brute answered with pride. "Just you remember that name. I'm the one that's claiming the bounty for the two of you."

"Two of us?" Thorne asked.

"You and this dumb bitch," he said, shaking Teska.

Baggy Eyes pawed her hair. "She's a right pretty little thing."

"End this. *Now!*" Cabbott roared. His voice tore across the clearing.

"Uh, say what, Grandad?" Lynch asked. Baggy Eyes and Crossbow looked at Cabbott with a mixture of surprise and humor.

It was all Teska needed.

Give men enough time, she thought, *and they always do something stupid.*

She kicked Baggy Eyes. The blade protruding from the toe of her boot sunk into his groin. The sudden movement caused Lynch to loosen his grip just enough for Teska to wiggle out of his grasp.

Baggy Eyes collapsed, shrieking like a little girl, hands to his bloody crotch.

Cabbott leapt forward. He thrust Crossbow's weapon toward the sky so hard that the man's finger tightened on the trigger, releasing the bolt into the treetops. Cabbott screamed like a soul damned to the Twelfth Hell and ripped his saber free.

Thorne and Tua got to their feet just as Cabbott plunged the sword into Crossbow's gut. The blade emerged from the man's back. Cabbott left it there and grabbed the crossbow off the ground. He turned on Lynch. With a scream of fury, he brought the crossbow down on the man's skull.

Teska bit Lynch's hairy arm, eliciting a bellow of pain and rage. He yanked her to the ground by the hair. She kicked at his legs, but the boot blade missed.

Cabbott struck him a second time. Lynch teetered, then careened to the ground. Cabbott stood over him, eyes wild. He slammed the broken crossbow into the scarred face again and again. Blood flew with each swing until there was nothing but mushy pulp and bone shards above the shoulders. With a demonic grin, Cabbott turned to Baggy Eyes.

The bounty hunter remained doubled over, sobbing and howling, his hands slick with blood. Cabbott yanked a dagger from the man's side.

Thorne helped Teska to her feet while waving a hand toward his friend. "Thurl, no! Wait! We need to interrogate—"

Cabbott slammed the blade into the man's back. Over and over.

Tua lost count after nine. He tried to pull Cabbott away from the twitching man.

Cabbott brushed him off with a snarl and resumed mutilating the body. Blood covered his tunic, hands and face. "I said no!" he snarled, spittle flying from his lips. "No more! This ends now! You do not—*you will not*—threaten us again! Is. That. Clear?" On the final blow, he left the dagger between the shoulder blades. Cabbott spat on the body and stood up, dripping blood.

Thorne, Teska, Tua and Amelia stared at him in disbelief.

Cabbott walked past them, breathing heavily, but made no eye contact. He threw his tunic away and climbed into the wagon to get a clean one. When he reappeared, his friends were still rooted to the spot, mouths agape.

After dumping the bodies in the woods by himself, Cabbott refused to discuss the incident. He kept to himself until time for dinner. Afterward, around the campfire, Thorne broached the subject once more.

"Thurl, what happened? Earlier today."

The now-familiar gleam in Cabbott's eyes danced in the firelight. He leaned back against a log and looked at Thorne. "I suppose I do owe you an apology. But you must admit, it was them or us."

"I'm not disagreeing with what happened to those bounty hunters. I'm concerned about *how* it happened."

"Thank you, by the way," Teska said from the other side of the fire. "But you could've gotten me killed. That bastard would've had no qualms about slitting my throat. The bounty was alive *or* dead."

Cabbott apologized to Teska. "I guess I just…cracked. Maybe it has been the strain of all the travel. Or maybe"—his tone became thick and tough as leather—"I am just sick and tired of being hunted and jumped and attacked."

Thorne studied his friend. "In all our years together, I've never seen such bloodthirstiness, such intense rage from you," he said. "And afterward… Well, you just went off and sat in the woods for hours. I understand that you maybe needed some time, but—"

Cabbott raised a hand to stop him. "I let my emotions get the better of me. I acted without thinking." He apologized to Teska again. "I am not proud of what I did." He seemed to be searching for the right thing to say. "I just—I do not know…"

Thorne and Teska looked at each other as Cabbott stared into the fire. After a moment, Thorne said, "We're just worried about you, old friend. We know you've been struggling ever since Last Chapel. If I knew what to do for you, I'd do it."

Cabbott seemed somewhat perturbed that Thorne wanted to continue the conversation. "I know," he said curtly. "And I appreciate that." Then he rolled onto his side, away from the fire.

The next day, they bypassed Baymouth. The Church still hunted them, and Thorne had no idea how many more bounty hunters might still be out there. They remained hidden on the outskirts of the city while Amelia slipped into a market to pick up some supplies. They kept to less-traveled roads and made camp again as evening fell.

They arrived outside the village of Corinthia on Thursday morning. Thorne instructed them to stay out of sight while he was gone. He returned after several hours, informing them that Dubose and Carden would meet them later that night. They settled down among tall pines to wait.

Around eleven o'clock, the two men emerged from the inky darkness. Rich DuBose stood shorter than Thorne and Cabbott. Long blond hair arched down over one eye, and his smile was playful against the hard jawline. He wore a dark-green tunic, black breeches and boots, and a woodsman cape.

With him stood Murnau Carden. His black skin and dark clothing melded so well with the nighttime forest that at first all anyone could see were his eyes and teeth. As he moved closer to the fire, they saw his black mohawk that tapered to a long braid at the back. The letter T had been branded into the back of one hand. Multiple earrings hung from each lobe. He stood as tall as Thorne, with what seemed like twice as many muscles.

Thorne, DuBose and Carden bypassed the clasped-forearm greeting and went straight to bear hugs. They did the same with Teska, but Cabbott merely nodded and smiled, not allowing them close. Thorne introduced Tua and Amelia. She blushed when Rich offered her a flamboyant greeting and kissed her hand. Her attention was fixed on his smile and dimples. Tua frowned and looked away.

"You ready to go, mate?" Rich asked Thorne.

Carden slipped back into the darkness and returned with horses. Tua helped Amelia onto the driver's bench, then climbed up beside her. With their mounts tied behind the wagon, the group left the forest and made their way down a deserted dirt road. The fragments of the moon glimmered like distant suns.

On the way, Thorne broke the news about Merrick, but DuBose and Carden already knew. The Fifth Order had made a public proclamation of his capture and execution. They had silenced the renegade and reaffirmed the Church's supreme authority.

"Except it wasn't an execution," Thorne spat. "It was cold-blooded murder." He told his friends the details of what had happened in Last Chapel and about their journey to the Tex'ahn lands. They talked of the information Thorne had gleaned from his search.

Shortly after midnight, DuBose and Carden brought them to the ruins of an ancient building. Upon seeing it, Thorne's heart caught in his throat. It was the high school where he had first met Traugott—and discovered that the man he hated and hunted for so long was actually his former mentor. Thorne stared at the empty frame where the school doors had once stood. His mind carried him back to breakfast in the library and a life-changing conversation in the office. His heart felt as empty as the derelict building in front of him.

"Get some rest," Carden told them, his voice deep in the still night air.

"We'll be back tomorrow with some supplies. We've got a lot of catching up to do." With that, DuBose and Carden slipped away as if they had never been there.

The two men returned under a graying sky early Friday afternoon. They stabled their horses with the wagon and other mounts inside what had once been called a "gymnasium." Back outside, they sat on a ring of logs encircling a fire pit.

"You've only been gone a few weeks," DuBose said, "but since Last Chapel fell, things have moved like greased eels. Those damn Crusaders don't ever seem to sleep."

Thorne scratched his goatee. "We've heard talk ever since we made it to Baymouth. What's the Fifth Order up to?"

"Well, mate, the biggest thing is the compliance camps."

"We've heard those mentioned in whispers," Teska said. "What are they?"

"The Church—really the Fifth Order—has been constructing them all over the realm. They're holding facilities for certain people."

Thorne frowned. "What people?"

"Heretics. Traitors. Basically anybody the Fifth Order considers dangerous or potentially rebellious," Carden said.

DuBose continued, "Once there, they undergo 'reeducation,' as they like to call it. Some stay a week or two, others for longer. But those who come back are… different."

Teska leaned forward. "Different how?"

DuBose raked the hair out of his eyes. Amelia watched him with unabashed infatuation. Tua observed it all with disapproval.

"It's like they've been brainwashed," he replied. "They're the same people, but they're not. They come back full of piss and vinegar about how great the Fifth Order is, how the Church is going to have a golden new millennium and that complete obedience to the Fifth Order is our duty."

"But how can the Church condone this?" Thorne asked. His brow furrowed in confusion.

"That's just it; the Fifth Order has assumed control of the Church. They run the whole thing now. The other Orders do their bidding, no questions asked."

"How many of these compliance camps are there?" Teska asked.

Carden shook his head. "We're not sure."

"Word through the underground is that every major city will have at least one. There's one in Covington, outside Baymouth. Opened about a month ago. Two weeks ago, a camp opened in Anlin, outside Nashton. That was a week before Nashton fell," DuBose said.

"When you say 'fell'…" Thorne began.

"I mean the entire city is under the dominion of the Fifth Order. New laws are put in place. Crusaders replace the constables, deputies and Witchfinders who won't go along. Everything's about the Fifth Order now."

Teska wrapped a strand of hair around her finger as she spoke. "How many cities have fallen?"

"Four that we know of: Last Chapel, Baymouth, Nashton and Three Waters," Carden said.

"Three Waters?" Thorne leaned forward, his voice filled with anxiety. "When?"

DuBose and Carden looked at each other. "End of July, beginning of August."

"Damn!" Thorne said. Teska laid a hand on his arm.

Now it was Dubose's turn to question. "What?" He looked from Thorne to Teska.

Thorne stared at the charred fragments in the fire pit. "You remember Dario, Tycho and Solomon? My men who were with us last time we were here? They were going to Three Waters."

No one spoke. Birds sang in the nearby treetops. A light breeze eased by, bearing the distinct scents of dead leaves and pinecones.

Thorne broke the silence. "What about your meetings? The freedom movement?"

DuBose stretched his legs out in front of him and crossed his arms as he leaned back against a log. He shook his head. "It's harder to do now. There're more sweeps and roundups, more arrests—"

"We still meet," Carden interjected. "When we can. With whom we can."

"When Traugott"—DuBose nodded at Thorne—"that is, when Merrick didn't come back, we just… He was the mortar that held everything together." He dropped his gaze to the ground. His shoulders slumped.

Carden snarled and gritted his teeth. "We wanted to keep it going. But the damned Church and those fucking Crusaders…"

DuBose looked up at Thorne again. "The fire's still there. People want to know. Hells, they *need* to know. Now more than ever."

"We need someone like Traugott," Carden said. "A leader. Someone who isn't afraid to stand up and be the face of the movement."

"You are talking about a martyr," Cabbott said, speaking for the first time.

"Only if they're caught," DuBose said.

Cabbott smirked. "You mean like Merrick?"

"Shut up, Thurl," Teska said.

Thorne motioned for silence. "It's hard to believe that so much has changed in such a short amount of time. But things are different than when Val did this. His battle was against the Church. Ours"—he looked around the ring of faces—"is against the Fifth Order. Yes, the Church has its problems. But it once stood for something great, and I believe it could do so again. But not as long as the Fifth Order exists. They're the real enemy. They have been all along. They're a hidden plague at the heart of the Church."

"So what, then?" DuBose asked, uncrossing his arms. "What do we do?"

Thorne leaned forward again, a glint in his eyes and a captive smile on his lips. "We begin by giving the people what they need," he said. "A leader. Then we come up with a way to bring down the Fifth Order."

"How would you do such a thing?" Tua asked, having taken everything in.

"I don't know yet," Thorne said. "But first we need to stoke the fire again." He looked at DuBose and Carden. "Teska has to get to Attagon. Could we meet with your groups on the way there? Like Merrick did?"

Both men nodded.

"They won't follow me if they don't know me or trust me. I've got to become more visible to them. I'm sure you don't know every group Merrick had contact with, but they must be familiar with one another. Like a chain. Each group connects to the one behind it and in front of it." He stopped to catch his breath. "Will you take me?"

Once again DuBose and Carden looked at each other. They grinned. "Damn right, we will, mate!"

"Can I ask the two of you one more thing? Will *you* join me?" Thorne asked.

Carden stood and placed a clenched fist over his heart. "You have my sword and my loyalty, my friend."

DuBose likewise stood. With a wide grin, he extended his hand.

"What's so funny?" Thorne asked as he grasped the forearm.

"Not amused," DuBose said. "Just pleased. Before we split up outside Nashton, Merrick told us that one day you'd carry on his work."

Thorne felt a wave of warmth touch his heart, and he smiled, too.

7
IDEAS

SATURDAY, SEPTEMBER 26, 999 AE

"We don't have a lot of time."

Tycho Hawkes kept his voice low and glanced around Camp Three's yard. Prisoners gathered at firepits between the mess hall and barracks Number Six. Deputy Edgar Sousby watched from the closest tower. Hawkes liked Sousby. They were about the same age, and Hawkes thought he could detect some discontent in the deputy's demeanor.

Around one fire were Hawkes and Hart, Darien and Warner, Landrew and two new allies. Rian Clancy was a balding, middle-aged man with thick hands and a protruding lower lip. His beard was sparse—as if the hairs had drawn lots to see which would stick out and which would stay hidden—and his heavy jowls made him look like a hound dog. He was a metalworker by trade and assigned to make the barbed wire.

The other man was tall and lanky, which was only exacerbated by poor nutrition. Hawkes guessed that Oliver Wycroft was at least fifty. He had high cheekbones and an aquiline nose, and more wrinkles around his brown eyes than anywhere else. Before being sent to Saxonburgh, Wycroft had been a teacher in the Abthanian Order. He taught mathematics, philosophy and history to Advanced Catechism students. Refusing to surrender some of his students to the Fifth Order had landed him there.

"Don't everybody sit the same way," Hart whispered. "This needs to look like we're just enjoying our free time." He looked at Warner, slapped him on the back, and laughed out loud.

Warner squinted his good eye. "What the hells you do that for?"

"Selling it to the guards," he said. "Report." Hart leaned forward and poked the fire. Sparks rose into the air and vanished. "Dario?"

"Unfortunately, I have nothing new to report. There hasn't been a single thing worth noting."

Landrew spat into the fire. "We been doing this for nine days now," he growled. "And you saying there ain't been one thing we could use?"

"What kind of ideas do we have?" Hawkes asked, pushing on.

"Forget diggin' out. Ground's too cold for that now," Warner said.

Clancy spoke for the first time. "Aye, an' we need weapons."

"We have a few," Hart said, keeping his head down. Prisoners who spent too much time looking around caught the attention of the guards. "Mostly just shivs we've been able to smuggle out of the repair shop. We've got maybe half a dozen."

"Need more 'n that," Clancy said.

"I agree. But all the weapons are locked in the armory in the Fifth Order's offices."

Head down, Hawkes spoke to the fire as he poked it again. "I've been wondering about scaling the wall."

Warner hooked a thumb at his friend. "He could do it, too. Raised in a travelin' carnival. He can jump like a cricket on a hot stove."

"If I could get on top of our latrine, I think I could make the jump to the wall."

Wycroft was a man of medium build, and he wore his thinning hair parted to the side above a slender brow with deepening creases of worry and fatigue. His cheeks were hollow, his ashen mustache and beard unkept. Green eyes, filled with wisdom, peered into the fire.

He cleared his throat like an instructor in front of a class. "My dear Master Hawkes, while I do not doubt your acrobatic prowess, you'd have to clear almost ten feet from the roof of the—ahem—outbuilding to the wall. And the wall is easily ten feet taller than the roof." He shook his head as if he'd just graded a particularly poor paper. "I don't see how you could traverse such a distance without the aid of a rope."

"Wow, Oliver, thanks for pissin' down his back," Warner grouched.

Clancy jerked his head in the direction of the watchtower. "Aye, an' we got those bloody shites t' consider, too."

Landrew nodded, eyes narrowed. His teeth were bright in the orange glow of the fire. "Kill 'em," he said and spat on the ground.

Darien massaged his left knee. "I hesitate to bring this up, gentlemen, but someone has to do it." He looked at the men around him. "*Are* we going to kill all the guards?"

"They'll kill us if ordered to," Clancy replied. "Hells, might not even need a bloody order."

Landrew leaned toward the fire, elbow resting on his knee. He stared hard at Darien. "Fuck right, we're gonna kill 'em. Like Clancy says, they'd do it to us without a second thought."

Darien chewed his lower lip. "But how do we know *all* of the guards are supportive of the Fifth Order? Some may have been forced into this, just as we've all been forced to do things we disagree with." He looked at Landrew and Clancy.

"Dario, I sympathize," Hart said. "But how would we know who is being coerced and who is doing this willingly? We can't just go up and ask them."

Darien's hands trembled from the cold. He tucked them under his armpits. "But there's got to be a way—"

"We don't have the time." Hawkes interrupted. "I'm sorry, Dario. I really am."

Wycroft cleared his throat again and said, "Gentlemen, we could consider all the moral and ethical arguments related to this situation. But I do feel it necessary to point out that there is soundness to Master Darien's question."

"How so?" Hawkes asked.

"As I told you before, I am here because I refused a direct order from a Crusader. I would not turn over my students without proper parental authorization, which I did not have. As I was being arrested and my students taken by the Fifth Order, the Crusader who chained me said something. I had actually forgotten about it until I started talking with Masters Darien and Hart—"

"Get on with it already," Clancy said.

Wycroft stuck out his chin. He looked away from Clancy, his mouth pinched. "Yes, well, as I was saying, the lumbering brute told me, and I quote: 'No harm will come to them unless it comes to us first. Your precious charges will be well looked after. I swear on my life.' Then he laughed and rousted me from my classroom."

Hart's eyes smoldered. Darien's filled with tears.

"Which means what?" Hawkes prompted, glancing around the yard. They would have to break up soon. About half of the prisoners had started shuffling toward the barracks.

"As we've speculated," Darien said to Hawkes, "there's some sort of link between the children and the Crusaders. 'No harm will come to them unless it comes to us first,' implies a connection."

Hart turned pale. "Are you saying that if a Crusader is harmed…" Trepidation filled his voice.

"It could mean harm to a child," Wycroft said.

"We don't know that for sure," Clancy pointed out.

"No, we absolutely do not," Hawkes agreed. "But it adds another obstacle to our plans. Shit."

"We need to find out more about this," Darien said.

"We ain't got the time," Landrew growled. "We gotta move, and we gotta do it soon."

"We're gonna need horses," Warner said. "And a wagon, too. Ain't no way Dario can ride a horse through this country in winter."

"The livery," Wycroft said, casting a quick glance toward Camp One.

"Aye, except how the hells do we get 'em?"

Hawkes shook his head. "Same problem. Just like the weapons."

"Whatever we do, it needs to happen at night. We'll have the darkness for cover. Maybe even some drowsy guards. Plus, we'd have more time to pull it off. We've only got a few hours between roll calls during the day," Hart said.

Hawkes snapped his fingers. "I've got it!" His grin spread from ear to ear. "We've been thinking about this the wrong way."

"Huh?" Landrew and Clancy both said at the same time.

"We've been looking at this from the standpoint of getting out."

Clancy snorted. "Aye, that's kind of the fucking point."

"It is," Hawkes agreed. "But in order to do that, we've got to have access to weapons, horses, food. I mean, even though Saxonburgh village is close by, and Three Waters is a few miles down the road, we're going to need supplies. Especially when the snows come. Plus, we've got to think about those in the infirmary. And the old. Getting out means tangling with all those guards. It's a lot to account for."

Wycroft steepled his thin fingers. "So, if you do not believe that extricating ourselves from this prison is the solution, what exactly do you propose?"

"We'll escape. Have no doubt about that." He was still grinning. "And when we do, we'll ride right out that gate." He made a subtle gesture across the yard.

They looked through the barbed wire, past the processing building, to the wooden front gates.

Landrew chuckled, but there was no mirth in it.

"An' they're just gonna let us ride right through, pretty as ye please?"

"I think we'll have a better chance at escape…if we take over the camp first."

Clancy's eyes bugged. "Yer fucking nuts!"

Warner scowled. "That's gotta be the strangest thing I've ever heard you say. And I've heard some mighty strange stuff from that yap."

"Listen, listen!" Hawkes hissed under his breath. "Just give me a minute. I don't have all the answers. But I think it could work."

"Tycho, there's a handful of us. How would we take over the whole camp?" Hart asked.

"We get all the people who're on our side. We assign each of them a task. It's almost time for another work crew to go cut firewood for the officers' quarters and the barracks. If I could take the place of one of the work crew guards—"

Clancy rubbed his face with his palm. "Holy shite! We really gonna listen to this bloody madness? I thought we're planning an escape, not a fucking fairy tale."

Hawkes dropped his smile. "Clancy, shut the hells up. Unless you've got a better idea."

"Aye, I got a better 'n. How about I smash yer fucking face!" The burly metalworker stood up, fists clenched, jaw set.

"For the Church's sake," Hart whispered, ducking his head. "*Sit down* before you call the guards down on us!"

Wycroft nodded. "Master Clancy, perhaps if you would do as he suggests—"

"Fuck you! An' fuck this whole idea. Yer all crazy as shithouse rats!" He stomped across the yard and into his barracks.

Deputy Sousby appeared disinterested from his perch in the watchtower.

"Is he going to be trouble?" Hawkes asked Landrew. His tone was as cold as the ground and twice as hard.

"I'll talk to him. He'll come around. He's just—"

"High strung?" Wycroft interrupted. "Excitable?"

Landrew spit. "Nah, I was just gonna say he's an asshole. But he'll be there for us."

Hawkes threw Warner a glance that said, "keep an eye on him."

Warner nodded.

Hawkes leaned forward and kept his voice low. "Here's what I'm thinking. At the end of the day, I can get the work crew back into the camp as the sun's going down. If I can manage to delay the crew a little bit, we might be able to make it back after dark. If you've noticed, the guard always opens the gate before we ever get close. Once we're in Camp One, I'll give the signal. Our people will take out the guards in the towers. We'll need several groups to handle specific jobs when the time comes."

Hart leaned closer to the fire and looked across it at Hawkes. "So, you bring the crew in. I'll lead a second group to take over the watchtowers."

"We'll need a third group to simultaneously move against the guards on the ground, and a fourth group to move against the barracks. While all that's going on, a fifth group can raid the armory." Hawkes smiled.

Hart looked doubtful. "Tycho, getting five different groups to work in unison will be extremely difficult. And you *do* remember there are Crusaders here, don't you? This might possibly work if it was just deputies or constables. But Crusaders?"

Hawkes ran a hand over his scalp, forgetting his hair was no longer there. "I know, I know. It'll take the strongest, most courageous people we've got. If we could catch the majority of the Crusaders in their barracks and burn it down—"

"But again, what if they are somehow connected to the children?" Darien asked.

"How do we fight them without gettin' the weapons first? And can we trust that many people with this plan?" Doubt had also filled Warner's face.

"We pick one wrong person, this all goes to shit, and we die," Landrew added.

Hawkes sighed in frustration. "And if we stay here, we're going to die one way or another." He raised one finger for each possibility. "If the guards don't kill us, or we don't drop from exhaustion, or get sick from the cold, then we'll starve to death!" He held up four fingers. "We can't wait around for any of that to happen."

"I agree," Hart said.

Darien looked at Hawkes and laid an arthritic hand on his arm. "Tycho, you don't have to figure all of this out by yourself. Lighten up, lad. You look like you've been through a torture session. We can help. I think you've got a good beginning."

"You really do," Hart said. "I have to admit I was skeptical when you started talking." He grinned. "If we can come up with a way to get those weapons, I think we'd have a fighting chance. And that's all any of us can ask for right now, isn't it?"

8
DWALE

MONDAY, OCTOBER 5, 999 AE

Clouds like bloated corpses covered the sky like a mass grave. The wind howled and cut through the thin camp uniforms like a razor. By noon, six inches of snow blanketed the camp. Hawkes knew it was six inches because that's how high the hem of his breeches were from the ground. He could not feel his feet. He could not remember the last time he did.

He breathed heavily as he rammed the shovel against the frozen ground. Sweat stood out on his skin despite the frigid air. He wanted to get this over with and get back to the pitiful woodstove in the barracks. He glanced over at the sled. Two more to go. He stabbed at the earth again. Brown chips of dirt flew into the air and fell with the snow. Exhaustion threatened to bury Hawkes as he buried the dead. He just wanted to lie down. If only he could sleep for a little while.

Out of the corner of his eye, he saw Warner approaching but kept digging. Deputy Weller was watching. He was an oafish taskmaster who forced prisoners to work no matter what the conditions. The elements never seemed to bother him.

"Hey, buddy, need some help?" Warner asked. Without waiting for an answer, he plunged his shovel into the area marked out for the grave. *Another* grave.

Two days ago, they had upset Witchfinder Supreme Gries, although neither had any idea what they did. Of course, it really did not matter. Gries needed no reason for his cruelty. After sound beatings for both of them, Gries had taken away their food rations and assigned them to the burial detail.

"H-H-How many?" Hawkes shivered as he worked.

"How many what? Days we been doin' this?"

"No—bodies."

Their shovels crunched in the dirt. Warner paused to adjust the flimsy excuse for a scarf around his face, then went back to digging. "Four in the past two days. Six since last Wednesday."

"Weller…l-l-let you help me?"

"Weller? Hells, no!" Warner chuckled.

It sounded warm, and Hawkes wondered if it could help his frostbite.

Warner dug as fast as he could. "He hauled himself back inside. Probably drinkin' ale and eatin' beef right now." His breath billowed as it hit the icy air.

"So who—"

"Deputy Sousby. He replaced Weller."

Hawkes paused for a moment and looked over his shoulder. Sousby stood thirty feet away, a crossbow halfway pointed in their direction. The man stomped his feet and shivered. When he made eye contact, he offered an apologetic smile.

The snow creaked under their feet like warped floorboards. Hawkes tried to flex his fingers but found them nearly frozen around the handle. He stared at Sousby's lambskin-lined gloves with longing.

"Got some good news," Warner whispered as they worked.

"Sousby's g-gonna let us build a s-s-snowman?"

Warner smiled. It appeared lopsided behind the scarf. Snowflakes hit his face and vanished. "Glad to see you ain't lost your sense of humor."

"I'm fucking freezing, J-Jester, get on with it."

"There's goin' to be a guard rotation next Monday."

"And?" Hawkes stumbled to the other side of the grave and continued digging.

Warner lowered his voice even more. "It'll be the perfect time for the takeover."

Hawkes shot him a confused glance. "H-H-How is having *more* g-guards in camp supposed to help us?"

"That's just it; there won't be more guards. There'll be *less*. Dario saw the message. On Sunday, they're movin' a few guards out. On Monday, the rest'll leave and be replaced by a new group."

Hawkes stopped shoveling. He felt nothing below his knees. He had to look to be sure that he had not accidentally buried his feet under the dirt. "Less guards," he whispered into the wind.

"We could make our move sometime Sunday or early Monday mornin'." Warner leaned on the handle of his shovel.

"Get back to work!" Sousby yelled.

"And that ain't all," Warner continued out of the side of his mouth. "We've got more people who're ready to help. At least four dozen, according to Hart."

"Nearly fifty people?" Hawkes asked in surprise.

"Not countin' us, Dario, Landrew or Hart."

Hawkes blew on his hands to warm them, but it was a futile gesture. "Wh-What about Clancy?"

They heard Sousby stomping his feet and the raw howl of the wind over the noise of their digging.

Warner shook his head. "I don't think so. Seems he was seen talkin' to Witchfinder Clement the other day."

"Do we n-n-need to kill him?"

Warner stopped shoveling and stared at his friend. Hawkes's eyes were weak, and his complexion was only a few shades brighter than the clouds. His hands were chapped, caked with dirt and verging on blue. He bore too much resemblance to the bodies they had been laying to rest. A shiver that had nothing to do with the cold ran down Warner's spine.

"C-Come on. Hurry it up!" Sousby shouted into the wind.

"You want to *kill* Clancy?" Warner asked. He pushed his shovel into the deepening grave and tried to wrap his mind around his friend's question. Tycho Hawkes was a fun-loving, easygoing fellow. Gregarious. A natural showman. Warner had seen his friend do some harsh and nasty things in service to the Paracletian Order. But he had never known him to speak about murder with such bluntness. The camp was not only taking a toll on his body. His spirit was flaking away.

Like those wax dummies in Last Chapel, Warner thought, *just before Rann captured us*. He remembered knocking one over and how it disintegrated into dust. He looked at Hawkes. His friend was upright, for now. But he was falling all the same.

Hawkes paused, his shovel halfway between the grave and the pile of dirt. "Do we need to k-k-kill him?" he demanded.

Warner sighed. "I don't know. Maybe. Let's just get this done so we can get inside."

For dinner, Hawkes received a bowl of warm soup that was actually just water with three chunks of potato in it, along with a finger-length strip of chicken. The others at the table snuck bits of carrots, leeks and chicken from their bowls into his. He would have cried at the generosity, but his tears were frozen like the rest of him. He shook so badly he needed two hands to hold the spoon.

"You're going to the infirmary after this," Darien told him. Hawkes did not object.

He was so ravenous that Darien and Warner had to keep him from eating too fast. When the soup and bread were gone, he looked around for more like a child searching for a missing parent.

Warner could not take it. "Come, showoff, let's get you some help."

Hart and Warner put Hawkes between them, and Hart convinced the Crusader by the door to let them leave. It was colder now, and snow continued to fall. It had to be close to a foot deep. The snow crunched as they tried to walk in the footsteps left by others. The sound reminded Warner of the cemetery. He gritted his teeth and checked his burning rage at the thought of having to dig his friend's grave.

"Hurry up," he urged as they stumbled through the freezing night.

Two women huddled around a small stove in the infirmary's front section as Hart and Warner dragged Hawkes through the door. Snowflakes followed but disappeared in the warmth.

"Close 'at damn door!" a woman shouted. She had dark skin and wore the same garments as they did, but hers could have been used to make four full sets with some left over. She rose from a chair and waddled toward them. Hart shut the door while Warner eased Hawkes down on a bench.

Beyond the stove, chairs and a desk, the rest of the building was divided into individual bays separated by curtains. Two more stoves sat equidistant down the central walkway. Coughs and moans floated on air that tasted like mold and smelled of roots and bitter herbs.

"Camille, go get 'at healer," the heavyset woman instructed. She stood in front of Hawkes and looked him up and down. "What's wrong with 'im?"

The other woman—thin, pallid and dressed the same—pulled a tatty blanket around her shoulders and left.

"Overexposure," Hart said as he closed the door behind the woman.

"Burial detail," Warner added. "Past two days."

"Mm-hmm," she mumbled as she poked and prodded Hawkes. She lifted his hands one at a time. "Ooh, 'at's bad, 'at is."

Warner watched her. She was no more than five foot six at most. He guessed her weight somewhere between two hundred fifty and three hundred pounds. She had plump cheeks, a wide mouth and two chins. Her eyes were dark but bore a kindness that Warner never thought he would see in a compliance camp.

"Looks like malnutrition, too," she said as she went back to the desk. She sat down and wrote something on one of the many parchments that covered the top. "Number?" she asked without looking up.

"Mine or his?" Warner asked.

"His."

"Twenty-four. His name is Tycho Hawkes."

"Don't need no name. You know they don't let us use no names." She scratched some more lines on the parchment before pushing herself up and plodding down the center walkway. "Bring 'im down here."

Hawkes had regained a little of his strength, so he shuffled behind her. Warner remained by his side. Each cubicle they passed held a prisoner on a hard, wooden bed.

At least they got their own pallets and blankets, Warner thought. It galled him to think that someone had to be so close to death to be allowed the simple luxury of comfort.

"What's your name?" Warner asked as he helped the woman stretch Hawkes out on a bed.

"Told you we don't use no names here."

"Apologies," Warner said. "I just heard you call the other woman Camille."

"Yeah, well… We work together."

The woman fussed the edges of the blanket around Hawkes. She gave him a drink of water and pointed a sausage-shaped finger at him. "You stay right there. Don't you go getting up." She returned to the makeshift office.

As they arrived, the door opened. A gaunt-looking man whom Warner first took to be a prisoner limped in. Camille followed behind him, her eyes watching the floor. Hart closed the door again.

"What is it?" the man asked with an annoyed, nasally whine. He removed his cap, and the remains of his white hair lay around his ears like snow on mountaintops. He pulled a pair of spectacles from his pocket, wiped the lenses, and slipped them on his bony nose. His eyes became twice as large.

"Prisoner Twenty-Four, down in bay seven. Looks to me like frostbite. Starved, too." She paused. "But ain't that the way with all of 'em?"

"Not you, Eighty-One." The old man chuckled. His voice was raspy. "You've got enough to live on for a full year." He limped off toward the bay.

The woman showed her middle finger to his back. "Damn ol' son of a bitch."

"I'm sorry," Warner said to her in a soft tone.

She grinned a toothy smile. "You be sorry for him. One a' these days, I'm gonna sit my fat ass down on that scrawny little turd an' make a greasy spot of 'im."

"Pop him like a grape, eh?" Warner said, returning her smile.

"Mm-hmm. Gonna get outta this place one of these days, find my three young'uns. But before I do, I'll flatten 'at ol' son of a bitch."

"Eighty-One! Seventeen!" the physician barked. "Get the surgery table ready."

Hart's eyes widened. "Surgery? What for?"

The physician returned. His white goatee and mustache made him look like he had been hit in the face with a snowball. Warner choked back a giggle.

"Two of those fingers on the left hand have to come off," the healer said without a hint of compassion or care. "If not, it'll be the whole arm within a week."

Warner seethed inside but kept a straight face. He looked at Hart, who had the same expression and simmering eyes.

The old man flopped his hand at Camille. "Seventeen! Don't forget the dwale! And be careful with it, you clumsy heifer. Keep it away from those stoves."

Warner gave the big woman a questioning look. Camille drifted by, clutching a glass jar full of liquid. The emptiness in her eyes made Warner want to look away.

"What's in the jar?" Hart asked.

"Dwale," Eighty-One said as if the word explained everything.

Down in the cubicle, the physician issued orders.

"It's something new from the Fifth Order," she added as an afterthought.

"*Dwale?* What's that? I've never heard of it before," Warner said.

"Some concoction. He pours a bit on a rag and puts it over a patient's face. They go right to sleep and don't wake up for a while."

Hart rubbed his chin. "Why'd he tell her to stay away from the stoves?"

"You get it around fire"—she held her hands together as if praying and then pushed them up and apart—"BOOM! Dwale blows right up. I hear some of them Fifth Order sons a' bitches burnt themselves up making it. Good riddance." She spat on the floor.

Warner and Hart looked at each other.

"And how much of this dwale do you keep around here?" Hart asked in what he hoped was a nonchalant manner.

She sat down. The chair creaked beneath her weight. "Just got two more bottles in last week. With winter coming on, these sons a' bitches expecting a lot more amputations."

Warner flashed Hart a devilish grin.

"You boys best git," she said. "Ain't nothing you can do for Twenty-Four now, 'cept wait."

Hart opened the door on the hyperborean weather.

Warner looked at the woman again. She had a mother's worry lines on her forehead, but unlike Camille, something burned in her eyes. There was still purpose. She still had reason to live.

"Thank you, Eighty—" He stopped. He did not want to refer to her as a number.

She glanced down the length of the infirmary, where they could hear the physician berating Camille. She looked back at Warner.

"Lillia," she said, using her hand to shield her words from the rest of the building. "Lillia Pittman."

"Solomon Warner. Pleased to meet you." He gave her his best smile and nodded. "I'll see you soon, Lillia," he said before closing the door behind him.

9
CLANDESTINE

FRIDAY, OCTOBER 9, 999 AE

Valerian Merrick had always been a father to Thorne after the death of Thorne's parents in a fire. Merrick had taken the lad under his wing. He had sponsored Thorne's journey through the ranks of the Church, and his example had shaped Thorne into the man he was today. Thorne had sought to imitate all that Merrick was. These remembrances were like a well-worn bearskin robe.

However, there remained a bittersweetness to these memories because of how Merrick had died. No loss was ever easy, but Thorne believed his heart would feel less empty if he could have said goodbye. He had imagined he would carry the numb incompleteness with him the rest of his life. Now, he was not so sure. Over the past seventeen hard, unrelenting days, he had found a sort of unexpected closure from Teska's presence and their feelings for one another.

A couple days of laying low outside Corinthia had been just what Thorne's beleaguered group needed. There had been no push to get anywhere by any particular time. DuBose and Carden had shown them a natural spring in the forest not far from the high school. They had rested, tended to their mounts, made repairs on the wagon and enjoyed the luxury of a bit of distance from each other.

Thorne and Teska took walks together, using the time to talk about their families and experiences, their hopes and dreams and fears.

"Malachi, who was Elaine?" Teska asked one day as they sat near a small leaf-choked pond. "When we first met Merrick, he said I reminded him of someone named Elaine."

"Huh, you still remember that? I'd forgotten."

"A girl has to know her competition." She flashed her dimples.

"No competition; trust me. I've never known anyone quite like you. There's a—"

She wagged her finger at him. "Hey, this isn't about me. Elaine, remember?"

Thorne nodded. "She was a girl I knew in Rimlingham. Val and I had been there for about two weeks. This was right before Toadvine, where I thought he had died. She and I met, had dinner a few times—the usual." He surprised himself at how effortlessly he admitted this to her, especially after keeping it bottled up for so long.

"Did you love her?" she asked. She swept all of her hair to the side so it hung down over one shoulder, the way Malachi liked it. Like a crimson waterfall.

"No," he said. "I don't think so. It probably wasn't anything more than infatuation for both of us."

"Dario once told me that you didn't like to talk about her."

Thorne shook his head and bit the inside of his lower lip.

She looked over at him. "Wanna tell me why?"

He couldn't decide how to answer. Part of him wanted to tell her—another barrier between them coming down. But he instinctively pulled back, confronted again by his old specters of sadness, anger and guilt.

"Malachi?" Teska put a hand on his arm.

He picked up a pinecone and threw it into the pond to give himself something to do. "I guess because it's something I've always been ashamed of." He sighed, and Teska encouraged him to continue by rubbing his shoulder.

"The night of the raid on the farmhouse—the night I thought that Merrick had died—Elaine and I were together. I had a rare afternoon off. The raid was scheduled for the next night. However, Val got word that the traitors"—he paused, realizing that he was now just like those men and women at the farmhouse—"had changed their meeting. So the Order moved up our timetable. They couldn't find me to tell me about the change in plans because I was with Elaine. So they rode out to Toadvine without me. When I finally got word about an hour later, I charged after them as fast as I could. But I arrived just after Val had entered the burning farmhouse."

"And that's why you blamed yourself for his death," she said, a statement instead of a question.

He nodded.

Teska leaned over and put her head on his shoulder. She took his hand, her thin fingers splayed between his larger, calloused ones. "I can see why you'd think that," she said. "But being with her had nothing to do with it."

"Yes, it did," he said, tensing. "If I hadn't been so concerned about mak—" He snapped his mouth shut and shook his head. He continued in a softer voice. "I wasn't thinking. I was young. Full of myself. Given the reason we were in Rimlingham, I shouldn't have let myself be distracted."

Thorne knew that he had not been responsible for Merrick's death. As Merrick himself had told him, there could have been hundreds of Churchmen there, and it would have made no difference to the course of events. He tried to take solace in that.

During the break at Corinthia, Tua'Ahtaki had kept them in meat. A skilled outdoorsman, he had attempted to teach Thorne how to track, but the former Witchfinder Imperator did about as well with it as he did with the long bow. Tua also entertained them with history stories about his people and the Tex'ahns. When Thorne was not with Teska, he was often found in the company of Tua.

Teska continued to instruct Amelia, teaching and guiding her in the ways of the Communion. A week ago, during their stopover near the village of Meridell, Teska had found another Nahoru'brexia, Katherine Breem. The brevity of their visit meant Teska did not get to teach her, but she promised to contact her again.

Amelia Sloan prepared all their meals, something she took great pride and enjoyment in doing. She mended clothes, kept stock of their provisions, carried water, and helped care for the horses. Teska taught her a few simple spells that required little energy, and she practiced them. Amelia gained more knowledge of the Communion's origin, history and sisterhood. She also chose Mother Depresja as her Source.

Every brexia who became part of the Enodia Communion pledged allegiance to one of the Three Witches. While all three were venerated, a brexia could only draw magical energy from one of them. Teska had chosen Maiden Mallumo, mainly because she was the first of the Three that Teska had come in contact with. Plus, Matriarch Trahnen, the Witch of Tears, scared her.

Each of the Three had a particular sphere of influence. The Maiden, the Witch of Darkness—youngest and cruelest of the Three—ruled the earth element. Her totem was the serpent. Mother Depresja was the Witch of Sighs, whose element was fire and whose familiar was the rat. The Witch of Tears was known by the spider and represented water. The element of air was reserved for Hecate, Supreme Goddess of the Three and the Source of their power.

Thurl Cabbott kept to himself, working on his journal and maps. He ate most of his meals alone, either in the wagon or the surrounding countryside. He spoke little and rarely engaged in jovial conversation, even with Tua, with whom he shared a love of the outdoors. He seemed content—in fact, Amelia had privately pointed out that he seemed *pleased*—to just watch and listen. There had been two more nocturnal outbursts, and while they were brief, it reinforced Teska's belief that Thurl was trying to warn them about someone in their group. Twice, Thorne had found the constable wandering alone, talking to himself, seemingly out of his mind. "It was as if he were having a conversation with someone invisible," Thorne had said. Most nights, Thurl sat by the fire, the peculiar gleam in his eye now accompanied by a disquieting smile.

They had departed Corinthia on Monday, September 28th. Thorne wanted to meet as many different groups as he could while making sure that Teska was in Attagon in time for the Feast of Michael the Second. To do this, he planned to follow a zigzag course, traveling south before turning northeast, and then repeating the pattern until they arrived at the capital city.

Thorne spent one night each with the underground freedom movement in Corrona, Old Troy, Sparta, Akermun and Maridell. Each village was little more than a few huddled buildings and outlying farms. At the conclusion of the night's meeting, a member of the group escorted Thorne and his friends to their next destination. This not only offered the safest route, it also provided a point of contact and a verifiable reference to the group in the next community.

They had spent October 3rd and 4th in Skonmesto. Rich DuBose and Murnau Carden had accompanied them that far before they headed back to Corinthia on October 5th. That had also been the first snow. Just a few flurries throughout the day, but evidence that winter had settled in.

They followed the same pattern on the next leg of their journey, moving northeast and stopping overnight in such hamlets as Walnut Grove, Phila-delph, Brooksvale and Aberdeen. They kept to side roads and rutted tracks, someone always riding point so they would not be surprised by what lay ahead.

Tonight, they gathered in the remains of an ancient farmhouse on the outskirts of a village called Sullivant. A fire crackled in the fireplace, casting elongated shadows and leaving much of the large room shrouded in darkness. The wind gusted through cracks in the walls. Two dozen men and women sat on the cold, warped floor. Cabbott and Tua stood off to the side. Teska and Amelia sat in the front row. With a nod from the man who had been serving as his Sullivant contact, Thorne rose from his place beside Teska and stood in front of the fireplace. The light cast a gossamer aura around his form.

"My friends," he said as he scanned the expectant faces. "Thank you for coming here tonight. I know how much you risk by doing so, and I'm grateful that you have allowed me this opportunity. Henry"—he gestured toward his contact—"has told me of your desire for freedom and the discussions you've had among yourselves." He paused. "Did you know the man called Traugott?"

Several people shook their heads.

"Never met 'im," one man said, "but we knew of 'im."

Thorne nodded. "He was a close friend of mine. His real name was Valerian Merrick. He took the name Traugott to hide his true identity from the Church. You see, Valerian Merrick had once been a Witchfinder Imperator. In my younger days, I apprenticed under him."

A current of unease rippled through the crowd.

Thorne raised his hands as if surrendering. "You have nothing to fear. Please believe me. I, too, have left the Church, just as Merrick did. I wanted to meet you tonight to tell you that his movement—of freedom from Church dominion—did *not* die with him. My friends and I are going to continue the fight that he started.

"I've spent the last few months outside of Deiparia, in a land to the southeast—a land that Merrick once visited—trying to learn as much as I could about freedom. About what it means. About how to achieve it. About how to keep it."

He put his hands behind his back and stepped closer to the audience. His shadow stretched over them like an ebon tapestry.

"We all know that a world existed before the Great Cataclysm. We see evidence of it in the tall towers of Rimlingham and Attagon and Skonmesto; in the twisted metal signs that line our trade routes; in the tales our Storicos tell us. I've discovered"—Thorne held up a leather case such as those clerks used to carry and store documents—"much about that world that the Church hasn't told us."

As he handed the case back to Teska, a voice rose from the group. "What's in that thing?"

"While I was away, I discovered a great many ancient documents that predate the Great Cataclysm. I copied as much as I could from them, and I keep them with me so I can continue to study them. The original documents were so old that some of them nearly crumbled to dust at the merest touch."

"So a buncha letterin's gonna make us free?" another man asked, not hiding his skepticism.

A third man hooted. "Oh yeah, Muldoon, didn't ya know? All we gotta do is whomp them Crusaders over the head with them writings an' they'll fall like chestnuts from a tree!" Laughter swirled through the room. Thorne waited for it to die down.

"Well, my friends, those documents are a kind of tool. We all use tools to help accomplish different tasks. Those"—he pointed toward the case in Teska's lap—"are tools that will help us in our fight for freedom."

"How?" an elderly man asked as he tugged a woolen blanket tighter around his shoulders.

"Long before the Great Cataclysm, our ancestors lived in this land and called it the United States of America. It was a collection of fifty kingdoms—"

"Fifty kingdoms?" someone exclaimed. "Hells, how did they all get along?"

"That's just it," Thorne replied. "They didn't always get along. But they were all united together under one form of leadership called a 'democracy.' A democracy was where every person had a vote—a voice or a say—in things that happened. Unlike the Church, which makes and enforces rules according to its own desires, the Americans could choose how they wanted to respond to things."

"What a load of manure!"

"Sounds like a buncha chaos ta me!"

Thorne motioned for silence. "No, it was orderly. Structured. In that respect, not unlike the Church. But where it differed from the Church was in the flexibility that people had to make their own decisions. They could vote for who they wanted with no fear of repercussion. They could do what they wanted—so long as they didn't break the law. They married whoever they chose. They worked at whatever best fit their skills and interests.

"Now, of course it wasn't always perfect. People disagreed, as they always have. Sometimes one of the kingdoms didn't like something the larger kingdom suggested or did—"

A woman near the back asked, "What's this 'larger kingdom'?"

"It was called the 'federal government.' It had the authority to make and enforce laws, protect the citizens, make treaties and trade agreements, produce money and so on. Just like the Cartulian Order does now. Every one of the fifty kingdoms voted for people who made up the larger government. That way, everyone was included. Everyone had a voice." Thorne paused to take a drink of water. The wind was a frigid howl through the boarded-up windows.

"Are you saying that Deiparia should be like that?" a different woman asked.

Thorne nodded. "I think the *idea* is worth pursuing. It would mean a different life—a better life—for all congregants. Merrick knew this. He gave his life for it. And he wasn't the only one. Throughout the history of the United States, there were countless people who sacrificed their lives for the cause of freedom. What we're talking about isn't new. It only sounds new to us because we've never been exposed to it before. I believe that democracy, the freedom of the individual to make his or her own decisions, is what Deiparia needs."

"Let's say you is right," a skinny man said. "How you 'spect to do it? What would that look like?"

"A good question, friend," Thorne replied. "The people of the United States weren't handed their freedom. They had to fight for it. According to what I've read, there was another land, another realm, where the Americans originally came from. They made colonies in these lands. But the motherland wanted to keep them under control, so it levied one tax after another against the colonists. We all know what paying taxes is like."

A chorus of grumbles and curses eddied around the room.

"The colonists were being oppressed by the motherland far, far away. And they finally had enough of it. They armed themselves and set about winning their freedom from the motherland. Many of them died doing so. Of course, the motherland sent more men to fight the colonists, but it was too late. Those Americans had tasted freedom and wanted more. And they weren't going to be stopped by the motherland, or her warriors or her taxes.

"Outmanned and with fewer weapons, the Americans prevailed. They earned the right to be in charge of themselves, to not be tethered to the motherland anymore. And they formed their new government, the democracy. They made their own laws, levied their own taxes. They even kept a huge legion of warriors to protect all they had fought for. And every colonist had a say in all of it. They selected the best men to represent them. They created their own realm, not beholden to anyone else. They fought whenever necessary to protect what they had created."

"So we attack the Church, is that it?" one man asked in disbelief. "We'll be hanged as traitors or burnt as heretics. Probably both!"

Thorne nodded again. "I won't lie to you. Many of the freedom fighters among the Americans *were* hanged for being traitors. There was one man"—he turned to his contact, paused and smiled—"his name was also Henry. To those who tried to take away this freedom, he said, 'Give me liberty or give me death.' Another man told the people about to hang him, 'I regret that I have only one life to give for my country.'" Thorne paused. "What we're about to do…yes, it's dangerous. It *is* a life-or-death struggle. No one is forcing you to participate. You came here tonight to meet my friends and me. You came to hear what I have to say. Only you and your families can decide what you want to do. No one will force you. That is the essence of freedom—being able to choose your own path, to make your own choices. But know this: you are free to choose, but you're not free from the consequences of your choices."

"Meaning what?" a different voice asked.

"Whatever you choose—whether it's to fight for freedom or not—comes with consequences. Some may be good, positive, welcome; others may be harsh and ugly and painful. Freedom is never free. There are extreme costs associated with it. If you choose to join with us, you must be prepared to accept the consequences of doing so. You can't blame me, or your neighbor or Merrick when a decision backs you into a corner. You can't point fingers at the Church or the Heiromonarch. You have to take responsibility for your own decisions.

"I used to be a Witchfinder Imperator in the Paracletian Order. I chose to walk away from that—and believe me, it wasn't easy. I elected to believe in and follow my friend and mentor, Merrick. I have suffered much because of those choices, and I have been blessed because of them. I have sacrificed more than you can know. But I have gained so much." Thorne took another drink of water.

"Do you got a plan? For doing what yer talkin' about?"

Thorne handed the cup to Teska. "I don't have a firm plan yet. I'm working on one. I know that we've got to find a way to stop the Fifth Order. They've corrupted the Church for far too long. They are the ones behind the Crusaders, the compliance camps, the takeover of our cities. If we can eliminate them, we'll be in a much better position to confront the Church. Believe me, once we have a plan, you'll know of it."

"All this sounds so…impossible," a young woman said from behind Amelia. "And there're no guarantees, are there?"

Thorne smiled at her. "No, there are no guarantees. Nothing in this life is guaranteed to us except death. We tread into unknown territory, which means we'll face unknown peril. Merrick knew this and died for what he believed in. Despite the danger, I, too, will see this through to the end. No matter what."

There were more questions about freedom, the Americans and their democracy, and the Fifth Order. Around midnight, people began to drift back to their homes and warm beds. A few hung around, soaking up as much information as they could.

When the last person had departed, Thorne and his friends lay down to rest in front of the fire. Cabbott kept watch.

"Merrick would be so proud of you," Teska said the next day as their journey continued. "How many commitments did you get back there?"

Thorne pulled his dark-green cloak tighter around his neck. The wind whistled around them, snowflakes dancing on the currents. The sun struggled to make its presence known through clouds that appeared as hard as a breastplate.

Tua said, "There were nine men who agreed to help. Five women."

"That seems pretty good for a group that size," Amelia said from the driver's bench of the wagon.

"It is," Thorne said. "Tua, how many does that make since we started?"

His friend, draped in a thick bearskin hide, hunched over the mane of his mustang, attempting to hide from the bitter wind. "Let's see…" He mumbled figures to himself for a moment. "We have firm commitments from 166 men, and forty-nine women."

Amelia grinned. "That's over two hundred in less than three weeks!"

"Skonmesto was the biggest place we visited. If we'd had more time to meet with people there—"

"Malachi, remember," Tua said from beneath his bearskin, "it's not just about you meeting with people. If this is going to work, they have to find and meet with others. You lead and inspire. Others connect and build."

"I know. But if we didn't have to use these back roads—if we could travel faster, I could make contact with more communities."

"Yeah," Teska replied. "And we'd all get arrested by the Church—or killed by bounty hunters."

"Speaking of which," Tua said, "we haven't seen any of them for weeks. Of course, they could just be tracking us, waiting for the right opportunity to attack."

"They had better not be," Cabbott said as he brought up the rear.

Another few miles passed with minimal conversation. The rutted path they followed beneath snow-laden boughs made progress slower. Their contact from Sullivant rode a mile ahead, and they had no trouble following his tracks. By late afternoon, as the sun's pasty light weakened and the land turned as gray as the clouds, they arrived in the village of Tollgate. After a thorough check to ensure there were no Churchmen around—and no familiars to snitch on them—they stabled their mounts and wagon and spent the evening in front of the tavern fireplace.

Shortly after midnight, a cart clattered to a halt outside the inn. Thorne and his companions snuck through the icy blackness and climbed on board. It carried them along to their next gathering, and hopefully more commitments.

10
ESCAPE

SATURDAY, OCTOBER 10, 999 AE

Tension among the prisoners had been high since Wednesday. That was when the escape plan had been finalized. Everyone with a central role had been briefed but could not say anything to their groups until a few hours before the attempt. That would hopefully alleviate the risk of a nervous prisoner accidentally blurting something out. Each group leader had been assigned their task in private so that if compromised, the details of the rest of the plan would remain unknown. Only Darien, Hawkes, Warner, Hart and Landrew knew the whole thing.

The plan had not changed much since Hawkes first pitched it. Upon closer inspection, the leaders liked what was there. They tweaked it a bit and nailed down the rest of the details.

On Sunday evening, Hawkes—disguised as a guard—would lead the work crew back into camp and give the prearranged signal. Warner would lead the second team to take out the guards in all the towers, except the one by the main gate. Some of the work crew would handle that one. Hart and team three would slip into the infirmary and get the bottles of dwale. Wycroft, being unskilled with weapons, would lead team four in preparing prisoners for escape. Erik Landrew and team five had the hardest assignment. They had to keep the guards occupied using only the shivs and a few tools they had managed to hide. This suicidal mission had brought a smile to Erik's wide face. He relished the idea of hand-to-hand combat, even if his chance of survival was slim.

The moral dilemma over what to do about the guards had been resolved, at least by some. Where possible, the guards would be given the opportunity to surrender. If they accepted, they would be put to sleep with the dwale and locked up Downstairs. Should this courtesy be rejected, or if the guards fought to the death, then so be it.

Above all, they wanted to keep from killing any Crusaders. They would knock them out or tie them up or use the dwale—anything to avoid killing them. If there was even the remotest chance they were somehow linked to the missing children, the resistance leaders refused to authorize lethal force. Of course, there was no way to monitor every prisoner and every situation. Some, like Landrew and Clancy, made no guarantees.

Once the guards were incapacitated, the prisoners could escape. Darien, Hawkes and Warner planned to get a wagon and some horses, along with as many supplies as they could, before setting out. There was a limited amount of time before the guards would be able to free themselves. They needed to be as far away as possible when that happened.

Today's work schedule had been light. Prisoners still cleared snow from the grounds, but no work crews had been sent out. It was as close to a holiday as they got.

Hawkes, Warner, Hart and Landrew sat around the small stove at the back of barracks Number One. They reviewed the plan and tried to anticipate potential problems. Other prisoners lay on their bunks or sat on the floor playing with a dingy deck of cards. Some merely stared off into space. No one paid any attention when the door opened and Darien hobbled in. He moved between the rows of bunks, straight for the stove.

"Slide over," Warner said. "Let him get warm."

"No time!" Darien whispered. Anxious to the point of trembling, he leaned closer.

"What's going on?" Hart asked.

"The plan—" He doubled over coughing. He caught his breath and stood up. "The plan—the message I just saw!" His breath rasped from his throat. "We've got to change the plan!"

"Whoa, whoa. Hold on. What're you talking about?" Hawkes asked. He massaged his bandaged hand. He could have sworn he still had his two missing fingers. The stumps ached in the cold.

Darien steadied himself with his cane and Warner's shoulder. He took a deep breath and forced himself to calm down. He looked at the men around the stove.

"A message just came in for Gries, but Fairchilde left it on my desk since the commandant is out. No one was around."

"You saw it? What'd it say?" Warner asked.

"The Fifth Order is alerting all the compliance camps. Some of the children are being relocated to Attagon."

The men looked at each other in confusion.

"Why would they be sending children to Attagon?" Hawkes asked.

Darien shook his head. "I don't know. But there was a list with the message—a list of the children being reassigned." Tears filled the old man's eyes. "Cassidy and Cassandra are on the list! We've got to rescue them!" Before anyone could respond, he looked at Hart. "Your daughters are on it, too."

Hart looked as if he had been hit in the face with a cold fish. "Y-You're sure?"

Darien wiped away the tear that rolled down his sunken cheek. "The names on the manifest said Juliette Hart, Clara Hart and Sara Hart."

The former Witchfinder swallowed hard and stood up.

"Lillia Pittman's children were listed, also. The children's caravan is following the 79 trade route south. We can't wait for tomorrow night. We've got to move *now*!"

Everyone around the stove spoke in quiet but intense voices, reconsidering their options in light of this news.

Ten minutes later, Hart said, "This actually works in our favor. Everyone's on edge, waiting for tomorrow. All it would take is one anxious word or overstressed, exhausted prisoner to alert the guards. If we act now—tonight—we can put all that pent-up energy and tension to use and cut down on the chance of someone giving us away."

They talked for another thirty minutes before they had a revised plan. They jettisoned the idea about Hawkes bringing in the work crew. But everything else remained the same.

Hawkes set his jaw and nodded. "Let's do this, then. Alert your groups. Give them their orders. Tell them we move tonight on my signal."

At midnight, while the stars sparkled like tempting jewels forever out of reach, Tycho Hawkes sloshed some of the dwale inside the carpentry shop. After stealing it from the infirmary, it had taken him nearly an hour to cross the camp. He had stayed low, cautiously picking his way from shadow to shadow, eyes darting from one guard tower to another. He thought he had seen some movement around the barracks, blobby shapes disengaging from the darkness only to disappear again.

A group of three men crept through the night on their way to the guard tower by the main gate.

Landrew's team edged toward Camp One like a pitiful militia armed with shivs, axes and shovels.

Hawkes squinted at the nearest watchtower. Two men were ascending the ladder. He waited a little longer.

A door in Camp One opened, pale yellow light leaking out into the night. A man stepped out carrying a small lantern. Hawkes saw him stop.

"Hey! What're you doing?" the man yelled.

Damn! Hawkes thought. He raked a match across a board and flicked it into the carpentry shop. He dove aside, tucked into a forward roll and came up running toward the main gate.

A whoosh of air from the carpentry shop was followed by a thunderous BOOM. Flames roared through the building, licking from the windows and illuminating the work area.

"Sound the—" The guard's voice silenced. The lantern fell and broke against the frozen ground. The oil caught fire. The guard collapsed.

Hawkes ran as fast as he could. The night air seared his lungs. His feet had only just recovered from the frostbite. *Thank God I didn't lose them, too.* He hoped everything was going according to plan. Prayed it was. But there was no turning back now and no way to know until it was all over. Or until it was too late.

He scuttled through the gate connecting Camps One and Two. To his right, men and Crusaders poured from the doors like wine from a busted skin. Landrew's group screamed and charged, and all Hawkes heard was yelling, grunting and the sounds of battle.

Looking left, he saw past the processing building and through the barbed wire into Camp Three. Men and women scampered from the barracks, holding one another up, tripping, yelling, crying.

A scream caught his attention. He looked toward the main gate. A guard plummeted from the tower. He smacked the ground with a cold thud and did not move. Hawkes grabbed the man's dagger. Two prisoners hurried down the ladder. One of them had the guard's sword.

One at a time, Hawkes thought. *One at a time.*

By now the carpentry shop was engulfed in flames. The camp collapsed into chaos. Hawkes and the two men reached the front gate. They removed the security bar and shoved. The well-oiled doors swung open.

"Go, while you can!" he ordered the two prisoners. One nodded and sprinted toward freedom. The other kept a tight grip on the sword and ran toward the officer's buildings to join the fray.

Hawkes knew his dagger would be of limited use there. He made for the stables.

Four tower guards were dead. Two had surrendered. Warner directed his men to take them Downstairs where dwale-soaked rags awaited them.

Every guard and a dozen inmates near the barracks were dead. The majority of Saxonburgh's 196 prisoners streamed toward the gate, a river of terror and misery rushing to freedom. A number of men veered off and joined the battle around the Fifth Order's buildings.

Another fire had started inside one of them. Despite their superior armor, weapons and stamina, the Crusaders were pushed back by the growing tide of screaming, bloodthirsty prisoners eager for their pound of flesh.

In the stable, Hawkes found a wagon. It was long, fully enclosed and had a tongue for two horses. He led two from their stalls and hitched them up. He tied two more to the back. Through the livery doors, he heard shouts of delight and cries of hope as prisoners fled the camp. The unceasing clamor of battle carried on the wind.

Bong bong bong!

A bell resounded across the camp. Someone had managed to sound the alarm.

Hawkes crept to the front of the stable, keeping to the shadows, and looked out. He saw the rear of the Crusader's barracks, the central building, the mess hall and the kitchen. Flames danced inside the main building. Crusaders climbed out windows and ran around to join the fighting in front. The mess hall and kitchen were dark.

The carpentry shop fire had spread. It now devoured the repair shop next door.

Hawkes found two lanterns hanging from the wall. He lit them and waited until no Crusaders were around. He hustled across the yard in a crouch and flung both lanterns inside the barracks. Shattering glass and the whoosh of blossoming fire made him smile.

He turned back to the stables. Bright lights exploded in front of his eyes. Then the world went dark.

"Tycho! *Tycho!* C'mon, man, get up!"

It sounded like Solomon Warner's voice, but far away and slushy. The blackness called to him and promised him rest. Rest was good.

"Shit! Somebody gimme a hand over here!"

Hawkes floated down a river. The choppy current took him where it wanted. It was a black river, just like everything else was black. But it made him feel good, so he relaxed and let the warm waters carry him.

It did not seem long before the river turned cold. Hawkes did not like it as much now. The water remained rough, like moving through ice floes. He had trouble distinguishing his skin from the river. They felt the same.

Suddenly, something touched his face. It felt like an icicle. He tried to back away but didn't know where his arms or legs were.

Where am I?

The cold thing still lay against his head. Somehow it was pulling him out of the river. Out of the current. Even out of the darkness. He began to see shades of gray.

His head shrieked in pain as if his skull was on fire.

How could my head be on fire if I'm in a river?

His body felt coated with lead. Cold lead. His skull throbbed in rhythm with his heartbeat and would not stop. He forced his eyelids apart even though he knew it was a bad idea. They immediately closed again.

"Wh-Wha—?" a voice said. He thought it was his voice, but that was not possible. His voice sounded much better and stronger than that.

"Easy now, child," a different voice said.

That was not his, either.

"Mister Hawkes, can you hear me? It's all gonna be okay. You jus' take it easy now."

"M-M-Momma?" How had his mother gotten here? Where was here? Maybe she could make his head stop screaming.

"Sorry, showoff, that ain't your momma," a familiar voice—Warner's voice—said. "Can you open your eyes?"

Doing so was like trying to pull a stuck hog out of the mud. Something cold touched his head.

"It's f-f-freezing."

"I know, child. But it's just water. Trying to clean up this mess."

Hawkes did not know about any mess. He did not even know who the voice belonged to. His skull felt like he had been scalped. He thought he heard the river calling him again. He relaxed, and sure enough the current embraced him once more.

When next Hawkes opened his eyes, the light hurt them. He clamped them together before easing them open again little by little. Had he been thrown down the side of Heaven's Peak, believed to be the highest mountain in the Great Appian range? He moaned and lifted his head. Something hard and sharp and relentless stuck in the side of his skull. He raised his hand and felt a heavy bandage. Grazing its surface sent a bolt of pain down his spine.

"Ahh! Damn."

He let his head sink back into a pile of clothes that served as a pillow. He looked around. He was laying inside a wagon, lit by three lanterns hanging from the ceiling. A beautiful, quilted blanket covered him. The sides of the wagon held tack for horses, some swords, even two pairs of manacles. He saw some sacks and boxes to his left, but it hurt to turn his head too far in either direction. The wagon smelled like stale sweat and leather. Or maybe that was just him.

The back door opened. A bulky shape filled the doorframe. Hawkes blinked several times, and the form came into focus. A woman.

Lillia Pittman huffed into the wagon, mumbling under her breath.

"I thought I heard something," she said. She smiled and towered over him to look at the bandage. "Mm-hmm, 'at's gone to bleeding again."

She smelled like cook smoke. And the compliance camp. She seemed familiar. "Wh-Who're you?"

"Hey, there he is!" Warner's voice bounced around inside the wagon.

Hawkes tried to raise his head, but it hurt too much. "Sol?"

Warner stepped into his field of vision. "Yeah, yeah, it's me. Man, am I glad you're okay."

If this is okay, I don't want to know what not *okay feels like,* Hawkes thought.

The heavy black woman did her best to maneuver around the cramped confines. Warner stood at his feet, near the door. Although he was smiling, Hawkes saw concern on his friend's face.

"What happened?" he croaked and smacked his lips.

"Just hold on, I'm getting you some water," Lillia said.

Warner stepped closer, grinning like a fool. "We *did* it, man." His tone was soft but filled with emotion. "We escaped!"

Hawkes knew he should be elated, but the best he could manage was a smile. "Wh-Where—?"

Warner glanced out the window above Hawkes. "We're followin' the caravan. Tryin' to catch up."

Lillia came around, a ladle in her hand. "Here, help 'im set up a bit," she told Warner.

Hawkes gritted his teeth but could not suppress the agony that coursed through his skull, down his neck, along his spine, as Warner gently raised his torso off the bunk.

"Sorry, man."

Lillia held the ladle to his mouth. "Drink," she said.

Hawkes did. The water was ice cold and tasted woody and sweet.

"Lay 'im on back down now."

"My head—s-something cold," Hawkes mumbled. He raised a hand to his head but remembered not to touch the bandage.

"That was just me," Lillia said. "I was cleaning off all that blood yesterday."

"Yesterday? I don't understand. What happened?"

She patted Warner on the shoulder. "You catch 'im up. I'm going to finish my dinner. But don't you go tiring 'im out, now. Boy needs his rest. Yell when you're done. I gotta change that bandage."

"Thank you, Lillia." Warner put his hand on top of hers.

She smiled and left the wagon.

Hawkes could see better now. It was dark outside. He saw the flickering light of a campfire.

Warner pulled a crate over and sat beside Hawkes. His eyes were filled with a mixture of gratitude and doubt. "You had us worried. We didn't think you were gonna make it."

Hawkes smiled.

"Like I said, we made it. Thanks to you. Most everyone escaped—at least as far as I know. We lost at least thirty men, though. Maybe more. I found you behind the barracks. A Crusader had knocked you out. I guess he thought he had killed you. You got a nasty sword cut across the side of the head. You bled, man. Damn, did you bleed. I swear we thought you were already dead."

"So that's it. Bastard caught me from behind."

"You're lucky he didn't run you through. Guess he was aimin' for decapitation."

Hawkes closed his eyes. "Nice."

"We got all but two of the Crusaders into the holdin' cells. Used the dwale to put them to sleep. Some of the other guards surrendered. Once it became obvious the guards weren't gonna keep us all in, some of them just gave up. Motioned for us to leave and didn't stand in our way. I found this rig in the stable. We loaded you in and took off, just in case the guards changed their minds or let the Crusaders loose. That was last night."

"What time is it now?"

"Probably around eight or nine. You been out nearly a whole day."

He opened his eyes. "Are they following us?"

"Haven't seen any pursuit. But they're out there."

Hawkes tried to raise his head again, but the pain slapped him back. "Fuck, this hurts."

"It's deep. Lillia says you need stitches. Only we don't have any physicians around. Got a bad concussion, too."

"What about…the children?"

Warner nodded. "We're behind them. We've got their trail. It wasn't hard. They've got a dozen wagons, I'll bet. Plus supplies, a bunch of horses. But we've got the advantage. We can move quicker than they can—and they don't know we're comin'. I figure we catch up in three or four days."

Hawkes nodded but even that simple motion turned his skull into a sea of fire and made him nauseous. He grimaced.

Warner patted his arm. "That's enough for now. You need to rest."

Hawkes did not reply. He was already sinking back into the warm, soothing river.

Warner descended the two steps and joined Darien, Lillia and Hart around the fire. He ate his ration of food they had managed to take from the camp. In two or three days, it would all be gone. Then they would have to resort to stealing. He wished Teska was here to do that—even if she had tried to kill him twice. He wondered where his friends were and hoped they were doing better than his little group.

A few lazy snowflakes fell. As they touched his face and melted, Warner stared east into the darkness—toward the towering crags of the Great Appian Mountains. The trail led that way. Once they rescued the children, they were going to have to brave that treacherous, unforgiving expanse if they expected to get away.

With four horses, a wagon, a woman, an old man, and now an invalid, Warner thought. He and Hart were the only ones capable of fighting.

In the frigid blackness, Warner could have sworn the eastern wind laughed at him.

11
PANTOMIME

THURSDAY, OCTOBER 15, 999 AE

"What time is it?" Teska asked.

"Shouldn't be long now," Thorne replied.

He stared out of the glass door. If the wind was not blowing so hard, he would have enjoyed standing on the deck, overlooking the gentle incline that led to the cliff's edge and, beyond it, the three-hundred-foot drop to the rocks below. Up there, the icy wind howled with vicious delight.

Most of the surrounding trees had been used to build the lodge they were in. Those that remained still held patches of snow on their boughs. The north, east and west sides of the grounds sloped down into the thickly forested mountainside. The back of the lodge faced south, with its breathtaking views of the surrounding countryside and the town of Gilmotier far below.

Thorne was grateful for the wide stone fireplace and the cheerful fire. And the fact that he could conduct a gathering where wind and snow did not blow through holes in walls or where fires were too risky. Each of them would have their own bed tonight, courtesy of Edward Averitt, owner of the hunting lodge, wealthiest man in town and a fervent believer in freedom.

Thorne turned from the door and looked around. Averitt Lodge was constructed of smooth pine logs, the sweet, prickly scent present everywhere. Five couches, three times as many chairs and numerous small tables were arranged throughout the room to facilitate conversation. A bearskin rug covered the floor in front of the fireplace, and mounted heads of moose, deer, elk and bear stared vacantly into space. Doors led off to the kitchen, dining room and lower level on one side, and to bedrooms on the other. Curved stairs on either side of the room rose to a second-floor landing and more bedrooms. Directly beneath where he now stood was a well-appointed stable, a small armory and doors leading onto the grounds.

Thorne walked to the fireplace and added another log. Embers swirled up the chimney. He looked at the mechanical timepiece on the mantle, one of the few he had ever seen in his life. Even the majority of the Church's upper echelons did not have such devices. It read 10:49.

Teska and Amelia sat across from one another on the other side of the room. Heads bowed, they held hands across the table. Tua had explored the entire lodge and now sat with his feet up in front of the fire, smoking his pipe. Cabbott had not budged from the front door since they arrived four hours ago.

"They are running behind," Tua said. "Probably the weather."

Thorne turned from the mantle and faced the chair that nearly swallowed his friend. "It's not snowing, Tua. Hasn't for two days. You saw the road up here. Did you put the horses behind the lodge?"

Tua nodded through a veil of smoke. "In the smaller stable. They are out of the wind and probably fast asleep by now." He turned his attention to Amelia and watched her.

Thorne looked at Teska. She was talking to Amelia in a low voice. He let his gaze wander over Teska's face. Its symmetry was perfect, which added an almost ethereal quality to her beauty. Eyes closed, lashes fluttering, she silently mouthed words. He watched her lips, remembering how they moved against his, and the taste of her passion. He realized his heart was beating faster. When he looked away, he noticed that Tua was staring at Amelia with the same intensity. He grinned.

"Let me ask you something," Tua said, missing Thorne's smile. "Do you truly believe you can overthrow this Fifth Order? Can you bring freedom to your land? It is a monumental task." He searched Thorne's green eyes.

A full minute passed before Thorne spoke in a voice that would not carry through the cavernous lodge. "I want to, Tua. I believe in these concepts—freedom and democracy and voting. Having been on the inside of the Church, I know that there must be a better way for people to live."

"But…?"

Thorne sighed. "But I don't know if I can. I don't know if what I'm doing will make any difference." He paused to search his friend's face. "I'm scared, Tua. I feel like I'm making this up as I go along. I don't feel like I have any plan."

"I am glad, Malachi Thorne, that you did not answer right away. This tells me that you have doubts. You are unsure of yourself and your goal. This is good."

Thorne raised his eyebrows. "Good? How so?"

"It means that you are open to new ideas. You are not locked into only one perspective. And you are not thinking too highly of yourself."

"Sometimes—*most* of the time, actually—I feel very inadequate for all of this."

"Nothing great is ever accomplished without inadequacy. It is what keeps us humble and yet always striving. I wonder, what is it that you fear the most?"

This time Thorne did not hesitate. "Losing Teska. That, and failure, of course. Of not being able to give people freedom."

Tua smiled and put his pipe back in his leather belt pouch. The firelight shone off his black braids. "If it is any consolation or encouragement, I believe you can do what you say. I have seen you study to find answers, to find the truth. I have heard you speak eloquently and with great zeal. You would have made a fine chief of my people back in the Long Ago. I think, from now on, I shall call you 'Chief-Who-Wins.'"

"Why not? One of my deputies calls me 'Boss' all the time." Thorne glanced at the clock again. It was 11:05. They were now over an hour late.

The front door burst open. Edward Averitt and another man scampered inside. Cabbott slammed the door behind them. Teska and Amelia looked up.

"Master Averitt!" Thorne shouted. "What's going on?" The two men stumbled into the middle of the room. Their spooked faces made Thorne's stomach drop. "What happened?" he asked, dreading the reply.

Edward Averitt gasped for breath. At seventy-two years of age, he still had a full head of silver hair. Panicked eyes stared from behind rectangular spectacles. The left side of his face drooped slightly, and he limped, favoring his right leg. He motioned for his companion to speak while he caught his breath.

The caramel-skinned man, Thorne had learned earlier, was Custis Newsome, a close friend of Averitt's and another merchant in town. Newsome had a thick nose with flared nostrils, a heavy mustache, round spectacles, and short, felt-like black hair. Both Averitt and Newsome wore collared black shirts with bone buttons, black trousers and riding boots.

Teska and Amelia moved to join Thorne, Averitt and Newsome. Tua watched from his chair. Cabbott remained by the door, occasionally peering through the leaded glass pane in the center.

"Ambush," Newsome wheezed. "They knew…we were coming!"

"How?" Thorne demanded, his stomach sinking further.

"Are you hurt?" Amelia asked.

"Nah, nah," Averitt said, having caught his breath. "We got away. Barely. But the others…" He sank into a chair and cradled his head in his hands.

Thorne looked to Newsome, who shook his head. "All dead."

Thorne's stomach hit bottom and turned to ice. "Crusaders?"

"A few," Newsome replied. He walked to a cabinet and filled two glasses with a dark-brown liquor. "I think I saw two—"

"Three," Averitt said, looking up and accepting the drink. He downed it without hesitation and sat the glass on a table. "A Witchfinder, too. Some constables and deputies."

Thorne cursed. "Thurl, you see anything? Did they follow them?"

Cabbott stared through the window. "No one is coming."

"Master Averitt, are there any other ways up here?" Thorne asked as he glanced around the room that now seemed to be closing in on them.

"Nah. The mountain narrows until it reaches this point. There's a squirrel path down the west side of the cliff face, but it's treacherous. Doubly so in this weather. Horses probably couldn't do it."

"Tua, you've got the best eyes," Thorne said. He pointed upstairs. "Let me know if you see anyone coming."

Tua jogged upstairs. Thorne told Amelia to lock every door and shutter every window. "Teska, get our weapons. Thurl, bolt the front door."

He looked at Averitt and Newsome. "How did they know? Who tipped them off?"

Averitt shook his head. Newsome shrugged. "Nobody—an' I mean *nobody*—knew about this except those participating. I made sure. It doesn't make sense."

"Malachi!" Tua's voice bounced down the stairs. "They have arrived!"

Thorne ran to the front of the lodge. He cracked the shutters just enough to look through the thick glass. He made out a group of mounted riders all carrying torches. The wind whipped the flames in every direction so he could not get a solid count. He estimated eight or nine.

Teska returned, arms loaded with weapons. Tua came downstairs, retrieved his bow, quiver and knife and hurried back to the landing. Newsome helped Amelia check the rest of the doors and windows. As Thorne slung his bastard sword across his back and checked the dagger in his belt, Cabbott walked into the middle of the room.

"This is where it all ends, Malachi," he said, his voice strained.

"Not if I have anything to say about it."

Cabbott chuckled. It sounded like bones clattering together. "But you do not. I am not making a prediction. I am stating a fact. You—and this ridiculous pantomime—are finished."

Thorne narrowed his eyes. "Thurl, what're you talking about? You're not making any sense. What pantomime?"

"Your pitiful attempt to overthrow the Fifth Order and the Church."

Thorne studied his longtime friend. Other than the unusual gleam that they had come to accept in Cabbott's eyes and the stiff smile tugging at the corners of his mouth, he seemed normal. Without taking his eyes off Cabbott, Thorne yelled at Newsome. "What're they doing out there?"

"Oddly, nothing at all. They're just…waiting. I count three Crusaders, one Witchfinder—the other eight are constables and deputies."

"Thirteen, actually," Cabbott corrected.

Cabbott was breaking out in a sweat. He blinked furiously, as if something was in his eyes, and his arms and hands twitched. His mouth opened and snapped shut, a fish out of water. Thorne laid a hand on Cabbott's shoulder. Heat radiated through his heavy tunic and vest.

"Thurl, you're—"

Cabbott's eyes bulged as the gleam faltered. He shook harder. "M-M-Malachi—get away! Save yourself! I can't—" The constable shook his head, saliva flying from the corner of his mouth. He panted like an overworked mule.

The gleam returned. "That is enough of that," Cabbott said through a rictus grin.

Teska edged close to Thorne. She grasped his arm.

Thorne scowled at Cabbott. "What's wrong with you? Are you sick? Where's the thirteenth man you mentioned?"

"He is right here," Cabbott said, the grin stretching. He threw his arms open as if to give a hug. "But he is more than a man. Oh, so *very much* more!"

Cabbott jerked as if being prodded with a hot poker. The gleam disappeared and left behind pleading, dilated pupils. *"Please, go!* He'll destroy you all!"

"Silence!" Cabbott roared as the gleam flickered in the firelight once more.

"Wh-Who—? What's happening?" Thorne said.

Cabbott bent over, grasping his stomach as if he were about to vomit. When he stood up, the smile had disappeared. It was replaced by a smirk layered with ice and hatred and arrogance.

"You still do not understand, do you?" Cabbott asked. "Fool! Your constable is mine! I control him. I *rule* him! Just as I will soon rule all of you."

Cabbott glanced around at the perplexed faces that surrounded him. "Little witch, you have had suspicions," he told Teska. "You too, Co'manche." He glanced up at Tua, crouched on the landing, arrow notched and aimed between the bannisters.

"We're not speaking to Thurl Cabbott right now, are we?" Teska asked in a slow, dreadful manner.

"So you understand after all. If all the congregants of Deiparia are as ignorant, pitiable and so easily deceived as you lot, our conquest shall be a simple matter."

"Who the hells are you?" Thorne demanded, anger burning in his eyes. "What conque—"

Cabbott smiled. Or rather Cabbott's mouth stretched into the mocking, imperious grin. "My name is Maggard Blackscar," he declared with haughty condescension. "I am one of the Crimson Fathers."

"You're one of the—?" Thorne gasped. "H-How? Why?"

"Oh no…" Teska whispered. She gripped Thorne's arm tighter. "By the Matriarch, Mother and Maiden."

"Ah, yes, little witch… Go on. Put the pieces together. Last Chapel. The purple light." He paused. "Sneaky."

At the mention of the name, Teska's mouth dropped open. "Oh shit, Malachi."

Amelia clasped her hands to her chest and looked around, confused. "I-I don't understand. What's going on?"

"Holy bloody hells," Teska said. She shook her head and looked into Cabbott's eyes. "You did it, didn't you, you son of a bitch? You *transmigrated*."

Cabbott—or Blackscar—continued to smirk.

"What's 'transmigrated'?" Thorne asked in complete bewilderment.

Teska looked at him. Dread filled her face. "You remember Sneaky—that little shit I corralled in Last Chapel when everything was going to hells? That's him." She pointed at Cabbott. "He's *in there*. At the time, I thought he was just some cowering little toad. But he was actually one of the Crimson Fathers." She closed her eyes and shook her head. "I knew I should've killed you when I had the chance."

"B-But, Thurl. Mallory healed him," Thorne said, grasping for a mental foothold.

Blackscar sneered. "She did save his life. But he was so weak he became the perfect receptacle for me. When my brothers cast the spell that decimated the Communion's power, I was the conduit. The force of the magic annihilated my corporeal form—but I had made preparations for that. Your constable's body was nearby. It was weak and unable to resist. He became the perfect host. Thurl Cabbott's essence—his personality and memories and soul—have been conquered. He is a prisoner within his own body.

"Once I realized what you planned to do, it was easy enough for your beloved friend to tag along, helping out however he could. And in the process, you helped the Crimson Fathers more than you can know."

Teska paled. "You. You're the one Cabbott tried to warn us about. You've been spying on us this whole time." She looked up at Thorne's confused but sinking face. Once more her mouth hung open. She found herself wishing she could take back the last several weeks. It felt as if everything inside her body had turned to marble.

"What's wrong?" he asked.

"Oh no, Malachi… We've done their work for them." She started to cry, pressing her face against Thorne's chest. She hated to cry in front of people, especially men. And especially this Crimson Father. But she could not help it.

"Oh yes, yes! Spying, yes," Blackscar crowed. "Every meeting you have held, I have been there. I know the names and locations of every traitor who participated. And the Nahoru'brexia she found? I know every one of them."

"No…" Thorne whispered.

Blackscar twisted Cabbott's grin into feral malignancy. "All those times you thought your constable was meditating or just taking time alone, I was in contact with my brethren. I relayed everything to them. And after we departed for our next rendezvous, Crusaders went in and arrested everyone involved. All those traitors and witches you have been with the past few months?" He chuckled, an evil sound devoid of humor. "They are all in compliance camps now—the ones who were not executed on the spot, that is."

"You called off the bounty hunters," Thorne said. His heart felt leaden. He had difficulty swallowing around the tightness climbing his throat.

"Of course. I could not let Zadicus Rann's petty vengeance interfere with the knowledge I was gaining."

"It was you who mutilated those men before we got to Baymouth," Thorne said. With each realization he grew more nauseous. "And the attempts to warn us—"

"Yes. Unfortunately, when I rested, Cabbott's spirit drew closer to the surface."

Teska wiped her tears. "The warning wasn't about Tua or Amelia," she said, eyes puffy but now narrowed in disgust. "The traitor in our midst—"

"Was your precious constable," Blackscar said. "You are alone, Thorne. Hopelessly, completely alone. Your grand dreams are nothing but dust. Yours, too, little witch. The Crimson Fathers are supreme. The Crimson Fathers are eternal."

Thorne could do nothing but hold Teska against him. He yearned to throttle Blackscar, to make him suffer. But that would mean hurting his friend. He ground his teeth together. His head ached. Tua and Amelia watched with growing hopelessness. Averitt and Newsome sat in benumbed silence.

"You are all under arrest," Blackscar said in triumph. "There shall be a special tekoya for the lot of you, a public execution that will crush your freedom movement irrevocably. Take them!" he bellowed.

The front door swung open. Three Crusaders entered, weapons drawn, and advanced into the middle of the room.

12
DESPAIR

THURSDAY, OCTOBER 15, 999 AE

Thorne always had an escape plan. As soon as they arrived in any location, he scouted the best ways out in the event they were compromised. He had done that at Averitt Lodge. But now their plan was useless because Blackscar knew it.

Just like he knows everything we've done.

The thought surged through Thorne's mind like rising bile. He stood transfixed, unable to take his eyes off the friend who had just betrayed him and everything he had worked for.

"Malachi!" Teska yelled. "We've gotta go! *Move!*"

Behind the Crusaders, a Witchfinder entered whom Thorne did not know. Constables and deputies poured in after him. All had weapons ready.

"Damn it, Malachi! This isn't the time!" Teska shouted again.

He was not sure he could move. He tried to process everything that was happening. Thorne's arms felt as if they had soup in them instead of bones.

Cabbott sneered, arms crossed, as the Crusaders and Churchmen filled the room.

"You can surrender, or we can kill you," one of the Crusaders said, his voice like a growling bear.

"Shit!" Teska snarled through her teeth. She elbowed Thorne in the gut as hard as she could. "Get your head together!"

He heard the twang of a bowstring. Grunts and cries of pain. Two deputies collapsed.

"Yes, yes…" Thorne said, the fog lifting from his mind. He whipped the bastard sword from its sheath across his back.

One Crusader stood beside Blackscar and the Witchfinder. Another Crusader led two deputies up one set of stairs. On the other set of stairs, a Crusader and two constables did the same.

Tua's arm was a blur as he yanked arrows from his quiver, drew and alternated fire in both directions. The constables and deputies crouched behind the broad Crusaders. Some of the metal-tipped projectiles thunked into the walls or bannisters. One hit a Crusader in the chest, but the plate armor absorbed it. The giant pulled it loose and tossed it aside.

The sword in Thorne's hand grounded him, gave him focus. It was solid. It was something he could trust—and most importantly, control.

Unlike my friend.

He forced the thought away. There was no time to think about that right now. He glanced around, assessing the situation.

Teska stood to his right. She wore look on her face that said she was glad to have gotten through to him. Short sword in hand, she pushed Amelia behind a chair.

Averitt and Newsome had scuttled to the fireplace. Averitt gripped the poker with trembling hands, and Newsome held a short sword. Both were prepared but neither seemed ready.

"Who in blazes are you?" Averitt demanded. He stepped forward, holding the poker low. "This is my property. You have no business—"

The Crusader backhanded him. The poker clattered to the floor, and Newsome had to grab the old man to keep him from falling.

"Teska," Thorne said under his breath. He did not look at her but kept his eyes forward. "Take Amelia. The hallway to your right. Find a room; barricade yourselves in. Then get out through a window. Get the horses ready."

"I hear you whispering, Thorne. Making more futile plans?" Blackscar said.

"The only plan right now is to kill you."

Blackscar laughed, bitter and callous. "The Crimson Fathers are immortal. You cannot kill us."

"On my mark," Thorne muttered to Teska.

Upstairs, the hail of arrows ceased. Tua turned and fled down the hallway. The Crusaders and Churchmen on the stairs raced up after him. They reached the landing, and a deputy cried out. He fell backward with an arrow in his shoulder. Tua slipped through the window at the end of the hallway. He skittered down the angled roof and hit the ground before the Crusader appeared at the window. Slinging the bow across his back, he drew his knife and went for the Churchmen's horses.

He severed the reins loose from the trees with deft cuts. Whooping and yelling, Tua slapped the horses' haunches. They stampeded away into the stygian forest. He ran toward the rear of the lodge.

Thorne crouched, sword in front of him. The Crusader, face grim as a tombstone, did likewise. The Witchfinder unsheathed his rapier and crept into a flanking position. The two Crusaders, constables and remaining deputies poured down the stairs, cursing and shouting to Blackscar what Tua had done.

Thorne parried the Crusader's attack. Metal sang against metal.

"GO!" Thorne yelled as he blocked another strike.

Teska grabbed Amelia's hand, and they sprinted toward the hallway. The Witchfinder moved to intercept. Teska held her breath. It was always satisfying to see someone's expression change the first time she did this in front of them. It never got old.

The Witchfinder's eyes darted back and forth—saw only Amelia—and he dropped his rapier to grab his crotch, his face reddening.

Teska released her breath and became visible again. She shouldered the groaning Witchfinder aside, and the two women dashed down the hallway.

Thorne seized the opening. Instead of striking with his sword, he stepped closer to the Crusader. It was a risky move, but he needed the element of surprise. At close quarters, neither of their swords would be of any use.

Getting in close, he threw his fist into the Crusader's jaw. It was like hitting a sack of wet grain. His hand immediately started to ache. Ignoring it, Thorne ducked beneath the Crusader's retaliatory punch. No way he could match strength for strength with a Crusader. Better to use his speed against the giant's clunky movements in his heavy armor. Thorne scurried into the hallway on his left that led to the kitchen, dining room and lower level.

He charged down the steps, praying he did not miss one in the dark and break his neck. Behind him came shouts, booted feet, curses. He reached the bottom of the stairs as the Crusader followed.

The Witchfinder had recovered enough to point the second Crusader and two deputies down the hallway where the women had gone. A door slammed somewhere in the darkness. The Crusader checked the doors on the left, the deputies the ones on the right. The last door on the left was locked.

The Crusader threw his armored weight against it. The wood creaked but held. He hit it again with his shoulder. The frame cracked around the hinges.

"Out you go," Teska said.

She dangled Amelia by the wrists from the window. It was only a drop of a few feet to the ground. Teska breathed heavily as she followed Amelia. Even that brief use of her gift weakened her more than it used to. They ran to the back of the lodge.

Tua met them there with their horses.

Suddenly, a door on the other side of the lodge flew open. Thorne bolted out and slammed it behind him.

In the main room, Blackscar grinned. "There is nowhere for them to go," he said to the third Crusader. "They cannot use the path out back. If they try to follow the road down this mountain, they will be captured by those we left below. And if they try to separate and flee through the forest, we will still end up with some of them. They are trapped. Come, let us watch the little birds realize they have nowhere to fly." He spun and left the lodge, the Crusader hard on his heels.

"Wh-Where are we gonna go?" Amelia asked as she scrambled into the saddle. "They're right behind us!"

A Crusader and two constables appeared around the left side of the lodge. From the right came another Crusader and two deputies. Behind them was Blackscar, the Witchfinder and the third Crusader. They moved confidently, boxing Thorne's group against the edge of the cliff.

"This way!" Tua shouted. He turned his mustang and urged him onto the dark, spidery trail that wound down the side of the mountain. Amelia followed reluctantly. Teska waited at the trailhead, watching Thorne.

Up on the deck, two deputies held Averitt and Newsome captive as they watched the drama unfold.

The semicircle of Crusaders and Churchmen tightened. Thorne stood beside Nightwalker, bastard sword still in hand.

"Malachi, let's go!" Teska pleaded.

Blackscar stepped forward. The Crusader and Witchfinder flanked him.

"I know your escape plan is compromised, but you cannot flee that way," Blackscar said, gesturing to the path. "Even mountain goats would not use that. You and your friends will break your necks if you try in this darkness."

"What difference does it make to you?" Thorne fired back.

"I would prefer to take you alive. Think of what a tekoya we could have—executing all of you in public—proving once and for all that the Fifth Order is supreme, that nothing can stand in our way."

"Sure," Thorne said. "I'd saw my own fucking head off with a rusty trowel before I'd let you do that."

Blackscar stepped forward again, but this time he staggered. The Witchfinder grabbed his arm to steady him.

"Malachi! You've got to get away!"

It was Cabbott's voice. Thorne had almost forgotten what it sounded like. "Thurl?"

Blackscar shook Cabbott's head as if trying to shoo away a scorpion fly. He chuckled. "Your friend thinks he can overpower me."

"Malachi! For fuck's sake, come on while we still have a chance!" Teska yelled.

Cabbott's body jerked as if hit by lightning. The Crusader and the Witchfinder each held an arm to keep him upright.

"You *can* stop them," Cabbott grunted, his head twitching. "Find the Flame. That destroyed them before—" His back arched, and a defiant scream erupted from his mouth.

"Silence!" Blackscar hissed. A strand of saliva dangled from his lower lip. "Your friend is persistent, I will give him that."

The remaining Crusaders, constables and deputies watched the spectacle.

"Fight him, Thurl!" Thorne yelled. "Fight him!"

"He cannot win," Blackscar replied. "I am supreme. I am one of the Crimson Fathers!" Again, the gleam fled his eyes, and the body convulsed.

"You're…a mouthy bastard," Cabbott said as he struggled to regain control. His eyes locked onto Thorne's. Pleading. Apologetic. "I can't…hold him. He's becoming…more powerful."

"You can fight him!"

Cabbott shook his head. Another tremor ravished his body. The Witchfinder and Crusader held him tight.

"Stop him!" Blackscar shouted. "He is—"

Cabbott snapped his mouth closed so hard he nearly bit his tongue in half. Blood seeped from the corners of his mouth. His eyes were normal, filled with determination. "Can't do much more," he said, still looking at Thorne. "Besides, I'm…getting too old for this shit anyway."

He winked at Thorne. "The Flame! Find it!" Then he grabbed a handful of the Witchfinder's tunic as well as the Crusader's arm. Cabbott flung himself to the side. His momentum, aided by the off-balance men, carried them to the edge of the cliff.

Cabbott jumped.

"NO!" Thorne screamed. He reached out instinctively even though he was too far away. His hands closed around air. "Thurl! *No!*"

Three distinct screams were heard fading to the bottom. The Witchfinder. The Crusader. And Blackscar.

"Thurl," Teska said in a stunned whisper. "Oh no…"

The Churchmen jogged forward and peered over the lip of the cliff into the cold darkness.

"Malachi!" Teska shouted. *"Malachi!"*

He turned and stared as if seeing her for the first time. He looked back to the edge and the men clustered there. He wanted to scream again, but the air had gone from his lungs.

Nightwalker's snort beside his head got his attention.

Teska stared down at him with tear-filled eyes, but her mouth was set in a determined line. "Come on. While they're distracted." She reached down and put a hand on his shoulder. "This is our last chance to go."

Thorne nodded stiffly. He heard the commotion at the cliff's edge as the Churchmen saw him climb into his saddle. He saw them coming toward him, but it felt like a dream. His eyes trailed back to the spot where Cabbott had gone over.

Teska slapped Nightwalker's haunch. The horse whinnied and shot forward, hitting the meager trail head so fast that it almost tumbled tail over mane. The winter wind in Thorne's face snapped him alert. Behind him, Teska and her horse clattered down the perilous, stony path. Above them, their voices growing distant, the Churchmen bellowed orders and stumbled their way onto the trail.

Thorne pulled hard on Nightwalker's reins as he leaned back in the saddle, trying to counterbalance the horse's wild plunge. The wind whistled past, stinging his eyes and nose. He felt the tears on his cheeks begin to freeze.

The horse half fell through the chilled night, hooves slipping and clattering over loose stones and broken tree limbs. Tua navigated them swiftly but carefully. Amelia helped him by using her Nahoru'brexia gift as much as her strength allowed. Her ability to see in the dark was a boon to the Co'manche as she warned of obstacles that lay ahead.

To Thorne, the mad descent felt like a twisted dream. Branches swatted him. His horse leaned from side to side as it skidded down the path. Rocks clattered constantly. He knew he needed to guide the animal, to control it, but he could not remember how. Nightwalker plowed downward. The wind bit Thorne's face and hands, the world around him a blackened smudge.

He had no idea how he stayed in the saddle. His heart felt as heavy as a cathedral bell. He wondered if the mountainside was caving in behind him, chasing him down into oblivion. A bough whacked him in the face, snow flying past his head. Thorne rushed headlong into darkness, and he did not care if he survived it or not.

"Undying One, we have a problem."

Vaelok Strang, First of the Crimson Fathers, turned hooded eye sockets toward the speaker. His pupils shone with feverish light above the gaping nasal cavity.

When he moved, his stringy black hair raked across gaunt shoulders. He stroked the braided silver beard that lay upon his red-robed chest. "What is it?" His voice was the void of the grave.

"It's Blackscar. He's dead."

Strang's head whipped around with an audible crack. These new bodies were already failing. "What did you say?" The light within his sockets darkened.

"Maggard's host—the constable with Thorne—is dead. He killed himself."

Strang turned his face toward the ceiling and growled. "And Blackscar had no receptacle prepared for such an eventuality?"

"No."

Strang locked his emaciated hands behind his back and walked to the nearest window. He looked down at the Celestial Akropolis, Attagon, spread out below the Heiromonarch's Palace.

The messenger joined him at the window. "There is something else."

Strang turned to his companion again. Temias the Bonesorrow, dressed in the flowing red robes that distinguished all the Crimson Fathers, did not return the gaze but likewise looked down upon the city. He was the third of the Fathers to have been resurrected.

Vaelok was the tallest of the Twelve—eleven now—at over six and a half feet. Temias was a foot shorter. He had the same desiccated form as Strang, but his head was completely bald and laced with graying, protuberant veins. His skull was elongated, drawing his bulbous eyes closer together around a razor-thin nose. A fanged mouth spread above a black goatee. His tongue licked flabby lips before he spoke.

"They know of the Flame."

"*What!*" Strang shouted. A servant by the door on the far side of the room cowered, trying to make himself invisible.

"Yes," Temias continued, "it would seem that despite his age, the constable was more *resilient* than Maggard had anticipated. While our brother was learning through him, the host was also learning. About us."

Strang was silent for a long moment. His bony fingers clutched the rock windowsill. "Where is it?"

"Safe. It rests within the hidden chamber."

"In all these years"—Strang sighed, the most human sound he had yet made—"we still cannot find a way to destroy it."

Temias raked a taloned hand through his goatee. "We need not worry about it. No one knows of the chamber except us."

"And how do we know the host didn't learn that detail as well?" Strang challenged.

Temias shook his head. "No. We would have known. Something of *that* magnitude? Maggard would have alerted us."

"True."

"And since it cannot be destroyed, we ensured that it would be well guarded. Forever."

Strang paused, then said, "Come. Jaccomus and Callodin are ready. The others are on their way. It is time to begin preparations for the eluruum." Temias followed Strang out of the room.

Thorne hunched inside his cloak as the freezing rain pelted his face. They raced through the endless night, putting as much distance as possible between them and their pursuers. But the farther they ran, the heavier Thorne's numbness and grief became.

They had managed to survive the torturous descent but not without casualties. Amelia's horse had broken a leg halfway down, and she now rode with Teska. They did not have time to put the horse out of its misery, a kindness that Thorne knew Cabbott would have insisted on. As a lover of the outdoors, it would have devastated him to leave the horse alone and in pain.

But he left me alone and in pain, he thought. He tucked his head close to Nightwalker's icy mane, smelling the horse's sweat. No, that was not fair. Or accurate. It was not Thurl's fault. Blackscar was to blame. Those damned Crimson Fathers.

"They'll pay," he snarled to his horse. "I swear by God and the Church and anyone who's listening. I'll make them pay." It felt good to take the pain and direct it elsewhere. But the ache in his heart pulled at him. It wrapped miserable claws into his soul, dragging him back no matter how fast the horse ran.

It was just like Merrick's death. As those memories flooded his mind, the agony tugged harder. Persistent. Uncaring. It wanted to devour his heart and soul and spirit. Surrender would be so easy. Just let go. Give in. Fighting only prolonged the inevitable.

"Malachi! We need to find shelter!" Tua yelled through the rain as he rode up beside him. Thorne paid no attention.

"The horses are done in! If we don't stop soon, we're going to kill them!"

Done in. The horses are done in.

The thought settled in Thorne's mind. Amelia's horse was done in. It was whimpering in pain on the side of the mountain.

Thurl's done in. His body…

The meager path from the lodge had emptied onto a talus pile at the base of the cliff. As they had picked their way over the stones, they came upon Cabbott. He lay facedown atop a boulder, arms and legs splayed at gruesome angles. Blood, black in the winter night, splattered the surface of the rock. They had no time to even retrieve the body. Their pursuers had pressed hard after them. Thorne left his friend broken and unburied. Alone.

"Malachi!" Teska called.

He wished they would just leave him alone.

"I think we're near a village. Let's find a barn or cave or something. We've gone as far as we can tonight."

What little strength he had left dissolved. Fatigue and grief washed over him like the rain. He nodded, although he did not know—or care—if she saw him.

Half an hour later, they sheltered in the ramshackle remains of a barn nearly obscured by a field of weeds and bare trees. They were too tired to start a fire, but they could not risk one anyway. No one had any appetite. They tried to air-dry their cloaks as best they could and found suitable places to sleep. Thorne sat in a numb haze on his bedroll.

Teska sat down beside him and took his large hand in hers. She laid her head against his shoulder. He smelled the rain and sweat in her hair and put his arm around her. Outside, the crackle of the rain continued. They sat that way for a long time.

Finally, Teska broke the silence. "Do you remember me telling you that Marco and I had once talked about going west? Just dropping everything and riding and riding and riding until we ran out of land?"

He nodded.

Her voice was tender but serious. "Why don't *we* do that?"

Her heart ached to see how grief had hollowed his face. Wet hair stuck to his forehead, and he shivered in the drafty barn.

"I mean it," she continued. "To hells with the Church and the Communion. Fuck the Crimson Fathers and freedom and everything else. Let's get as far away from here as we can."

Thorne tried to process the words. He looked at Tua and Amelia, already asleep back-to-back for warmth. He looked at Thurl—no, he looked at where Thurl *should have* been—beside the animals or off to the side keeping watch. But no one kept watch. No one took care of the horses, wiping them down and checking their shoes.

Just go? Thorne thought.

He forced the idea to come together in his detached mind, as cold as his body. Leave everything? Why? How?

"We're survivors, you and I. We can go. We can create something new if you want. Maybe we could go back to the Tex'ahns for a while?"

"But—but we can't just…" They were the first words he had spoken since discovering Cabbott's body hours ago.

Teska squeezed his hand and held his arm. "Yes, we can," she said in a gentle but insistent manner. "There's nothing to hold us here."

Thorne sighed. "What about the Communion? You said they would punish you if you disobeyed them."

"Piss on them. Let them do what they want. I don't care. You and I need a fresh start. How much more are we expected to give? How many more losses do we have to accept?"

The words hummed in Thorne's mind, teasing and tempting. They *had* given so much—too much—for the cause. Merrick and Cabbott, both gone forever. Dario and Tycho and Solomon. He had no idea where they were or if they were even still alive.

He had tried to undertake Merrick's cause and carry it forward. He had devoted his time to studying and learning, to examining and planning, to meeting and unifying. And for what? Every freedom fighter they had met, every Nahoru'brexia that Teska had found, all had been rounded up, arrested and thrown into compliance camps. Who was left to help him? How could the movement grow, much less progress, when all his work had been undone?

"Malachi…?"

"I-I don't want the Communion to hurt you. There's been too much hurt—"

"You let me worry about the Communion," she said, sticking her chin out.

Thorne nodded toward Tua and Amelia. "What about them?"

"They could come with us if they want. They could go back home if they want. I'm sure they'll understand."

Several minutes passed. The rain stopped, but wind continued to quarrel with the corners of the barn.

"I've—I've got nothing left to give," Thorne finally said. His voice was haunted and weak.

"I know."

"All that we've done, all the plans we were making…"

Teska nodded. "I know. Let somebody else take it. If it's meant to happen, someone else can carry the banner. It doesn't have to be you."

"I c-can't believe he's gone."

She squeezed his hand again. "Just think about it." She laid down, her back to him, and was asleep in minutes.

When he eventually laid down, he snuggled up against her back. He laid an arm around her waist. Thorne stared into the darkness, his imagination showing the two of them chasing the sunset. He drifted off to sleep with a hole in his heart.

13
RAID

SATURDAY, OCTOBER 17, 999 AE

"We get the kids out tonight. Can't wait any longer," Warner said. He wrapped the heavy fur coat around him, thankful for the winter garments they had found stored in the wagon.

"I've been thinking," Hawkes said, "why not just keep following them—see where they're going? We know they're not going to hurt the kids."

Darien shook his head. It was a bony-looking thing inside the fur-lined hood. "We don't know that for sure. We have no idea what they plan to do to those kids."

"And I ain't going to Attagon," Lillia Pittman said, crossing her arms over a bosom wide enough to shelve books on. "Nuh-uh. I'm getting my kids and going back."

Hawkes raised his hands. "Okay, sorry, it was just a thought."

"How are we going to do this?" Hart asked. The minimal rations in Saxonburgh had taken their toll on him, too.

All of them, with the exception of Lillia, were far below their normal weight. They had consumed all the food scavenged from the camp. For the last two days, they only had a few runty, hard vegetables that Warner had managed to steal from snow-covered farms. They had seen some game, but the longbow in the wagon was broken. They had nothing to use as a bowstring.

They had caught up with the caravan on Wednesday, four days after fleeing the compliance camp. And for the past forty-eight hours, they had trailed behind, out of sight, learning its routines.

There were twenty-five wagons. Each bore the symbols of the Four Orders, with the symbol of the Fifth Order painted in the middle. Fifteen wagons carried children. According to the message Darien had intercepted, there were six children per wagon. Unfortunately, all the wagons looked alike, and the children flitted between them all the time. Six carried food, plus grain for the fifty horses. The remaining four wagons were for the adults. Four grooms cared after the horses. The guards numbered an even dozen—nine deputies, two constables, and a Witchfinder.

Due to the caravan's size and the uncooperative weather, it only covered about ten miles per day. A deputy rode point, looking for suitable places to stop. They traveled along one of the pre-Cataclysm trade routes, and in the evening set up camp beside or on the four-lane road. They circled the wagons for added protection from the wind and predators.

After dinner, the Witchfinder assumed the role of pedagogue and instructed the children about the Fifth Order, the new ways of the Church, the golden age of the upcoming millennium and the importance of their obedience to the future of the realm. The lectures always ended with a prayer and the common phrase, "the Church is God."

In the two days since they had been watching the convoy, no one had seen any children attempt to escape. Perhaps they were afraid to be on their own out here, so far from home. Perhaps they knew to stay near the food. Maybe they knew they would be punished if they attempted to escape. Yet there was no evidence that the children were afraid. As dinner was being prepared, they sprang from the wagons and played games. They laughed and threw snowballs. The children's wagons were not locked at night, although guards were on duty.

It's like one great big adventure to them, Warner thought. Traveling to unknown destinations, the promise of seeing the capital, new friends, new sights along the way. Did they have any idea what was really happening? And if they knew, why were they still so happy and carefree?

"Hey, Jester, you got snow in your ears or something? Matthias asked you a question," Hawkes said. He leaned against the side of the wagon, trying to stay out of the wind. His head remained bandaged, but his color had returned. He had even felt well enough to take his turn at the reins.

"Huh, what? Oh, sorry. What'd you say, Matthias?"

"I was wondering how we're going to do this raid."

Warner finished making their fire despite the wind's efforts to prevent it. He sighed. "You and I'll sneak into the camp tonight just before the guard change. That way the one on duty might be a little drowsy." He stood up, dusted off his hands and shoved them into his coat pockets.

Snowflakes covered his shoulders and hood like dandruff. The sun had almost been swallowed by the western hills, and overhead the sky had already turned purplish blue. Lillia placed a metal bar over the fire and hung a small pot from it.

"We go in; I'll find Cassidy and Cassandra. You get your girls. And we bring them back. We stay in other footprints or wagon tracks as much as possible."

Lillia stopped stirring the pot and stared at them. "What about my young'uns?"

"I'll go back for them," Warner said.

"And what if they find out them kids 're gone *before* you can do that?" she challenged.

"They won't," Warner lied. "I promise." He prayed that did not happen because if it did, there would be no way to get any more children. And none of them would get away, either.

Lillia said nothing but looked away and added a few paltry vegetables to the pot of water.

"I'll go with you," Hawkes volunteered. "I'll get Lillia's kids."

"That won't be possible, Tycho, you know that," Darien said as he crouched as close to the fire as he could get. "You can barely climb up on the driver's seat, much less round up three children and get them out."

"I can do it," he declared.

Hart looked skeptical. "Tycho, it's only been a week since you took that hit to the skull. I'm afraid I agree with Dario—"

"I don't care who you agree with," Hawkes interrupted. "I've been feeling better every day. We're only going to get one shot at this. If you bring some of those kids up here but can't get all of them…" He said in a softer tone, "Look, I know I can't fight right now. So if one breaks out, I'm no good to you. I get that. But I *can* walk. And I *can* lead kids back here."

"Two trips would be difficult," Hart conceded.

Warner furrowed his brow, causing his one eye to squint. He worked his jaw from side to side as if the idea were a piece of jerky. He looked at Lillia. His expression softened. "What do you think?"

She pushed herself off the ground and stood beside him. "Let 'im go," she said. "I'd rather try than risk not getting to see my babies again." Her tears sparkled in the firelight. "Oh, Church, protect 'em."

Hart crept within viewing distance of the caravan and returned shortly thereafter. It was about half a league from them, atop a low, domed hill of naked trees. Clouds layered the sky, making it difficult to see the stars.

"I know which wagons they're all in," Hart told them.

"Let's wait a little longer, then we'll make our move," Warner said.

Lillia waddled to each of the three raiders and handed them a folded piece of cloth. They were cold and slightly damp.

"What's this?" Hawkes asked.

"There's a rag in there, got some dwale on it. I hope 'n' pray you don't need it. But it's hard to say what kinda nonsense they been filling them kids' heads with."

Hart offered her a smile that was part gratitude, part pained realization. "It's a very good idea."

Warner pocketed the cloth. "Here's how we do it: each of us sneaks into the wagon where our kids are. If any of 'em asks any questions, pretend you're a guard. Make up a lie, tell 'em a joke—anythin' to get 'em out as quickly and quietly as you can. Stick to the footprints as much as possible. There's plenty goin' off into the surroundin' woods where the kids have gone to the bathroom. Stay low, keep your head down. Keep the kids quiet as best you can."

"What about a distraction?" Darien asked. "Maybe a fire?"

Hart shook his head. "That would put everybody on alert. The guards would lock those wagons down in the blink of an eye."

"What if you all stampeded their horses?" Lillia suggested.

"That's a better idea, but again, as soon as it happens, everyone knows something is going on," Hart said.

Warner studied what he could see of the stars. They looked like ice crystals. The snow had stopped for the moment. Their fire burned low. "We'll wait another hour," he said. He sat down on a log and stared into the glowing embers.

Warner grimaced with every step. He had shed his heavy coat so he could move quicker, and the night air gnawed at his flesh. Even though he was using a pathway of small footprints, his boots in the snow sounded like bells tolling in his ears. He stopped every few feet, breathing hard, praying, watching. From his position, he could see Hart doing the same thing. Hawkes was on the other side of the wagon ring.

Two guards patrolled the circle, one on each side, usually equidistant from each other. Tonight, however, both walked together. They talked in low voices and smoked tabáks.

Warner hunkered behind a snow-capped rock while the guards strolled by some thirty yards away. Once they vanished, he crept toward his wagon, keeping on his tiptoes to help diminish the noise. He crouched behind the rear wheel until he saw the guards on the other side. When they disappeared behind a wagon, he climbed up the two rear steps. He grasped the door latch, lifted it and stepped inside, closing the door behind him.

The wagon smelled of unwashed clothing. He waited for his eyes to adjust. Two windows did little to illuminate the interior. Along one side of the wagon was a set of bunks. Two more sat against the opposite wall. A child slumbered in each.

No shouts or alarms so far. His heart pounded in his throat, and his hands were sweaty. He studied the small forms in the bunks. Cassidy and Cassandra were in the first set to his right. He eased toward it.

Now that he was here, Warner realized he did not know which of the two to awaken first. Should he wake Cassandra since she was younger? Or would it be better if she saw her brother already awake? He decided to rouse Cassidy first.

The boy was on the top bunk, slightly above Warner's bald head. He stepped on the side of the lower bunk and pulled himself up, so his mouth was close to the boy's ear.

"Cassidy," he said, so softly he was not even sure he had made any sound. He tried again, a little louder. "Cassidy."

The boy moaned and moved a little.

"Cassidy, wake up. It's Uncle Solomon."

He moved again, mumbling something incoherent.

"Cassidy, come on, *wake up*." Warner risked saying it a bit louder. In the confines of the wagon, his voice sounded like a hammer on an anvil.

The ten year old smacked his lips. A small fist rubbed an eye. "Huh?" he said, groggy.

"I need you to get up, Cassidy. Uncle Dario wants to see you."

Cassidy raised up on his elbows and blinked like an owl. "Wh-Who are you?"

"Uncle Solomon. You remember me. Let's get your sister and we can go see Uncle Dario."

Cassidy sat up in bed, staring. Warner eased aside to give the lad room to climb down. Instead, the boy opened his mouth and shouted.

"HELP!"

Warner's heart all but leapt out of his body. He clamped a hand over Cassidy's mouth. As the lad started to thrash around, Warner groped for the rag in his pocket.

Two children turned over in their bunks.

Warner felt sweat trickle past his eye. He anticipated them sitting up and raising the alarm. But they remained asleep. He held the rag over Cassidy's face. The child took a deep breath for another yell but received only a lungful of dwale. In less than thirty seconds, he was as limp as wet parchment.

He waited, breathless, to see if anyone would respond to the boy's cry. He heard no shouts or alarms being raised. He exhaled and checked Cassidy's pulse. Slow but strong. He was not going to make the same mistake with Cassandra. He held the rag underneath her button nose, and after a moment her pulse matched Cassidy's.

He wrapped them in blankets and waited until he saw the guards go around again. He cracked the door and pushed it open with his foot. He hoisted Cassidy over his right shoulder and Cassandra over his left. With a silent prayer, he descended the steps.

Shit! I can't close the door!

He considered laying the children down in the snow and closing it, but he did not know how long he had until the guards returned. They would just have to assume that a kid had gone to the bathroom.

Crouching as best he could with two bundles on his shoulders, Warner fled back to the rock. He dropped into a slide and hit the ground as the guards came into view. He lay still, trying not to breath hard and give himself away. He heard the guards stop walking, followed by the sound of a match being struck. Then the two men continued their patrol.

Warner waited until they were out of sight. He gathered up Cassidy and Cassandra once more, and with their legs flopping against his chest, he raced for the shelter of the forest.

Warner was the first one back to the wagon. Darien and Lillia had extinguished the fire in preparation for departure. They awaited him in the darkness like parents expecting a prodigal. When Darien saw his niece and nephew, he broke into tears.

"Thank you, Solomon! Oh, thank you!" he cried.

He followed Warner into the wagon and waited until the children were laid out on the folding bunk that Hawkes had used. Darien stroked their cheeks with palsied fingers. His chin with its small growth of white beard trembled as he wiped tears from his face.

"I had to use the dwale," Warner told him. "Cassidy was about to raise the alarm."

Darien nodded. As Warner turned to leave, the old man laid a hand on his shoulder. "Thank you," he repeated. His smile was the purest and brightest Warner could ever remember.

Outside, Lillia yelped and clapped her hands. "Praise the Church!"

Hawkes appeared from the darkness with two small boys at his side and a girl in his arms. His face was flushed, and he walked on unsteady legs. When the children saw their mother, they bounded through the snow into her arms. Lillia wept and hugged all three at the same time.

"Any sign of Matthias?" Warner asked Hawkes.

He shook his head. "He got inside the wagon, I know that."

"Get inside and rest. You about did yourself in," Warner said.

Hawkes plodded toward the wagon. As he did, Lillia stood up and bear-hugged him. Her cheeks were wet, and her skin was cold as a salamander, but the warmth of the embrace was undeniable.

"Bless you!" she said. "May the Church bless you for what you done!"

He looked at the three tearful children and smiled before climbing into the wagon.

Twenty minutes later, as Warner stomped his feet and blew into his hands, Hart stumbled into view. He held two daughters in his arms. The third ran behind him, gripping the back of his coat.

"Sorry we're late. The guard change happened just as we were about to leave. I had to wait until that was over."

Warner smiled at the three girls. They looked at him in bewilderment and clutched their father tighter. "I'm just glad you made it."

"What about Tycho?" Hart asked, standing the two girls in the snow. They looked to be about seven years old. The third, still using her father as a shield, was perhaps ten.

"He made it. Got Lillia's kids."

"And you?"

Warner nodded, smiled. "Got 'em both."

"Thank the Church! Then let's ride," Hart said.

Once everyone was in the wagon—Warner grinned at the thought of so many people crammed in there—they descended the gentle slope of the hill, snow crunching beneath the wheels. He turned east. They were already in the foothills of the Great Appian Mountains. In less than an hour, they would begin their ascent. That was when things were really going to get difficult.

The dwale was potent on small bodies. Cassidy and Cassandra slept for hours. Darien remained by their side in the back of the wagon, but after a while its rhythmic swaying lulled him to sleep as well. A familiar voice pulled him back to wakefulness.

"Cass'dy, where are we? Cass'dy?"

Cassandra pushed her brother's shoulder to rouse him. He moaned and his eyelids fluttered. She put her mouth close to his ear. "Cass'dy, please wake up. I'm scared. I-I don't know where we are." She looked around at Darien and froze.

He smiled at her, joy swelling his heart. After so many difficulties, he could hardly believe that his niece and nephew were finally with him again. He felt sure his face would crack from the widening grin.

But Cassandra just stared at him, her eyes large and filled with fear.

"Cassandra, it's okay, don't be afraid," he said as he kept his voice soft. "It's me, your Uncle Dario."

The little girl took a step back. She studied him but there was no recognition on her face. She shook her brother, harder this time.

"Mmmm, wha…?" Cassidy said, smacking his lips.

"Cass'dy, get up!"

Darien raised his wizened hands to show he was not a threat. "Cassandra—"

Her lip trembled. Tears filled her eyes. A small sob leapt from her throat.

Cassidy bolted upright. Still blinking away the sleep, he grabbed his sister and pulled her close. He saw Darien and frowned.

"Cassidy, take it easy. You're safe. It's me, your Uncle Dario."

As his sister had done a moment before, Cassidy searched Darien's face. The old man felt the warmth in his heart begin to cool as no recognition dawned on his nephew's face. He was about to speak, to reassure the children, but Cassidy interrupted.

"Who are you?" he demanded. "Where are we?" He glanced around the wagon.

Darien kept smiling. Surely they would recognize that? Maybe it would just take them a few more minutes to flush the grogginess from their minds.

"You remember me, don't you?" Darien said. "I'm your Uncle. Uncle Dario."

Cassidy shook his head. "No you ain't!" Cassandra shook her head, too.

"Yes, yes, it is me. You have to believe me. I've—I've… Something's happened to me. It's…hard to explain. But you have to believe that it's *really* me. I'm your Uncle. My friends and I, we got you away from that caravan."

Cassidy frowned. "I don't believe you. You ain't our uncle. Take us back."

Small cracks began to race across Darien's heart. His niece and nephew stared at him defiantly. Cassandra's lower lip stuck out. Cassidy wrinkled his nose to show he meant business.

"I-I can't take you back. Please, just listen to me. I can explain everythi—"

Cassidy screamed as loud as he could. Cassandra joined in. The shrill sound hit Darien's eardrums like a white-hot awl.

"HELP! HELP US!" the boy yelped.

Darien rose uneasily in the bouncing wagon and took a step toward them.

Cassandra shrieked in terror and burrowed against her brother. Cassidy held her tighter and continued to yell for help.

Darien tried to say something that would calm them. He tried to remember a story or adventure, anything that might prove his identity. But he could not concentrate. Cassandra cried and Cassidy called for people that Darien assumed had been adults in the caravan. The cracks in his heart widened and chipped.

Finally, Cassidy stopped. He breathed heavy from his outburst but still glared at Darien. "I don't know you," he said. "You ain't our uncle. And you better take us back, *right now*, or you gonna be in big trouble with the Church."

Darien's lip quivered as he tried to think of what to say. There was so much to tell them, so much to explain. But they did not recognize him. It was not the lack of recognition that comes from not seeing a loved one for a while. This was different. He saw it in their eyes. He had changed so much that he was nothing more than a stranger to them.

"Oh, my two poppets…" he whispered as a tear slid down his face. "Please… please believe me. I'd never lie to you."

"You stay away from us," Cassidy said and wrinkled his nose again. "You ain't our uncle. You stay away."

Pieces fell from Darien's broken heart.

Warner pushed the horses as hard as he dared. They were rested but hungry. There was no grain left. Vegetation was dead or buried beneath the snow. They were managing okay for now, but he knew that would not last much longer.

The terrain grew rockier as they climbed into the teeth of the mountains. In the wake of the Great Cataclysm, the earth buckled and separated and reformed many times. What had once been a mountain range of softly rounded hills became a granite spine that remained unexplored in places a thousand years later.

Bits of ancient roads and ruined buildings could be found all across the face of the mountains. Unreadable twisted signs, odd metallic carriages that must have been some form of pre-Cataclysm transportation and collapsed bridges appeared among the wild flora as if they'd been dropped there by accident. Dead grass and weeds gave way to scrub brush, and skeletal trees clawed the heights with snow-covered limbs. The wind howled down the peaks.

Warner guided the wagon along narrow paths between towering boulders that loomed out of the darkness like angry gods. And he took them higher still. His ears popped twice. The horses slipped several times, and on each occasion, he held his breath, imagining them all cascading to their deaths in a crevasse or valley. When he looked down and behind them, he saw pinpricks of fire in pursuit.

Warner had no idea how high they were. He did not know how far their pursuers were behind them. So he kept going, through evergreen-filled canyons and along precipices that made him dizzy to look over. Clouds completely obscured the stars. The incessant wind turned his skin to ice. Around them, the massive peaks thrust ever higher. Their snow-capped summits scraped the floor of the First Heaven, their forested slopes and alpine ridges shadowed and silent. Warner imagined he could almost hear the snow falling. The jostling of the wagon kept him awake, but he could feel his body slowing down, needing rest. His ears popped two more times before he found the shell of an ancient building. He set the handbrake and climbed down, his limbs all but frozen in place.

Three walls remained, but there was no roof. The floor had rotted away ages ago. But at least it offered some shelter. While Warner looked for firewood, Hart tended to the horses. Lillia did her best to find something for everyone to eat. Hawkes still slept, as did all of the children except Cassidy and Cassandra. They huddled together, throwing sharp glances at Darien, who watched over them like a beatific sentinel.

How are we goin' to feed everybody? Warner fretted as he piled some wet sticks together. *And the horses can't keep goin' like this. Neither can we.*

He was also worried about how Lillia would get back home now, how close the guards were behind them and what would happen if they were attacked tonight. He worked for fifteen minutes before coaxing a feeble flame into life. He sat back to enjoy the warmth and never knew when he fell asleep.

14
LEADER

TUESDAY, OCTOBER 20, 999 AE

On the day that Thorne, Teska, Tua and Amelia fled Averitt Lodge, the capital city of Attagon fell to the Fifth Order. But to say it was a fall implies a grandiose collapse when, in reality, very little changed. Some constables and deputies were replaced by Crusaders. Laws were tightened. The Crimson Fathers remained unseen in the Palace of the Heiromonarch. The economy was strong, so few complained. The Northgate compliance camp had opened a few weeks before, after months of work for architects, stonemasons, metalsmiths and laborers. For the majority of congregants, life went on as before: paying obedience to the Church of the Deiparous, earning a living, raising families.

And making preparations for the millennium.

In a little over two months, the realm would welcome the year 1000 and the new golden age of the Fifth Order. It was to be an extravagant affair. The Church planned to hold a worship service at noon on December 31st. The rest of the day was devoted to feasts and festivities. No labor would be done on that day or the next. Already, congregants who could afford to do so made their way to the Celestial Akropolis. Thespians and acrobats, jongleurs and craftsmen, pilgrims and merchants slowly trickled in. Thorne and his friends had no difficulty entering the city.

They had been stopped briefly so their wagon could be searched. Thorne and Teska had hidden inside the boxes that ran along both inside walls and served as benches. Tua and Amelia had opened the rear door, proudly displaying the jumble of pots, pans, clothing and bric-a-brac they had methodically scattered about.

Tua had jabbered to the guards the whole time, claiming to be from Skonmesto, how it was his first time in Attagon and how excited he was to see the Heiromonarch—more words than Thorne had heard his friend string together in two weeks' time. The guards had been more than willing to wave them on if it meant silencing the garrulous stranger. Thorne and Teska had crawled from their hiding spots and sat side by side, watching the city through the barred windows. Thorne saw familiar buildings and smelled familiar aromas. The streets buzzed with activity as people carried out their business.

Despite Teska's presence, being home brought a pang of loneliness. Thorne felt disconnected, a foreigner in a place he once called home. He looked toward The Bluff, where he used to live. Someone else would be living there now. The property and possessions of a heretic were forfeit to the Church. He wondered if his manservant, Ames, was still up there. Or had the Church reassigned him?

The scent of winter's muddy chill, bread fresh from stone ovens, animals and smoke replaced the staleness inside the wagon. Yells and curses, laughter and conversation, braying donkeys and squeaking wheels punctuated the general din and hum.

Thorne was preoccupied with the traffic around them and did not notice Teska looking at him. He would not have liked the worried lines that furrowed her brow and creased the edges of her eyes.

While Tua had rattled on like a runaway carriage to the guards, Thorne had been just the opposite for the past four days. Taciturn and depressed, he had spent one full day just riding inside the wagon, the agonies of Averitt Lodge consuming him like starved rats at a corn crib. He had eaten little, and sleep eluded him. Not even the comforting words and encouragement of his friends made a dent in his grief.

Teska had tried talking with Thorne, looking for some way to assuage his pain. But he had only sighed, deep and forlorn, and stared off into space. He would not talk about their future, plans for the movement, or even Dario, Tycho and Solomon. Each day, he retreated a little further and fortified the walls between him and everyone else. Nothing Teska said made any appreciable change in him. She was frustrated. There was nothing she could do to ease his suffering.

Nothing except pray.

Teska had never been religious. Even as a child, she was not awed by the pomp and majesty of the Church's cathedrals or its liturgies and services. The Church had never helped her after her mother died or when her father and brothers decided to use her for their own pleasure. She had never believed that the Church was God and refused to worship it as such. She had never really prayed. Throughout her twenty-two years, she had lived by her wits, her luck and her Nahoru'brexia gift.

But after visiting the Tex'ahn lands, she found herself thinking more about God. She tried to remember some of the things she had heard and had questioned

Amelia a few times about her faith. Amelia prayed. She talked to the invisible God as if he were sitting right beside her, a devoted friend listening and appreciating every word. It seemed odd to Teska.

It had felt even odder the first time she tried it. She had been alone and did her best to imitate what Amelia did when she prayed. It had been awkward for Teska. She spoke to nothing and heard no reply.

Over the last few days, she had prayed more.

God, if you're really there, help Malachi. He didn't do anything wrong, but he won't stop blaming himself. I don't know what to do to help him. So if you're up there, do something. Fix this.

She and Thorne had talked a little more about running away together, but Thorne became more detached the closer they got to Attagon. She did not know if he simply remained undecided or if it was just inconsequential—a dream with as much substance as an early morning fog.

And then there was the Communion. Now that she was in Attagon, as the Maiden had instructed, what happened next? But she knew the answer. She would wait. That was the way of the Communion. When the time was right, they would contact her and tell her what to do.

Tua and Amelia guided the wagon onto a side street. Excrement from chamber pots lay in slushy puddles, and the stench burned their nostrils. A cat watched them from a windowsill, tail twitching. A few people passed by but paid them no mind.

Tua set the handbrake, dismounted and checked the horses tied behind the wagon. Amelia also got down and opened the back door.

Teska knelt in the doorway. "Everything all right?" she asked, scanning the street behind them.

"Everything's fine. We just need to know where we're headed." She looked past Teska. "Malachi?"

He looked over at Amelia and did not try to hide his dour expression. He reluctantly got up and walked to the door but stood behind Teska.

She glanced up and over her shoulder. "Malachi?"

"Do we have a place to stay?" Tua asked. "The horses are in need of rest. We all are." He said the last sentence into a horse's ear as he brushed its neck.

"Where are we?" Thorne asked. He, too, watched the traffic along the main road at the end of the street.

Tua and Amelia explained that they had passed the campus of the Abthanian Order and its cluster of educational buildings on the northern shore of the River

Tense. They had entered the business district that began at the riverfront, and Thorne asked what specific businesses they had passed in order to find his bearings.

A group of men on horseback came from the other end of the street, and Thorne withdrew deeper into the wagon. Teska turned away and pretended to be searching for something. The clop-clop-clop of hooves and the men's conversation eased by them and melded into the traffic at the other end. Thorne stuck his head out the door and, with a few brief sentences, instructed Tua and Amelia on their destination.

It was past noon.

"Is anybody else hungry?" Amelia asked. "I sure am."

Tua nodded.

"Teska, is there anywhere around here to get something to eat? I suppose I could whip up something from what we've got in the back."

Teska glanced at the sky from between the two large buildings. It had been almost an hour since Thorne had halted them, order them to wait, rapped on a warehouse door, and slipped inside when it creaked open.

"I wouldn't go anywhere," she replied. "I'm not sure what's around this area, and we don't want to risk getting tangled up with a Crusader or Churchmen."

Amelia opened the back door of the wagon. "I think there's some jerky left. We can just have that for now." As she rummaged through the sacks in the wagon, Tua sat on the lowered step, smoking his pipe. Teska stayed between the wagon and the building, shielded from any prying eyes that might pass through the alley.

She had been to Attagon before but did not know the city like Thorne did. Plus, they remained wanted fugitives. Even with the preparations for the new millennium, she knew the Church would be thrilled to slap them in irons and roast them at the next tekoya.

The warehouse door opened, and Thorne peeked out. "Teska, have Tua and Amelia take the wagon and horses around back. We'll meet them there."

The smell struck her as she walked through the door. Rose oil, camphor, cinnamon and balsam mixed with vanilla, clove, ginger and orange in a sweet and ethereal concoction. She sniffed and snorted, attempting to clear her nasal passages.

For the first time in nearly a week, Thorne laughed. "You'll get used to it. It is a bit intense at first. Let me introduce you to a friend." He indicated the man standing in front of them.

He was Teska's height, with short black hair worn in a bowl cut. Cheerful eyes turned down into a small nose. He looked at ease in the smile he wore.

"Teska, this is my friend, Ryoma Takata."

The man stepped forward and took Teska's hand in his bejeweled, plump one. He bowed, letting his right leg slip behind his left. His eyes never strayed from hers. "Hail and blessing, Beautiful One," he said in an elegant voice with a faint feminine tone.

Takata wore a dark-green woolen tunic. Short breeches ended just below the knees with the rest of his legs covered by white stockings that disappeared into long-toed shoes. A scarlet coat, trimmed with fox fur, hung nearly to the floor. Two gold necklaces lay upon his chest, and a wide belt strained around his waist. He was like a gaudy barrel in the midst of all the real ones around them.

The pungent, aromatic war that hung in the air deadened Teska's sense of smell.

"Takata is an oil merchant," Thorne said.

"No shit," she mumbled, rubbing her nose and looking at the rows of casks.

"Come, my friends, come!" Takata said. "My men will attend to your conveyance and steeds." He spun on his heel and led them along an aisle between stacks of crates. He babbled about his business as they walked. Thankfully, Thorne did not see anyone else around. If they could avoid meeting the men Ryoma had mentioned, so much the better. He wanted as few people as possible to know they were here.

Despite laughing a moment before, Thorne remained enshrouded in his depressive pall. He wanted to cast it off and return to his normal self. But it stuck to him like pitch—no, like a parasite that had made its home in him. He knew he could not continue in this manner but had no idea how to stop it. He cursed his own weakness.

I'm a Witchfinder Imperator, for God's sake! Or I used to be, he corrected himself, and felt the inward prick of another failure on his part. Merrick, betrayals, Cabbott's death, losing his vocation, being labeled a heretic and traitor—his failures stacked up like the barrels and crates in Takata's warehouse, threatening to crush the life out of him.

Takata excelled at two things: smiling and talking. He flitted from one subject to another, often leaving ideas and sentences unfinished, though Thorne was barely listening anyway.

Teska held Thorne's hand as they walked. He knew he did not deserve her or Takata. Or Tua.

The weight of his failures was unbearable, and he wanted to just lay down and sleep. Even the simple act of following the merchant across the warehouse felt like trudging through a snowbank.

Whenever Takata glanced back, Thorne smiled and nodded. It was amazing how quickly he had learned to switch masks back and forth—like a thespian playing dual roles. It was something else he hated. He felt like a fraud but knew of no other way to cope. He forced himself to interact with his friends when necessary, but doing so drained him, which only increased his guilt.

"Here, rest yourselves," Takata said as they entered his office. Two tables, burdened by piles of documents and stoppered vials of oil, sat off to one side. Boxes and crates lined the opposite wall. Ryoma's desk was in the middle of the room. The merchant ushered them to several thickly cushioned chairs that faced it. He returned to the door, still jabbering about sales and distributors and tariffs. A man delivered Tua and Amelia to the room and left. As they sat down, Takata closed and bolted his door.

"Drinks?" he offered, and before anyone could decline, he filled a tray with glasses.

"Who the hells is this guy?" Teska asked under her breath as she nudged Thorne in the side. "Do you trust him?"

Thorne nodded and faked a smile. "We wouldn't be here if I didn't. Takata and I are old friends. We met when I was just starting as a Witchfinder. He was my second case."

"Yes, and I am forever indebted to this man," their host said, grinning so wide that his eyes almost disappeared. He handed each person a glass half full of a daffodil-colored liquid and sat down behind his desk.

"Honeyed wine," he said. He lifted his glass and sipped daintily. "Malachi saved my mother and my sister. Both had been accused of witchcraft—can you believe such horror? My own dear, frail mother and sister! But Malachi uncovered the truth." He pulled a handkerchief from his sleeve and dabbed at the corner of his mouth.

"An old grudge," Thorne said, emptying his glass. "Typical stuff."

"Well, it may've been typical for *you*," Takata protested with an affable grin, "but it left me a nervous wreck. I was so traumatized I couldn't sleep for weeks afterward!"

Thorne sat his glass on the edge of the desk and looked at his friends. "Takata has graciously offered to keep us out of sight," he said. "There's a small basement here we can stay in."

Takata waved his arms back and forth. "You are welcome to traverse in and out as your needs require. I have a few men in my employ here, but they will cause you no problems and are completely trustworthy."

"Completely trustworthy doesn't mean much these days," Teska said, rolling her empty glass in her hand.

Takata clucked his tongue. "Yes, yes, Malachi has informed me of your recent disagreeable experiences. I am deeply sorry for what you've had to endure. But rest assured: my men have no love for Crusaders or the Fifth Order. You're as safe as a baby bird in a nest here." He turned to Thorne. "What are your intentions now?"

Thorne gave a drawn out, pained sigh. He stared at the floor for a moment. "I can tell you what we *need* to do. The Crimson Fathers need to be stopped. They control the Fifth Order. Once they are out of the way, we can begin to address the issue of freedom as it relates to the Church. But…I have no idea *how* to do it." He sighed again. Teska could almost touch the defeat in his voice.

"You sound unsure, Chief-Who-Wins," Tua said. "Are you questioning your goal or yourself?"

"Don't call me that!" Thorne snarled. "I haven't won anything!" He looked away only to find his other friends watching him with concern. He closed his eyes, seeking refuge in the darkness.

"I-I'm sorry, Tua. You didn't deserve that. It's just…I can't do it. I can't be the leader that Merrick was. I've already ruined everything we've done." He opened his eyes and looked at the faces around him, searching for agreement. They needed to say he was right. They should blame him, point accusing fingers. None of that happened.

"We have had a setback, nothing more," Tua said.

"Ha! A setback? You call losing every Nahoru'brexia and compromising every resistance cell a *setback*?" Thorne shook his head. "They've beaten us before we even got started."

"Okay, so those Father guys have won this battle," Amelia offered with a precocious grin. She did not like conflict and tried to lessen it whenever she could. "But it's not the end of the war, is it?"

"No, it's not," Teska said with firmness. "I'll be damned if I'm going to let my sisters rot away in compliance camps—not when the Communion still has options." She glared at Thorne. It was time to try a different approach. "And you've still got options, too."

His shoulders slumped. "What options? H-How can I lead after what I've done?"

"You haven't *done* anything!" Teska snapped. "Which, I'd point out, pretty much sums up this conversation so far."

Their eyes locked in a battle of wills.

She spoke first. "Yes, you got suckered by Blackscar. We *all* did. If that's the issue then all of us here, with the exception of our host, are guilty. And Thurl's death is not your burden to carry. He made his choice. *He* decided to do what he could to help us escape. He believed in you—"

"And look where that got him!" Thorne shot back.

Teska bit her tongue.

"Malachi," Tua said, "have you considered that Thurl died in the way he wanted? He died with honor, protecting his friends, fighting against a great evil. What happened to him is not a burden to shoulder. It is a symbol to imitate."

"My people, the Nermernuh, believed that to offer one's life in exchange for another was a high honor. Your friend—*our* friend—believed in what you are doing. As Teska said, he believed in you enough to entrust the future to you, by buying us time to flee." He paused. "We lament his death and honor his sacrifice."

"No one's going to follow me," Thorne said. "What good is a leader who has no followers? Once word gets out—and you can be sure that the Fifth Order will see to it—there won't be anyone who would listen to me tell a bedtime story, much less follow me in this movement."

"Might I offer a perspective?" Takata asked. "Give the people a *reason* to follow you."

"And how in hells am I supposed to do that?"

The question hung in the spice-laden air. No one said anything, each lost in their own thoughts.

After a moment, Teska brightened. She rubbed Thorne's shoulder. "The Flame!"

He looked at her, uncomprehending.

"It was what Thurl said just before— Sorry. Anyway, he told you to find the Flame. That's what you need to do."

Amelia sat her empty glass on the desk beside Thorne's. "What's the Flame?"

"That's just it," Teska told her. "We, uh, don't know."

Thorne shook his head. "Never heard of it before."

Takata chuckled as if he had heard a joke meant only for his ears. "You can rest assured that there is someone who does."

"Who?" Teska asked.

Takata shrugged. "I don't mean to imply that I have congress with any *specific* individual who might be in possession of such knowledge. However"—he let the word hang in the air for the space of two heartbeats—"if such a thing does exist, would the information pertaining to it not be within the archives of the Cartulian Order?"

Thorne looked up. The wheels began to turn in his mind.

"I-I don't remember a lot of details about that night," he said. "Other things I remember…too well." He turned to Teska. "What did Thurl say, exactly?"

"His exact words were 'find the Flame.' He said that *you* could stop them and that whatever it was had stopped them before."

Thorne mulled the words over. It was like a child's jigsaw puzzle. He had a few pieces but did not know what the final picture was supposed to look like. Yet the thought—the *possibility*—of something that had stopped the Crimson Fathers before, and might do so again, sparked in his mind. It was small and its light meager, but it glowed in his inner darkness. For the first time in weeks, some of the weight in his soul began to lift.

"How would Thurl have known this?" Thorne asked, fishing for more pieces.

Tua finished his drink. "If Maggard Blackscar occupied space in Thurl's brain or possessed his body, would some of him have rubbed off on Thurl?"

Thorne leaned forward in his chair. "You mean that if Blackscar knew what Thurl did, then it's possible that Thurl knew something about Blackscar—or the Fathers? Say, some secret they were hiding?"

"By the Church," Takata said, putting his palms on the desk, "I do believe you are on to something!"

Again, Thorne paused. His eyes darted from one thing in the room to another without really focusing on them. He rolled possibilities around in his mind, pushing bits here and there, looking for connections.

Teska smiled.

Thorne slapped his thigh, a sudden movement that caused Amelia to flinch. "Thurl was giving us a clue! He discovered a weakness that can be exploited."

The atmosphere in the room had changed. No one knew exactly when it had happened, but they were all aware of it. A level of expectancy, of possibility—yes, of *hope*—had crept in. Everyone sat up straighter. Their eyes were quicker, more alert.

Thorne gestured in the air as he talked. "If we had this Flame, it would be much easier to unite the movement here in Attagon. It would be a symbol for people to rally around."

"Ooh, stop the Fathers *and* bring people together," Takata said.

"But we still don't know what this Flame is. Or where it is," Amelia said in the way people do when they do not want to break the mood of a moment.

"But Takata's right," Thorne said. "The Church has always kept meticulous records of everything. If there's anything to know about the Flame, there will have to be a record of it. Somewhere."

"How would you find it?" Amelia asked.

Thorne got up and started to pace. "Well, we can't just walk in and ask for it. No, first we have to figure out where such information might be."

"That will be an exceptionally arduous and lengthy task, I'm afraid," Takata said, "since the Cartulian Order occupies nearly three times as many buildings as any other Order."

Thorne nodded. "We'll just have to put our ears to the ground. Ask around. I still know a few people here who won't turn us in."

At least I hope they won't.

"If I can get to them, I can ask them to see what they can find out. Teska, do you have any contacts in Attagon?"

"Maybe one or two, if I could find them."

Thorne stopped behind her chair and put his hands on her shoulders. "What about the Communion? Could you work through them?"

"I don't know. I could try."

Ryoma clapped his hands together. His rings sounded like miniature cymbals. "Oh, well met! I know many people whose assistance I could solicit—surreptitiously, of course," he said, winking at the group. "How delightful! 'Tis like a quest from bygone days!"

"Easy, Takata," Thorne said. "What we're talking about is dangerous. If anyone gets caught, it'll be a tekoya for them—if the Crimson Fathers even bother with that anymore. They could just execute us on the spot."

"Oh!" Takata paled.

"We're outlaws," Thorne continued. "Heretics. Traitors. Anyone who aids us becomes the same."

Takata tapped his fingertips together and swallowed hard. He glanced around his office as if expecting Witchfinders or Crusaders to leap out and arrest him.

Thorne smiled at him. He put his hands on the desk. "You don't have to do anything, Takata. You've offered us your hospitality. That is more than sufficient. I am grateful."

"But," Thorne said, leaning across the desk, "if you could put in a good word for us with those you trust—surreptitiously, of course—you'd have our gratitude."

Thorne stood up. "We need to move quickly. The longer we delay, the stronger the Crimson Fathers become. Let's get some rest and think on this." He snapped his fingers. "We'll need to alter our appearances, too. Teska and I will stand out like melons in a winepress. Tua, you and Amelia are fine. You're new here. Nobody knows you. That'll work to our advantage, too."

Takata had regained his composure. "I'll return later tonight with food and drink to warm your bellies and strengthen your hearts! I may be ill-suited to pursue vigilante activities in the streets, but I can keep you well fed and safe!"

"You have our thanks, Takata," Thorne said. They clasped forearms.

That night, Thorne and his friends made their plans. Once they knew the correct location, they would break into the offices of the Cartulian Order and track down the Flame.

Shortly before midnight, Takata returned, snow flurrying into the warehouse behind him.

15
MOUNTAINS

WEDNESDAY, OCTOBER 21, 999 AE

Warner's group had run out of food the day after the raid. Tempers were short. Cassidy and Cassandra had repeatedly demanded to go back to the caravan and threw tantrums when the adults refused. They refused to acknowledge Darien's relationship to them, which kept the old man in a constant state of anxiety.

They had been close to giving up hope when Hawkes steered them into a small village nestled among the towering peaks. It was not much as far as villages went, but it had a picturesque quality with an air of serenity, as if it had been lifted out of a fairy tale, carefully placed there and forgotten. In spite of its size, Brookhaven had a blacksmith and a mill for turning lumber. Small homes with gardens, deadened by winter's touch, hunkered against the crags and beneath tall pines. The main road snaked between gutted pre-Cataclysm buildings. Most of them had been cleared away, and structures of log and stone—still quite old—had taken their place. One of these was the Earlcore Inn, a quaint tavern with gabled windows and a moss-covered roof.

The proprietor had greeted them with a surprised but welcoming smile when they pulled up. He had leaned on a snow-clotted broom, which he was using to clear a path to the door. The children had spilled from the wagon, and the man laughed as if it was the most wonderful thing he had ever seen. Inside by the fire, he had listened to their story with great interest. He gave them some leftovers, and while they could not pay for rooms, he offered them as much space in his tidy little stable as they wanted.

In order to make some much-needed repairs to the wagon, they had stayed a second night. Their presence turned out to be big news. The Earlcore had filled with people asking questions and listening to news of the outside world. They were devout supporters of the Church, so Darien, Hawkes, Warner and Hart had agreed to say nothing that might jeopardize their goodwill with the people. Lillia kept the children out of sight as much as possible. It would be awkward, and potentially dangerous, if the villagers learned that they had all been abducted from a Church caravan.

Provisioned by the generosity of the villagers, they had departed on Tuesday, October 20th—but with a lighter load and lower spirits. Matthias Hart and his daughters needed to return home. Lillia had agreed. She did not know if her husband was still alive, but she meant to find out. Hart said the same about his wife.

They had thought about hiding out in the surrounding hills until their pursuers got tired and gave up, but they could not risk the villagers turning them in. Since they had said nothing about the Fifth Order or recent developments in the Church, they could not expect the devout congregants to take their side. As much as Darien, Hawkes and Warner wanted their company and felt better having them around, the truth was that these people needed to start putting their lives back together. Even, Hart said, if it meant risking their freedom again. He owed it to his wife and children. He owed it to himself. Lillia seconded him every step of the way. After leaving Earlcore, they planned to make their way back down to one of the villages in the foothills, and from there find the best route home.

So with a few bundles of bread, some cheese, jerky and a barrel of icy mountain water—along with a small amount of grain the villagers could spare for the horses—Darien, Hawkes, Warner, Cassidy and Cassandra set off south. They followed the winding road until it had become blocked by a rockslide. From there, it was back to rutted wagon tracks in the crunchy, snow-covered ground. They climbed higher as the paths took them deeper into the heart of the range. Their ears kept popping as they traversed the monstrous granite peaks that pierced the slate-colored sky. It was said that some of the mountains in the Great Appian range were over twenty thousand feet tall, and as the little brown wagon rolled among them, they could easily understand why.

Dusk came quickly in the narrow valleys, and the group sheltered in a thick copse of conifers a short distance from the trail. Ravenous wolves—and who knew what other horrors—lurked in the darkness beyond their tiny campfire, so they kept watch all night. The thought of losing their horses and being stranded up here was too horrible to contemplate. The next morning, they pushed on, following an ice-choked stream that gurgled like a baby until it disappeared underground. The woods grew darker and wilder, and their horses became skittish. Several times, Warner led them by the reins to keep them calm.

❖   ❖   ❖

Birds circled against flat, steely clouds that promised a heavy snowstorm. The wagon and its occupants trundled across a small valley ringed by mountains so high it made them feel like an insect crawling across the scalp of some primordial giant. They reached the other side and navigated into an even thicker forest where limbs grew together hundreds of feet overhead, and the ground held only the faintest dusting of snow.

Warner halted the team and slipped down from the driver's bench.

"What's wrong?" Hawkes asked him from the seat.

"Just checkin' this wheel. That last rock we hit sounded awful." Convinced there was no problem, he was about to climb back up when movement caught his eye. "Shit, they're still back there. And they've just about caught up with us," he said, nodding toward the back of the wagon.

The snowy bowl of the valley lay below them, dotted with trees. A wagon and six or eight horses followed in their tracks.

"They don't give up, do they?" Hawkes asked.

Warner shook his head. "We didn't when we were them."

"You think we can fight them?"

Warner chewed the inside of his cheek and stared into the trees ahead.

"They're going to catch us eventually," Hawkes added, as if it would hasten Warner's decision.

It was ironic how this relationship had changed. Hawkes and Warner had been the same rank—Paracletian Order Deputies—under Thurl Cabbott and Malachi Thorne. Hawkes had been assigned first. Warner had always been the new guy. But now he was the leader.

Hawkes was recovering nicely from his head wound. His hair was growing back, although there was no way it would ever fully cover the scar that ran from his temple to behind his ear. His strength had returned. But he joked less with Warner, his demeanor more pensive and distant.

Dario Darien was another story altogether. The old man grew frailer. He rode in the back of the wagon all the time. Several nights ago, they had caught Cassidy and Cassandra trying to run away. Their defiance and rejection of Darien's identity caused him great suffering. He had almost broken completely when they called him a traitor and a heretic. Cassidy quoted verses from the Testament at him the way a snake spits venom. Cassandra kept to her brother's side, her mouth set in a firm line. Since then, Darien had only nibbled at his food and spent much of his time watching his niece and nephew with a mixture of pity and grief.

"I can't fight off that many. And I don't think y—" Warner stopped himself.

Hawkes frowned. "And you don't know if I'll be of any help, is that it?"

Warner was unsure how to answer. If he said no, Hawkes would know he was lying. If he said yes, there would be an argument. There had been a lot more of those since Hawkes took that shot to the head. Warner climbed back on the driver's bench and urged the horses forward.

"Just say it," Hawkes demanded. "I'm useless."

"You're *not* useless."

Hawkes scowled and crossed his arms. "That's what you were thinking."

"An' how the hells do you know what I'm thinkin' and what I'm not?" Warner snapped.

"You think I'm a liability—that I'm not pulling my weight."

"Oh, for shit's sake, Tycho, nobody thinks that. You're recoverin' from a nearly fatal head wound. Nobody expects you to be your old self immediately."

"I can *still* fight," he said softly, as if convincing himself.

"I know, buddy."

Hawkes watched the trees go by for a moment. "Do you want to hide?" he asked.

Warner shook his head. "Don't know that we could. Tracks'll lead them right to us. Plus, the kids…"

Hawkes nodded. "It's killing him, you know? Dario. He tries to reach them, but whatever brainwashing they did on them is really strong. I think that's killing him quicker than his age or the cold."

Warner agreed. Cassidy and Cassandra were belligerent and arrogant. They rebelled against anything the adults said, especially if it had to do with the Church. Tears filled the old man's eyes more often than not.

"We can't outrun them," Hawkes added.

"I know, I know…" Warner pulled his hand down his face.

"What if we left the wagon and the horses—took off and hid in these mountains until they go away?"

Pity stabbed Warner's heart. The old Tycho—before the blow to the skull—would have never suggested something so obviously flawed and unrealistic. He glanced out of the corner of his eye. Hawkes watched the way ahead. On the outside he was the same, aside from the scar. But inside something was different. Warner tried to force his sadness back down.

"No good, buddy," he replied. "If they didn't find us by our tracks, and if some animal didn't eat us, they'd take our horses and wagon. We'd die up here with no shelter and no food."

Hawkes nodded again, and it pained Warner to see his friend struggle to understand something so obvious.

Warner snapped the reins, pushing the horses faster. The wagon rattled and thudded over stones and branches.

Without warning, both animals came to a dead stop. They whinnied and pranced, eyes rolling in fear. Warner searched the ground. It was too cold up here for serpents. Even the deadly two-headed carghella snakes were hibernating. He scanned the forest on either side.

Wolves, maybe?

Both horses broke into a frenzied gallop. The wagon lurched forward, bouncing from side to side. Warner and Hawkes gripped the edges of the seat. Warner stood and threw his weight back against the reins. Pine needles whisked across his face. He managed to ease the horses back, but they continued to stomp and chafe at their bits.

Both men looked around again. Other than the faint chirping of a few hardy birds in the canopy overhead, everything was peaceful.

The horses bolted again, and this time Warner lost his balance. He tumbled from the seat but managed to grab the side handle. The toes of his boots raked across the hard ground as he dangled off the side. Hawkes took the reins and likewise stood up to stop the team. They had been carried down into a small gulley.

"You okay?" he asked as Warner got his feet under him.

"Yeah. What's gotten into them?"

"What's going on?" Darien's voice floated from the back of the wagon. The old man held the door open, peering out with owlish eyes.

"Everybody back there okay?" Warner asked him. "Horses just took off like they'd been set on fire."

We're lucky we didn't break an axle.

Then they heard voices above them. As Warner and Darien watched, several men on horseback appeared at the top of the incline and stared down at the fugitives. They wore the standard wine-colored leather armor of Paracletian Deputies beneath their heavy cloaks. They were also having trouble controlling their skittish mounts.

"You, men!" one said, drawing his saber and pointing it into the gulley. "You're under arrest. Don't try to flee."

Two more deputies arrived.

Five so far.

"HELP! Help us!" Cassidy yelled through the wagon window. "We're in here!"

Warner kept his hand on the hilt of his short sword. His face fell when he saw the wagon appear over the rise.

Two more. No, four mo— Aw shit...

Cassandra joined her brother at the window and yelled.

A Crusader stepped up and surveyed the situation. He was easily two heads taller than any of the other men. His helmet looked dull in the dusky light beneath the trees.

"Listen!" he bellowed. His deep voice boomed through the gulley as his breath swirled in front of his face. "Your flight is over. Lay down your weapons and come up here. You have to the count of three. After that, we come down there. And it will be extremely unpleasant for you if we have to do that." He paused. "One!"

"Help! Save us!"

Every horse at the top and bottom of the incline bucked and shrieked in terror. Those attached to the wagons struggled to break away. It was all the deputies could do to keep them in place.

"Calm those horses down!" the Crusader shouted at the mounted man next to him.

"W-We're trying, sir, but they won't…"

For a second, Warner thought about making a break for it. But two things held him back. One, his own team was now foaming at the mouth. He doubted they would respond to anything in such a spooked condition.

And two, he saw the trunks of several trees *move*. They rose slowly, pulled out of the ground, clotted soil falling from them.

They can't be trees, the rational part of Warner's brain told him. *They don't have any roots.*

Sure enough, the bottoms ended in a pointed, chitinous tip. As his eyes followed the bark-like surface up, he realized there were no branches—just spiny-looking hairs that reminded him of thorns. And there was no bark, just more dark, bony material.

Every horse squealed in terror. One man was thrown from his mount, and the animal galloped away. The Crusader looked around dumbfounded while his men did their best to keep from joining their colleague on the ground.

A peculiar chittering sound came from the canopy above. One of the tree-legs descended and jabbed into the ground; another did likewise. All around them the jointed legs rose and fell with a stabbing motion, kicking up dirt and dead leaves. The sound grew louder, more aggressive.

Men and horses scattered. Warner held onto the wagon wheel, sword still in hand.

Darien peeked out once again, but one of the legs javelined into the earth near the rear of the wagon. He yanked his head back and slammed the door shut.

Warner stared at the legs, transfixed. Each was thick as a man's body and they moved like those of a crab.

Or a spider! His heart caught in his throat.

"Tycho!" he yelled over his shoulder. "Get us out of here!"

A hysterical scream rose, then was cut off. One of the legs had impaled a deputy. His arms and legs dangled beneath him. The chitinous surface below his body darkened with blood.

Another leg flew down like an arrow shot from the sky. It barely missed the Crusader, who sidestepped without much apparent concern. Another scream, another man skewered. The angry chittering filled the canopy.

Warner ran to the front of the wagon. He heard an insectile shriek and looked up just in time. He threw himself to the side and landed on his back. One of the legs stabbed into the ground where he had just been. Dead sticks rained down as something large moved through the canopy. Looking up, Warner saw a round shape. The segmented legs all led up to it, were attached to it—

He saw…a chimney? A door?

That's a window!

He stared in amazement at the round house made of logs and dried mud, a wisp of smoke rising from the roof, supported on eight spiked arachnid legs.

The men on the hill fled as another of their number screamed and died, clutching the leg that pierced his torso.

The hut crashed through the canopy and showered branches to the ground. Roots and vines hung beneath it as if it had been pulled out of the earth. The legs rose and fell, stabbing at the ground the way a child might stomp ants.

Tycho offered an outstretched hand to help Warner up on the driver's bench. Warner grabbed the reins from Hawkes and immediately dropped them. With the tension gone, the horses burst into a horrified gallop up the far side of the gulley. All the two men could do was hang on. Warner prayed that they did not break an axle. The wagon behind them creaked and rattled. The chittering diminished.

The horses ran blindly, heedless of brush or branch. Hawkes kept his hands up in front of his face. The forest was a cold gray blur around them.

Warner's heart pounded. He was covered in cold sweat. Like everyone, he knew what was said to lurk in the Great Appian Mountains. Whispered stories claimed that Matriarch Trahnen, the Witch of Tears, kept her abode among the lonelier peaks—but was not restricted to them. No, the Witch of Tears had a home which was said to stalk the forests on spider legs. It moved wherever she willed, scuttling and creeping to whatever blasphemous destination awaited her.

After a while, the horses slowed, and Hawkes picked up the reins again. Warner frantically scanned the landscape behind him, his eye wide. But he saw no indication of pursuit. As his breathing slowed and he wiped his brow, he wondered what would happen to all those impaled bodies. He shivered and realized he did not want to want to know.

16

ELURUUM

MONDAY, OCTOBER 26, 999 AE

The Palace of the Heiromonarch had been built into the side of Outlook Mountain, halfway to the summit. It had taken 218 years to construct. Most of the stone blocks had been quarried and transported in from as far away as Skonmesto and Colobos. The palace was surrounded by a wall that snaked across the face of the mountain. Its fortifications and position made it nearly impervious to any kind of attack. In fact, none had ever been attempted. The palace consisted of 102 rooms, most of which were administrative offices for the Heiromonarch, his chief advisors and administrative staff.

When there had been a living Heiromonarch. Now he was simply a simulacrum created and controlled by the Fifth Order.

Created in secret in 318 AE, the Fifth Order served to protect the leadership of the Church, guard its secrets, ensure proper succession and transitions of power and handle delicate matters from the shadows. No record of membership had ever been discovered, and the exact composition was known to only a select few across the centuries.

In 873 AE, their paranoia and lust for power untempered, the Fifth Order moved to make the Heiromonarch subservient to them. With the inauguration of Heiromonarch Peo the First, they succeeded in placing a simulacrum at the head of the Church. Whenever they deemed it appropriate, the Order would instruct the Church to announce the death and subsequent election of a new Heiromonarch. In that way, the Church always had its leader, the "Avatar of all existence" as the Deiparian Creed phrased it.

Since then, the Heiromonarch made few public appearances, and none in which he would have to be among people. The Order saw to that. The simulacrum was convincing but not perfect. They knew that overexposure would lead to questions, so they circulated stories of the Heiromonarch's failing health, his age or his travels as reasons for the rare appearances.

Today, the wind whipped the banners of the Four Orders that flew from the top of each palace turret. The blue of the Kyrian Order had the word *FAITH* embellished in bold black letters. The Abthanian Order's green showed the word *WISDOM*. There was a red banner for the Paracletian Order and its word, *OBEDIENCE* and a white one for the Cartulian Order with the word *LOYALTY*. The purple banner of the Fifth Order proclaimed *DOMINION* in glossy black embroidery. It hung from the rampart above the main entrance.

Snowflakes swirled like ash from a volcano. Wisps of smoke rose from chimneys across Attagon, which looked like a patchwork quilt spreading out from the base of the mountain. In the distance, the River Tense was dark as molasses.

Vaelok Strang stared out of the arched, glassless window. He did not feel the biting wind that ruffled his robe. He turned and walked to the chairs in the middle of the room. Aside from some faded tapestries and a fireplace full of cold ashes, there were no other furnishings.

The chairs were arranged in a circle upon a round mystical symbol carved into the floor. Filigreed runes and sigils intertwined across its surface. Words in an strange tongue were etched across every wall. To anyone other than the Fathers, the words seemed to squirm and pulsate. Staring at them too long caused physical illness and a creeping sense of madness. That was only one of many reasons why few living things ever entered the chamber.

Strang sat down, steepled bony fingers in front of him and looked around at the other Crimson Fathers. "It is time, my brethren," he said. The air whistled through the gaping cavity where his nose should have been.

"Ready to make for the eluruum, then?" Phaeddark Deathlord asked. His voice was a mutilated gurgle as it seeped from the hole in this throat. Eyes like boiled eggs gleamed above a mouth held together by heavy stitches.

Strang nodded, his bony neck creaking. "We are. Our dominion over the Church, and over the realm of Deiparia, is complete. Those who resist are reeducated in the compliance camps. Or they are executed."

"We possess their children," Kaige Paleblight said. He was the only Father without skin. His hands were the only thing visible to indicate this. A scarlet veil hung from the inside of his hood to mask the moist, glistening face.

"The information we have gained," Callodin Valhalla said, "it is good."

Strang looked across the circle at him. Of all the resurrected Fathers, Valhalla could most readily pass as a normal person. He was plump beneath his voluminous robe, and his face, although the skin was waxy and stretched too tight, had all its features. His body held no deformities or aberrations. In any city in the realm, he could be a butcher, a lawyer, a merchant.

"It is," Strang acknowledged. "Through our lost brother, we have been able to cripple the pitiful attempt at rebellion and freedom. We have found Nahoru'brexia, whose power we have fused into our own. And we have discovered a whole new land to conquer."

Oste'warg Braun grinned, the lipless mouth curving across his face, causing his second row of teeth to be more prominent. He rubbed his temple with one taloned finger. "Ah yesss, thossse Tex'ahnsss," he hissed. His tongue flicked along the first set of teeth.

"Think! Think!" Tejharmal the Abomination blurted out, wiggling the three remaining fingers on his left hand in anticipation. "So much space! So much! We shall expand! We shall conquer!" His yellow eyes gleamed, and a pearly strand of spittle leaked from the corner of his mouth. When he sat back in his chair, the hairy, clawed appendage that served as his right arm was briefly visible.

Strang motioned for Tejharmal to calm down. "Eluruum is our right by birth. It is our right as new gods. We must add more land so that our progeny have a place to live and so that we can expand our rule. Our congregants will spread out into the land of the weakling Tex'ahns, and we shall claim it for ourselves."

Klaus Lodaec drummed his fingers on the arm of his chair and looked at Strang. "We shall need our army," he croaked through a full mustache and beard that crawled with small insects. His single eye burned with a feverish intensity. The other, he wore as an amulet around his neck.

"Such is prepared for," Nem'kai the Masaga replied. "Soon our army will be at full strength. It is our destiny to subjugate the new land and the new millennium."

"What I look forward to," Jaccomus Veidt said, "are all the…children." He said the last word almost reverently, his lecherous grin like a scythe blade across the pockmarked skin of his face. His right eye drooped below the left, which sparkled with unspeakable ideas.

"You may have *some*, Jaccomus," Strang said. "You know we need the majority of them for the Crusaders."

Veidt rubbed sweaty palms together, and his breath came in short, almost sensual, gasps. "Only two or three, that's all I seek. I can make them last for a while."

"I believe that Last Chapel should be the staging area," Paleblight said from behind his veil. "We already know Zadicus Rann can be trusted."

"Rann! He is but flesh. Weak! Unreliable!" Avorhus Godfury shouted. He pounded his fist on the arm of his chair.

While all of the Fathers could experience pain to certain degrees, Godfury was the exception. No amount of agony or suffering troubled him. As a result, he intentionally bore the most horrific visage, to better strike terror into those who came near him.

Godfury's head was misshapen, pointed near the top and widening as it descended. He was bald and had wrapped the majority of his face in barbed wire, leaving strips open for his baleful eyes and crooked mouth. His nose poked between the wires. Dried blood coated his head, and fresh wounds constantly oozed. He had severed the fingers of his left hand and replaced them with a metallic gauntlet of wide, fishhook-like blades. Avorhus Godfury was the chief torturer of the Fathers—when such persuasions were necessary.

"Zadicusss Rann hasss proven hisss loyalty to the Order."

"Agreed," Deathlord said. He had no eyelids, so he never blinked.

"Mad! He is mad! Insane!" Godfury shouted around blackened teeth.

Strang raised a hand and waved Godfury's concerns away. "Of *course,* he is insane. That is what makes his devotion to us assured."

Lodaec nodded. "Last Chapel is perfect for our needs. We gather the army there. We move against the Tex'ahns."

"My Lord Strang," Temias the Bonesorrow asked, "what of the Flame?"

"What of it?"

"Do we need to be concerned, Undying One?" Valhalla asked. "Its existence has become known. We all remember what happened last time—"

Strang stood up. "The Flame is safe. No one knows its location. It is buried in the past, protected by our magic. Even if people know its name, none remain who know its power."

"Destroy it! We must! Destroy, destroy!" Godfury bellowed.

Nem'kai the Masaga shook his head, a misshapen lump that matched the one on his left shoulder beneath his robe. His eyes were impossibly narrow, as if they had been stretched toward his ears like wax. The thin mouth held a smattering of different-sized teeth. He looked toward Godfury. "You know we cannot destroy it, Avorhus. We tried before."

Godfury growled in his throat. "It will be a problem! A problem! Mark my words!"

"If Vaelok says it is safe and of no import, I believe him," Braun said, still showing his sets of teeth.

Lodaec leaned forward and rolled the eyeball amulet between dirty fingers. "Why don't we use it? The power rightly belongs to us."

"Impossible," Strang replied.

"Remembering our past, hard for you still," Deathlord said. He pointed a gloved finger toward Lodaec's head. "Brain inside, working poorly. Still not fully back."

Temias the Bonesorrow looked at the eye still in Lodaec's face. "The spells placed upon it during its creation extracted our power. And its protective spells prevent us from reclaiming it."

"It must first find a new host. Only *then* can we finally recover our true power," Valhalla added.

Their bones popped and cracked as the Fathers nodded.

"Dismissed, my brethren. Go forth to set the plans for eluruum in motion and continue to build our army. Soon—very soon—we shall rule *all things* as it was meant to be."

17
FAMILY

FRIDAY, OCTOBER 30, 999 AE

Dario Darien's aged heart thumped in his chest with all the grace of a one-legged rabbit. He could feel the faltering muscle constrict a little more each day. It worked as best it could, but he was just like the sun clinging to the western horizon. It would not be long before he slipped into eternal night.

His gaze drifted from the darkening hills to the people around the campfire. Hawkes sat to his right, Warner to the left. Cassidy and Cassandra were on the opposite side of the fire. Everyone ate in hungry silence, huddled in their heavy coats, as scattered snowflakes drifted in the air.

From what they had been able to surmise from the occasional ruined road sign, they were traversing a pre-Cataclysm land once known as West Virginia. Several days prior, in a village called Greenbank, Warner had been able to get their bow restrung. They traded news of the realm for a handful of arrows and some grain for the horses.

On Wednesday, Hawkes had successfully brought down a small buck, and since then they had enjoyed venison every day. There was enough to carry them for another week, at least.

At these elevations, finding sufficient food for the horses remained an ongoing problem. They rarely found edible vegetation. When they did happen upon a bush that flourished in the frigid heights, it was always picked clean. The horses grew thinner and slower as they had to subsist on pinecones, roots, bark and the occasional basket of barley from a compassionate villager.

Darien watched his niece and nephew while he chewed the meat. Several of his teeth had fallen out, and although the venison was delicious, it was not friendly to those that were left. But he was grateful for the food and savored the seared taste as he swallowed.

"Cassandra, in another few weeks you'll be able to see your mother again," he said, smiling.

At least I hope and pray you can.

He did not know what had become of his sister since he had last seen her in the Talnat dungeon. It was possible she had already been executed for the charge of witchcraft. The thought turned his stomach sour, and he hesitated to take another bite.

The little girl chewed her meat and stared at him with wide brown eyes.

"Leave her alone," Cassidy said. "She don't wanna talk to you."

"Well, maybe she does today." He kept smiling at his niece. "What did you think of that ice cave we passed earlier? Or that nest of Appian redvalks? I'd never seen a nest before."

Cassidy leaned over to his sister. "Don't say nuthin' to him." He eyed Darien suspiciously, just as he'd done ever since the raid. "He's one of *them*."

Darien, Hawkes and Warner had learned quickly who "them" were. Heretics, traitors and anyone who did not embrace the Fifth Order's new world. Both children had made it clear that they were the only *true* believers in the group.

"Cassidy, are you afraid your sister will say something wrong? Something she isn't supposed to say?"

The boy frowned as he looked at Darien and chewed his venison.

Hawkes leaned over and whispered to Darien, "You might as well give it up. I hate to say it, but they're just not going to break. Whatever the Fifth Order taught them, they've swallowed like a starving dog."

A familiar pain stabbed Darien's heart once more. He saw his niece and nephew, heard their voices, had them close—yet they remained as distant as the bits of the moon that littered the sky. Nothing he said had gotten through to them. Even Hawkes and Warner had been upbraided by the ten-year-old zealot when they had tried to help.

Comments about seeing their mother again had not affected them. Stories about times they had shared together as a family made no impact. Pleas to their hearts went unanswered.

At least by Cassidy.

Darien believed that Cassandra was weakening. He thought he had seen flashes of awareness in her eyes, old memories resurfacing for a moment.

Twice since rescuing them, he had been awakened by her soft crying in the night. The first time, as he fumbled from his bunk to comfort her, he stopped. His heart told him to go to her, but his head said stop. If he was going to break the Fifth Order's stranglehold, she had to come to him. He had climbed back under his fur, his heart breaking as he listened to the pitiful whimpering. He had slept no more that night as he cursed himself.

The second time it happened, he sat up and was about to go to her, but again he had forced himself to stop. He desperately needed to pick her up, cradle her, comfort her and tell her it was all going to be okay. Climbing back into his bunk required more courage and determination than he thought he possessed. But he did it. He had spent the rest of that night praying she would break free of her conditioning and holding back his own tears of frustration.

Undaunted, Darien continued. "When we get home, I guess you'll be the man of the house now, Cassidy." Darien's heart skipped as he stood on the precipice of the one tactic he had avoided until now.

"I mean, with what happened to your papa and all…"

He left the thought unfinished and worked over another piece of meat, staring into the fire. He could feel the little girl's eyes on him. He wanted to tell them the truth and hold them close. But instead, he swallowed, took a drink of water and broke into a coughing fit.

Warner patted him on the back until he regained his breath. Cassandra held her stick of venison halfway to her mouth, eyes still wide. Cassidy's eyes shifted around, looking at everything and nothing.

"Papa's dead." Cassidy said it with finality, but he was not old enough to know how to mask his sorrow.

Grief clutched Darien's heart. The regretful look on Cassidy's face as real as the mountain beneath them. "Yes, yes he is. That's why you'll have to take care of your sister and your mother from now on."

"I can do that," Cassidy said with bold confidence, his moment of loss forgotten. He crossed his arms. "The Fifth Order says that a man—"

"Children, your papa wasn't killed by bandits," Darien said. He swallowed hard. The words floated in the air with the snowflakes. He silently prayed that he knew what he was doing.

Cassidy frowned and pursed his lips. "He was too! Robbers attacked him. You're just saying that 'cause you wanna hurt us!"

Darien's face crumbled. Tears spilled down the crevices of his cheeks. "Oh, Cassidy, I would *never* hurt you. Never. You and your sister are precious to me. I love you!"

"Then why'd you say somethin' like that?" the boy challenged.

"Because it's true," Hawkes said. He leaned forward and put his elbows on his knees. He stared at the children, his face golden in the firelight. "I was with your uncle when he…found out about your father. He's telling you the truth. I give you my word. Your father was… He was…" Hawkes mumbled himself into silence, unsure of how to say it.

Darien built up his courage, though he imagined how the next few moments could go horribly wrong. He sighed. "What Tycho's trying to say is that your papa was killed, but not by bandits. I did some research, just like I used to do in my job. And I found something…awful. Something mean."

"Wh-What was it?" Cassandra's soft voice cut through the night. She put her stick of meat down and focused on Darien.

"'Sandra, hush!" her brother demanded.

She shook her head. "No, I wanna know."

"I told you before. We can't trust what they say," Cassidy said.

Cassandra turned to face her brother. "Why would Uncle Dario fib to us?"

"'Cause's he's one of *them*! An' they wanna take us away from the Church."

Cassandra mulled this over, her brows knit together. "They *did* take us from the caravan."

"That was just to protect you," Warner said.

"We wasn't in no danger!" Cassidy shot back. He looked at his sister. "See? They're tryin' to confuse us. That's what the Preceptor said would happen."

Cassandra nodded at her brother and turned wary eyes on Darien.

He did not give her time to speak. "Your papa found something—something very important. It was one of the Church's relics. He was on his way to return it to the Church when he was killed. By Crusaders."

Please, please, let this work.

The little girl looked up at her brother again. "Why would Crusaders kill our papa?" Her voice held a tremor of uncertainty. "They're supposed to help people."

Cassidy threw down his stick and the remains of the venison. "Darn it, 'Sandra, it ain't true! He's fibbin' to us!"

"Cassidy?" Hawkes said. When he had the boy's attention, he continued. "I will swear to you on the Bones of Michael the First that your uncle's not lying. What he said, it happened. Crusaders—well, they…they did kill your father. And they made it look like it was bandits."

"Cassidy, did the authorities bring your papa's tools and horse and wagon home to you?" Darien asked.

The boy nodded, but his face was hesitant, as if he was not sure about agreeing with the adults.

"Then tell me why the bandits didn't take any of those things?" Darien said. "If *you* were a robber, would you have left them behind?"

"You could sell all those things for a lot of money," Warner added.

Once again, Cassandra looked at her brother, doubt shadowing her round face. "Cass'dy?"

He thrust his chin out and said, "They prob'ly just forgot." But the words lacked conviction.

"Well, that would be silly! They wouldn't be very good bandits," Cassandra said.

"I don't know!" her brother exclaimed. He scratched behind his ear as he looked at her.

Darien's heart jumped, and he suppressed a smile. Scratching behind his ear was something Cassidy did whenever he was scared or insecure. The old man pressed his luck with a different angle. "Cassandra, was your mother a witch?"

Both children looked at their uncle.

"Did you ever see her do, you know, witchy things? Did she ever make the runes, or recite incantations or fix potions for people?"

Cassidy frowned.

Cassandra shook her head. She started to wring her hands.

"Did your mother ever speak ill about someone? Did she have an image of one of the Three Witches?" Darien asked.

This time both children shook their heads.

Darien pushed himself off the broken log and limped halfway around the fire. He sat down on a rock near the children but still far enough away that they would not feel threatened. The snowflakes had stopped floating and now fell straight to the ground. The children's wiry black hair looked like it had been dusted with sugar.

Darien smiled. "Your mother was no witch. We all know that. She's my sister. I would *know* if she were a witch. I picked on her a lot when we were your age. She was always mad at me about something I'd done to her." He winked at the children. "If your mother was really a witch, she'd have turned me into a salamander a long time ago!"

Cassandra giggled. Cassidy cracked a slight smile.

"He'd have made a nice toad, wouldn't he?" Warner said. He puffed his cheeks and stuck out his tongue.

Both children giggled.

"My darlings, your mother is not a witch. That was a lie so they could take you from her. And your papa wasn't killed by thieves. That was also a lie because some very powerful, bad men didn't want anyone to know the truth. Those powerful, bad men are in the Church—but they don't want to help people. They're doing some mean, awful things instead."

Hawkes and Warner both nodded in support.

Darien broke into a coughing fit. When he regained his breath he said, "I'm not a heretic. Neither are Tycho or Solomon. But we *are* trying to stop those mean, awful things from happening. And because of that, people call us names. They tell lies about us to make it harder for us to show everyone what those mean, awful things are."

"What are they?" Cassidy asked. "The mean, awful things?"

Darien patted the air with a trembling hand. "It's very complicated. It's like a puzzle inside another puzzle."

"I like puzzles!" Cassandra grinned, showing her mixture of baby teeth and snaggled adult teeth.

"Just like your Uncle Malachi," Darien said to encourage her. "I've seen the two of you working puzzles before."

"I did some puzzles with Uncle Mal'chi, too," Cassidy added with pride, unwilling to be left out of the memory.

Darien pointed a crooked finger at the boy. "Yes, you did. If I remember correctly, *you* figured it out before he did. And he's a Witchfinder Imperator."

Cassidy's grin spread from ear to ear.

"You really are our Uncle Dario, ain't you?" the little girl said.

The old man nodded. "I most certainly am. And very proud of that fact. I've got the smartest niece and nephew in all Talnat!"

"In all Deiparia!" Cassidy stood up and stuck out his scrawny chest, his teeth slightly straighter and bone-white in the light.

Cassandra walked over to Darien and studied him for a moment. She giggled.

"What's so funny?" he asked, his tone jovial.

She pointed to his head. "You got snow on you, but it looks just like your hair."

Darien made a show of shaking his head, tossing flakes onto his shoulders.

"How come you got so old?" Cassidy asked. "You're older than our pa—" He closed his mouth as if the word was too important to be set loose. His lower lip trembled.

"*Do* we get to see mama again?" Cassandra asked, looking at her uncle with doe eyes. "I-I miss my mama."

Cassidy sniffed and began to cry quietly.

The moment Darien had prayed about and dreamed about for months was finally upon him. He opened his arms.

Cassandra moved inside them and wrapped hers around his neck. She smelled of campfire smoke and the inside of the wagon. His own tears began to fall again.

Cassidy did not move. His shoulders jumped up and down as he cried. He rubbed his eyes with his fists and looked at his uncle. Uncertainty and longing warred across his tear-streaked face.

Darien motioned for the boy to join them.

He did, collapsing into the old man's shoulder, sobbing. Cassandra began to cry as well.

They remained that way for a long time.

18
STEALTH

FRIDAY, OCTOBER 30, 999 AE

From their hiding place, Thorne watched the shadows of every building, tree and bush. Snow was falling. Not a lot, just enough to trick the eyes. There was no wind, but the temperature had plummeted once the sun disappeared.

"Are you sure you can do this?" he whispered, his breath a milky vapor.

Teska grunted as she worked at the window seal. "I told you I could the last time you asked. Now shut up and let me finish!" Her fingers were numb since taking off her gloves to manipulate the delicate set of tools she had borrowed from a friend.

To get inside, Teska needed to cut out a pane of glass three hands high and three hands wide. That would allow her access to the interior shutters. In order to unlock them, she had to release a metal latch on the other side using only the narrow space between the shutters.

Thorne shivered even though he wore a long black leather coat lined with rabbit fur. His head felt too light—*and damned cold!*—since Teska had cut his hair and shaved off his mustache and goatee. It was short on the sides, longer in the back and in front, part of it swept down over his forehead. She'd done a good job, even if she did make him look a little like Rich DuBose. He rubbed the back of his neck, surprised once again at how cold the bare skin felt.

Amelia had helped Teska change her hair as well. Thorne did not realize how much he loved her curly red tresses until she appeared with her hair solid black, like his, and nearly as short. It barely reached the nape of her neck. She reminded him of a Novitiate just beginning his career in the Church.

"Amelia, do you see anything?" Thorne asked.

The young woman, wrapped in a heavy brown woolen cloak, knelt beside him, scanning the area. "All clear so far." Her Nahoru'brexia gift was a blessing.

Her eyes could see in the darkness as well as anyone's could in broad daylight. They had to be careful, though. She weakened quickly if she used her gift too much. But that was true for every member of the Communion now.

There was a soft snap followed by Teska's sigh of relief. She folded up the tool pouch and slid it into a pocket of her furry parka. She started to shift the pane of glass from the frame when Amelia hushed them.

"Guards. To the left."

Teska dropped behind Thorne and Amelia. Tua hunched in the brittle shrubbery beside them, buried in a fur-lined hood and coat, silent as the falling snow. The bushes that lined the side of the building had lost most of their leaves. Thorne felt too exposed, as if the two deputies were heading straight for them. He gripped his dagger in a gloved fist, praying he would not have to use it.

The deputies talked as they strolled along the pebbled sidewalk, the tips of their tabáks glowing, the smoke trailing them like vengeful ghosts. They stopped in front of the bushes. The taller one attempted to remove something from the bottom of his boot. His partner smoked and looked around the courtyard, surrounded on every side by the dark, brooding Cartulian Order buildings.

The first deputy cursed and continued working at his boot. The second crushed his tabák on the sidewalk. He turned and looked in their direction.

The bushes in front of Thorne had shed most of their leaves for the season. From a distance, he was certain no one could see them. They would just blend in with the shadows. But if anyone got too close and looked—

The deputy started toward the bushes. "Aw, fer fuck's sake!"

Had something about the window attracted his attention? Had he seen them—their breath, maybe? Or their footprints?

Damn it! Thorne tensed, hands sweating inside the gloves. Teska and Amelia were as still as stone effigies.

The deputy stopped less than ten feet from Thorne.

Teska's hand curled around her dagger.

"D' you believe this?" the deputy asked.

Thorne's leg muscles were taut, ready to leap.

The deputy bent over, picked something off the ground and returned to the pathway. "Fer this, I joined the bleedin' Order." He waved a scrap of parchment at his partner, who waited impatiently in the cold.

"What is it?"

"Bit of trash, innit! Can ya believe this? Horses can take a shit in the street, people dump their bleedin' chamber pots in the road. But we gotta keep this bleedin' place neat an' tidy. I hate bloody guard duty."

"Come on, let's go," his partner said. They disappeared around the corner of the building, the second man still complaining.

Amelia's hand was over her heart. "Oh my…" she whispered.

Thorne realized that he had been holding his breath. He released it slowly. It looked like steam rising from a blacksmith's quench bucket. He glanced over his shoulder. "Go on," he told Teska.

A moment later, she had the glass pane out of the frame. She sat it behind the bushes. Then she set to work on the shutters with a long, narrow pick.

"How long until they return?" Tua asked.

Thorne kept checking the shadows. "Twelve minutes, if they don't lollygag. Amelia, anything?"

She shook her head inside the hood of her cloak. "All clear."

"Only two guards to patrol the grounds of all six buildings?" Tua asked. "Your Church does not seem to take security very seriously."

Thorne chuckled. "They don't need to. Nobody in their right mind would *ever* think of breaking into Church buildings."

Tua looked at Thorne. "And what does that make us?"

"Suicidal," Thorne replied.

It had taken them nine days to discover the most likely location for the information they sought. Thorne had made contact with two associates—a constable named Witten, and Naomi Kestring, assistant to Regent Sempect Brior Lachlan—neither of whom believed that Thorne had turned traitor. They had helped him narrow down the correct group of buildings on this quad.

Ryoma Takata, true to his word, kept them well fed and sheltered. He brought them tidbits of information about guard rotations, areas to avoid, incidents that were taking place in the city and the best times to pursue leads. He had also outfitted them with proper winter attire so they would not freeze as they scouted locations and skulked through alleys waiting for a contact to arrive.

Teska had used a former contact from her thieving days, and he had put word out to those he trusted. In less than three days, she had the specific building identified. Two days more and they had pinpointed the most likely room.

If it's not the right one… Thorne did not want to think about that.

They had little time, and according to their reports, at least a dozen potential rooms in this building to check. And all they had to go on was a name. Before his death, Valerian Merrick had told Thorne about something he had discovered long ago. He claimed there was a link between the ninth Heiromonarch of the realm—the mad Okafo Kobina, or Okafo the Dark—and the Crimson Fathers. Their only stroke of luck so far was the fact that this building stood only a single story. The other five on the quad were two and three stories high.

"Got it!" Teska whispered.

She knelt and put her tools away. Once they were sure no one was around, Teska pushed the shutters open. She hauled herself over the sill with little effort then stuck her hand out. Amelia grabbed Teska's hand and struggled through the window. Tua followed, silent and graceful as a cat.

As soon as Thorne was through, he closed the shutters again. "We need to move quick. The next time those guards come around, they're likely to notice the missing glass in the window."

Teska steadied Amelia; she was beginning to tire from using her gift. But she smiled and continued to scout the darkness ahead, guiding them across the room and into a hallway that smelled of musty documents and brittle parchment. They checked the placards beside each door, searching for the right room.

Thorne cherished the scent from his childhood. Merrick used to take him into rooms like these, choked with bound manuscripts, and read to him the tales of Heiromonarchs, the Church and the Great Cataclysm. As Thorne moved along behind his friends, the memories filled him with wistful yearning. He wanted to open one of these doors, slip inside and lose himself in the past.

But that was not possible. He had a job to do.

Teska halted. "This is the one. Let's hope our information was accurate."

The door was made of heavy wood bound in iron. Like all the others it was locked, so Teska unrolled the flap of leather that held her tools. They waited while she worked, the only sound the metallic scratching that came from the lock. It released with a click. They stepped inside and closed the door behind them.

"Everyone remember their job," Thorne said.

They fanned out. Amelia closed all the shutters, leaving one partially cracked so she could watch for patrols. This room had thin, narrow windows that were too small to climb through. Tua drew matches from his pocket and lit several small oil lamps around the room. Then he moved to the doorway so he could watch the hall. The scent of burning oil competed with the mustiness, and shadows flitted around the room.

Thorne felt at home. His fingers shuffled through sheaves of documents, searching them for a clue that would tell him anything about the Crimson Fathers. As they rifled through page after page, dust floated in the air. Amelia sneezed twice, as softly as she could. The lamps kept their hands and faces warm, but their toes cramped from the cold. As they searched, sweat broke out on their foreheads.

After nearly half an hour, Thorne shoved a manuscript back on the shelf. He rubbed his nose with fingers that smelled like a dry tomb.

"Anything?" he asked Tua and Amelia. Both replied in the negative.

"What about you?" he said, walking over to Teska. "We're running out of time."

She dropped the leather portfolio full of pages back on the desk and stretched her arms over her head. "Not yet. I think I'm getting close. But hells, I don't know…"

Thorne nodded and rubbed his stiffening neck. This was like looking for a pinch of snuff in an ash pit, but they all resumed their searches. Tua aided them as best he could from his post at the door. Thorne handed him manuscripts and parchments to look over. He did the same for Amelia, although not as often. He needed her attention focused outside. Another half hour passed.

Thorne looked at Teska. "What're you doing?"

She was bent over a manuscript, picking at its surface with one of her tools. She looked up. "Trying to get this damned thing open. I think it's important. It's got three different locks on it."

Thorne nodded. "Let me know when you get it."

Amelia had just finished skimming through some scrolls and was returning them to Malachi when she stopped and looked down. The floor near the wall was scarred, as if something heavy had been pulled across it. She pointed it out to Thorne, and when he arrived with the lamp, the gouges were clearer. They disappeared underneath a bookshelf against the wall.

Thorne knelt and ran his fingers across the marks. "Interesting…" he said. He thanked Amelia and directed her back to the window.

"Malachi!" Teska's voice sounded like a cathedral bell in the hushed antiquity of the room.

The metal-bound manuscript sat before her on the table. She had opened it to the first page. It was covered with a delicate, pinched script. She tapped the page as Thorne leaned over her shoulder. Her hair smelled of the walnut tree bark she had used to dye it.

"Damn Church does keep records of everything," she said. "This is about Okafo the Dark. Must be something special to be locked up like this."

Thorne sat down beside her and put the book in his lap. The metal was ice cold. His eyes darted back and forth across the page. His brows furrowed. He said nothing for ten minutes, his finger tracing each line of painstakingly inked sentences. Finally, he put the book on the desk and leaned back. The chair creaked like a rusty hinge.

Teska smiled, her dimples shadowy pits in the marmalade-colored light. She squeezed his arm. "Is that it?" she asked.

"Did you find something useful?" Tua asked. He sat cross-legged in the doorway, looking from the hall to the pile of parchment in his lap and back again.

"Yes!" Thorne replied, his tone strong and confident. "Val was right. According to this, the Crimson Fathers were formed in 261 AE."

"What is AE?" Tua asked.

"It means 'Apocalypse Era,'" Teska said. "It's how we measure the years since the Great Cataclysm."

Thorne jumped up and walked over to Tua. "Put this in the bag."

Tua stood, sloughing off the lapful of documents like a snake shedding its skin. He pulled a burlap sack from inside his coat and stuffed the book inside. "What does it say, Chief-Who-Wins?"

"The Fathers were formed at the behest of Okafo the Dark," Thorne continued. "Their task was to enchant the bones of Michael the First, as a way for the Church to ensure the people's loyalty. It guaranteed the Church's dominion over the realm. The Fathers completed their task in 268 AE and were executed immediately thereafter, again on orders from the Heiromonarch."

"Why would your Church want to enchant bones?" Amelia asked, still watching the snow.

Teska snapped her fingers. "The rank pins! Every one of them has a sliver of bone inside—"

"From Michael the First," Thorne said.

"Merrick was right all along." Teska smiled.

Tua picked up the documents he had dropped on the floor and put them on a table. "How were these Fathers killed? Does it say what happened to them?" he asked.

Thorne grinned. "A special weapon was forged. A sword called 'Imperator's Flame.' One of Okafo's private guards murdered the Fathers. The corpses were buried in a secret tomb—along with the Flame."

"Where's the tomb?" Amelia asked.

Thorne groaned. "It doesn't say. I guess there are *some* things the Church doesn't want to remember."

Teska wore a haunted expression as she searched Thorne's eyes.

"What?" he asked, growing uncomfortable.

"I was just thinking. If all the Crimson Fathers were killed—then who brought them back to life?"

Thorne digested the question and found it sour and foul.

Amelia gasped. "Guards! Lots of them!"

Thorne pushed past tables and chairs, cracked a shutter and peered into the night. A contingent of men—perhaps ten or more—ran toward the building. He spun around. "Tua, make for the west exit. That's closest."

"What about the other rooms?" Amelia asked. "Can we hide in one of them?"

Faint pounding came from the direction of the main doors. More sounds came from a different direction.

"No good on the other rooms," Teska told Amelia. "It'd take me too long to pick a lock."

"And they'll search them all," Thorne said, rushing back to join Tua at the door. He was about to step into the hall when he heard doors slamming. Muffled voices echoed through the lonesome halls. "Damn it, they'll be here in a few seconds!"

He reached inside his coat and drew a falchion sword from its sheath. Teska did likewise with the short sword at her side. Tua saw them and unsheathed his short sword as well.

"The windows!" Amelia shouted, forgetting that they were too small for anyone to get through. She opened a shutter. "Oh no."

"Ain't that a piss down the back," Teska groused.

Through the swirling flakes, more men approached the building. It looked like half of the Paracletian Order was converging on the building.

Running feet and shouting filled the hallway.

Thorne raced to the bookcase. "Tua, give me a hand! I think there's a door behind this!"

Both men grabbed the shelf. "Pull!"

They tugged on the piece of furniture, but nothing happened.

The voices and footsteps came closer. Teska slammed the door and locked it.

Thorne stepped back and slapped the side of the bookcase in frustration. Tua continued to push and pull, dislodging manuscripts and scroll tubes. As they fell around his feet, something heavy thudded against the hall door.

Amelia jumped like a trapped animal.

"Open this door! We know you're in there! You're all under arrest!"

Tua was on his hands and knees, fingers racing across the wainscoting beside the shelf.

The pounding on the door intensified. "In the name of the Church, you are ordered to open this door immediately!"

"Here!" Tua announced. He pressed on a section of board that bore faint scuff marks. Something clicked, and the bookcase separated from the wall.

"Excellent, Tua!" Thorne grunted as he gripped the bookcase and pulled it away from the wall. It weighed at least two hundred pounds but opened smoothly without a sound. It stopped with just enough room for a grown man to slip into the icy black void behind it.

Keys rattled on the other side of the hall door.

Tua clutched the burlap sack to his chest, grabbed an oil lamp and slipped behind the case.

Thorne motioned Teska and Amelia inside. He squeezed in behind them. A handle on the back of the shelf made it easy to close. The latch clicked again. A few seconds of silence followed as they waited in the wavering shadows, oily smoke being pulled down into the darkness behind them.

Inside the room, the door burst open. Thorne waited, ready to strike the first man who opened the bookcase.

At least I'll have the element of surprise.

Shouts and orders filled the room. Tables and chairs scraped across the floor while books, scrolls and portfolios tumbled from shelves. Thorne had no trouble imagining the horrified reactions of the Cartulian Order's fastidious librarians when they discovered this room tomorrow. It would not be pretty, and woe to anyone who was around them.

Amelia stifled a sneeze.

Tua's dark eyes reflected the lamplight as he tugged Thorne's sleeve. He said nothing but motioned behind them. Thorne looked.

They were standing on a small landing. A set of rusted metal stairs led down into a cold, stygian darkness. A faint current of air teased the smoke, offering promise of an exit.

"Where the hells did they go!" someone in the room shouted.

"They couldn't have gotten by us!"

"Check the windows."

"Bleedin' windows 're all closed."

"Hey, look at this."

Thorne heard men gathering on the other side of the bookcase. Unless they were the village idiots, it would not take them long to figure out what had happened to their quarry.

"Search every inch of this place!" a different voice boomed. Thorne heard footsteps, curses, fists against the wall.

"Sir, I think I've got something!"

Tua was already descending the stairs, his lamp bobbing in front of him. Teska nodded at Thorne and tilted her head in the direction of the stairs.

Underground again? he thought. Their narrow escape from Honvale and the Vulanti'nacha a few months ago still made him shiver. Reluctantly, he turned and followed Amelia and Teska across the landing and down into the freezing depths.

19
DISCOVERY

SATURDAY, OCTOBER 31, 999 AE

The stairs vibrated under their feet. Supports had been built into the stone walls, but more than once Thorne saw flecks of rust sifting from them in the lamplight. They were probably not accustomed to bearing so much weight at one time. The air smelled earthy, but a hint of rot lurked behind it.

The secret door did not surprise Thorne. He knew the Church had them in various places, although he had never known where any were located. They were mostly used by high-ranking officials to move about unseen. But he had no doubt they had also been used for a host of illegal activities as well, with or without the Church's approval. The Palace of the Heiromonarch was said to be honeycombed with hidden doors and passageways.

During his time in the Paracletian Order, Thorne had heard rumors of a whole city beneath the streets of Attagon. He had never put any faith in those rumors, but now, as they descended the ancient steps, he was less sure.

Maybe the Church keeps things down here? Thorne imagined forbidden knowledge or artifacts from before the Great Cataclysm. His heart beat faster at the prospect of stumbling upon archaic treasures that the Church had buried in the depths.

They arrived at a small room and followed Tua inside. Thorne estimated they had to be at least twenty or thirty feet below ground. In the meager lamplight, what they found surprised them.

A dozen cloaks hung from pegs on the wall. A table contained a variety of hand-held weapons, lamps like they carried, torches and two empty scroll tubes. Several chairs of comfortable design sat in various places. There was one closed door opposite where they stood with a barred window in it.

"What do you want to do?" Tua asked Thorne as they moved around the room. They lit torches and blew out their lamps, placing them on the table. More light was safer.

Thorne glanced back at the stairs. "We need to avoid a fight. There're too many of them. We'd have an advantage on the landing or the stairs. They couldn't come at us all at once. But that's not an advantage I'd put much faith in."

"What's this room for?" Amelia wondered.

Tua handed her the burlap sack since his fighting skills would be more useful compared to hers. She tossed the sack over her shoulder and held her torch higher. The smoke gently floated toward the closed door.

"It's more than likely a safe room," Thorne replied. He ran his hand through a pile of tunics, stockings and robes on a second table, all four colors of the Orders represented.

"Whatever for?" Amelia asked.

Thorne tested the closed door and found it unlocked. He pulled it open.

"Church officials use them," he said. A rough manmade passageway led away from him into the darkness. For some reason, it reminded him of a hungry maw. Maybe it was the distasteful odor just beneath the smoke and stone and age around them. "If there were some sort of disaster or attack, they could sit it out down here. Judging by the look of those clothes, they still use it to get from one place to another."

"Sh!" Tua hissed and waved his hand for silence. "Listen."

Several seconds slipped by.

"I don't hear anything," Teska said.

Amelia shook her head. "Me either."

"Quiet!" Tua whispered. He put a thin finger to his lips.

They waited. Finally, Thorne moved over beside him. "What did you hear?" he asked.

"Noise, up there." He pointed toward the steps. "The guards are coming down."

Thorne whirled around and jerked a torch from the wall. "That's our best option," he said, gesturing toward the door he had just opened.

"But we don't know where that leads." The earth muffled Amelia's voice.

"No, we don't," Thorne replied. "But we can't fight all of them." He paused. "Amelia?"

"Yes."

"Can you fall in beside me? We'll likely need your gift from time to time."

The passageway floor was smooth. It was wide enough for two people to walk abreast. A faint air current tugged at the smoke. Thorne and Amelia led the way.

They heard no other sound apart from their footsteps and the crackling of torches. The passageway was cold enough to be felt through the soles of their boots. After about a hundred yards, it sloped down at a gentle angle.

The first side passage they came to was impassable. The ceiling had collapsed a few feet in, and, judging by the condition of the debris, it had happened decades ago. They pushed on.

Teska clenched her jaw to keep her teeth from chattering. She watched Amelia's blonde hair bounce and sway as she walked ahead of her. Teska had never worn her hair short before. She shook her head like she had done so many times already, as if her hair would suddenly return to its former weight and density. It felt unnatural. Her ears were cold and exposed, her neck covered with gooseflesh. She cursed under her breath.

Time had little meaning down here. There was no way to mark its passing, so they could only guess at how long they had been walking. It felt to Thorne like it had been fifteen or twenty minutes. But it could have just been five. He stopped and asked Tua to listen for any pursuit.

He shook his head. "Nothing."

Thorne knew the guards were still pursuing them. They were not going to give up just because their quarry had gone down a tunnel. He resumed walking. It occurred to him that if someone could map these passages, the freedom fighters could make good use of them. It would be an excellent way of moving around the city unobserved. He tried to think if he knew someone in the Cartulian Order he could trust—someone who might know something about the tunnels or could help make a serviceable map.

Amelia tapped his arm.

"What?"

"I'm sorry," she said. "You didn't answer when I called you."

"My apologies. Just lost in my head."

She pointed into the blackness. "We're coming to a big opening."

He looked, even though he knew he could not see beyond the light of their torches.

"How far?"

She shrugged. "Sixty, maybe seventy feet?"

Thorne glanced back at Tua and Teska. "Keep your weapons ready. And watch our backs. We don't want to get ambushed from behind."

They crept forward again, the smoke continuing to lead them. The foul odor—like fishy mud and decay—grew stronger. Thorne thought it seemed brighter up ahead. As they reached the opening, he saw why. There were phosphorescent fungi everywhere. It clung to the walls, offering them ghostly translucent light. It covered boulders, and patches dotted the tunnel floor.

And the buildings in front of them.

Thorne stopped. His eyes widened, and his mouth fell open. He stared in disbelief.

"It's a…city," Amelia gasped.

Tua and Teska stepped up beside them.

"Damn, would you look at that," Teska said in surprise.

"A city," Thorne whispered. In the peculiar light, his face seemed to glow with amazement. *So it was true after all!*

Stalactites hung from the ceiling like fangs. The sickly green light created a disorienting, alien panorama. Parts of pre-Cataclysm buildings the color of turds leaned like gravestones. Their tops disappeared into the earthen roof of the cavern. Rows of sagging windows showed only darkness inside. Entire walls had collapsed, and piles of rubble lay in what had once been streets. Rusted shells of auto-mobiles sat here and there, half buried in rock and debris. Two parallel rusted rails lay in grooves down the middle of one street. Water dripped in soft, hollow plops.

The forgotten city sprawled throughout the cavern. They could vaguely see more buildings in the distance. How far it spread beneath Attagon was anybody's guess. Their footsteps were drumbeats in a mausoleum. The light from their torches sent shadows crawling over stones, doorways and twisted signs, whose messages had long been erased. A series of rocks, too crude to be called steps, led down a few feet into the city. The tunnel continued to their left, winding farther away into the earth.

For several moments, no one spoke. They stood transfixed, gawking in awe at the ancient ruins of yesteryear. It was Tua who broke the silence, his breath forming wispy clouds.

"The guards are coming."

"Any idea how close they are?" Thorne asked.

"Five minutes, give or take?"

Thorne looked at the passageway to his left, then back at the undercity. He stepped onto the first rock.

"What're you doing?" Teska asked

He moved down to the next rock. "Hiding," he said over his shoulder.

"Have you lost your mind? We need to get the hells out of here!" Her voice had grown in volume as she spoke. The last few words drifted back as echoed frustration.

"They are getting closer," Tua reported.

"Yes, hiding," Thorne said. "They'll think we kept to the passageway. We can wait for them to pass."

"And what if they come down there looking for us?" she snapped.

Thorne smiled. Teska Vaun might have black hair, but there was no covering up her redheaded ferocity. "If they come down, which I don't think they will, we'll have the element of surprise. We can choose the best place to make a stand, if necessary."

"Did you eat crazy bread for supper?"

Tua followed Thorne. Teska looked back into the tunnel. She cursed, motioned Amelia ahead of her and joined the procession down into the silent, freezing necropolis.

Thorne had never imagined a city actually existed beneath Attagon. When he was small, he had wondered what such a city would be like. But as he got older, he came to believe—as adults do when they lose their childhood curiosity—that it was all just a myth. Tunnels for Church officials to move about unseen, he could accept. But an entire city, fallen and forgotten beneath the streets? That simply was not possible.

And yet here he was, staring at the impossible as he stepped off the last rock and onto a street that had not seen the sun in well over a thousand years. Probably more. Tavern talk claimed that Attagon rested atop a pre-Cataclysm city once known as Chattanga or Chantoga or Chantanooga or something like that. As the River Tense rose and fell and flooded over the years, the land around it shifted and sunk. After centuries of silt deposits, sinkholes, erosion and earth turbulence, the lower part of the old city disappeared. And every few hundred years, the city streets had been raised, regardless of whatever was below them. Overhead, Attagon still had the remains of some of its pre-Cataclysm structures. But down here, the foundation of the city dug its roots into a bygone era.

Thorne led them quickly but carefully into the city. He avoided areas where they might leave footprints that would give them away. It felt like walking through a mummified corpse. The death that surrounded them was so archaic that it had crumbled to dust, ground into powder for the earth to reclaim. They were in the midst of atrophied history.

As they picked their way around rubble that was antediluvian when the first Heiromonarch was chosen, small creatures fled in all directions. Most were rats, sleek and dark, their eyes glinting blue in the abnormal light of torch and lichen. Thorne preferred not to guess what they lived on down here. The creatures disappeared into the numerous piles of rubble, avoiding the large holes that speckled the ground. Each hole was about a foot in diameter and sank straight into the ground.

He recoiled from the first one he bent over to inspect. The stench of rotted meat rose from it.

"Keep your eyes open," he instructed as he gave each hole a wide berth.

A few insects skittered from the invading torchlight, but most were dormant until warmer weather returned. There were plenty of cockroaches, however, and again Thorne was clueless as to what they found to eat. They were unafraid of the torchlight, probably because they lived in this half-lit world. This was their domain, and they did not scatter like those above. Thorne's boots crunched them into gooey smears when they moved too slowly.

They saw an occasional snakeskin, cracked and flaky white, but it was too cold for them now. Bats screeched and took flight whenever the group ranged too close to a building. Their leathern wings sounded like rain as columns of them spiraled up into the darkness.

Crumbling buildings like decayed teeth stood to their right and left. Some leaned; some had collapsed into their foundations. Once-stout wooden walls were reduced to pulp or desiccated by vermin. Arches had collapsed. Once-decorative millwork had rotted away. Rusted pipes crossed overhead or simply ended in mid-air. Gritty sand mixed with the stone and dirt, indicating that at some point it had been used to fill in depressions or shore up foundations. Bricks lay scattered about, the mortar on them having turned to powder ages ago. Ice filled the mudholes and potholes.

They found bones here and there. Most were from cats, raccoons and rats. They did see an occasional human skull or ribcage. Aside from the stench rising from the holes, the place smelled like a muddy riverbank.

Not surprising, Thorne thought, *considering how easily the river floods.*

"In here," Thorne said. He pointed toward a building with arched windows. They navigated over detritus and slipped inside the hollowed-out framework. Then they waited.

Not long after, they heard voices. Thorne peered through a hole in what remained of a wall. A knot of constables and deputies emerged from the tunnel. They halted and looked around, dumbfounded. Two Crusaders pushed through them.

Thorne motioned for everyone to stay low and remain quiet. He had been sweating while they walked but now found himself shivering. He dug his hands deeper into his coat pockets. Thanks to the acoustics of the cavern, he had no trouble hearing their pursuers.

"What in all the bleedin' hells is that?"

"By the Church…"

"…bloody cold down here."

"…it's a bunch a buildin's!"

One Crusader turned to the stunned Churchmen. "Silence!" His voice tolled like a death knell and echoed back.

"You think they're down *there*?"

"Go back, all of you," the second Crusader said. "Return to the surface."

A brown-skinned deputy with long black hair looked at him. "Whatta ya mean go back?"

"Go back. That's an order. We'll follow them from here."

"The hells you will!" someone said. "We gotta run those thieves down!"

Cockroaches scurried around and over Thorne's boots.

Teska, Tua and Amelia were out of sight but positioned so they could see what was happening.

The Crusaders grew irritated. The first backhanded the brown-skinned deputy, sending him careening against the rock wall. The second Crusader slid the broadsword from the scabbard across his back.

"Never question our orders!" he barked. "Do as you are told, or I will gut you where you stand."

"You shits!" a tall deputy exclaimed. "We ain't afraid of you! There's four times as many of us as there be of you."

The second Crusader swung the sword as if it weighed no more than a quill pen. The blade finished its arc, trailing blood. The tall deputy's head struck the floor, bounced and rolled down the stone steps. The first giant unsheathed his sword and leveled it at a constable's midsection.

"Go," he growled, "while you still have life in you. We will track the fugitives."

Grumbling, but not too loudly, the men gathered up the corpse. One went to retrieve the head. The first Crusader held the constable at sword point. The other cleaned his blade.

"Ye going down in there?" a different constable asked. He was sufficiently out of sword range.

"No need," the Crusader said. "They will have stayed with the passageway."

"Begging yer pardon, but how do ye know? There's a million hiding—"

A scream reverberated throughout the necropolis.

Everyone except the Crusaders flinched.

The deputy who had picked up the head was entangled in what appeared to be roots coming out of the ground.

"That's why," the second Crusader said as he watched without emotion.

The deputy screamed again. Then Thorne realized they were not roots.

They were tentacles.

Dozens of them wrapped the deputy as he continued to shriek. More tentacles encircled his torso and legs. His arms were pinned to his body. Between screams there was a moist, slurping noise.

A constable started toward the stone steps, but the first Crusader stopped him with a hand on the chest. "No," he said, his voice detached and hollow. "He is already dead. You go down there, you will be as well."

"B-But we can't just leave 'im t-to *that*!"

By now the deputy's agonized shrieks had become hiccupping squeals. More tentacles latched on to his body.

The creatures the tentacles were attached to wiggled out of the holes. They were like earthworms, pale white in color, almost transparent, and reeked of putrefaction. Thorne had heard of them before but had never seen one in person. He estimated them to be two to four feet in length. Shiny, viscous slime covered their ringed bodies. Fifteen or twenty of them slithered toward their catch, their tentacles stuck to every available piece of skin. They had no eyes, only lamprey-like mouths nestled inside the ring of tentacles.

"You cannot save him," the Crusader reiterated to the assembled Churchmen.

"What the fuck are those bleedin' things!"

The first Crusader sheathed his sword. "They are called Galorme. 'Madworms,' by their more common name."

The deputy continued to twitch but made no further noise. More Galorme surfaced. Tentacles quested here and there. Thorne held his nose and breathed through his mouth.

"M-Madworms?" Amelia whispered to Teska.

"Move out!" the second Crusader yelled. The men took their headless colleague and retreated into the tunnel. The two Crusaders turned and continued forward into the other passageway.

Thorne silently counted to a hundred before moving. His knees hurt from crouching. Tua indicated that he heard nothing beyond the squelching and sucking of the worms.

"I-I have never seen anything such as this," Tua mumbled. He buried his nose in the crook of his arm.

"Me neither," Amelia said, horrified. Even in the phosphorescent light, she looked pale. "Wh-What are those things?"

Thorne rubbed his knees before straightening up. He sounded funny as he tried to talk without breathing through his nose. "Like he said, they're known as Galorme, but people usually just call them madworms."

Tua frowned. "Why madworms?"

Several of the creatures slithered toward a black opening beneath a rubble pile. A dozen or more worked together, using some of their tentacles to drag the deputy's body. They quested along the ground, feeling their way toward the gaping hole as effortlessly as if they could see it.

Thorne paused and swallowed. The back of his throat tasted like phlegm, and he felt his stomach roll. He used the fingers on one hand to block his nostrils.

"It's because of what they do to their prey," he said.

More tentacles appeared from beneath the debris, guiding the body down into the earth. Thorne closed his eyes when he heard a faint moan as the deputy slipped out of sight.

"Oh my God!" Amelia cried. "H-He's still alive!"

Thorne nodded. "Madworms drain most of the blood from their prey. Then they take them into their warrens. They'll"—he cleared his throat—"they'll keep him alive and incubate their young inside his body. When the offspring are old enough, they'll…chew their way out."

Amelia gagged and covered her mouth.

"And their prey remains *alive* the whole time?" Tua asked. Even his tanned complexion had lost color.

"Once a madworm starts drawing blood, they inject a kind of paralyzing poison. Victims can't move, but they can see and hear and feel everything that's happening to them. That's why they're called madworms. Their prey goes insane *long* before they ever die."

Amelia turned away. She bent over with her hands on her knees and vomited.

"It's a cruel, vicious form of death," Thorne agreed. "But madworms aren't intelligent. They're simple creatures, like ants or birds. It's just their way of surviving."

"Yeah, nasty way of doing it," Teska said.

Amelia shrieked. She stood trembling, finger pointing toward the archway they had used to get into the building.

Dozens of madworms crawled over stones and debris toward them, leaving pearly trails behind them.

Amelia screamed again, hands clenched in front of her mouth. She remained frozen as the foul-smelling things wiggled closer. Thorne moved across the rubble to help her. As he did, a deep rumbling came from beneath his feet.

"Shit!" He threw himself forward.

The rumbling grew louder. Stones grated together. The ground shook. A loud crash blasted through the cavern. The place where Thorne had just stood collapsed. The gaping pit sucked in rotted wood, stones, bits of metal and everything else nearby.

Thorne hit the debris hard, knocking the breath from his lungs. His hand flew open, and his sword clattered down the newly opened slope and into the sinkhole. The sound of tumbling rocks echoed from below. Dirt billowed in the air. Thorne lay on his back, holding his chest, mouth working like a fish.

Teska and Tua grabbed Amelia's arms. They pulled her back and away from the madworms. More slithered through the arch.

Teska leaned out a window. Madworms crawled from their holes, tentacles flailing. She knelt beside Thorne. "Are you okay? Can you get up?"

He wheezed an acknowledgement, but she had to help him. More debris tumbled into the sinkhole.

"Back against the wall!" Tua yelled. He extended his arm for Teska to steady herself and Thorne. Amelia cowered behind him.

Thorne finally pulled in a lungful of the rancid-tasting air into his lungs. "D-Damn it! L-Lost my sword—"

"Never mind," Teska said. "Head that way." She pointed to the right. There was enough room to navigate the edge of the sinkhole and keep them away from the madworms. She led the way, Thorne at her back, Amelia behind him. Tua brought up the rear.

They climbed through a window on the other side of the building. There were no worms here, so they hurried down the buckled street.

Behind them, the rumbling came again, louder this time. The ground shook so hard it threw them off their feet. Rocks and dirt rained from the darkness overhead. Bats flitted and screeched through the air. The ground kicked and groaned. The building behind them shuddered and broke apart, collapsing into the hole with ear-splitting finality.

Coughing dust from their lungs, everyone stood and surveyed the damage. Nothing remained of the building except a handful of stones on top of one another. The pulped, glistening bodies of madworms writhed and twitched throughout the rubble, their stench even more abominable in death. A hole at least a hundred feet across blocked their path back to the safe room.

"Come on," Thorne said, wiping cold dirt off his hands. "That's bound to have alerted those Crusaders. We need to find another way out of here. Fast."

20

UNDERGROUND

SATURDAY, OCTOBER 31, 999 AE

Leaving the necropolis and those disgusting worms suited Amelia just fine. She feared she would never get the screams of the poor deputy out of her head. The horrifying fate that awaited him would haunt her the rest of her life. She shivered from the cold but also from the thought of being buried alive while worms ate their way out of her.

Tua noticed her complexion. "Are you all right? You are not using your gift right now, are you?"

"No, just cold."

She appreciated the concern in his tone. They had shared many conversations over the past several months—on the road, over meals, whenever time and opportunity presented. She thought that maybe Tua'Ahtaki liked her, and she was flattered. But he was far too old for her. Besides, since the death of her husband, she had felt more insecure about herself—her looks, her figure and most importantly her ability to make a worthwhile contribution. Thorne did not know it, but when he asked her to walk with him and guide them through the tunnel, it had made her feel good. Valued. Needed. Instead of just fixing meals—which she truly did enjoy—or tending to the animals, he had made her an indispensable part of this journey.

It had to be the work of God that brought these people into her life. For weeks before meeting them, she had been weighing her options as a new widow. She knew she could not stay on the homestead. There was too much work for one person.

There was too much for both of us, she thought. She remembered the hard days of trying to coax something good from the baked Tex'ahn soil and the frigid nights when the wind swept the warmth from the prairie.

She did not really have any family. There was an aunt who lived near Magnolia City, but the two of them had never gotten along all that well. Not only would it be an imposition on her aunt's hospitality—she also knew it would not have lasted more than a month, at best. Their temperaments were too closely aligned.

She could have gone back to Dallastown or maybe Road's End in a pinch, but even that would have worn thin after a while. She knew she wanted—she *needed*—to be married. She had known since she was a little girl. Her talents were centered around the home and hearth, and she was proud of that.

Of course, there were eligible bachelors in both cities, but she had not been ready to remarry so soon after Alec's death. In time she would. But not yet. It had been difficult enough just walking away from his simple grave for the last time.

Remember how long it took to scrub the dirt from your hands?

She did. She had just about rubbed them raw, as if the soil had somehow caused Alec's death and her grubby hands were complicit in it.

Amelia had never been an impetuous person. It was not what the card players called her strong suit. She planned and organized. Try as she might, she could not remember the last time she had done something on the spur of the moment. Saying yes to Teska's invitation to join the Enodia Communion—that had been a huge step for her. But agreeing to leave her home and accompany them to Deiparia? That had taken more courage than she thought she possessed.

But if the past few months had taught her anything, she was stronger than she gave herself credit for. She had tried to tame the vast emptiness of the prairie. She had endured tornados and wild dogs and, during lean times, had scraped together enough food to sustain her and Alec. Amelia had chosen to undertake this strange voyage and accept her place in this sisterhood of magic.

Something tightened in her stomach. It was a visitor she had come to know well. It arrived whenever she thought about the Communion, and it ate at her as she struggled to reconcile her faith with the sisterhood.

She had been raised to believe and trust in God. Alec had owned a small book called a New Testament. He used to carry it in his pocket. It belonged to her now. The book was ratty and bent, with a broken spine and dirt-smudged pages that felt like lace. They had read it together by the hearth, wondering what the words meant. They had followed the story of Jesus in the first four parts, but the rest of it became harder to untangle.

She had been conflicted ever since agreeing to join the Communion. Some of the things Jesus said seemed to be at odds with her gift and the purpose of the sisterhood. How could she worship God and one of the Three Witches? Was she supposed to? Would God be angry with her?

Sometimes she wondered if her gift was really a curse, a punishment bestowed by God for something she had done wrong. But her gift helped her. It helped other people. Especially now.

So how could it be bad? Why would a good God give me something that was bad?

Maybe these questions and feelings stemmed from the fact that she had kept her gift secret from everyone. Even Alec. He had never known what his wife was capable of. She felt guilty for not sharing the truth with the man she loved.

But would he have accepted me if I'd told him? Would he have thought of me as damaged goods or called me a monster? The questions made her stomach as cold as the rock beneath her feet.

She focused on the passageway, on marshalling her strength as Teska had been teaching her.

"It's like taking water from a bucket," Teska had explained. "You draw out a ladle of water, the level in the bucket goes down. Draw it all out and the bucket is empty. Every time you use your gift—and the incantations later on—your level of energy and strength goes down. Use too much energy too fast, or too often, your bucket is empty. It will replenish from the natural world around us, but it takes time."

Teska had given her exercises to help her become more aware of her spiritual energy and ways to recognize the magic of the natural world and draw upon it. Since coming down here—*how long ago was it? It feels like months*—she had used her gift numerous times. Right now, she felt like someone who had gone two days without sleep. Thorne had told her to conserve her strength. She was grateful, even though using her gift made her feel more like one of them.

"Where are we?" she asked.

Thorne spoke but did not turn around. "I've got no idea." The earth ate his voice.

Unable to circumnavigate the pit, Thorne had led them across the dead city. It was so wide, it had taken them an hour—*at least it felt like an hour*—to reach the other end. At first it appeared they had run into a dead end, but Teska discovered another tunnel nearly hidden by debris. It was different from the previous one. This one was completely natural, more treacherous and went deeper.

Some distance back, they had emerged into a high-roofed cave. Five tunnels had radiated out like spokes on a wagon wheel. Two of them, they discovered, had collapsed. The third ended at a sheer drop. They couldn't see the other side, if one even existed.

The fourth tunnel descended sharply, narrowing as it went. It finally constricted to an opening no bigger than a pumpkin. They had returned to the hub, frustrated and tired, and selected the one they were on now. As if they had a choice.

Every so often, Thorne halted and asked that Tua listen. His sense of hearing was excellent. But each time, he shook his head, black braids wiggling, and they moved on.

Amelia prayed that this tunnel would soon lead back to the surface. She was beginning to feel trapped. She had never been afraid of small spaces, but this was different. She was buried—*alive, like with the madworms!*—beneath tons of earth and the entire city of Attagon. She felt it pressing down, closing her in, forcing the breath from her lungs. Her fingertips brushed along the icy stone wall, reminding her there was no way to dig out, no way to escape—

She cried out. It echoed away like ripples across a pond. Her heart threatened to burst from her chest and flee for light and air. Her pulse exploded in her ears, and she trembled as her legs became jelly.

"Hang on, I have you," Tua said tenderly.

Amelia swayed and fell into him.

He steadied her against the wall. "Her hands are clammy. I think she may be going into shock."

Amelia's hair stuck to her forehead. Her eyelids fluttered.

Teska eased her to the hard floor. "Amelia, can you hear me?"

Somehow, she nodded. She opened her eyes, and two Teskas shimmered before her, wavering like reeds in a wind. "Got to…get out of here," she said.

"I know. That's what we're doing. Just rest for now."

Everyone's breath formed miniature clouds. Tua removed his coat and covered her. He rubbed his arms to keep warm and walked over to Thorne.

"We cannot stay here," he whispered so his voice would not echo. "We will freeze to death."

Thorne nodded, his shadow doing likewise on the tunnel wall. "I'm going to scout ahead, try to see if there's something to tell us where we are. Stay with them."

Tua and Teska knelt in the tunnel, their torches burning lower. They watched the darkness in both directions for signs of movement. Color slowly returned to Amelia's cheeks. Her breathing returned to normal.

"Thirsty," she mumbled.

"We'll get some water soon," Teska reassured her. She looked at Tua and mouthed the words 'I hope.'

Both saw the pinprick of light coming toward them. They tensed and went for their weapons, but it was only Thorne. His torch guttered.

"Tunnel goes up not far from here," he said. "Indications of a breeze, too. How is she?"

Amelia felt good enough to smile, although she needed help getting to her feet. "I'm…okay," she said. "I'm so sorry. I-I don't know what came over me."

"Do not worry," Tua comforted her. "There is nothing to be sorry for. Take my shoulder and let's get out of this place."

Thorne led the way, their torches dimming by the minute.

Amelia closed her eyes as Tua held her arm.

Maybe if I get used to the darkness it won't be so bad when the torches die.

They climbed up the tunnel, trying to reach *something* before they lost their light completely. They could not count on Amelia's gift now. She was too weak and terrified. Thorne did not know if he could handle being down there in the pitch black, with no hope of rescue.

A faint, almost translucent light—like they had seen in the undercity—shone ahead. But the closer they got, the more the tunnel narrowed. Fear surged through Thorne. What if they got this close but were unable to reach the light? The thought lent speed to his aching legs even though he dreaded what he might find.

He almost shouted when he realized the narrow spot did not thwart their progress. They squeezed through one at a time, and the tunnel widened again. The light brightened. Another incline. Small patches of glowing fungus splotched the walls. They crawled through a hole and emerged in another high-roofed cavern.

It looked exactly like the one they had been in before.

Thorne's spirit crumbled as he reached back into the tunnel to help the women up.

Tua scrambled out, breathing heavily. "I do not much care to be a mole."

"Oh shit," Teska said as she looked around.

The phosphorescent lichen illuminated five tunnel openings that led off into darkness.

"What? What!" Amelia cried, one step from complete hysteria. She hunted for hope in Teska's eyes.

"We are— By my ancestors, we are right back where we started," Tua said, his voice filled with hopelessness. He slumped against the cold stone wall.

Amelia's watery eyes danced with fear. "Oh no. No, no, no!" She twirled around and around, looking, despairing. "NOOO!" she screamed.

Teska held Amelia up, her own face a mask of futility and despair.

"Wait a minute," Thorne said. He picked his way across the uneven floor to one of the openings.

Thank the Church and God and whoever else there might be!

He spun around, grinning. "This isn't the same place!" he yelled.

Everyone stared at him, not daring to hope.

"Look, look at this." He pointed to a tunnel opening. Bolted to the rock beside it was a small, rusted metal square. Time-worn engraved letters spelled out CATHEDRAL.

Thorne dashed to each opening and read the signs aloud.

PALACE.

PARACLETIAN ORDER.

RIVER.

CARTULIAN ORDER.

"We're back in the Church access tunnels!" he yelled.

Amelia began to sob with relief.

"So which way?" Teska asked.

Thorne paused. "I don't know how long we've been down here. If we head back toward the Cartulian Order buildings, we're likely to run into those Crusaders or guards. And I'd guess the river's a long way from here."

"Which place is closest?" Tua asked.

Thorne shrugged. "I don't know. I have no idea where we are." His torch sputtered and went out. Tua's followed a moment later.

"I say we head for the cathedral," Teska said.

"We can't just go charging off again," Thorne replied, his tone weary and short. "We might be close to a way out, and if we start in the wrong direction, we could end up wandering around down here longer."

"I still say the cathedral."

"Malachi, let us check them out, just for a few hundred feet," Tua said. "We may find something to help us make a better decision. If each of us tears off a few strips of cloth from our garments, I will try to make a fire. We can use the leftover strips to wrap the torches. They will not last long. But anything is better than this darkness."

A few minutes later, everyone had torn off a sleeve—and put their heavy coats and cloaks back on quickly. Amelia felt better. She wrapped the torches after Tua managed a pitiful fire with a few scraps of cloth.

"This will not burn long," he said.

Torches relit, Thorne entered the tunnel toward the cathedral. Tua selected the one to the Paracletian Order. Teska and Amelia talked softly in the cavern and tended the dwindling fire. Both men returned to report that neither tunnel offered any indication of distance. Or escape.

"You take the palace," Thorne said. "I'll check the one toward the river."

Thorne returned five minutes later, shaking his head. "That one won't help. It descends almost immediately. We definitely don't want to go down again."

Tua's deep voice cut through the cavern. "Malachi, I think you need to see this."

He led them through the tunnel, which was wider than any of the others they had found. The floor was smooth. Not far inside, while the tunnel continued straight, Tua stopped at a crevice in the right wall. It was low but large enough to admit one person at a time. Tua crouched and motioned for them to follow him.

"Where're you going?" Thorne asked. "The tunnel goes this way."

"It is not the tunnel you need to see." Tua's voice floated back through the crevice.

Sighing, Thorne sent Amelia and Teska ahead of him, then slipped through the gap. On the other side was a wide cavern. More of the phosphorescent lichen grew from the walls, bathing the empty space in sickly, wan light.

Except it was not completely empty.

Tua pointed. "Look."

A hundred feet from where they stood, two heavy iron doors sat in the stone wall. Some type of intricate filigree—or was it words—decorated both, but Thorne could not make it out at this distance. Each door had an iron ring in the center. One of the biggest chains Thorne had ever seen ran through them, secured by a lock with no keyhole.

As they walked closer, their torchlight played across the iron, throwing the carved designs into sharp but fleeting relief. The doors had to be at least twice Thorne's six-foot-three height.

"Oh!" Amelia exclaimed as if someone had just cut her. She rubbed her hands together.

"I feel it too," Teska said.

Upon closer examination, an unknown script covered the doors, punctuated by sigils carved into the iron. Both doors looked as if they had been tattooed from top to bottom. Even the frame, lintel and capstone were inscribed. The letters seemed to move if stared at too long.

"What the hells is this?" Thorne asked, removing his glove and sliding his fingertips across the iron. He drew his hand back and stared at the door.

"Cold?" Tua asked.

"Just the opposite. It's *warm*."

He checked and found it just as Thorne said.

Teska stuffed a glove in her pocket and laid her palm against a door. She stood still, then her body jerked.

"Teska?" Thorne asked. "You okay?"

Suddenly, her head lolled to the side. Her legs gave out. She looked like someone who had fainted—yet she remained standing with her palm still against the door. It seemed to be the only thing keeping her upright.

"Teska!" Thorne shouted.

She was not sure what had happened. Everything faded away. It was just her and the door. A rush of warmth made her skin tingle like pins and needles. She saw the letters and sigils before her glowing with an eerie light. Thorne called to her from a great distance. Had he gotten lost in the tunnels?

Drowsiness settled on her. She had trouble remembering how long they had been underground. Why had they come here in the first place? Her memories did not work right, and when she focused on one it was as elusive as a fistful of water. Then something that felt like a wave washed over her. It buoyed her up as if it wanted to take her somewhere. It felt so good. Its warmth seeped all the way into her bones. She relaxed and floated on the wave.

She could not keep her eyes open. Just before she succumbed to sleep, something emerged from the tranquility. It was like a shadow on smoke, a whisper in the snow. She felt it burrow under her skin. It trickled behind her eyes.

And it spoke to her.

It murmured promises of respite and security. Of power. All she had to do was let go. It would hold her, protect her, welcome her.

She heard Thorne's voice again, farther away than before. Was he leaving her here? Why would he do that? The shadow consoled her. It said she did not need to worry. She would be taken care of. She just needed to say yes and let go.

She was tired—tired of running, fighting, hiding. The warmth surrounded her like a bearskin blanket and lulled her deeper into its embrace. If she wanted to rest, all she had to do was—

"Teska, snap out of it!"

Suddenly, the warmth disappeared and the wave vanished. The promises of the shadow were silenced. The sigils and letters stopped glowing. Everything around her came back into focus. She felt as if the breath had been stolen from her lungs. Gasping, she blinked and looked around.

"Teska! Talk to me," Thorne said. He held her wrist, her hand no longer in contact with the door.

"Wh-What happened?" she asked, her voice groggy.

Thorne looked in her eyes. "Are you okay? What happened?"

"I-I'm fine. I—" She started to collapse.

Thorne held her until she could regain her strength. She felt frail and tiny in his arms. "Just take it easy."

Teska shook her head. "I'm okay."

He let her go, and she remained on her feet, although her eyes still had a distant, unfocused quality about them.

"Can you tell us what happened?" Tua asked.

She nodded and told them about the experience.

"All we saw was you going limp as soon as you touched the door," Thorne said. "I-I thought something had happened to you." He glanced at the massive portal in doubt. "When you didn't respond I pulled your hand off the door."

Teska nodded. "That would explain why everything vanished all of a sudden. It snapped me out of… Well, whatever I was in."

"What about the wave? And who was whispering to you?" Amelia asked.

Teska looked at the sigils on the door. "I'm not sure. But just when you pulled my hand off the door, the shadow…howled. The whisper cursed. And I felt very *empty*." She was silent for a moment before looking up at Thorne, eyes like those of a spooked deer. "It's magic, *powerful* magic. Something was leeching my magic away." She looked back at the doors. "We've got to get in there."

Thorne raised his eyebrows. "What, why? You just said—"

"It's in there," she replied. Her voice was low, steady but demanding. "We've *got* to go in."

"Whatever for? What's in there?" Thorne asked, edginess creeping into his voice. He loved puzzles, but this was not the time or place for one.

Teska grinned, a mixture of relief and glee. "The Flame," she said. "It's *in there*."

21
FLAME

SATURDAY, OCTOBER 31, 999 AE

"Would you like to run that by me again?" Thorne asked, hands on his hips. The sallow, crystalline light from the fungi painted his face a cadaverous blue.

Teska sighed, an angry but exhausted sound. "The Flame—it's behind these doors. We have to break in there and get it."

"How do you know that?"

"It told me. I think it wants to be found."

Thorne raised his eyebrows again. "It *told* you?"

She started to put her hand against the door but stopped. She glared at him instead. "You really try my patience sometimes. Do you think I'm making this up?"

Thorne shook his head, releasing the tension in his face. "Of course not. I believe you. It's just so—"

"Strange?" Tua interrupted.

"Weird?" Amelia said.

Thorne scratched his chin, forgetting he no longer had a goatee. Did it itch, or was he doing it out of habit? He took a deep breath and started over. "What did it say to you? Is all that"—he gestured at the doors—"some kind of warning? A spell, maybe?"

"Could it just be decoration?" Amelia asked.

Teska's eyes roamed over the bizarre language painstakingly engraved in the iron. "Nobody put that kind of time and effort into decorative design—certainly not with glyphs and sigils incorporated into them—and most certainly not to be hidden away beneath the earth. It's got to be some sort of protective barrier."

"It is, maybe, a curse to keep out thieves?" Tua asked. "Or is it to…keep something in?

Teska looked pale. She nodded at Tua. "I-I think that's it." She turned to Thorne. "You asked what it said. I didn't hear a voice. It was more like an *impression*. An intuition?" She did not know if that made any more sense.

Tua looked at her. "And it *wants* us to find it?"

"Yes. It was reaching out, calling to me."

Amelia offered a smile that was half serious, half lighthearted. "I heard a story about a singing sword once."

Thorne put his hand on one of the rings. It was still warm, as if a fire were slowly dying inside of it. He tugged. The chain rattled; bits of rust fell from the links. The door did not budge.

"How do we get in?" Tua asked. "The lock has no keyhole."

Thorne picked it up. It had the same temperature and was as big as his two hands. He turned it over. The keyhole was on the bottom.

"Can you pick it?" he asked Teska.

"I'll try."

"Do not let your skin touch the lock," Tua advised in a parental tone. "It may have the same effect on you as the door did."

Teska removed her other glove and unrolled the lockpick set. She worked intently for a few moments. Their torches sputtered. There was a grating click, and the lock released.

Teska replaced the tools, put on her gloves and stepped back.

Thorne tossed the chain aside. He grasped the iron ring and pulled. Nothing happened. He tried again with the same result. Cursing, he placed his left foot against the left door and tugged on the right ring with all his strength. He grunted through gritted teeth. Metal scraped together.

"Tua, lend me a hand; this thing's bloody heavy."

Both men planted their feet and grabbed the ring.

"One, two, three!"

They pulled hard. The metal protested this interruption of its sleep but slipped an inch.

Panting, they shook the tightness from their hands before trying again. The metal squealed, finally surrendering. With loud growls of exertion, Thorne and Tua hauled the towering portal open.

A hard wind gusted over them. It reeked of fossilized tombs—like the undercity, except dry and dusty. They shielded their eyes from the flecks of rust swirling in their faces.

As quickly as it came, the wind disappeared. The cavern was still and silent.

They forced the door wide enough for one person to walk through at a time. Lamenting the loss of his sword, Thorne crept through the gap, senses alert. Teska, Amelia and Tua followed. Tua collided into their backs after they suddenly stopped. He peered past them to see why.

They stood before a circular chamber. Four massive columns held up the vaulted ceiling. A stone footbridge led across a sheer drop that connected to a smooth circular floor that sat in the middle like a bullseye. A massive column of rock below supported the floor.

Thirty yards away were piles of rotted clothing scattered across the circular floor, along with bits of debris and rock. A rectangular, altar-like stone stood near the back. Something lay on top of it.

They did not need their torches despite the absence of the lambent growths they had come to appreciate. A glacial wind swirled up around the bullseye.

The hair on Teska and Amelia's arms stood up. They looked at each other and nodded.

Thorne stomped on the footbridge. It seemed resilient in spite of its obvious age. He stood on it and waited for a moment. The wind toyed with the hem of his coat and fur-lined hood. He took another step.

"Be careful," Teska said. The wind captured her voice.

The bridge did not move or make a sound, so he walked the rest of the way. None of them looked down as they crossed the abyss.

The circular platform was approximately fifty feet in diameter. The columns, two on the right and two on the left, were pitted and cracked by time. Each had a series of glyphs around its base.

The piles of clothing had once been robes—red ones—although they were now faded to a dull terra-cotta. Inside each lay a human skeleton. Amelia gasped and stepped back against a pillar.

Teska and Tua moved carefully around the bones sprawled across the platform. Closer inspection revealed a smooth-edged slit in the front and the back of each robe. Rusted daggers and short swords also littered the floor.

Thorne walked straight to the stone rectangle.

"What happened here?" Tua asked.

Teska walked the perimeter of the platform, peering over the edge that dropped away into oblivion. She studied the robed skeletons. "These were the original Crimson Fathers." Pronouncing the name sounded like a nail being driven into a coffin. "I count twelve. That'd be right."

"And these cuts?" Tua asked. He used the tip of his sword to lift a robe off the floor.

"They were murdered, remember," Teska said.

"No doubt with this," Thorne said.

A broadsword with a ruby-colored blade lay upon the altar. Light glinted off the razor-sharp edges. It looked to be five and a half feet in length. The handle was wrapped in golden wire and was one-fifth of the total length, with a rounded pommel and a gently curved cross guard. Above that, an unsharpened section—designed as a secondary handle for leverage—terminated at a false guard of curved spikes. These protected the second hand from enemy blades, and prevented it from slipping up onto the sharpened edge. Intricate flames had been etched onto the blade, beginning at the base and tapering at the point. A scarlet scabbard lay beside it.

Thorne's eyes glowed with admiration. "How did they make a red blade?" Removing a glove, he slid his finger along the flat of the blade, feeling the flames. They were as precise as if they had just come from the engraver.

Teska also took off a glove and touched the hilt. Immediately, she stiffened as if struck by lightning. As before, everything around her lost its color and became insubstantial. Her friends were nothing more than wisps of smoke in a fog. The wave came upon her again, harder this time, and threatened to pull her under. There was no drowsiness but rather a heightened alertness. Every nerve ending felt aflame. It was frightening and exhilarating at the same time. The shadow's voice returned, caressing her mind, promising, teasing, whispering things dark and forbidden. She saw fire and destruction, a blackened world tainted with madness—and *power*. So much power. There was power to create and to destroy. Power to rule. Power to live forever.

One act of will is all that is needed, the shadow told her. *A simple decision to let go. It takes so very little to gain so very much. All you have ever wanted—and more! Surrender. Surrender.*

If she said yes, it could all be hers. She felt as if something was trying to force its way into her body. She wanted it badly even though it filled her with terror.

Just let go.

"Damn it! Teska!"

Without warning, it all vanished again. The world around her came back into focus. Once more, Thorne held her wrist. Her fingers hovered above the gold-wrapped handle.

"What happened?" Thorne asked.

Teska shook her head. "S-Sort of like the doors—but more intense. The shadow…it showed me things. Images of ruin and destruction. There was a…foulness…about it." She eyed the blade as if it were a venomous serpent, but the promise of power and eternal life clung to her memory. She decided not to say anything to Thorne about that.

"Are you sure you're okay?" He narrowed his eyes as he searched for answers on her face.

Teska nodded and ran a hand through her hair. "Yeah, yeah…I'm good."

Thorne eyed her a moment longer, then looked at the sword.

"So this is what killed the Crimson Fathers," Thorne said. He appraised the weapon from point to pommel.

"And will do so again," Teska replied, her voice now firm and assured. She pulled her glove on and softly laid a finger on the blade.

"Wait! What're you doing!" Thorne said. He tried to grab her arm but was too late. Teska's finger touched the metal. Nothing happened. "Amelia, whatever you do, don't let any part of your skin come in contact with this."

"Why not?"

"It seems to…siphon off energy. It's magical, just like the doors. When I touched the doors, it was like floating on water. If I'd given in, I'd have probably lost every bit of my power. But this?" She shook her head at the sword. "This is darker. There's an evil here that wanted me, wanted to use me. Wanted to be *inside* me." She shivered yet studied the blade with a fascinated expression.

The power could be hers. So could eternal life. She would not risk Amelia taking them by accident. *Or on purpose.* Teska glanced at Amelia and felt a twinge of wariness.

Tua frowned. "That is strong medicine."

His voice sliced through her thoughts. "Yes. We need to be *extremely* careful with this," she said.

Thorne looked at her. Even in this peculiar light and with her dirt-smeared face, she was beautiful. "You're saying the doors leech magic from people? But the sword tried to *give* you magic? I don't understand."

She nodded.

"Why? What for?" he asked.

"I-I don't know."

"Why would it do that?" Amelia added.

Teska suddenly felt dirty. Foul. Violated. An abhorrent taste lingered in her mind. "I don't know. And I don't like it."

"Well, let's get the hells out of here," Thorne said. "We've found it. Now we can get back to the surface and figure out what to do next." He slung the scabbard across his back and picked up the sword.

Something rattled. It sounded like sticks of chalk being shaken together. It grew louder and came from all around them.

"What the—?" Thorne gasped.

The rattling and clacking increased. Clothing ruffled and swished. The wind became icier and bore a hateful stench.

Teska put a hand on her forehead. Her face contorted in pain.

"What's wrong?" Thorne yelled.

"It's the— It's the shadow again. In my m-mind. Promising me—" *But why should she tell them? The promise was for* her, *not them. If they knew they might try to take it away, give it to someone else...* She wanted what it offered, yet she didn't. But it would be so easy to—

"Don't do it!" Thorne shouted.

Amelia screamed as the Crimson Fathers rose from the floor.

Their robes, eaten by time, hung in tatters. Cracked skulls turned on the intruders. A malevolent purple-red hue gleamed within the recesses of their empty eye sockets. Several had wispy remnants of mustaches and beards. The bones sounded like wheat beneath a millstone. Centuries of dust caught in the wind. They closed in, anxious fingers clawing at the air.

Thoughts of the Flame and its spectral promises did not matter at the moment. Teska held her sword and stood behind the altar. Thorne, at one end, gripped the Flame with both hands. Tua was in the center of the platform, and he drew his sword as well.

The skeletons raked weapons off the floor and advanced. One stayed near the footbridge like a sentinel.

Amelia screamed again. She trembled, unable to move. Two skeletons veered toward her, jaws creaking open. They trapped her against the pillar. She dropped the burlap sack with the stolen book and fumbled for her dagger.

A third skeleton, its robe nearly disintegrated, stepped in front of Amelia. She opened her mouth to scream, but it grabbed her by the throat. Her strangled cry turned into gurgling coughs. She tried to free herself, but pieces of robe just shredded away as she beat on the unfeeling limbs.

She felt herself being lifted off the floor. The Father slammed her against the pillar with a thud. She wanted to cry, to scream, but had no air. Eye sockets blazing, it pulled her back and slammed her head against the stone again. On the third hit, her vision went gray. She smelled blood. The back of her head felt warm and mushy. Pain charged through her with every heartbeat. She moaned.

The skeleton still held her aloft. The two others watched. The Father pulled Amelia close, as if looking deep into her glazed eyes. Clacking its jaw, it rammed her against the pillar a fourth time. Amelia Sloan made no more noise. Strands of hair stuck in the blood on the pillar. The skeleton dropped her in a heap, and all three turned to assist their brethren.

Skeletons four and five leapt at Tua. They were unnaturally quick. Each grabbed an arm and held tight. He felt the pressure even through his parka. A sixth with its broken jaw hanging loose clattered toward him. With an upward stroke, the weapon caught Tua in the stomach and finished near his throat. His cloak parted. His tunic fell open. A thin curve of blood marked the weapon's passage.

Tua gasped, surprised to still be alive. The sword only grazed his skin.

Broken Jaw raised the sword over its head.

Tua kicked with all his might. His foot connected with the thing's ribcage. The bones cracked, and the Father twisted to the side, dropping the sword. Tua began to kick as hard as he could at the legs of the two that held him. Another crunch and number four let go and fell to the floor. Number five still had him by the arm. Broken Jaw regained its balance and picked up the sword.

Now that his arm was free, Tua's sword whistled through the air. Number five's skull burst open in a cloud of dust and bone fragments.

Broken Jaw's sword descended upon Tua. He parried and struck back.

Skeletons seven and eight came at Teska.

"Hit these bastards hard!" she snarled. "They're just bones!"

She assumed an offensive posture and swung at them. Both parried easily. She blocked one of their swings. The other sheared a hole in the arm of her parka.

"Shit!" she yelled as she backed up against the altar. She faced the rear of the platform, her back toward the footbridge. The skeletons attacked again. This time she managed to deflect both blows but had no opportunity to follow up.

They continued to rain blows on her from two directions. She protected herself as best she could, but their relentlessness gave her no chance to retaliate. It was all she could do to keep them busy. Her arm began to tire and weaken. Breathing heavily, she did what she really did not have the energy to do.

She held her breath.

Both skeletons halted their attacks, skulls twisting on bony necks as she vanished.

Teska slipped between them unseen, but she already felt her strength flowing from her like water through a sieve. She raised her sword, arms trembling. Once behind them, she released her breath.

They were searching for their prey when she sent one of the skulls flying. She decapitated the second before it could defend itself. Both collapsed in on themselves, clattering to the floor. As she watched, the bones cracked, broke apart, and turned to dust. Only mounds of powder and rotted cloth remained.

Teska looked up. She saw Amelia crumpled at the base of the pillar. *"NO!"* she screamed.

She launched herself at the three Fathers turning away from her friend. It was only when she was halfway there that she realized her mistake. She was getting weaker by the minute. Using her gift had depleted her too much.

She could not reach Amelia. Her arms were heavy as the stone pillars. Her feet felt like anvils. Skeletons one, two and three surrounded her. They did not slow. They did not offer surrender. They continued to slash at her, blades tearing her parka to ribbons. She attempted to defend herself but collapsed, tasting blood as she hit the platform. She curled into a fetal position and waited to die.

Fucking…stupid…of me…

Number nine came directly at Thorne. Skeletons ten and eleven flanked him. He could have sworn he heard a gasp from the empty jaws as he raised the Flame in front of him. But it was probably just the swirling wind.

Fiery hatred burned deep within cobwebbed sockets.

The Flame felt good in Thorne's hands. Despite its massive size, it was as light as a dagger and felt as if it had been custom-made for him.

The skeletons on his flanks charged. The one facing him swung for his head. Its rusted blade shattered when he parried with the broadsword. Thorne stepped back, planted his feet and gauged the oncoming attacks. He dodged and spun.

He reduced skeleton number ten to moldering dust with a swing that separated backbone and sent the torso over the edge of the platform. Teeth bared, he shattered the spine of number eleven.

Skeleton number nine slashed his shoulder but failed to draw blood. Its blade spun in a dizzying whirl of silver as Thorne parried. He feinted left, spun right and brought the crimson blade up through the Father's ribcage. With a silent howl, the skeleton exploded in a cloud of dust.

Panting, he turned. Fear gripped his pounding heart.

Teska and Amelia lay on the floor. Neither moved. Blood, already coagulating in the cold chamber, pooled around Amelia's head. Blood leaked from Teska's wounds. Three Fathers, blades spattered red, looked up from Teska and started toward him.

"DAMN YOU!" Thorne screamed. He ran toward Tua and plowed into skeleton number four as it regained its feet. The impact sent it sprawling toward the footbridge. Thorne pursued and stomped the base of its spine while stabbing the blade into the skull. The skeleton disintegrated into fine white dust.

Thorne returned and stood beside Tua. They still faced Broken Jaw as well as Fathers one, two and three. The Flame was large enough to counter the blades of numbers one and two. The men grunted. Steel rasped and clanged. Because of the ease with which he wielded the Flame, in less than a minute Thorne had destroyed both skeletons. Tua exchanged thrusts and parries with Broken Jaw. The wind blew dust and cloth through the air. Bones clattered.

They did not see number one—who had attacked Amelia—and number twelve at the footbridge, creep into position.

Tua lunged at Broken Jaw. Both careened to the floor. The skeleton was quick, but Tua was quicker. He got to one knee, swung and decapitated Broken Jaw. He stood, wiping sweat and watching the bones crumble to powder. The last two skeletons came up behind Thorne.

"Behind you!" Tua yelled through the turbulent wind.

Thorne could not turn in time.

The Father's sword whistled through the air and cut into Thorne's left shoulder. He screamed in agony and dropped the Flame. His leather coat darkened with blood. He fell to one knee, sucking air through his clenched teeth.

The skeleton dropped its weapon, and its eager hand reached for the Flame. Bony digits scratched across the golden wire. It lifted the sword but stopped halfway off the ground. Through tear-filled eyes, Thorne saw the Father quivering, the sword trembling in midair. The thing threw its head back, jaw open in a silent scream. The light in its sockets pulsated a vile purple.

The wind spiraled around the platform.

Number twelve had both claws around the handle. The sword vibrated like it had struck an iron bar. The wind swirled faster, harder. Then, with a sound like stone breaking, the wind plummeted from the vaulted ceiling, plunging itself into the twelfth skeleton's chest. It lifted it off the ground. The bones shook. Needle-thin rays of purple light shot from holes in the calcium. The Father dangled in the air, unable to release the Flame, countless purple needles jutting from its form. As the last of the dark wind disappeared into the robe, the skeleton jerked one final time. It exploded in a burst of bone, cloth and light.

The Flame clanged against the stone floor, a mysterious purple aura dying around it.

The explosion knocked skeleton number one off its feet. It scrambled to stand, but Tua stood over it. He stomped it back down, pinning its shoulder blades against the platform. It clawed at him, jaw clacking its hatred. With a primal yell, Tua slashed the skull in half.

As the wind sucked up the bone dust, Tua turned and ran to Thorne.

"Are you okay, Chief-Who-Wins?" he asked.

Thorne panted through his teeth. Sweat beaded his forehead. "Forget…about me." He pointed with his good arm. "Teska. Amelia. I'll be…all right."

His shoulder burned as if molten metal had been poured in the wound. He watched Tua bend over Amelia, then Teska.

Tua stood and looked over at him. "We must go. *Now.*"

Thorne did not like the expression he saw on his friend's face.

Tunnels, Thorne thought. When had it not been tunnels? Just how long had they been burrowing through the earth?

He carried Teska in his arms and shuffled up the incline, trying to ignore the pulsating pain radiating from his shoulder. Tua was behind him holding Amelia, who still had not regained consciousness.

Thorne cradled Teska to his chest. He was unable to describe the joy and relief he felt when she had opened her eyes before they left the chamber. For a few moments, she had not responded to his attempts to rouse her. His fear of losing Teska had almost made him panic. When she finally came around, his sigh was so large and loud he almost extinguished their meager torch. He could not imagine carrying on without her.

She was awake enough to hold the torch for him. He was thankful. If she had been unconscious, they would have wandered down there forever. Thorne could not carry her and a torch at the same time. Neither man had any strength left to fight. If they ran into guards or Crusaders they were finished.

They had fled the vault into the passageway that led toward the palace. After a while, they had found a side tunnel marked *CEMETERY*. They had veered off into it, and it began to climb upward. Thorne felt as if it was taking three times as long to get back up as it had to come down.

"How're you doing?" he asked Teska. The parka hung from her in strips, and her blood had already thickened on his gloves. He no idea how many wounds she had, or even which ones were still bleeding. The skeletons had done plenty of damage, but none of it, from what he could tell, was particularly deep.

God, if you're really up there, thanks for that. Now please get us the hells out of here!

"Bastards…got me good." She looked up into his face. "Thank you." She did not wait for a reply but lay her head against his chest once more.

"Thank you for that torch," he said, sounding more upbeat than he felt. "We'd never find our way out of here without it." What he did not say was, *Of course, we wouldn't have to be doing this—we wouldn't have needed the Flame—if I hadn't compromised months of work.* He forced the thought aside. *First, we get out of here, then I can feel sorry for myself.*

They continued up the tunnel until they arrived at a wooden door with a barred window in it. There was no light on the other side. Thorne tried the latch and breathed a sigh of relief to find it unlocked. The room was identical to the safe room they had found earlier.

When was that? Yesterday? The day before? Last week? Thorne placed Teska in a chair, took the torch and lit several more on the walls.

Tua placed Amelia's limp body on top of a table.

"How is she?" Thorne asked.

Tua gently lifted her head. Tacky blood covered his gloves. Her complexion was waxy, the skin cold to the touch. He shook his head. "If we cannot find a healer soon, I do not think she will survive." The gravity of his voice matched his worried expression.

Thorne found two skins of water. He gave one to Teska; he and Tua shared the other. It tasted like honey, and ice flecks crunched between their teeth.

"Wait here," Thorne said. "I'll go up and see where we are." He exited through the door on the opposite side of the room.

As before, a metal stairway led up to a landing with a freezing stone wall on the other side. The light from his torch showed a metal handle bolted into the stone. He lay his good shoulder against the door and pushed. Pain seared his torso. After two more hard pushes, it opened enough for him to step through.

He stood at the back of a dusty, cobwebbed mausoleum. There were ten niches on the walls to his left and right, but all were empty. He crossed the floor, mounted a few stairs and found himself before an iron portcullis covered in dead vines. Cold air blew against his face. He took a moment to savor the smells of Attagon, and to appreciate their survival, before returning to the room.

"Wh-Where are we?" Teska asked.

Thorne smiled. "We're in the Forest Hills Cemetery, south of the cathedral. Do you want me to carry you?"

She shook her head. "No, but I could use a good strong arm to lean on."

They pushed the rusted portcullis open and crossed the cemetery. Halfway up the side of Outlook Mountain, torches flickered around the Palace of the Heiromonarch. Judging from the sky, Thorne estimated it was between three and four o'clock in the morning. Had it only been a little over six hours that they had spent roaming the bowels of the earth? It felt like an eternity.

"Amelia's pulse is very slow," Tua said them. "She is barely holding on."

"We all need tending to." Thorne grimaced through a flash of pain. He was beginning to weaken also. "We've got to hurry."

They could be at Takata's warehouse in less than an hour—before much of the city stirred to life. That was their first priority. The second was securing the services of a trustworthy physician as soon as possible.

"Hang on, Amelia," Tua whispered as they hurried through the predawn gloom. "Just stay with us."

22

TALNAT

WEDNESDAY, NOVEMBER 18, 999 AE

"We're home! We're home!" Cassandra shouted as the twisted metal towers that marked downtown Talnat came into view. Both children, giddy with anticipation, rode on the driver's bench, squished between Darien and Warner. Hawkes rode inside but opened the door and peered toward the city that, before the Great Cataclysm, had been called Atlanta.

"I never thought…I'd see this place again," the old man said, struggling to get his breath. He was hoarse. The illness he had contracted two weeks ago was only just leaving him. Sunken eyes and cheeks made him look almost mummified as he huddled inside several cloaks and a heavy fur.

They were down to one horse. The other had died two weeks ago before they left the mountains. It had only been a week since they had completed their trek through the southern foothills that marked the end of the Great Appian range. Much of the wagon's paint had been chewed away by the elements, and the back wheels wobbled like loose teeth. Warner knew the front axle was close to breaking, and the inside smelled of body odor and sickness.

As they rolled over the smoother road toward Talnat, Warner looked at Darien. "Where do you wanna go?"

Despite the fact that the old man had been unsure of their survival several times over the past months, he had never relinquished hope of reaching his goal. It was the sole force that drove him, the fire that refused to be extinguished.

"To my sister's house," he wheezed before coughing. It was a moist, rattling sound that made Warner uncomfortable.

"We get to see Mama!" Cassandra said, clapping her hands.

Cassidy's eyes sparkled with renewed light. The influence of the Fifth Order waned with each passing day. Children were resilient. Darien hoped that one day both would be able to forget everything that had happened to them.

"Can we sit on top, Uncle Dario?" Cassidy asked.

"Please, please, pleeeease!" Cassandra begged.

The old man smiled and nodded from inside the layers of clothing. "Just…be careful."

"We will," Cassandra promised. Her brother climbed on top of the wagon and helped her up. They moved to the middle and sat down.

"Dario," Warner said so the children would not hear, "is their mother at home? I mean, has she been released?"

"I don't know."

"Do you think it's a good idea to go back there? The Order might still be watchin' the house."

Darien sighed, the sound tired bones would make if they could. "I doubt it. They've got…too many other things…to worry about. The millennium celebration. Compliance camps and…who knows what else." Even talking burdened him to the point of exhaustion.

"Okay," Warner said. "Just rest."

The Grays and their children lived in a small house not far from Stonemason Street. A snow-covered yard separated it from the muddy road. The stone fence had collapsed in several places around the property. Behind the house was a small stable where Jairus kept his wagon, animals and tools.

Had kept, Darien thought.

The sight of the little home filled him with longing. He remembered celebrating Feast Days here whenever his scheduled allowed. Cassidy and Cassandra were born here. The last time he had seen Jairus alive had been right there in the front yard. Black shutters hid the windows, and the door was closed—not unusual in a Deiparian winter—but he saw no trace of smoke from the chimney. His heart slipped into his stomach.

Warner steered them into the stable. As Hawkes helped the children down from their perch, Warner found a feed bag that still had a little grain in it. After unhooking the skinny horse and stabling it, he attached the bag to its head. It was munching greedily before he could close the stall door.

Cassidy and Cassandra stood beside their uncle, fidgeting and eyeing the back door of their house. Suddenly, their excitement uncontainable, they bolted across the yard, snow scrunching under their feet. While the weather was nothing like what they had experienced in the mountains, Talnat still lay beneath half a foot of snow.

"Mama! Mama!" the children screamed. Cassidy tugged at the door handle, but it would not open. Cassandra pounded on the wood with her small fist.

Hawkes and Warner aided Darien through the snow. They exchanged worried glances when no response came to the commotion at the door. A surge of alarm and heartache climbed Darien's chest. He dreaded what he might—or might not—find inside. He had been trying to steel himself to the possibility that his sister might well be dead.

Hawkes pointed. "Somebody's in there. That shutter just moved."

Cassidy and Cassandra continued their assault on the door.

"I'll go check the front," Warner said. As he turned to leave, a lock was drawn back on the other side of the door. Cassandra danced from one foot to another, her smile bright enough to melt the snow. Cassidy watched the door intently.

It creaked open an inch. A face peered out, but Darien could not make out who it was. Suspicious eyes flicked back and forth at the men before dropping to the children.

Then the door swung open. Demerra Gray stood stunned and speechless.

Cassidy and Cassandra threw themselves across the threshold, shrieking with delight, and wrapped themselves around her waist.

Hawkes and Warner smiled. Darien wiped tears with the back of his hand.

Demerra knelt and pulled both children to her. Tears spilled from her eyes and coursed down her cheeks. "Oh, my darlings! My darlings!" she exclaimed, laughing and crying at the same time.

Demerra had an oval face that clearly showed the ravages of incarceration—poor nutrition, worry, terror and lack of sunlight. As she continued hugging her children, the men could see scars on her arms and ligature marks on her wrists.

Hawkes and Warner helped Darien inside and bolted the door behind them.

They stood in the kitchen. A cold fireplace with stones missing from the hearth occupied one wall. There was a table and chairs, and a rack of wooden dishes. A cupboard held dry food and cooking implements. Several thick tapers provided the only light. The faint aroma of bread and meat could be detected, like ghosts that had passed in the night. Mostly it smelled of disuse. A doorway led off into the rest of the house.

Warner eased Darien down onto a chair. He gave Hawkes a candle and told him to check out the other rooms.

Both children chattered at once, telling their mother about everything that had happened. It poured out of them—fears and sights, adventures and mountains, walking houses and Fifth Order training—and they gestured wildly as they talked over each other.

Darien smiled as his heart grew full. Against almost insurmountable odds, he had accomplished what he set out to do. This reunion was worth more than the greatest treasure anyone could ever possess. It was captivating as the sunset, overflowing his heart with joy. He imagined he could almost reach out and touch the love that filled the room.

Darien knew his sister wanted to say something to him. When the children were not vying for her attention, her eyes strayed to his wizened black face. He could tell from her expression that she was perplexed about his identity.

Hawkes returned, informing Warner that the rest of the house was clear. Most of the rooms were closed off and unused. He sat down at the table and added his gregarious smile to the joy that filled the kitchen.

After twenty minutes, Cassidy and Cassandra finally slowed down. Demerra instructed them to get a fire going. They scampered to the hearth to set about their task.

Demerra stood up and looked at Darien. Her dark-green eyes searched every line of his face. She twisted the wedding ring on her finger as she stared in disbelief. He looked like her brother, but his *age*… Trembling, she pulled up a chair and sat down across from him.

He nodded slowly. "Yes, sister. It's me."

"D-Dario? What— How?"

"It's so *good* to see you."

"But you— What happened? How is this possible?" She studied his face for answers. Darien noticed that her eyes had lost much of their sparkle, and she looked fifteen years older.

"Wh-What did they do to you…down there?" he asked. Consternation filled his voice. He traced the lines of her brow with a quivering finger.

She grabbed his hand in hers and held it to her mouth. She kissed the feather-soft skin that was too loose, too wrinkled. Fresh tears slipped down her cheeks. "How?" she kept repeating. They leaned toward each other, smiling but still absorbing the changes that had transformed them both.

With the fire started, Warner told Hawkes to see if he could find some tea. Cassandra filled a dented kettle with water from a barrel. As they made the tea, they heard Darien and Demerra weeping behind them.

An hour later, as the late afternoon shadows lengthened, the adults sat around the kitchen table with empty cups in front of them. Darien had asked the children to go to their room to clean up. Both were reluctant to leave their mother, so Hawkes said he would sit in the doorway. That way the children could see him when they looked out of their room. This satisfied them, although from time to time, Cassandra came to the doorway. Hawkes tousled her wiry black hair as she watched her mother.

Darien told the story of his bargain with the witch, Rebekkah Barlowe. He explained the truth about how Jairus had died. The revelation brought more tears, but then Demerra set her mouth in a hard line. Her eyes narrowed. Darien knew from childhood what that determined, angry look meant. She was furious and ready to take on the world.

The men told her about the rank pins, Last Chapel and the Crusaders. They told her about their experiences in the compliance camp and what had happened to the children. Her eyes blazed with furor, and she scratched at the tabletop with her fingernails.

Demerra was two years younger than her brother—or at least had been before he consulted with Rebekkah Barlowe. At thirty-eight, she was thinner than she should have been due to her incarceration. She had the same nose as Darien, wide with flared nostrils. Her hair was midnight black and cut short.

"Courtesy of the Southlake compliance camp," she spat as she ruffled her hair with her hand.

"They put you in one, too?" Hawkes asked.

She nodded. "They kept me in the Talnat dungeon for—I don't know—weeks. Then all of a sudden, they told me the charge of witchcraft had been dropped. After that, a bunch of us were transferred for reeducation." She said the last word with wicked derision.

"Then you heard the same madness we did," Darien said.

"How'd you get out?" Warner asked.

She offered a snide grin. "They let me go. Said I'd done well in the program, that I was ready to be an obedient, contributing member of Church and society again. Of course, I faked it. I told 'em what they wanted to hear. I was desperate to see my kids again." She paused. "That's why it took so long for me to open the door. I thought you might've been familiars, or Churchmen or those damned Crusaders come to take me back. Tell me something. Why'd the Church let the kids go? You said there was a whole caravan of 'em."

Darien struggled to catch his breath, so Hawkes answered. "From what we gathered from Cassidy and Cassandra, any of the children in the program who caught on and accepted the propaganda were being sent back to their homes."

"That doesn't sound like the Fifth Order to me," Demerra said, arching an eyebrow.

"It is," Darien managed to say. "It's all…part of their plan."

"The kids 're bein' sent back home to spy on their families. The Order's turned them into little familiars," Warner said.

Hawkes nodded. "They've been instructed to report anything they see or hear that goes against the Fifth Order."

Demerra's mouth remained tight, the lines at the edges more pronounced. "Those devious bastards. They're trying to turn our own kids against us!"

"Is my old pipe still here?" Darien asked as if he hadn't been listening. "I'd love a smoke."

She shook her head. "Once I was arrested, the Church came in and confiscated everything. You know how they do. It's just more money and goods for their coffers." There was no masking the scorn in her voice or on her face.

"Just as well, then," he answered. "It's past time I quit anyway." Immediately, his face grew stern. "So, you're not immune? To the effects of the rank pins, I mean?"

Demerra got up and poured the remainder of the tea into their cups. She looked up to see Cassidy and Cassandra standing beside Hawkes. When she smiled at them, they turned and went back to their room.

"I'm not," she replied as she sat back down.

"The kids ain't, either," Warner said. "They told us the Fifth Order had them do a bunch of tests related to the pins."

Demerra sipped her tea. "How do they know my kids aren't immune?"

Darien patted her hand. "The same way we know you're not immune. You're still alive."

She stared at him over the rim of her cup, eyebrows falling, the lines of her forehead deepening. "What?"

"When the Fifth Order identifies someone with a natural immunity to the pins…they're executed. They're trying to eradicate…every form of potential resistance."

Warner nodded. "If you're caught and they find out you've got that immunity, that's it," Warner reaffirmed quietly.

Darien cleared his throat. "Jairus was immune. That's why they wanted to find out about you and the children."

Demerra's eyes smoldered. "You mentioned resistance to the pins," she said to Darien. "I know there's an underground resistance against the Fifth Order. I know you're all part of it. I want in. I want to help."

Now it was Darien's turn to be surprised. "Excuse me?"

She looked toward the fire for a moment and seemed lost in the dancing flames. A tear crept from the corner of her eye. When she turned to face the men, her voice quivered, but her face was hard as iron.

"I hate them. For what they did to Jairus. For what they did to my kids. For what they did to me." She bit off each word as if tearing into a piece of meat. Her jaw worked from side to side in frustration. "I want to kill 'em. They have to *pay* for what they've done." She could not stop the tears.

Darien nodded. "I understand, Dee—I really do. We *all* do. But you…you have to take care of them." He indicated the doorway behind Hawkes.

"I-I know," she said in a tight, seething tone. She rapped her teacup on the table. It began as a soft tapping but escalated with each hit. Finally, she slammed it against the tabletop, and with a strangled cry of rage and frustration and pain, leapt up and hurled the cup into the fire. It shattered as it struck the logs. She began to weep and slumped back down in the chair. "I-I know," she said. "But I'm *so* angry—so full of hurt. I hate 'em so much."

Darien pushed himself up from the table and tottered behind her chair. He put his arthritic hands on her shoulders. He did not say anything, merely rubbed her shoulders until her sobs became hiccupping gasps of air. Cassidy and Cassandra came in. They stood on either side of her. Cassidy held her hand. Cassandra laid her head in her mother's lap.

Demerra eased the door to the children's room closed. She stood for a moment with her hand flat against the wood, as if touching them through its grainy surface. Turning, she put the candle on a small table beside the door and returned to the kitchen.

"What're you going to do now?" she asked the three men.

"To be honest, ma'am, we ain't really sure," Warner said.

"Solomon, I told you to quit calling me ma'am." She grinned at him. "I'm not *that* much older than you."

"We need to…lay low for a while," Darien told her, still short of breath. "If the Church or the Fifth Order finds us…they'll kill us outright. We're still wanted traitors and heretics. Plus, we don't know where…the rest of our friends are. Malachi and Teska and Thurl…went into the Tex'ahn lands." His voice dropped. "Who knows if they're even still alive?"

"But don't worry," Hawkes said. "We won't be presuming on you. The Fifth Order's already keeping their eye on you. We're not going to be the reason you get in trouble."

Darien nodded. "We'll find somewhere else. Someplace safe…and out of the way. We've put you at great risk…just by coming here." He was struggling to get a deep lungful of air.

"You brought my kids back to me," she said. "That means more to me than anything. Whatever I've got, you've got."

"I understand. And we may have to…take you up on that sometime. But for the present…we need to stay out of sight."

Demerra studied him. He knew what she saw. His once six-foot frame was now stooped, shoulder blades sticking out, arms thin as broom handles. His hands trembled constantly. And his breathing seemed to grow raspier by the hour.

Looking into her eyes, Darien smiled. Nearly half of his teeth were gone. The lines on his face looked deep enough to bury a treasure. Wrapped in cloaks and the heavy fur, he seemed like a miniature doll, fragile and precious.

"St-Stop worrying about me," he chided. "You're…just like mother was. I'll be fine. I just… I just need some rest." But he did not sound convincing.

She returned his smile. But when he looked away, she noticed Hawkes and Warner watching her. Warner shook his head, confirming what she already knew but did not want to accept.

Her brother was not going to live much longer.

23
DEFIANCE

THURSDAY, NOVEMBER 19, 999 AE

On Wednesday, November 4th—the day the Orestdale compliance camp opened outside Rimlingham—Malachi Thorne had met with the key leaders of the Attagon resistance. Ryoma Takata had made all the arrangements through his network of business contacts.

Thorne had been skeptical of the meeting. While he trusted Takata, he had not been as sure about the other seven men around the table. Any one of them could be a spy for the Fifth Order, and by extension, the Crimson Fathers.

He had known two of them by name and title, and another two by association. The rest had been new to him. Throughout the meeting, he had been overly cautious with what he said, gauging reactions and body language, assessing tones of voice and trying his best to uncover any deception or mixed motives. They could not afford another mistake like Blackscar.

The men who had shared the cold basement that evening listened to Thorne's story. And they shared theirs. But the group of men and Thorne were like two fighters testing one another's defenses. The guardedness had been thick. Everyone knew things lay on a razor's edge.

They had all heard about what happened to Cabbot, as well as Thorne's change of allegiance. Now that Traugott was discredited and dead, he had become the Church's number one target. Witchfinders, constables and Crusaders searched for him with the same zealousness that he had once invested in capturing Traugott.

The meeting had been brief, just an opportunity to get to know each other. Thorne had told them he wanted to call a special meeting of the key leaders, their closest associates and a select handful of people who were willing to see their cause through to the end. He had stressed the necessity of vetting these people with extreme care and patience. One slipup would end everything for all of them. With a little bit of convincing, Thorne had promised them something that would not only be worth their time—it would change the balance of power decisively. Intrigued, the seven men had melted into the darkness to make plans for this night.

Snow continued to fall with no sign of letting up. Several inches had already accumulated. It would make it harder for the resistance members to get here, but it would also hinder anyone out searching for them.

Here was the wine cellar of The Olde City Tavern, a well-to-do establishment near the southern edge of the business district with a broad clientele and excellent food, drink and accommodations. Someone suggested the meeting take place at The Four-Legged Fish, but Thorne vetoed that. The Fish offered Church-sponsored gambling, and the last thing he wanted was to be in close proximity to Church officials coming to collect their cut.

The Olde City Tavern occupied part of a pre-Cataclysm building that had once sported the words *Choo Choo* on its signage. Everyone assumed it had been a place to eat, owned by someone who could not spell. Much of the original structure no longer existed, its wood, stone or steel cannibalized for other buildings, but the part with the tavern had been refurbished. It did not look like much from the outside—a dull brown façade with a couple of small, lead-paned windows and a blue door displaying the name. But inside was a cozy, clean establishment that was decorated with artifacts from before the Great Cataclysm.

Tables and chairs covered the main floor. Each table had its own oil lamp that made for cozy dining. A long bar, with access to the kitchen behind it, ran along one wall. A hearty fireplace did the same on the other side. Two flights of wooden stairs led up to the second floor sleeping accommodations.

Odd bits of ancient debris decorated the walls of the common room. There were peculiar sigils with strange words like *Ford* and *Chevy* on them. Bits of rusted, pockmarked signage touted destinations such as *Aquarium*, *Market Street*, *I-24*, *Hospital*, *Riverfront* and *Museum*. There were odd-shaped blades and knives, painted bricks, a metal pole with something called a "meter" on top and even a contraption that the Storicos called a "bi-cycle."

The aroma of seasoned beef, piping hot bread and seasonal vegetables filled the air. A fire burned strong and cheerful beneath a mantle that displayed more curios such as a stuffed cat, a glass bottle and an unknown metal device that flipped open and had a series of buttons on one side and a busted screen on the other.

In the basement, Thorne cupped his hands and blew into them. Everyone stared at him. Waiting. He counted fourteen people, not including himself,

Tua'Ahtaki or Takata. The Co'manche sat on a sack of potatoes to Thorne's right. Takata fidgeted with his jewelry and talked in hushed whispers to two men. A long piece of oilcloth lay at Tua's feet.

One wall of the basement was given over to ale barrels laying on their sides like children in a bed. The other wall was a continuous shelf of bottles, flagons and casks of different sizes, in addition to the well-stocked wine racks. There were bags of flour and potatoes, baskets of dried herbs, pouches with mushrooms and roots, as well as a number of tools and kitchen utensils. There were no windows, and the only door led up to the pantry and into the kitchen. They had all arrived through the rear door and hurried through the kitchen, practically empty since the weather made for a slow night.

The owner of the tavern was Gwilym Scovell, a middle-aged man with black eyebrows, beard and mustache, all so thick it looked as if half his face wore a fur. He was bald except for a ring of black hair across the back of his head from ear to ear. He sat on an empty cask near the bottom of the stairs, the key to the basement around his neck.

Thorne stood, the top of his head almost brushing the centuries-old timber beams. He cleared his throat. The room fell silent.

"Thank you for coming tonight," he said in a low voice. "Each time we gather, it grows riskier, and we're running out of time. We have to strike soon."

There were several "ayes" throughout the cellar. A few men started peddling their favored avenues of resistance. Thorne held up his hands for silence.

"We have to be *smart*. Smarter than the Fifth Order. Word on the street is that they're increasing patrols and conducting more searches. They're expecting trouble. We need to assume that all the familiars have been paid extra to report anything unusual. We need to come up with the best approach, the best targets, the best plan. If we just go off doing our own thing, we'll be picked off like crippled ducks on a pond."

"Whatta you suggest?" a man with graying hair and sunken cheeks asked.

"I'd like to hear everyone's ideas. Let's put them all out there so everyone has a chance to be heard. Then we can sort through them and see what we can make work the best."

Nodded heads and murmured acknowledgments circled the cellar.

Scovell had excused himself at nine o'clock to go up and close his establishment. He returned an hour later to small clusters of people and hushed conversations. He joined Thorne's group and got caught up on what was happening.

They had taken five ideas with the greatest chance of success, and Thorne had assigned one to each group. They were tasked with developing the idea further and coming up with specific details as to how it would be carried out.

At a quarter to eleven, everyone took a break. Scovell provided liquid refreshment, and genial conversation flowed. When Thorne called them back together, the groups presented their ideas. Much discussion followed on the pros and cons of each plan. With Takata stretched out atop three ale kegs and snoring, the men and women debated. They played Archfiend's advocate and evaluated potential outcomes.

By then Thorne guessed it was nearly one in the morning. His eyes burned, and his throat, despite the excellent wine, felt like cracked plaster due to all the talking. But a boiling excitement filled him and made his heart beat faster.

We're close, he told himself. *If we can pull this off, we'll make a statement the people can't ignore. We'll send a message to the Fifth Order that true Deiparians won't sit still while they ruin our lives.*

"We need a symbol," a young woman of perhaps twenty-five said. She had braided brunette hair, hard green eyes, and carried herself like someone on a mission. "Something we can paint on walls or put on a banner. Something distinctive."

She reminded Thorne of Teska, and he wondered how her Communion meeting had gone tonight. He grinned at the young woman and nodded his head.

"I was thinking the same thing." He had already thought of a symbol weeks ago. But it needed to come from among the resistance themselves. They had to own it, believe in it. Stake their lives on it. He knew if it was *his* idea, it was less likely to find traction. The resistance needed something that was organic, that sprang up from the hearts and passion of the people.

But it never hurt to give things a little nudge.

Tua handed him the oilcloth.

"I'd like to offer this as our symbol." He pulled the cloth off, revealing the Flame. In the lamplight it gleamed yellow and crimson. The engraved flames along the blade seemed to flicker. Thorne grasped the hilt in both hands and held it in front of him.

"Wh-What is that?" someone asked, nearly breathless.

"Is that what I think it is?" an incredulous voice rang out.

Everyone talked at once as they stared at the massive weapon.

Thorne smiled. "This, my friends, is Imperator's Flame."

"I knew it!" the incredulous voice shouted. "I've heard stuff—rumors. But I didn't think it really existed."

"So it's a sword. Why's it all red?"

"Pipe down 'un let Mal'chi talk."

Thorne calmed them before sitting down and placing the Flame across his knees. It felt warm through his breeches even though the blade should've been freezing cold.

He told them about the original Crimson Fathers and the Church's dominion and control through the rank pins. He told them about Okafo the Dark's betrayal of the Fathers and their execution by this blade. Everyone listened intently to the history lesson they had never heard before. Thorne swallowed some wine to lubricate his throat. It did not help much.

"I have it on good authority"—*thank you, Thurl,* he thought—"that this weapon can destroy the Crimson Fathers again. And one way or another, I'm going to prove it. I think it would make a suitable symbol for the resistance."

Before he finished speaking, there were yelps of approval. The young woman who had brought the subject up took a small round container from her pocket. She opened it and rubbed her finger around the inside. It was some sort of pigment, perhaps meant for the lips. She reached over to the stone wall behind her and drew a stylized reproduction of the Flame in red. When she turned back around, everyone was smiling.

One by one, they took turns holding and admiring the sword before they left for the night. Only when they returned it to Thorne did one of the men say, "Glad I got gloves on. That hannel's cold."

"Cold?" Thorne asked.

"Yeah. It's metal. We're in a cellar. An' it's wintertime. Damn thing's cold!"

Thorne said nothing else. But after everyone had departed, he pulled off his gloves and held the hilt with both hands again.

It was warm, like a fireplace that had reached the exact comfortable temperature. He touched the blade and found it the same. He shook his head and covered it with the oilcloth. Putting his gloves on, he and Tua vanished into the darkness, snow crunching under their feet.

The following day—Friday, November 20th—would be remembered as the first act of resistance against the Fifth Order. The freedom fighters wore gray garments, cloaks and hats. They hid their faces behind red handkerchiefs tied around their heads.

A contingent led by a man named Diego Barrios ambushed a Crusader, two constables and two deputies at a place called Ros'land, near the River Tense. They painted the sword insignia on the side of a boat and across the backs of the five corpses before disappearing into the stunned crowd of fishmongers and fishermen, their flight scattering cats and sending panicked birds aloft.

On Saturday, November 21st, the early morning milkmaids, tradesmen and laborers discovered one side of the Avenue of the Lord barricaded by stone blocks. In places, the barricade rose as high as five feet. Scrawled between images of the red sword were the words:

> FREEDOM FROM THE 5TH ORDER
> FREEDOM FROM THE CHURCH
> FREEDOM FOR ALL

Later that evening, a Witchfinder was found dead in a wooden cart, the symbol painted on his face.

On Sunday—Worship Day—congregants arrived at the Cathedral of the Heiromonarch to find every door painted red and the word *FREEDOM* written across them in black. Worshipers did not get to see the true message, however. It had been removed by Church officials long before the doors opened. Aghast at the blasphemy, they'd taken the bodies of a Witchfinder and two Crusaders, red sword drawn up their backs, into the crypt. They sent every Novitiate they had in search of the heads.

Monday, November 23rd, found twelve resistance members charging through the business district on horses covered with red pigment. Effigies of the Crimson Fathers—straw mannequins with red cloaks and black numeral ranging from one to twelve painted on each—were dragged behind. When the group reached a pre-arranged intersection, the riders dismounted. They tossed the effigies in a pile and lit it on fire before riding off with cries of "Freedom!" and "Rise up!" filling the air. They grinned as applause followed them.

Late that night, Thorne led a group to the Northgate compliance camp a few miles north of the city. Some of the men set fire to the forest around the camp, drawing Crusaders and Churchmen out to assess the danger. They were ambushed and killed, and the freedom fighters loaded the bodies onto a sled to take back.

Thorne took some men, entered the camp and set fire to several buildings. In the chaos, they managed to free two dozen prisoners, who wept as they were being led out. Thorne drew the symbol on a wall before joining his compatriots. In the early hours of dawn, Thorne led his group to the middle of the bridge that spanned the Tense. All the sentries were huddled around fires inside their guard huts.

It was a massive risk. If any alarms were raised, both ends of the bridge would be blocked. Their only means of escape would be a jump into the river. Whoever might survive the fall would freeze to death in the black water before they could reach either shore.

As quietly as they could in snow packed hard by countless feet, hooves and wheels, they pulled the bodies from Northgate behind them. They could not risk bringing horses. Working swiftly because of the risk and the bitter temperature, they tied ropes to the railings and lowered the bodies down.

The next morning, every street and mart, alley and office, buzzed with news of the three Crusaders and five Churchmen swinging beneath the bridge, red swords daubed on their chests.

24
KNOWLEDGE

TUESDAY, NOVEMBER 24, 999 AE

Several miles southeast of Attagon, Winpeskah Lake lay beneath a glistening sheet of ice. Lingering around its perimeter were the remnants of what had once been a place of fun and recreation. The Storicos said it had once been called a "park of amusement." A few bits of rusted metal remained here and there. Sections of rail and wood in a wavy up-and-down pattern—like small hills that stretched for hundreds of yards—remained among the foliage that had grown up among it.

One building stood among the debris at the western end of the lake, the final soldier yet to fall in defeat. Inside, the members of the Enodia Communion gathered, overwhelmed by awe and a terror colder than the lake's surface. The Witch of Tears, the Witch of Sighs and the Witch of Darkness had arrived in their midst.

Twenty-two women of differing ages knelt, elbows at their sides, forearms extended, palms up. Everyone kept their eyes on the floor as they completed the invitation ritual, voices dying away like blossoms in frost.

The temperature inside the building had plummeted, and the light from the wall torches assumed a crystalline, sapphire color. The women strained to see one another through an aurora of wavering shadows. But they had no problem seeing the Three-Who-Are-One.

The Three Witches—manifestations of Hecate, whom they worshiped and served—ruled the Enodia Communion. Maiden Mallumo, the Witch of Darkness, radiated imperial beauty from behind three veils that rippled in an unfelt breeze. Dressed in a green gown, she wore a silver, moon-shaped tiara. Skin like alabaster bore no mole or freckle, blemish or wrinkle. She was youngest of the three and known by Communion and Church alike as the most sadistic.

"At ease, Daughters of the Moon," Mother Depresja said. "This is an informal gathering." The Witch of Sighs stood with oily, plump hands planted on wide hips. A stained gray smock, such as a cleaning woman might wear, covered her from neck to ankles.

The women lowered their arms, stretched, rubbed their hands together for warmth. Most stood. A few continued to kneel.

An elderly woman named Eugenia Lusk massaged her knees. She had thin, silver hair that fell below her shoulders. Sunken cheeks and a pronounced chin made it seem as if her flesh retreated from the bone. Set within the wrinkled skin were blue eyes that had lost some of their luster but none of their potency. She pulled out a pipe and lit it.

Teska took in everything. She had never seen the Matriarch or Mother and could have easily gone the rest of her days without such an opportunity. She wished that Amelia could be here to see all this, but the young woman's condition remained critical.

Matriarch Trahnen, the Witch of Tears, eldest of the three, was a crone of unknown age. Her saggy, blackened skin appeared to have been roasted in a fire. Pure white hair, thin as a drunkard's promise, hung lusterless beneath the diadem encircling her age-spotted brow. Her dark blue garment was shabby in comparison to the others and covered by patches.

Lusk addressed the Three-Who-Are-One in a raspy but reverent tone. "Praise the Three!" she declared. "Blessed be the Daughters of Hecate." She drew on her pipe, cheeks sinking even deeper into her skull, and exhaled. The smoke was indistinguishable from her breath as it hit the air. "We are assembled as you commanded."

The Mother smiled, but it was stern and lacked warmth. Her stomach draped over the belt she wore, and pendulous breasts sagged. Her sole accessory was a large key on a chain around her fatted neck. "You know the things of recent days here in Attagon and throughout the realm. We have been in consultation and have news to share," she said.

"You know what happened in Last Chapel," the Matriarch growled. Her face was narrow, punctuated by a hairy mole on one cheek and creviced with wrinkles. She glared at Teska, whose stomach turned to ice before dropping out of her body. She lowered her head.

The Matriarch smacked her gums. "The greater part of our magic was stolen from us. Over the last several months, we have remained out of sight, conserving what power was left. It is imperative that we regain what was lost."

"In light of that loss," the Maiden continued, her voice like honey-coated arsenic, "and due to the recent activities of the freedom movement here in the city, you are reminded to continue conserving your power. No magic is to be used without consulting us. Let the resistance do all the work." She toyed with a silver moon necklace that lay between her breasts.

"We shall wait," the Mother added, dusting her hands off as if that were the end of it.

Even though Teska had only just put her stomach back where it belonged, she raised her head. Looking at the Three, enveloped in the halo of misty, blueish light, made her dizzy. She did not want to do this but had told the others she would.

Swallowing the stone in her throat, she said, "Hallowed be the Three. I would ask—" She hesitated, unsure of herself or her words. It infuriated her to feel this way. She licked her lips and tried again. "I—we were wondering—"

"Here she goes agin'," an elderly black woman named Emmaline said. She crossed her arms and rolled her eyes.

Several voices agreed with her.

Teska clamped her teeth together. This had been going on for weeks. Every gathering now was the same. She resented it. She also resented the Maiden for agreeing with them. When she spoke again, her voice had found renewed courage, and she shot Emmaline a withering glare.

"As I was saying, we believe our gifts and skills can aid the resistance. They work for the same goal we do."

The elderly women cackled. Younger women voiced their support of Teska.

"I would not say our goals are the same," the Mother corrected. "We both seek freedom to live and worship as we choose. But there the similarities end. Much of the resistance still wants the Church to rule Deiparia. They fight to overthrow the Fifth Order but not the way of life they have always known."

"There are some who seek more than that," Teska said. "They want true freedom. For everyone."

Once more the older women laughed, hacking sounds like a hedge being pruned.

Teska stuck out her chin. "The Nahoru'brexia believe that together we can eliminate the Fifth Order."

Four women moved to stand around Teska. All nodded in agreement.

Lusk sneered and rapped the bowl of her pipe against the wall to call for silence. "Wise and Divine Three," she croaked, "these girls know not of what they speak. They are guided by their passions, untrained in the ways of the Communion—"

"Bullshit!" someone yelled.

The meeting disintegrated into shouts and confusion. The Matriarch, Mother and Maiden waited, allowing the conflict to rage about them like a stormy sea. Finally, the Matriarch spat and ordered them all to shut up.

Teska and the younger women stood to one side. The middle-aged and older women clumped together opposite them.

"It is as we foresaw," the Maiden whispered to Mother and Matriarch.

"Yet we did not foresee it this *soon*," the Mother replied. Concern tinged her words.

"We know of your division," the Matriarch snapped. She moved haltingly, but the vast array of keys that hung from her belt made no sound. "You believe we should aid our enemy, use what power we have in the fight against the Fifth Order and the Church." She turned from Teska's group to the other. "And you believe we should remain out of sight. Stay quiet. Regroup and return at a later date."

"We can lead," Auria said, pushing a strand of blonde hair behind her ear. She stood shoulder to shoulder with Teska. "We're learning and growing every day. Give us a chance."

Once again, the elderly brexia chuckled in disbelief.

"Isn't this what you've been preparing us for?" Teska asked.

Beatrice, a middle-aged woman with frizzy hair and missing teeth scoffed. "Hecate's blood! Are we supposed to follow *them* now? They know nothing of our ways."

"Piss off, Beatrice!" a woman behind Teska shouted.

The room fell into shouts and curses once more.

"Enough!" the Maiden yelled. Hair the color of a raven's wing and thick as the reaches of space swung as she shook her head. Her tone dripped callousness. Her eyes blazed behind the veils.

"They's pushin' us out!" an old grandmother named Isidore said as she adjusted her spectacles. "Wantin' it all fer themselves."

"We've been loyal!" another added.

"They can't jus' come in an' take over!"

Lusk put her pipe away. "They need us. Won't admit it, but they need us."

"What we need is to stop cowering!" Auria shouted. "Let's take the fight to them."

The Matriarch raised a wizened hand, long cracked nails clawing at the air. "Still your clucking tongues before I remove them!" The temperature in the room grew colder. Ice crystals began to form on noses, cheeks, ears.

"Our decision is final," the Mother said. "Use no magic without our approval. The time of the Nahoru'brexia is coming—but it is not now. You will work as one or else you shall be cast out. We will let the resistance be the focus of the Church's wrath."

Well, now's the time, Teska thought.

"Malachi has the Flame," she said bluntly, her voice strong as she played her trump card.

For the first time that any of the witches knew, the Three-Who-Are-One looked surprised. It was fleeting, but for a second it had been there. Lusk narrowed her eyes as she stared at the trio.

Gotcha! Teska thought.

The Three Witches turned toward one another, and the light around them pulsated. Their forms became vague, as if viewed through smoky air.

"What're you talking about?" Lusk demanded as she hobbled toward Teska.

She told them about the weapon. Where they had found it. The original Crimson Fathers.

"So that's what those markings are everywhere," one middle-aged woman said to another.

The Three-Who-Are-One became clearer, but only in the way someone appears through a rainy window. Teska told them about the burial vault beneath Attagon and the doors which had tried to draw her in.

"Strong magic," the Mother said. "Enchanted to protect against magical attacks. And which also obscured the vault from our view."

"When I touched the sword," Teska said, "it felt like something was trying to…push itself inside me. Like it wanted me." She paused and rubbed her arms. *And didn't I want it, too?* "It felt…ancient. And powerful. Evil."

"We will consider this," the Matriarch said. She turned to the Mother and Maiden. "We need to go."

They nodded.

"M-Matriarch?" The old voice belonged to Sylvaine Claremonde.

"Speak, my Child."

"I—that is, many of us"—she gestured to include all the women in the room—"have lost kids 'n' grandkids to the Fifth Order. They're not in no compliance camps. They've been taken…*somewhere*. The Church tells our families nothing 'cept that the young ones 're being taken care of and that they're receiving a special education. Some families have even gotten paid by the Church for the absence of their kids. But we don't know where they are." Her voice cracked. "Why haven't they come back? Do you know? Can you tell us anything?" Her eyes pleaded with the Three Witches.

"We do not have long," the Matriarch said to Mother and Maiden. They nodded.

"Still, they should know," the Mother replied. She sighed, an almost human sound. "The Crimson Fathers have created the Crusaders as a vanguard for the Fifth Order. You have no doubt noticed how all the Crusaders look very much alike. That is because they are not human—not fully human anyway.

"They are a magical-biological construct. Simulacrums. Grown in specifically designed chambers. The Fathers use dead bodies as starting material and then augment that with flesh and incantations. In order to animate them, the essence of a living being—a soul—is required. The best soul is that of a child."

Several of the women started crying. Others gathered around to console them.

Sylvaine wiped her eyes. "Wh-What happens if a Crusader—"

"If one dies?" the Matriarch asked.

The Mother shook her head. Greasy strands of hair hung loose from her bun. "When a Crusader dies, the soul dies as well." She paused. "To kill a Crusader is to kill a child."

The crying grew louder.

"Is the reverse true?" Emmaline asked. "If you free a child, does the Crusader die?"

"Naturally," the Maiden replied.

Teska put her hands on her hips. "Then we know what we need to do. We've got to find out where the children are kept and set them free."

"Most of them are being held in the Citadel of the Crimson Fathers," the Mother said. "Some are in the Palace of the Heiromonarch. Others are kept in Fifth Order strongholds across the realm."

"H-How do we save them all?" Isidore asked, her eyes brimming with tears.

"Time is of the essence," the Matriarch said in her guttural tone. "The Fifth Order is building an army of Crusaders."

"An army! What for?" a grandmother with a kerchief on her head pleaded.

"We do not know."

Once more, the room broke into a babble of conversation, but this time there was no acrimony, no accusations, no battle lines of old guard versus new. All were united in the maternal drive to rescue their children and obliterate the Crimson Fathers. But that didn't stop Teska from wondering why the Three knew nothing of the Flame or the army.

Late that night, just as she was climbing into Thorne's makeshift bed in the basement of the warehouse, a hiss caught her ear. It was all but inaudible to anyone except her. She had come to recognize the Maiden's call.

Upstairs, a voice echoed in her head.

A single candle in hand, Teska crept up the stairs, unlocked the door and walked into the warehouse. After so many weeks, her nose had become accustomed to the heady barrage of oils. Checking to make sure none of Takata's employees remained, Teska settled into a niche where she was surrounded by wooden cases. She assumed the supplication pose and waited.

The Maiden's appearance was always preceded by the arrival of serpents, her totem. When Teska heard no slithering or hissing, nor smelled any reptilian stench, she opened her eyes. There would be no manifestation.

Teska, the Maiden's voice spoke in her mind.

She tried to figure out what it sounded like but couldn't hold onto it long enough to make any connection.

My sisters and I have knowledge of the Flame.

"What is it?" she asked. She knew she could just think it, but hearing her own voice kept her grounded.

The Flame is a powerful weapon. This you know. What you do not know is the source of that power. The Flame is a reservoir.

"A reservoir?"

A wineskin holds wine. The Flame holds energy. Magical energy. As you said, it is ancient and evil. What you felt was the magical energy of the original Crimson Fathers. When they were struck down, their magic and essences were taken into the weapon and stored there.

Teska's mind raced. Where did these new Crimson Fathers get their magic if the old was still in the sword? Who resurrected them? And why? She wanted to ask all the questions but only ended up saying, "What I felt—the sense of something trying to get inside me—"

That was the magic of the Fathers. It has been stored in the weapon for centuries and is looking for a suitable receptacle. It sensed your connection to the magical realm and wanted you to open yourself and accept it. It is possible that the Flame may be… sentient.

"Could I have done that—taken the Fathers' magic into myself?"

Yes, but it would have killed you. This is dark and sinister magic. It predates the Communion. It cannot be held or contained by a single person. It would have torn you apart. That's why there were twelve Fathers—to disperse power of that magnitude among many.

"But Malachi—"

He has no connection to the magical realm. It cannot harm him. But it is *designed for one of his rank.*

Teska scowled. "His rank? He doesn't have any rank."

He was—and in many ways remains—a Witchfinder Imperator. The sword is called Imperator's Flame. Anyone can hold or wield it. But when one of such rank possess it, the weapon becomes easier to use. It lightens itself so the user is more agile in combat.

"I wonder if Malachi knows that?" she asked herself.

If not, he will soon learn.

There was a short pause.

We have a task for you. It is imperative that we possess the Flame. You are ordered to bring it to us. Only we can harness the power contained therein. We must have it before the Crimson Fathers realize it has been awakened. With such energy, we can rebuild the Communion in no time.

"Will you be able to take that power in?"

We are the Three-Who-Are-One—the Daughters of Hecate—the Witches of Tears, Sighs and Darkness. What it took twelve Crimson Fathers to do, we can do with only three.

Teska thought about the Flame, hanging from the wall beside their bed downstairs, and about what it meant to the resistance. And Malachi could certainly use it to its fullest advantage.

But steal it from him? she wondered. *I can't do that.*

"Could he— Is there a way we could just…borrow it for a while? Just until you can recover the magic?"

Your intentions betray you, Child. Be careful. Your feelings for this man grow stronger. They threaten your usefulness to us. We know not how long it will take to receive and distribute the power. We are the Three-Who-Are-One. We do not bargain. We demand the Flame. Bring it to us.

Teska tried to swallow, but her mouth was dry. Her thoughts spiraled out of control as her heart beat faster. *It promised me the power. It's mine! They have no right to take it. It wants* me.

Acknowledge our command.

She nodded and did her best to speak. "I-I acknowledge. It shall be as the Witch of Darkness commands." There was little strength behind the words. But within her heart, a tremendous battle began to rage that rivaled the conflict in her mind. She put her hand on her chest as if such a simple gesture could bring peace.

I am not unsympathetic to your plight. But the Communion comes first. You know this. You have vowed yourself to it. Bring us the Flame. We must have that power!

Although there were no further echoes in her mind, Teska remained seated in the cul-de-sac of crates, elbows on her knees, head in her hands.

25
PROPOSAL

FRIDAY, NOVEMBER 27, 999 AE

Teska crossed her arms and glared at Thorne as he walked toward her. His strides were purposeful and heavy. Anger pinched his face. "What?" he asked.

"Care to tell me what's going on?" she said, frustration coloring her words.

He sighed and looked away, jaw muscles tightening. He walked several paces past her, hands clasped behind his back, shoulders slumped.

The huddle of resistance fighters on the other side of the room continued to talk among themselves. They were animated about something and kept looking in Thorne's direction.

Teska went over to him and noticed his clenched fists.

"What's wrong?" she asked, less abrasive this time.

"Damn it," he said.

Teska waited. She had learned not to push him when he was awaiting the outcome of something over which he had little or no control.

Finally, he said, "I told them my proposal. But they're skeptical. They're going to *think about it*."

"Maybe if you told me the damned proposal—"

His chuckle held no humor. "Oh, it isn't the proposal as much as it is me. They're skeptical of *me*."

Teska pursed her lips. "Of you?"

He nodded. "They all know about Blackscar. They know I let one of the Fathers infiltrate all those resistance meetings. It's my fault they were all captured."

"It wasn't your fault. We've been through this."

Thorne sighed again. "I know. But *they* don't see it that way."

"But you've been risking your life with them—*for them*—ever since you found the sword. Why bring this up now?" She frowned at the group of men.

Thorne shrugged. "Maybe because I told them my idea. Now they're not sure just whose side I'm on."

She looked up into his eyes and put a hand on his arm. "Hey, you and I are in this together. Stop treating me like an outsider. Why haven't you told me anything?"

"Because it…it involves the Communion. I didn't want to say anything to you until I had the resistance on board. I didn't want them—"

"You didn't trust me. That's it, isn't it?" She narrowed her eyes and pulled her hand away.

"Tes, no, it's not that," he said. He tried to put his hands on her shoulders, but she resisted. "You know I trust you. It's just the Communion I'm not sure about."

"Meaning what?" she demanded, her voice rising.

His tone became clipped, each word bitten off into angry morsels. "Meaning I didn't know if your Maiden, or any of the other brexia, could read your mind! Or listen in on our conversations! I couldn't risk it."

Teska fumed. "We don't read each other's minds!"

"I don't know that!"

"You would if you fucking talked to me! Am I a liar now, too?"

Thorne pinched the bridge of his nose. His head ached as if a miniature blacksmith was using his temples to shape iron. He exhaled long and hard. "Of course not."

"Then tell me what you're up to! I have a right to know."

She was right, of course. And he trusted her with his life. But a niggling splinter of doubt regarding the Communion refused to be dug out.

"Look, let me finish talking with them." He tilted his head toward the other side of the room. "Then I'll tell you everything."

Teska jammed her hands on her hips and said nothing. Thorne walked away.

The men's voices carried well in the cellar. She heard them arguing, accusing Malachi of treachery and questioning his motives. He fired back, and the turmoil continued.

Teska walked over to a pile of empty sacks and prodded one with the toe of her boot. A rat squealed and disappeared through a hole in the wall.

She hated this. It seemed their arguments always started with something inconsequential, but both of them had a habit of blowing things out of proportion. In that respect they were too much alike. He was headstrong, in control and used to getting his way. Plus, he still kept trying to protect her.

But Thorne was only part of the reason for her heightened emotions.

It was almost a month since their encounter with the skeletons, and Amelia remained unconscious. She was alive, but there had been extensive damage to her brain. The physician did all he could to make her comfortable and address the external symptoms. But he gave them little reason to hope.

Teska remembered the sticky smear on the column and the long strands of blonde hair stuck in it. Her heart ached. She had grown fond of the Tex'ahn woman.

Even if she isn't worth a damn in a fight, she thought, trying to find a way to lighten her worry. But it only reinforced just how vulnerable Amelia had been.

Of course, she wasn't any good in a fight! She's a farmer's wife. She shouldn't have been anywhere near a fight. It was reckless of us to let her go down there. If she doesn't wake up…we're responsible for her death.

The physician had found a young woman who was willing to sit with Amelia. She gave her water and tried to spoon a few mouthfuls of soup down her throat each day. Amelia continued to lose weight. They all knew the truth. If she did not wake up soon, she would never wake up again.

And even if she did wake up, the physician had told them she would probably never be the same. He said she may not remember them or even her own name. She might be like a child, having to learn to walk and eat all over again.

Teska wiped tears from her cheeks. When she turned around, the men were dispersing. Thorne walked toward her. He wore the same furious expression, as if this moment was destined to be repeated forever.

"Come on," he said, his voice tight and controlled. "Let's get something warm to drink and I'll tell you everything."

"By the Twelve Hells! You're out of your fucking mind, you know that?" Teska exclaimed. "This is— It's—" She gave up and growled as she shook her head. "Out of your damn mind."

Thorne raised a hand as if to ward her off. "Look, I'll admit it's a bit unusual—"

"*Unusual!*" she yelled. "An albino is unusual. A snake with two heads is unusual. This? This is completely insane!"

"You were the one who was damned and determined to know."

They sat side by side at a table in the building beside Lake Winpeskah. The bitter wind blew snow through holes in the walls. The small oil lamp in front of them guttered, and Thorne cupped his hands around it to keep it from being snuffed out. It was after midnight, and beyond the pitiful circle of light was absolute darkness.

Teska shook her head. The tiny flame reflected off her black hair. "The Three-Who-Are-One have never met with a man. *Ever*."

"Then I've got nothing to lose but a night's sleep and the warmth in my fingers and toes," he replied, taking his hands from the lamp. He did not mean to sound spiteful, but his headache persisted. And he was worried. He knew the dangers inherent in this idea. It was worse than that time when Teska had been his prisoner, and he had cut her loose in the middle of a battle so she could join the fight.

"Sh!" Teska hissed and nodded toward the door.

A flickering light appeared. A dark shape came through the doorway. Snow whirled into the room until the door closed.

Thorne's hand went to the hilt of his dagger.

The form shuffled toward them, lantern in hand.

Thorne and Teska waited. He tensed, ready for anything.

The bulky shape placed the lantern on the table and sat opposite them. There were so many layers of clothing, it was hard to tell if a person was inside. Arthritic hands laid the heavy hood back.

Teska found herself staring at Eugenia Lusk.

Thorne glanced at Teska and back at the old woman. In the light, her face resembled a dried-out orange. He could have dug a furrow with her chin. Her blue eyes studied him with antipathy.

"Teska Vaun," Lusk said in a sour tone. "Can't say I'm surprised to find you here."

"Eugenia," Teska replied as courteously as she could manage. She was already biting her tongue.

"This the fool?" Lusk croaked. She wiggled a bony finger at Thorne.

He cleared his throat. "I am."

"Wasn't talking to you, Churchman."

"I'm no longer—"

"*Silence!*" Lusk tapped a cracked fingernail on the table in front of Teska. "I don't agree with this. None of it." She paused. "But it ain't up to me."

"You're just doing what you were told," Teska said.

The old woman nodded. "That's what we do."

"The Three-Who-Are-One know best."

Lusk scowled at her. "Don't pretend with me, missy. I know you. You're dangerous." She lowered her voice. "Don't know what they see in you."

"Excuse me," Thorne said, drawing the words out to get Lusk's attention.

She faced him with a sneer.

"Who are you?" he asked. "What are you doing here?"

The old woman chuckled, a rattling sound trying to escape her chest. She narrowed one eye and wrinkled her nose at him. "So cocksure, ain't you? You don't know nothing."

Thorne looked to Teska, his eyes pleading with her to intervene. But she had no chance.

"Name's Eugenia Lusk. I serve the Witch of Tears, Matriarch Trahnen, and have been part of the Communion for close on sixty years. I'm here"—she grimaced as she looked at them—"to hear what you have to say, Churchman."

Thorne raised his eyebrows. "The Three Witches aren't—"

"Silence yourself!" Lusk bellowed with more force than Thorne imagined possible from one so old. "You will *not* speak of them! Their names on your tongue are offensive! Did you truly imagine they would *deign* to appear before one such as *you*?" She shook her head, her chin thrust toward him. "Your arrogance is astonishing. You will speak to me. If they wish to speak to you—an honor you surely cannot comprehend or appreciate—they will do so through me."

Thorne raised placating hands. "Fine, that's fine. I didn't know how this would work."

"Are they… Are they here?" Teska asked, glancing around at the darkness.

Lusk leaned forward and placed her hands on the table. "In their own way. Now, time is short. You wanted this. I'm 'ginst it. So speak your piece."

Thorne also leaned forward, although he did not enjoy being closer to the old woman. She smelled of burnt cedar and mushrooms shriveling in a fire.

"I'm Malachi Thorne—"

"Know who you are," Lusk interrupted again, as if the knowledge was somehow poisonous.

Thorne tried his best to ignore her haughtiness. "I'm here to speak on behalf of the resistance in Attagon."

At least I hope to hells I am.

He paused, unsure if he was building up his courage or finally realizing the insanity of this idea. "I'm here to make a proposal, to ask for the help of the Thr—"

Lusk jabbed a finger at him.

"—the help of those who lead the Communion."

"Why should they care if you need help?"

"Because the Fifth Order and the Crimson Fathers are enemies to both of us."

"The Communion will deal with all of them when the time is right," Lusk said with confident ease.

"Maybe so," Thorne replied. "But how many more people will die in the meantime? How many more children will disappear? How many cities have to fall? We have an opportunity to do something *now*, not later."

"The Three ain't interested."

Thorne glared at the old witch. "Are they? Or are you the one who's not interested?"

Her wrinkled face pinched in rage. "I speak for the Three, you dimwitted scrotum sack!" She halted and took a deep breath. Her squinting eyes never left Thorne's. "You're lucky the Communion don't strike you down where you sit! Malachi Thorne, Witchfinder Imperator, the Hammer of the Heiromonarch, the Great Deliverer! Bah!" She all but chewed the words in her fury.

"All you've done is deliver us into the hands of the Fifth Order! Your stupidity and arrogance have cost the lives of many of our sisters."

"H-How do you know they're—"

"*We know!*" Lusk's eyes blazed like blue fire, and her chin quivered.

Thorne stared at the tabletop. The cold air felt like blocks of stone squeezing him. He could not deny her accusation.

"You come slinking to us, asking for help. After all that you've done. All those you've betrayed. All those you've put to death in your damnable tekoyas!" She spat on the table, and Thorne had to jerk his hand away to keep from getting hit. She pushed herself up and snatched her lantern off the table.

"Damn you to all Twelve Hells, Malachi Thorne," she snarled. "If I ever see you again, I'll make suppurating boils fill your eyes and peel your flesh from your bones! I'll turn your blood into sand!"

"Eugenia, please," Teska said.

The old woman spun around, her expression unchanged. "I'll see you cast out, you little bitch! You're a blight on the Communion. Hecate rue the day we thought your kind were important!"

Teska stood up slowly without taking her eyes off Lusk. "Try it, you miserable old cunt. I'll gut you like a fucking fish. I've had about all I'm going to stomach from you old hags." Her words ended in a snarl.

To Thorne and Teska's surprise, the old woman threw her head back and cackled. She looked at them as if they were waste in a chamber pot. She spat again, picked up her lantern and left the building.

For a moment, neither spoke. Then Thorne said, "Are there problems in the Communion?"

"Yeah, you could say that."

"You didn't say anything about it."

Teska shook her head. "It's private. Communion business. You know, like this proposal. Out of your damned mind…"

He ignored the bait. It was freezing, he was hungry and tired and they had a miserable ride ahead of them back to the city.

26
ALLIANCE

SATURDAY, DECEMBER 5, 999 AE

In the days following Thorne's failed proposal, the resistance continued their hit-and-run tactics across Attagon. But Crusaders had become more prevalent. Thorne and the other leaders had twice canceled planned attacks because patrols and guards were thick.

The revelation that the Crusaders were linked to the missing children also hindered progress. Some in the resistance thought it merely a ruse to reduce the number of attacks against the giants. Thorne did not agree. Teska told him what the Three Witches had said. To kill a Crusader was to kill a child. That put a stranglehold on their plans. They could still knock their opponents unconscious and tie them up, but that did nothing to diminish the number of Crusaders on the streets.

The news of a Crusader army generated even greater disbelief. Even Thorne questioned why the Crimson Fathers and the Fifth Order would need an army. They already had Crusaders. From Teska's report, the Fathers could create more of them whenever they wanted. They controlled every major city. They controlled the Church. How would an army benefit those who already dominated everything?

Congregants continued to stream into Attagon in preparation for the Festival of the New Millennium. Vendors, traders, urchins, pilgrims and revelers flooded the streets. It made things easier for the resistance; more bodies meant more cover. But it also hindered them as well. More bodies made it harder to get around.

Amelia Sloan remained unconscious. The physician had entrusted her to the care of the Cartulian Order, which was responsible for the health and welfare of congregants. She had been transferred at the beginning of December, when her caregiver took ill and could no longer look after her. The physician secured a room and bed for Amelia. There were always people in need of medical care in a city the size of Attagon. He concocted a story about finding her in an alley. No questions were asked. The beneficence of the Church had always included care for the body as well as the soul.

Her transfer removed some of the pressure from the resistance and their physician, who kept busy tending the wounded after raids. Teska grieved the transfer hardest because she could no longer visit Amelia when she wished. Now she could not take the chance of entering one of the Order's medical wards.

But Teska did pray. Like Thorne, she was not sure if the invisible Tex'ahn God was real. But if he was, she felt he needed to step in and heal Amelia. Her prayers were often angry and accusatory, but they were honest.

Tua'Ahtaki had become a vital part of the resistance. His bow skills, plus his stealth and tracking, made him one of the first men selected for missions. Some groused that was because he was good friends with Thorne. The majority, however, knew they could rely on him to have their backs. Several already owed him their lives.

Other members of the resistance had not been as fortunate. Since their assaults had begun on November 20th, six men had died. Nine more had been wounded severely enough to keep them out of action.

But it was to get much worse.

Thorne and the other resistance leaders stood around the warehouse basement in silence. One of their runners, a vibrant lad named Yarick, had just delivered the news. Both of the day's attacks had failed. All five men who had been attempting to raid a prisoner transport were cut down in an ambush. Four men assigned to set a fire had been captured. Two were executed on the spot. The others had been hauled off by the Paracletian Order for interrogation.

No one knew if the men had talked. But given the Church's skill at extracting confessions through torture, the resistance could not take chances. The leaders gave the order to evacuate the warehouse.

Thorne was the last to leave the building. He hurried down the alley to join the flow of traffic, keeping his head low. As he rounded the corner and glanced back, two Witchfinders he knew—Sebastian and Van Graf—forced their way into the warehouse. Crusaders followed. Constables and deputies converged on the front. Thorne trembled as he realized how narrowly the resistance had missed being captured and destroyed.

Two hours later, in the early afternoon, a man named Abner informed Thorne that Ryoma Takata had been apprehended in the street. The Paracletian Order issued a proclamation that everything he owned was now forfeit to the Church.

The sun shone with tepid reluctance through a blanket of gray clouds. The wintry air was brisk. Malachi headed east along slushy roads toward Mission Ridge and the resistance safe house he prayed was still safe.

By four o'clock that afternoon, the Fifth Order claimed to have broken the resistance and was rooting them out of their holes and hideaways. Ryoma Takata and two others had been sentenced to be burned at the stake for heresy and treason at the next tekoya. A dozen more men and women had been arrested after a freedom fighter had *cooperated* with the Church's investigation. Thorne knew that euphemism well. It meant at least one of the men had talked. And if one had talked, it would not be long before others did, too.

Elijah Corbyn bit off a piece of cold turkey leg and chewed. Aside from a loaf of bread, it was all they had been able to salvage when fleeing the warehouse. He walked to the door, cracked it and peered into the dying afternoon light.

It was an interior door of a house. The front half of the dwelling had been destroyed centuries before. Outside the door was a drop into the exposed foundation, filled with stones, snow and unidentifiable debris. Other similar houses hunched along the road out front. Snow lay heavy over everything. The middle-aged man closed the door, satisfied that they had not been followed. He turned back to what had once been a kitchen or dining area.

Also in the small room were Malachi Thorne, Bartholomew Fowler, Jon Cardwell, Michael Osman, Paul Keene and Christopher St. Jordan. All were haggard and sullen. Corbyn offered them the turkey leg, but none accepted.

"We cain't stay here long," Fowler said. Broad shouldered, with calloused hands befitting a farmer, he served as the main liaison between the resistance and the congregants on the outlying farms. The parts of his face not covered by his heavy beard were windburned from so much time outdoors.

"Are there any farmers who could offer us shelter?" Thorne asked.

Fowler shook his head. "They won't risk it. They'll support us with food and the occasional horse, but I cain't think of any that'd take us in."

"What about one of the other safe houses?" Keene asked. He was in his late fifties, with a receding hairline and a pointed nose.

Thorne said, "We can't chance it. We've got to assume that every place has been compromised."

"Well we can't just keep runnin'," Cardwell declared. "Gotta have somewhere to set up shop again." He squinted all the time as if he were constantly questioning the world around him.

"How about The Bluff?" Osman asked. At thirty, he was the youngest of the group.

"No good," Thorne said. "I used to live up there. Too many Church officials."

"Fraze Avenue?" Osman offered.

Cardwell rubbed the scar on the side of his neck. "Too close to the Abthanian Order headquarters."

"What about that place with all those empty cages?" Keene said. "There's gotta be basements or something like it underneath there."

Thorne nodded. "It used to be called a 'zoo.' And that's not a bad idea. But we'd need to scout it carefully."

"I wouldn't." Cardwell twisted the end of his mustache. "That's right near the Kyrian Order campus. And besides, it's too open up top."

No one said anything. The wind whistled through holes in the walls and roof.

"We've been hit hard," Osman said, uncomfortable with the silence.

Christopher St. Jordan stepped away from the wall, relying on his mahogany cane to compensate for his damaged foot. Thin and nearly as tall as Malachi, age pressed his shoulders down. With his silvery mustache and goatee trimmed to perfection and his matching slicked-back hair, he looked more like a lawyer than he did a cobbler. He spoke for the first time since they had arrived.

"We do need a safe location," he said, voice gruff but gentlemanly. "But I also think we need to reconsider Malachi's proposal. That may be the more pressing concern."

"How so, Christopher?" Corbyn asked.

The old man cleared his throat. "Individually, we can all lay low just about anywhere in this city. And there are plenty of unused places we can gather when we need to meet. We can send people out to scout locations. That will take time, especially since the Fifth Order grows stronger by the day.

"However, if we reconsider Malachi's idea, we can keep our momentum going. Right now, all we're talking about is a safe house. But we've got to keep the pressure on the Church. The longer we lay low, the more influence we lose among the people."

"His idea's preposterous," Caldwell said. "We've already decided that."

"Agreed," Fowler added. "Let's don't bring all that up again."

"But it could work. If the Communion—"

"Come on, Christopher, you know that's absurd. The Enodia Communion would never ally themselves with us. And I don't know if I'd even want them to. I don't trust them." Cardwell folded his arms.

"Gentlemen," Thorne interrupted, offering them his palms, "the Communion is hurting just as badly as we are. In the last few days, dozens of women have been arrested for witchcraft. The jails are filling up. There's even talk that the first tekoya of the new year will be two days long because they've got so many cases. I know you've all heard this as well."

Several nodded.

"The Church's familiars are making money hand over fist by accusing woman after woman. A good number are being held at Northgate, awaiting trial. I know the Communion wants their people released just as much as we do ours. Neither of us are going to make any difference on our own. We *need* each other's help."

"What makes you think the Communion would even entertain this nonsense?" Cardwell demanded.

Thorne offered what he hoped was a convincing smile. "They're willing to listen," he lied. "Some of their key leaders trust me."

Well, Teska trusts me. That's "some," right?

"I *can* make this happen," Thorne said with a confidence he was yet to feel.

The men looked at each other.

"Tell us your plan again," St. Jordan said. "Every detail."

Thorne did. When he finished twenty minutes later, they all looked at one another.

"You know, if we *could* pull this off…" Osman let the thought float in the air.

St. Jordan laid a wrinkled hand on the young man's shoulder. "Think of the impact it would have, not only for our cause but in weakening our enemy."

"We're wasting time," Fowler said. "Ain't none of this getting us any closer to a new safe house."

"We've all heard the idea," St. Jordan said. He leaned on his cane with both hands. "Let's take a vote. That *is* the essence of what we're doing all this for, is it not?"

"I'll abide by the majority decision," Thorne said. It killed him to say so, but he knew he had to lead by example.

When no one said anything else, St. Jordan raised his arm. "All those in favor of trying Malachi's plan?"

Corbyn, Osman and Thorne put their hands in the air.

"All those against the proposal?"

Fowler, Cardwell and Keene raised their hands.

"Four in favor, three against," St. Jordan said. He turned to Thorne. "Go make your proposal. In the meantime, the rest of us shall consider our options for a suitable meeting place."

Thorne made his way through the city with extreme caution. He scanned the streets and windows and took several detours to avoid patrols. He was grateful that he knew the city so well.

But so do your former friends and allies, he reminded himself. *Don't get cocky.*

The apartment he and Teska had been sharing was on the second floor of a pre-Cataclysm building that had been somewhat refurbished. Most congregants wanted nothing to do with the ancient ruins. The Church taught that many were home to demons and evil spirits, so the couple had few neighbors to notice their coming and going.

He found Teska inside, eating a bowl of soup. While he still missed her curly red hair, her new look had grown on him. He found it sexy. Their relationship had been rocky of late. Each shouldered too much responsibility. They had become the de facto leaders of their respective groups, although such leadership felt tenuous most of the time.

It was easier for Thorne. He had a rudimentary democratic process for making decisions. But Teska was caught in a burgeoning civil war between the Nahoru'brexia—whom Thorne understood to be the future of the sect—and the older witches who refused to give up authority and prominence.

If all the older witches are like Eugenia Lusk, he thought, *the Nahoru'brexia are in for a bloody rough time.*

"Hi, honey, I'm home," he said with a playful smile as he closed the door.

She grinned over her wooden spoon. "How'd it go?"

"We need to talk," he replied, dropping the smile and sitting down beside her.

It had taken less convincing than he imagined. It turned out the Communion was struggling just as badly as the resistance.

Thorne knew that he had people joining the resistance almost every day. Not all of them could fight, but at least they wanted to be part of the movement. Most of them had some kind of resource to share. After all, the resistance needed food. They needed clothes mended, weapons sharpened and places to hide. But the Communion… Well, they did not have people lining up to join them. Every witch they lost was like the resistance losing twenty-five.

Teska knelt in the middle of the floor in the pose of supplication. Thorne sat in a chair to the side. Despite the fire in their small fireplace, his hands remained cold. He leaned forward, elbows on his knees, and tapped his fingertips together.

God, she's a trooper, he thought as he watched her. *With everything going on around us, including Amelia's deteriorating condition, she's still willing to use her mag-*

ic for me. Thorne smiled at her profile. He was looking at her long eyelashes when she suddenly stood up. He leaned back.

"Tes?" he asked in a soft voice.

He saw his breath in front of his face. The tips of his fingers, nose and ears began to tingle.

Teska stood as rigid as a gravedigger's shovel, eyes wide open but solid white. It reminded him of the old witch in the holding cell in Colobos, and he suppressed a shiver. He held his breath when he saw Teska rise off the floor. She hung in the air, feet pointing down, toes inches from the wooden floorboards.

Thorne exhaled, swallowed hard. This was it.

"What are you doing, Daughter of the Moon?" The sensual young voice emanated from Teska's mouth but without a hint of warm breath hitting the cold air.

"Maiden Mallumo," Teska said. This time her breath clouded in the air. "Forgive my impertinence, but I seek your aid."

"You do this in front of a *man*?" the voice challenged.

"He has a request to make. You owe me nothing, but I pray you hear him out."

"Even though you are Nahoru'brexia, you push too far, Teska Vaun. You know this one is not to be trusted. You know the chaos he has caused us."

"Please, Maiden. I beg your indulgence just this once."

A cruel laugh echoed through the sparsely furnished room. "Just this once? Daughter, you have implored of me more than any other. Have you so quickly forgotten Last Chapel? You asked my assistance to free this man. Or when you begged that I aid his constable? You have met with Eugenia Lusk, who spoke our words to you. And now you come to me with this?"

The temperature dropped sharply. Thorne could've sworn the flames in the fireplace started to ice over.

"Most Revered One," Teska began, "I—"

"You waste valuable power and presume too much."

Thorne stood, hoping to enter the conversation as much as to get his blood flowing. He rubbed his hands together and blew into them. Then he did something he had never done before in his life.

"Maiden Mallumo," he said.

"Why does this impudent cur speak to us?" the Witch of Darkness demanded.

"My Lady, I—"

Thorne knelt on one knee and looked up at his lover, suspended in the air like a child's kite. Her sightless eyes looked at nothing. He dropped his gaze and focused on her feet.

"Maiden Mallumo," he said again. "I come to you with respect and reverence. I bring no malefic intent or hidden agenda. I know what I do is unorthodox. Please forgive my audacity. I asked Tes to do this for me—"

"We are well aware of the *influence* you have over her, Malachi Thorne."

"I knew of no other way to contact you. And it's imperative that I speak to you."

"Imperative?" The regal voice mocked. "You are a typical male. Presumptuous, vain and dangerous. You are the Witchfinder Imperator who sent many of our kind to the grave."

Thorne nodded at Teska's boots. "Yes, yes! I did that. But no longer! Now I fight for freedom from the Church. I wish to see the Crimson Fathers, the Fifth Order, the Crusaders and the Church done away with. I seek a world where people can live and work and worship as they please. But in order for that to happen, I need your help."

She chuckled. "We know of your proposal. Eugenia Lusk has spoken for us."

"That was several days ago. Since then, things have gone badly. For the resistance. And for the Communion."

"You know nothing of the ways of the Communion!"

"I know you've lost most of your magic," he said, closing his eyes so he could not see any repercussions that might be coming his way. "I know there's division in your ranks. And I know you need the Crimson Fathers and the Fifth Order out of the way just as much as we do." He paused. There was no sound except the crackling of the fire.

He glanced up. A chill swept down his spine when he saw Teska's sightless eyes fixed on him. Her short hair stood up. She gasped, but Thorne did not know if Teska or the Maiden made the sound. Her body trembled as if someone were shaking her. She lifted her head and stared at the wall again.

"You are in the presence of the Three-Who-Are-One," the Maiden said with great solemnity.

"I-I am honored," Thorne whispered. He lowered his gaze to the floor.

"Speak, lesser one," a brittle and hateful voice said from Teska's mouth.

"Th-Thank you." Thorne's heart raced. The air in the room felt charged, like before a lightning strike, and smelled of burnt flesh.

"As you know, we have a common enemy. The resistance is off-balance and on the run. Many of your witc—excuse me, brexia—are incarcerated or have been killed by the Fifth Order. We're losing good fighting men. You're losing more power. The truth is, separately we just aren't strong enough to take down the Fifth Order. And the longer we wait, the stronger they become. Left unchecked, they'll possess unimaginable power. We desperately need to strike them *now*. Hit them when they least expect it. Maybe even kill some of them."

"Continue," the Maiden's voice ordered.

"I propose...an *alliance* between our two groups, to remove the threat of the Crimson Fathers and the Fifth Order."

A hateful cackle erupted from Teska's throat. "You wish the Communion to ally itself with *men*?" The aged voice scoffed, imperious and acidic.

"Temporarily," Thorne replied. "Only temporarily. Then we can all go back to hating each other."

"Such a thing has *never* before been done." A new voice entered the conversation, more maternal, but with a sinister punitive quality.

"That's not exactly true," the Maiden said. "In Last Chapel, I sent aid to this man despite our misgivings. It was not an alliance. But we have joined before to contend with a common enemy."

"And what would such an alliance do?" the hoary voice growled.

For the first time tonight, the tension ebbed from Thorne's body. They were making progress. He allowed himself a brief smile.

"I have a plan," he said.

It took another hour, but after Thorne had explained the details, there was nothing to do but wait. He assumed the Three were debating. He hoped it was about the proposal and not on how to capture his soul and keep it in a jar. He shivered. His knees hurt. His legs were beginning to cramp from being in the same position for so long. *How do the witches do it*, he wondered, *when they meditate like this?*

"Yours is an intriguing and audacious plan, Malachi Thorne," the maternal voice finally said through Teska's immobile form. "We find it...to have merit."

Thorne exhaled loudly.

"We have consulted together," she continued, "and are willing to enter into this alliance. On one condition."

Thorne had been expecting something like this. "Go on."

"When our work is complete, we take possession of the Flame."

Thorne was surprised at how attached he had become to the blade. It was unlike any he had ever used. It felt as if it weighed almost nothing in his hand, and he would swear—only to his closest friends—that it somehow *guided* his movements. But losing it was a small price to pay for the Communion's help.

"Agreed," he said.

"In order to do what you suggest, we shall have to gather many brexia. The power required for the task will be considerable. It will be up to you to see that our sisters are protected when they reach this city."

Thorne scratched his chin. "I don't have that kind of influence in the Church any longer. But I may be able to set up something like a series of secure routes and safe houses they can use."

"How will you do such a thing?" the old woman's voice asked. "You have no safe houses for your resistance at the moment."

"I know, I know!" Thorne shot back. He didn't mean to sound aggressive. He could not afford to lose this opportunity. His heart thundered inside his chest like a runaway horse. "We're…working on that. We have places already lined up," he lied.

Please don't let them read minds.

"There is one brexia who will be instrumental in this plan," the middle voice said. "It is imperative that she get into the city unmolested. She has served the Communion faithfully for years and wishes to contribute in a meaningful way one last time before she dies. The Communion shall provide the power to do as you propose. Your resistance must make all preparations. It will be up to them to fight. To protect our sisters. To free the children."

Thorne nodded. "We'll arrange everything. I intend to circulate a rumor that the resistance is preparing something big at the Cathedral of the Heiromonarch on December 31st—the day of the new millennium celebration. That'll help draw Crusaders and members of the Paracletian Order away from our target."

"A wise stratagem. Then we are agreed," the Maiden said. "We shall do our part in exchange for the Flame."

"Listen," Thorne said, "one other thing. If all this works—if we're able to reclaim Deiparia and secure freedom from the Church—I want you to know that I'll do my best to see the persecutions against you stop. I can't promise anything. It may not be in my power. But if it is, I'll do what I can. Everyone should be free to worship and serve whoever they choose."

"Such a thing has never been said to us," the maternal voice replied. "It would be a…most welcome gift."

"We shall begin preparations," the wizened voice of the eldest said.

Thorne nodded. "As shall we. Time is against us. The festival is less than four weeks away."

"Do not think of crossing us, Malachi Thorne," the cracked and malevolent old voice warned. "We still have power. We can still make you suffer endlessly."

Thorne nodded again but said nothing. He realized he was smiling. He could not believe his fortune. It had worked!

Now came the really hard part.

27
FAVOR

SUNDAY, DECEMBER 6, 999 AE

Dario Darien did not remember what he had been dreaming about, but whatever it was had to be better than this.

He stood in the middle of a sprawling dirt field without so much as a weed, beneath a sky the color of moldy bread. He tried to move, but his body responded in the wrong ways, as if someone else was controlling it.

He saw something move on the horizon.

His heart pounded. His mind told him that he needed to escape. But escape was impossible. He did not understand.

He could not discern the temperature or see what he had on. And no matter how hard he focused on his arms and hands, he was unable to tell if he was young or old.

There was definitely movement ahead of him.

Something whispered that he needed to run while he had the chance. He tried, but his legs moved like stone. The racing of his heart filled his ears. He willed one foot, then another to work, but the ground held him like thick mud. It slurped at his bare feet—*Where are my boots?*—and squished between his toes. Then, somehow, he was stumbling forward, flailing through the ooze.

The skin on the back of his neck tightened. Something closed in behind him.

Darien tried to run faster, but his legs moved in slow motion. The harder he forced himself to run, the slower he went.

I'm dreaming, it's just a dream. I'm dreaming, it's just a dream.

He knew better than to look over his shoulder, but he did it anyway.

A serpent slithered along the ground behind him, getting closer and closer. Overtaking him.

The gangrenous light dimmed, but he could still see.

Darien felt the snake around his legs, its cold, sinuous form caressing him.

He tried to scream. Nothing came out. The serpent coiled about his feet and ankles, working its way toward his knees. He could no longer walk, much less run.

Curling around his waist, scales black in the decaying light, the serpent held him tight. Its head rose to his chest. Arching away from his body, it spread its hood and hissed. Black eyes stared at him. The tongue flicked in and out.

Darien tried to force his panic down. He could not flee, although his mind pleaded with him to try.

I'm dreaming, it's just a dream.

His heart hammered against his rib cage. The snake continued to coil around him, cocooning him in its cold scales. He did not know how long the creature was nor could he see a tail. The hooded head swayed as if to the tune of some invisible charmer.

"Dario Darien," a voice said.

Is that my mind? Or is it the snake? Or are they the same?

"They ain't the same," the voice replied.

It reminded him of somewhere, of someone.

"Yes, ye know me. I did ye a favor, once 'pon a time."

Rebekkah Barlowe!

The witch he had consulted—the one who had shown him how Jairus died. The one whose magic had prematurely aged him.

"Wh-What do you w-want?" His tongue felt like iron.

"It's time ye kept yer part 'a the bargain. I claim my right to collect on yer vow."

Something cold coursed through his body. He wondered if the serpent had slithered inside his skin.

"What do you want?" he repeated. His voice sounded hollow, unsure and tinged with dread. He could not tear his eyes from the hypnotic gaze of the snake mere inches from his face.

"Ye be lucky, and that's sure. My favor be only a wee thing, compared to what was done for ye."

"A-And what if I refuse?" he asked in a timid voice, already suspecting the answer.

The light vanished. Musky darkness pressed against him like living tar. The serpent still coiled about him, but he no longer saw it. Instead, before him like a seam in the darkness, a horizontal rip widened. It pulsated with an alien rhythm. He thought he could see stars the way a child might peek between his fingers at the night sky.

Something moved behind the gap, bulbous and pale, eclipsing the stars. Milky veins lay against a field of pus-filled skin.

Darien tried to push himself away, to bolt from the abominable veined eyelid that lifted slowly. He screamed and this time found his voice. He writhed helplessly against the serpent's body. He screamed again and again as the lid opened fully, revealing several pupils of differing sizes. All focused on him. All malefic.

IT'S JUST A DREAM! IT'S JUST A DREAM!

He heard a bizarre word, something that should not have come from a human throat.

Or did it come from the snake? Or that—that abomination?

The eye disappeared, as did the opening. The darkness seemed to detach from him. Bathed in cold sweat, Darien was sure his heart would shatter his sternum.

"That be yer answer, Dario Darien!" Barlowe promised. "And even worse, b'sides."

"T-T-Tell me. Tell me what you w-want." His breath came in shallow gasps, and he tasted bile in his mouth. "I'll honor the vow. Just please d-don't make me see *that* again."

Solomon Warner lowered his spoon and stared across the grain sacks that served as a makeshift table. He sat his bowl of oatmeal down and glanced at Hawkes, whose expression of disbelief mirrored his own.

"You want us to do *what*?" he asked Darien.

"You don't have to do it, Solomon. I can…see to it." He coughed hard, his entire body shaking with the effort.

"You barely got out of bed," Hawkes told him. "You can't go riding off into the countryside in this weather on some crazy errand."

"I have no choice. It has to be done."

"No, it don't!" Warner yelped. "What you're talkin' about, it'll—" He snapped his mouth shut and looked to the cold dirt floor. Something soft touched his arm, like a bird settling down. Darien's hand, frail and palsied, rested there.

The old man's smile was weak but genuine. "Kill me? I'm dying—we all know that. There's…nothing wrong with saying it."

"But you need to stay here," Warner said, "where we can take care of you. You need more medicine."

Darien shook his head. "The medicines"—he coughed again—"haven't helped in weeks." The sorrow in his voice was not for himself or his condition, but for his friends who had done more than could ever be repaid.

Warner's heart clenched, and he closed his eyes, desperate to blot out the truth.

Amid the stillness, they heard the wind around the foundation of the pre-Cataclysm building. They had left Demerra's shortly after arriving so that their presence did not attract unwanted attention. Demerra had begged them to stay, especially her brother. He did not need to be out in the cold in his condition. However, she could not persuade them. A day later they had made their temporary home in the basement of this building, which appeared to have been empty for centuries. They had no idea what it had originally been, nor did they care overmuch. They could make a fire, stay out of the elements, and rest in relative security.

Hawkes sat like a statue, staring at the grain sacks. "I don't understand," he said.

Darien sighed. It sounded like air slowly leaking from a balloon. "My aging… was the price I paid to find out what happened…to my brother-in-law. But there was also a price for the witch. Rebekkah Barlowe. She said I would owe her a favor of her choosing…when she asked for it." He gulped at the air like a starving man at a morsel of bread.

"And your dream last night? That was her tellin' you what she wanted?"

He wheezed, unable to speak, but nodded his head.

"She wants to go to Attagon?" Hawkes asked. "That's all?"

Again, Darien nodded. He held a trembling hand to the front of his oversized woolen tunic, his face ashen.

He looks like he's going to die any minute, Warner thought, and hated himself for it.

Hawkes chuckled. "I guess I figured she'd want you to undertake a quest to find some rare scroll or the hand of a hanged man, something like that."

"Yeah," Warner agreed, "somethin', you know, a little more unique."

"Or witchy," Hawkes added with a crooked smile.

"She…wants to go to Attagon. She didn't say why. I…didn't ask. All I know… is that I've got to get her there." He dipped his spoon in his oatmeal but left it there.

Warner rubbed his thickening beard and looked at Hawkes. "Shouldn't take more than a day," he said. "Get up there, pick her up, head back."

"What about Dario? We can't leave him here alone."

Warner shook his head. "We won't. We'll take him to his sister's. That okay with you?" he asked Darien.

The old man nodded.

"You want to go tomorrow?" Hawkes asked. He glanced up through the narrow, glassless ground-level window. The filmy gray winter light mimicked Darien's complexion.

"Don't think we got the time," Warner said so Darien could not hear. "We need to do it today. It's still early. I don't know how much longer—"

Hawkes shoveled in a few bites of oatmeal, wiped his mouth on his sleeve, and stood up. "I'll get us two horses. Be back quick as I can."

"Dario, we're goin'—" Warner stopped as he turned around.

The old man slumped against the wall, fast asleep.

Following Darien's directions, Hawkes and Warner made the journey to Rebekkah Barlowe's cottage. It took them four hours to get to the village of Stockshire because of the snow. From there, it was another two hours as they trudged through snowdrifts up into the hills, like trying to walk in half-set mortar. They were starved and exhausted when they knocked on the door of her house surrounded by naked trees and conifers. They were not surprised to find her waiting for them.

The old witch's feeble body could not make it through the hip-deep snow, but thankfully she had a small sled. Hawkes and Warner towed her and her dog, Grizzel, sapping their strength even more and making her snide comments difficult to endure. She seemed to enjoy asking if Warner would like a new eye, promising that the cost would not be too high. Grizzel growled at them whenever they looked at the old witch.

Barlowe said nothing about why she wanted to go to Attagon. "That be none 'a yer affair," she scolded them. "Ol' Rebekkah knows what she knows." Her two mules left it at that as they pulled her sled down the hill.

The trip back to Talnat took only three hours since they pushed their horses hard. Rebekkah hunched behind Hawkes, cheek to his back, claw-like hands gripping his coat. It made him uncomfortable. He could not shake the feeling there was a massive leech on his back. He thought he could feel himself growing colder, imagining his blood being drawn out little by little. He could not get her off the horse fast enough when they reached Demerra's house.

Once inside, Rebekkah made herself comfortable in a rocking chair in front of the fire, the light flickering over her rugose features. Grizzel lay at her feet. He made no noise but watched every movement in the room.

Barlowe accepted the steaming cup of tea that Demerra offered. Twice Demerra had to shoo Cassidy and Cassandra out of the kitchen because they kept creeping back to stare at a real witch. Rebekkah said nothing. She stared into the fire and sipped her tea.

Darien, Hawkes, Warner and Demerra sat around the table. Darien instructed his sister to take the children and flee Talnat. "Get out of this city," he said. "Go stay with our cousin, Tamlin. They live on the coast, not near any major cities. Get your…things together tonight. You can leave when we do tomorrow. I don't know…what's going to happen next. But I want you all safe."

Demerra excused herself to gather up her meager belongings.

Darien got up and shuffled to the fireplace. He sat down beside the old witch. A wave of cold anger swept through him as he looked at her. *She* had done this to him. Her magic had made him this way. He resented her, and yet part of him was oddly grateful. She had shown him the missing pieces of a puzzle, helped him find answers to provided closure and information that had led them all here, now.

He cleared his throat. "Rebekkah, I want you to know…here in front of these witnesses"—he gestured at Hawkes and Warner—"that I will honor my vow. The favor I owe you will be paid in full."

"Then ye'll be free of obligations, Dario Darien. My word on it."

He leaned toward her. "Why do you want to go…to Attagon?" he asked.

"Ol' Rebekkah's done got one final role to play in this saga," she croaked.

"Meaning what?"

She closed her eyes. "I be serving the Communion one last time. Then I die."

Darien remembered an old woman in a dungeon in Colobos, and an Elder Demon.

Hadn't she also been serving the Communion one last time? Is that what's going to happen to Rebekkah?

A chill that had nothing to do with weather or age touched him.

"What…will you be doing? How will you serve?"

Her jaw worked side to side, and she looked at the aged clerk. She sighed. "The Communion be preparing an attack, Dario Darien. They done made an alliance with the resistance up there."

"We've heard stories…about what's been happening…in the capital."

"We ain't strong enough ourselves. Resistance ain't strong enough alone, neither. They's done some things 'ginst the Fifth Order, but it ain't enough. So, there's gonna be one big strike, something that'll destroy the Crimson Fathers—so the leader of the resistance tells it."

Darien leaned back in his chair. "Who's their leader?"

"Malachi Thorne."

"Malachi?" The old man's voice rose in surprise, and he sat up again, almost to the edge of his seat. "Malachi's the *leader*?"

"That's just what I said. You goin' deaf now?"

Darien blinked several times, as if each could help process the information better. His heart rose at the knowledge that his friend still lived.

Are Thurl and Teska with him? As he mulled over the news, a tiny smile tugged at the corners of his mouth. The thought of seeing Malachi again flooded him with warmth.

He's doing it! He's taken up Merrick's mantle. He's continuing the fight for freedom.

But the warmth became tepid. His insides shrunk as he realized how extremely dangerous this attack would be.

"Rebekkah…what is Malachi planning to do?"

She shrugged, the gesture almost lost inside the thick cloak that covered her. "Ain't been told that yet."

"What does it involve?"

"Don't know that, neither."

"How many people…are in the resistance?" Darien could not help himself. The questions leapt into his mind one after the other. "It's hard for us…to get information. We can't go out very much."

The old witch snarled at him. "I don't know! An' I won't be a-knowin' until we get to Attagon."

Warner spoke up, his voice filled with suspicion. "The Communion didn't tell you what they need you for?"

She stopped rocking, craned her neck and pinned him to his chair with her gaze. "Hesh up, boy! This got nothing to do with ye. I've trusted the Communion for over fifty year—and when I die, I'll trust 'em with my soul. I got no need to know every little thing. I'll find out when I find out."

Hawkes yawned. "I'm turning in. I'm whipped."

Warner agreed and shot the witch a baleful glance as he left the kitchen. Labored breathing, the creaking of the rocking chair against the floorboards and the crackling logs in the fireplace were the only sounds.

"Whatever they're planning," Darien said, "it'll be big. If I know Malachi… it won't be easily missed."

"What know ye of that Witchfinder Imperator? Heard he turned traitor 'ginst the Church."

Darien laid his head back against the chair and stared at the shadowy ceiling beams. "I'll tell you…on the road tomorrow. It's too long to get into…now." He paused. "By the Heiromonarch, I'm so weary."

She looked at him, and her expression softened a bit. "Dying be easy. Getting old? That ain't."

"At least you…got to live a long, full life," he replied acerbically.

"For what it be worth, Dario Darien—that aging didn't come from me. I told ye: every spell cost something. Most times, the caster be paying the price." She hesitated. "Not all of this"—she ran a crooked finger down her cheek—"be natural, don't ye know? Anyway, the spell ye asked for didn't take nothing from me. Ye had to bear its full price."

"I understand," he said in a defeated voice.

They sat in silence a while longer. Outside a dog barked in the distance. Finally, Darien pushed himself from the chair, accompanied by a grunt and cracking joints.

"There's a pallet…in the room to the left…you can use," he told her.

She nodded. "Thank ye, Dario Darien."

He left her rocking in front of the fire, and when everyone awoke the next morning, she was still there.

28

REUNITED

WEDNESDAY, DECEMBER 9, 999 AE

Tycho Hawkes vaulted over a cart, scattering prayer beads and handmade crafts. Warner squeezed between tables to keep up. They overturned baskets and scattered livestock in their flight. They knew the streets of Attagon as well as anyone. But they were harder to navigate with so many people jamming the city ahead of the new millennium.

"Stop them!" someone shouted.

Everyone stopped but only to watch the chase. Cries of shock and surprise followed as the two men pushed through the throng. Two Crusaders pursued at full speed, cursing and shoving congregants aside. Their breath steamed the morning air like enraged bulls.

And they were gaining.

Hawkes and Warner fought their way forward, dodging and skipping around tradesmen, wagons, pilgrims and women running errands. The crowd parted for the Crusaders, giving them a clear path to their quarry.

"Halt!" one of them bellowed.

Snow fell, adding to the piles shoveled against walls and turning to brown slush in the streets.

Warner glanced back. "Damn!"

Hawkes also looked around. A constable and two deputies on horseback had joined the chase. They closed rapidly as the crowd fell away like wheat before a scythe.

Hawkes cut across Fountain Square, where the marble statue of Heiromonarch Michael the First stood. If they could get to the crumbling buildings of the Youteesee, they would have a solid chance of escaping. But they were still several blocks away, and the pounding hooves drew closer.

They crossed the Avenue Georga. Hawkes pushed himself harder, his legs burning from the exertion. Onto Vine Street. Just another block or two. Warner kept pace beside him. On the other side, the blurred form of a horse appeared.

"Duck!" Warner yelled.

A sword arced through the air as the horse sped past.

Hawkes threw himself into the dingy snow. He tucked into a forward roll and came up on his haunches. The second horse and rider arrived. The Crusaders were fifty yards behind, showing no sign of fatigue.

"Stand down!" the constable ordered. He turned the horse and leveled his saber at Warner.

The mounted deputy unsheathed his sword. Hawkes slowly stood up, hands open in surrender.

"You're under arrest," the constable said behind his graying brush mustache. "Your days of rebellion are over."

"We're…not rebels," Hawkes wheezed.

"Sure. And I'm the next Heiromonarch." He studied Warner. "Wait a minute." Nudging his horse closer, he leaned over and snatched the cloth from Warner's head. "I'll be damned! I thought so!"

Instead of a left eye, there was only a fleshy indention, the skin crisscrossed by scars.

"I know you!" the constable grinned in triumph. "Solomon Warner. The only cyclops we had in the Paracletian Order."

Warner recognized the constable but could not remember his name.

The constable looked Hawkes over and smiled again. "And that one's Tycho Hawkes. This is our lucky day, Beecham! We might just be up for promotion after this. We've got two of the boys who run with Malachi Thorne."

The prospect of a quick promotion brightened Beecham's young face.

The Crusaders arrived, one drawing his broadsword from the sheath across his back. The other pulled a set of manacles from his belt and walked toward Warner. "Hands front!" he demanded. "According to the Laws of the Divine Church, and as a Crusader of the Fifth Order, I hereby charge you both with sedition, heresy and aiding and abetting known rebels. The sentence is execution, to be carried out immediately."

"Death?" Hawkes exclaimed. "That's not the law!"

"It is now." The Crusader's voice was deep and devoid of emotion. "Kneel."

Hawkes looked at him. "But we don't know any rebels."

"Kneel!" He bellowed so loud that Hawkes flinched.

Warner picked up the cloth and wrapped it around his head. "We know the law. We're entitled to a Witchfinder—or at least a lawyer."

The Crusader shook his head. "Not for anyone who aids the resistance. Rebels are executed immediately." He smiled, but it seemed incongruous with the rest of his stony features.

"Hold a moment," the constable said. "Where is Malachi Thorne? What's he planning? How many men does he have?" he asked. "Tell me."

Warner shrugged. "How would I know? I ain't seen him in months."

"A likely story," deputy Beecham said.

The manacles were fitted around Warner's wrists.

"Stay the execution."

The Crusaders scowled at the constable with uncertainty. "Why, Leland?"

"Shackle them. Tie them behind the horses. They're known associates of Thorne. We'll take them in for questioning. They can tell us what they know."

"Ain't tellin' you shit," Warner said.

"You will," Leland replied. "As former members of the Paracletian Order, you know how *persuasive* our methods can be."

They reached the Avenue of the Lord, Attagon's widest street, that led to the Cathedral of the Heiromonarch, and from there to the campus of the Paracletian Order. All traffic moved aside to let them pass. No one wanted to be singled out by a Crusader for obstructing the progress of Church representatives and the prisoners stumbling behind their horses.

The party turned south, moving to the right of the median lined with skeletal, snow-laden trees.

Some congregants booed and hissed at the prisoners, but Warner got the impression their hearts were not really in the displays of disapproval. Some looked sorry, as if they were to blame for the arrest. Most just went on about their business. They had seen this procession too often in recent weeks.

The traffic going north on the other side of the Avenue kept moving. Congregants darted between carts and wagons, skipped over horse manure and often bumped into animals or other people. They crossed the median and wove their way through the southern traffic.

Warner had no idea anything was happening until the horse in front of him reared, whinnying in pain. A crossbow bolt stuck out of the horse's flank. Constable Leland yelled something and grunted in pain. He toppled from the saddle, crossbow bolts pin-cushioning his body.

Warner realized what was happening but had no time to act. Injured and startled, the horse yanked him off his feet. It galloped down the street. Warner was drug behind, bouncing and yelling.

He did not know when it happened or why, but suddenly everything went black.

Hawkes witnessed everything. The crossbow bolts had come from the tops of the buildings to his right. He saw dark shapes moving up there. Deputy Beecham slumped against his horse's neck, bolts buried in his body. The Crusaders ran for the protection of the trees in the median.

Across the median, a wagon stopped in the road. The top half of the side fell down, revealing armed men inside. They fired crossbow bolts at the Crusaders. More bolts from the rooftops whistled through the air. The Crusaders collapsed into the reddening snow and did not get up.

Two bolts hit Beecham's horse, shocking it into flight. The deputy's body flopped to the street. Like Warner before him, Hawkes toppled to the ground and was pulled along behind it. He was at the mercy of the spooked horse until it decided to stop.

Or until he died from being slammed into everything that came along.

Warner awoke to a circle of faces staring down at him. He thought he recognized one or two of them but was too shaken from his ordeal to be sure. He saw Hawkes sitting beside him.

"How are you feeling, young man?" The questioner was older, slightly stooped, with silver hair, mustache and goatee. He leaned on a dark, polished cane.

"Okay, I guess." Warner gave a soft chuckle. "Considerin'."

The man nodded. "From a cursory examination, I don't believe you've suffered any serious injury. Nor has your friend. But you'll both be quite sore tomorrow."

"These two are fortunate," another man said. He was shorter, with ruddy skin, a wide nose and wore his black hair in twin braids.

The three other men who had been standing around walked off.

Warner sat up. "Where are we?" he asked.

"You're in a safe place. You have nothing to fear." The older man's tone put Warner at ease. "As Tua said, you're quite fortunate. An ambush had been planned for the Avenue today. Our men were waiting for the right opportunity. And suddenly, there you were!"

"You—" Warner said, standing and helping Hawkes to his feet. "You ambushed them?"

"Why were you taken prisoner?" the man called Tua asked as he studied them with penetrating eyes. "Who are you?" There was a current of distrust in his tone, and Warner was not sure why he felt annoyed at him.

"That's none of your business," Warner said. "Just who the hells are you people? And where are we?"

Hawkes took a few steps, testing to see if anything was broken. Satisfied that he was in one piece, he said, "We're just travelers. Pilgrims. Isn't that right, Sol?"

Warner cringed at the abbreviated use of his name, but neither Tua nor the older man seemed to notice.

"Well, it's true that the Fifth Order has no compunction about who they harass. But if you don't mind my forthrightness, neither of you seem like pilgrims." The older man frowned. "I think I must agree with Tua. Who are you? What did you do to get arrested?" The soft, calming tone was still there, but a frown accompanied it.

Warner glanced around. They were in a basement or cellar. It was cold. The floor was just packed dirt. No windows, only one door. He assessed the area for weapons, clues as to their location or to the identity of these men.

The silver-haired man leaned over and whispered to Tua, "I'm going to tell Malachi. We'll see how he wants to proceed."

"Malachi?" Warner said. "Malachi *Thorne?*" The note of hopefulness sounded loud in his ears. He looked at the two men. "What? Just 'cause I only got one eye don't mean my hearin' is bad."

"How do you know of Malachi Thorne?" Tua asked, his tone wary. Both could read his body language. "Are you spies for the Fifth Order?"

"Spies?" Warner nearly choked on the word. "Hells no!"

"That is what a spy would say."

"Look here, you—"

Hawkes stepped between them and faced Tua. "If it's the same Malachi Thorne that *I* know, we were his deputies. Assigned to Constable Thurl Cabbott. Haven't seen him in a long time, though."

"What does he look like, your Malachi Thorne?" the older man asked.

Hawkes and Warner gave a quick description of their friend. "Used to be a Witchfinder Imperator. We had to separate back in the summer."

"Give me a moment, I'll be back," the older man told Tua. The way he limped out the door mirrored the urgency in his voice.

Hawkes and Warner sat on small barrels in the middle of the floor. Warner kept his eye on Tua, who was doing the same to them.

Ten minutes later, the older man returned. He stepped aside, and Thorne entered the cellar.

Hawkes and Warner shot past Tua, their faces nearly splitting with joy. Thorne gave each a bear hug, slapping them on the backs. They clasped forearms, grinning like madmen and laughing.

"By God, it's really you!" Thorne said. "I wondered if I'd ever see you two rogues again!"

"What happened to your hair? And your mustache?" Hawkes asked.

Thorne chuckled. "I could ask you the same thing. Where'd those long flowing red locks go?"

The men laughed again—deep, cleansing laughter—the kind that brightens the spirit and often leads to tears. Tua watched, the slight hint of a smile at the corners of his mouth.

They told each other about their journeys, the highs and lows of the past few months. Thorne introduced them to Tua and Christoper St. Jordan. Afterward, both left the three to their catching up.

"What about Teska? Is she…" Warner began.

Thorne nodded, still smiling. "She's fine. Fiery as ever!"

"Where's Thurl?" Hawkes asked.

"He's— I-I'm sorry. He's…dead," Thorne said to their boots. "It happened on the way back to Deiparia. One of the Crimson Fathers—I don't know—possessed his body or something. They used him against us. Nearly broke the resistance. Hurt the Communion, too." Some of the spark had disappeared from his eyes as he talked.

Hawkes and Warner stood in silence, coming to grips with the news.

"What about Dario? Where's he?" Thorne asked. "You said he got Cassidy and Cassandra back to their mother. Is he in the city with you?"

Hawkes lowered his gaze. Warner looked away before saying, "Yeah, he's here. He had to come. Some old witch made him bring her here."

"Why? What for?"

"He owed her for a spell she did for him," Hawkes said.

Thorne rubbed his jaw. "Where is she now?"

"We dropped her off at Winpeskah Lake. We didn't see anyone else around, but that's where she said to leave her," Hawkes replied. He studied Thorne's quizzical expression. "What, you know her?"

He shook his head. "No. But I think I might know why she's here. Anyway, about Dario—"

"It might be better if you see for yourself," Warner said.

The Tits Up Tavern lurked east of the city in an area of ramshackle buildings that housed some of Attagon's poorest. It was a miserable-looking establishment of crumbling stone and leaning walls, with a patchy thatched roof covered in snow.

No one paid attention as Hawkes, Warner and a disguised Thorne climbed the blackened steps to the second floor. The place reeked of smoke, urine and unwashed bodies. They walked down the hallway, listening to the boards complain under their boots. Thorne knew what awaited him at the door. He was all too familiar with the smell of death.

They stepped inside the cramped room. There were no windows, and the rankness of fever and age vied for supremacy. Darien lay beneath a ratty blanket, his head sunk into the sweat-stained pillow. His cheekbones and chin protruded from taut skin. Recessed eyes lined with dark circles were half closed.

Thorne had tried to prepare himself, but the sight of his friend still punched him in the gut. His heart collapsed in sorrow. He had to fight off a creeping sense of guilt that all of this was his fault. He sat on the side of the bed, Hawkes and Warner nearby.

"Dario?" Thorne said gently.

His eyelids crept open. "M-M-Malachi? Is that…you?" he asked through cracked lips.

"It's me, old friend." He took a gnarled hand in his own. It was like holding dry sand and felt clammy despite Darien's fever.

"I-I did it. I…got them home." He smiled, turning his face into a fleeting death mask that Thorne found simultaneously pitiful and unsettling.

"I know. Tycho and Sol told me all about it. You're a brave man. I know your family is proud of you. I am, too."

He closed his eyes again. A spasm racked his body.

"We'll get you some help," Thorne said. It was all he could think to say. And he needed to say something. Any sound would be preferable to Darien's labored breathing.

Darien rolled his head slowly from side to side. "No. The healers…can't do anything. It's…my time."

The hand that had punched Thorne in the stomach now grabbed it and twisted hard enough to bring tears to his eyes. "Well, you're not staying here." He turned to face Hawkes and Warner, the light flickering in his green eyes. He lowered his voice. "Why'd you bring him here, of all places? It's a sty!"

"W-We couldn't risk going much farther into the city," Hawkes said, taken aback. "We didn't want him to get caught."

"None of us wanted to get caught," Warner said, his voice hard.

"There are other places you could've taken him, where he would've—"

Warner bent down and hissed, "We ain't been here in months. We don't know what's been goin' on. We needed to make him comfortable and then find *you*." Anger flashed in his eye. "Although I'm beginnin' to wonder why."

Fury hit Thorne's face, but grief chased it away. He dropped his head, shoulders slumping. "I-I'm sorry, Sol. I didn't mean—"

"Forget it."

Warner felt himself going cold inside. He did not like it but had no idea how to make it stop. Darien was nearly dead. Malachi seemed to have found new friends, replacements maybe, for him and Hawkes? And what they had done for Darien was not to Thorne's liking? Thorne had no idea what they had been through to get this far. Warner was glad that Tua had waited outside the tavern. He was sure he could not have handled this crowded room *and* him as well.

Thorne acted as if he wanted to say something else but stopped. He looked back at Darien. The old man was asleep. Drops of sweat stood out against his pale black skin. His eyes moved sluggishly behind their lids.

Thorne sat in silence a few moments longer, just staring at his friend. Finally, he rose quietly and walked out. Hawkes and Warner followed, closing the door.

"Where're you going?" Hawkes asked as they headed toward the stairs.

"We can take him to one of the Cartulian Order wards. He'll be looked after there. At least it'll be cleaner than this cesspit."

Warner gritted his teeth. "Told you it was the best we could do."

"He's my friend," Thorne snapped as he reached the top of the stairs. "If he's to die, at least he'll do so without roaches and rats for company."

"He's our fuckin' friend, too!" Warner exploded. "What the hells you think we been doin' the past few months, *ignorin' him*?"

"Guys—" Hawkes said.

Thorne grabbed the banister, hung his head and sighed. "I-I know. I know you've taken care of him. That's not what I'm saying. I just—" He hesitated, cleared his throat. "I just want him to be in a better place. I'll take him to one of the wards. You don't have to go. I'll see if I can get him into the one where Amelia is."

As they crossed the common room, the tavern keeper put his hands on the bar and leaned forward.

"Oy, 'ey!" he yelled at them. "I want that damned plaguer outta here! He ain't spreading no diseases in my place!"

Thorne spun. Three strides of his long legs covered the room. He snatched the man by the collar and yanked him halfway across the bar.

Surprised, bloodshot eyes gawked back at him. The man's breath reeked of liquor and something that might have been bad meat stuck between the teeth. Thorne tried to ignore it. He leaned forward so his nose was inches from the man's baggy face.

"Listen, you sorry excuse for a son of a bitch! That man up there is my friend! He doesn't have any plague! I'm going to get a wagon to move him from this shithole." His tone was clipped and tight. Flecks of spittle flew from his lips as he snapped off each word. "I'd better find him alive when I get back. If he dies while I'm gone, I'll tear this place down with my bare hands and bury you in the middle of it. Are. We. Clear?"

The tavern keeper stammered, legs flopping in the air behind him, and nodded.

Thorne grabbed the back of the man's collar and slammed the side of his head down on the bar. He leaned in again and whispered in the man's hairy ear. "Take care of him. *Or else.*"

The owner stood up, rubbing the side of his reddening face, eyes spooked. "I'll, uh— I'll see to it 'at he, uh, 'at he gets some soup."

Thorne stomped across the room and threw open the door. "You do that," he said over his shoulder.

29
ASSIGNMENTS

THURSDAY, DECEMBER 17, 999 AE

A guard stood by the door in the small room that smelled of rotten flower stems. The fireplace was cold and dark since those huddled within could not risk smoke being seen from the chimney. The two rear-facing windows were covered by heavy black cloth. Pale yellow light glowed from three lanterns—one by the door, two on the table in the middle of the room.

Bartholomew Fowler, Elijah Corbyn and Christopher St. Jordan sat on a bench across from Teska, cantankerous Eugenia Lusk and a woman named Ana Maria Gallánica. Four brexia and several resistance fighters, including Hawkes, Warner and Tua'Ahtaki, filled the remaining spots on the benches. Thorne stood at the head of the table.

"Before getting to our assignments," he said, "I'd like to take a moment of personal privilege. The realm of Deiparia is rapidly changing. And while the new millennium will surely inaugurate many more changes, the most important ones are those that have taken place in each of our hearts.

"What we do here tonight is historic—not merely because of what we seek to accomplish—but because *you* are here. Look around. Right now, two disparate groups have united around a shared goal. Congregants of the Church have allied with the Enodia Communion. Never before has this happened.

"You've not only fought and bled and sacrificed for the cause of freedom and for the destruction of the Crimson Fathers—you've come together to join power and purpose. You've set aside centuries of enmity in order to make our world a better place. A freer place. Regardless of our plans or what may come of them, this night shall never be forgotten. Thank you for having the courage to do what has never been done, in the course of doing what must be done. You have my gratitude and my respect."

Everyone smiled or nodded except Eugenia Lusk. She glared at one of the lanterns as if her expression could extinguish it.

"Now to business," Thorne said as he sat down. "We all know that we haven't really hurt the Fathers or the Fifth Order with our hit-and-run tactics. We've taken out a few Crusaders—but even that has caused great moral confusion for most of us. While we have no direct proof that children are linked to them, we also lack any proof that they're not. So, our options for dealing with the Crusaders have become extremely limited. But they're just puppets of the Crimson Fathers. We can fight Crusaders all day long without ever reaching the true evil.

"We've all agreed that something big and unexpected is required—not only to make a statement and rally support, but to rid ourselves of the Fathers. The Church is readying December 31st as the Festival of the New Millennium. We intend to make it the day the Crimson Fathers are crushed forever.

"At noon, the Church will hold a worship service in the Cathedral of the Heiromonarch. Everyone will be there. Those who can't fit inside will be gathered on the grounds. Afterward, the Church is sponsoring a celebration carnival for the rest of the day. It will go all the way until midnight, when the Heiromonarch will pronounce a blessing for the new millennium.

"One thing we know about the Crimson Fathers: they never appear in public. So they won't be at the cathedral. They'll remain in the Heiromonarch's palace. We intend to strike them there, where collateral damage will be minimal."

Fowler raised a ham-sized hand and looked at Thorne. "The rumor still being planned?"

Thorne nodded. "We're going to circulate a rumor that the resistance will move against the worship service. That'll ensure the area around the cathedral will be crawling with Paracletian Order personnel. We want the focus to be there, so we'll have the best shot at pulling this off."

He paused and took a drink of water from a wooden cup. "The resistance doesn't have the *gifts* necessary to pull off this plan. And the Communion doesn't have the strength of arms to do it. But together? By doing what no one expects—by working in unison—we're going to pull the Palace of the Heiromonarch down on top of the Fathers while the worship service is underway."

"Preposterous!" Eugenia Lusk spat.

Ana Maria Gallánica laid a delicate hand on the old woman's forearm. "You know it isn't. The Three-Who-Are-One are in agreement. We can marshal the power necessary." Her voice was husky, at odds with her beautiful, light brown face and blue eyes. She looked at Thorne. "But there *is* the issue of getting our servant into the palace."

"We've got that covered," Thorne replied. "There's a secret system of tunnels beneath the city. I stumbled upon them not long ago. Church officials sometimes use them to move about unseen. Our guides will get you through them and underneath the palace. Once there, you can cast your spells to make the earth move. Gravity will pull the palace down the mountainside, killing the Crimson Fathers."

"How's that gonna work?" Fowler asked, scratching his beard.

Teska looked across the table at the burly farmer. "We'll be calling on all the brexia in Attagon and the magic of Maiden Mallumo, the Witch of Darkness. She controls the earthen element, which we need to disrupt in order to bring the palace down."

"And we shall be *vulnerable*," Ana Maria stressed. "Our sisters throughout the city will be weak during and after the casting. They will need protection."

"That's no problem," Thorne said before taking another drink. "The resistance will protect you."

"Aren't we also doing the fighting?" Corbyn asked. "Won't we be stretched too thin?"

St. Jordan shook his head. "No, Elijah. The resistance continues to grow with each passing day. With all the people coming into the city for the festival, there'll be more than enough to fight *and* protect our allies."

"The palace is fortified," Lusk groused. "You think you can pull it off the side of the mountain as easy as you pluck an apple from a tree?"

"There's one place it's not fortified," Ana Maria replied, a snippet of frustration creeping into her voice. She brushed some of her straight black hair behind her shoulder. "*Underneath*. The foundation is old, likely unkept. If we can compromise the stability of the rock and soil, gravity will do the rest."

"But what about our people under the palace?" a woman beside Ana Maria asked. "And everyone in the palace—the servants, Church officials… Are we going to let them all be killed?"

Thorne steepled his fingers. "No, we've addressed that. The resistance will send someone into the palace to contact the servants and anyone else who wants to get out. As I said, we want collateral damage to be minimal. Our scout will concoct a ruse to get people to leave. We're hoping that everybody will already be at the festival."

"Everyone will have the opportunity to escape," Ana Maria acknowledged, but she dropped her eyes and looked away as she said it.

"Except Rebekkah Barlowe!" Lusk barked. "She's going to be buried alive!"

Teska gritted her teeth. "We've been through this, Eugenia. Several times. Rebekkah's volunteering to serve as our conduit. Nobody's forcing her."

"Bah!"

Teska shook her head and looked at Thorne.

"It'll work," he said, although he knew his opinion held no weight with the old witch.

"I do have one question." St. Jordan looked around the table. "What do we do after the palace has collapsed? What comes next?"

"Do you mean that day or in the future?" Thorne asked.

"Both."

Thorne licked his lips. "With the power of the Crimson Fathers broken, we'll have the opportunity to become more visible. There are plenty of Churchmen who dislike the Fifth Order. Once all the chaos from our attack has subsided, we have to let the Church know that we seek discourse. With the Fifth Order leaderless, and the Church weak and unstable from the Fathers' machinations, it'll be a good time to be heard."

"And this discourse would pertain to…?" a man said from the end of the table.

"Freedom, of course," Thorne replied. "We cannot just usurp leadership of the Church. We're too few, and the structure of the Church too broad. We need to work *with* the Church to affect change. I believe we can begin that process once we have leverage."

"What'll be keeping the Church from just arresting an' executing us all?" a different man asked. Murmurs of agreement followed.

"We've considered that. Keep in mind that we'll have the Communion by our side, which, if I know the Church's hierarchy, will befuddle them completely. We also have momentum on our side, not to mention the goodwill and support of most of the population. Naturally, we'll have to be extremely careful with what we do and who we trust. But the Church has always been about order and stability. They'll do anything to get that back."

Lusk slapped the table with an age-spotted hand. "Do you honestly believe the Church'll take you seriously—that they'll just sit right down and forgive and forget? They'll see us all dead first!"

"Not if we play this right."

"You're a fool, Malachi Thorne. No, you're worse than that. You're an idiot. You and this trollop"—she wrinkled her nose at Teska—"are bringing ruination 'pon us all."

"Boss, you, uh, said somethin' about assignments?" Warner interrupted. He knew how to read Thorne's expressions.

Thorne appreciated his friend's awareness. Eugenia Lusk was a toxic presence. Just being around her gave him a headache. He massaged his temple. "Yes, there's plenty of preparations to be made. To begin with, I want you and Tycho to hit up the traveling carnivals—all the troubadours and minstrels you can find—any entertainers who've come to Attagon for the celebration. See if you can find people who're sympathetic to our cause. Stay alert for any news or information that can help us.

"When the time comes, Tua, I'd like for you, Elijah and a couple of brexia to escort Rebekkah Barlowe through the tunnels. Get her as close to the palace as you can." Thorne looked at Teska and Ana Maria. "We'll be counting on your ladies to help us find the best possible spot down there."

Both women nodded.

"Bartholomew, round up those you trust outside the city. See that they're armed. Reuben," he said to the man sitting beside Fowler, "you help him by getting fighters together inside the city. We need them in order to guard the brexia."

"The weetches all gonnah be inna same place?" Reuben asked. He chewed the question out slowly. He missed the glower from Lusk and the tightening of Ana Maria's mouth at the word "witch."

Nevertheless, Ana Maria forced a smile and shook her head, the light sliding up and down her hair. "No, that would put us at too much risk. Eggs in one basket, you know. We will be scattered across the city, behind closed doors."

"How meeny you gonnah have that need protecting?"

"At least one hundred and fifty," Teska said.

Ana Maria added, "Perhaps as many as two hundred."

Reuben whistled in disbelief. He was about Thorne's age, with golden hoops in each ear and a beard trimmed into twin points. "And you gonnah need…what? One guard fer each weetch?"

"At least," a brexia named Prisca said.

Thorne continued. "Lautaro, your task will be to work with some of the other men to plant weapons at key places around the city. We don't know what trouble we might run into before, during or after the attack. Our people need to be able to get their hands on weapons, if the need arises."

Lautaro smiled behind his black mustache but said nothing.

"Malachi, you want any of us around the cathedral—to cause a distraction? I mean, if the rumor's going to suggest we're doing something, do we want to—you know—actually *do* something?" The speaker was a tough-as-nails dark-skinned woman named Susara. She had found her niche in the resistance as a scout and spy. Thorne had often wondered if she might be Nahoru'brexia considering how successful she was at remaining unseen.

He shook his head but smiled at her. "No, we don't want to tie up any of our people that way. And with the Paracletian Order's increased presence around the cathedral, the risk of getting caught wouldn't be worth it."

Susara stared at him, her square face grim, but made no reply.

"But I do have a task that you're best suited for. I'd like for you to infiltrate the palace on the morning of the 31st. Come up with a plausible reason to evacuate and get as many innocents out of there as you can."

"You got it," she replied.

"Have we considered the possibility that this action may not kill the Crimson Fathers?" St. Jordan asked.

The room went silent.

"I don't know much about the Fathers," Thorne said with a sigh. "But their bodies are flesh and blood. If that palace collapses on them, there's *no way* they survive." His tone was confident, but a seed of doubt lodged in his mind.

Ana Maria folded her hands on the table. "And yet we are unaware of the kind of magic they possess," Ana Maria noted.

"You theenk they gonnah have enough magic t' keep from being buried alive?" Reuben asked, eyes bugged out.

"I don't know," Ana Maria said.

Thorne looked at her, then at Teska. "Is there any way to find out?"

Teska and Ana Maria leaned toward Lusk, who snarled at their intrusion into her space. They whispered back and forth for a moment.

Thorne turned to face the broad-shouldered man at the door. "Evan, I'm going to need you to form the resistance members in small units. I suspect all of this might spill out into the streets. We need groups of capable men—and women, if they can fight—in every section of the city, to protect the people and fight if needed. Like miniature militias in specific areas. Select a handful of men to assist you with this task. It's too big for one man alone."

He grunted in acknowledgement. "Where you want the groups, and when you want 'em in position?"

"I'll get with you later on that. For now, just find the men to help you get this going. A dozen or so should be sufficient."

Another grunt.

"Christopher, can you help get some of our less-noticeable people out on the street? I want them operating like familiars—watching and listening to everything and reporting back to us."

"I'll be happy to oblige."

"Malachi?" Teska interrupted. "Short of some serious scrying—which would require more magic than we're comfortable using—there's no real way to know just how protected the Fathers are."

"Then we need a different plan," a man beside Tua interjected.

Lusk pounced on the skepticism. "You get one shot at this," she stated, jabbing a finger at Thorne. "If you can't wipe out *all* the Fathers, the game's over. Communion won't have any strength or power left. If any Fathers survive, they'll come for you like all the demons of the Twelve Hells."

"I know, I know," Thorne replied. The throbbing in his head grew stronger.

St. Jordan spoke to the man. "Nigel, do you have an alternate plan to offer?"

"No, but—"

"Unless anyone can present a viable alternative—one that will accomplish our objectives with as minimal loss of life as possible—then we stick to this one." Nigel scowled from behind his spectacles, but St. Jordan's statement went unchallenged.

Thorne stood up and stretched. "The Festival of the New Millennium is exactly two weeks away. We'll meet again next Tuesday. Each group, be ready to report on your progress. Christopher, can you find us a place on the western side of the city? I don't want to push our luck by meeting in the same area too often."

The elderly man smiled and nodded.

Looking around the table, Thorne reminded them, "Don't trust anyone you aren't sure of. And if anyone gets caught…" He didn't need to finish the thought. It was understood. Capture meant no rescue attempts and almost certain death. From this point on, the plan was the only thing that mattered.

"Good night, be safe," he said.

A few people slipped out into the bitter night. The rest clustered in small knots, talking and planning, and trying not to think of all the things that could go wrong in the next two weeks.

30

GOODBYES

SATURDAY, DECEMBER 19, 999 AE

"Miss Vaun? I'm afraid I have some terrible news," Christopher St. Jordan said, his demeanor subdued. "You might want to sit down."

"What's going on?" Thorne asked.

St. Jordan looked at them before sitting down near the fireplace. He rested both hands on the top of his cane.

"What is it, Christopher?" Teska asked, searching his face and growing apprehensive at the glum expression.

"It's your friend, Amelia Sloan. I've…just come from her ward. A cleric from the Kyrian Order—he's just administered the Final Comfort." His voice softened with each sentence. Delivering bad news was hard enough. Being on the receiving end was worse.

"Oh God," Teska said. She covered her face with her hand. "Oh no! I'd prayed. I've *been* praying. But I hoped—" A small sob tumbled out.

Thorne went her, and she fell against his chest. Her body jerked as she wept. With one hand around her, he used the other to cradle the back of her head.

She looked at St. Jordan through watery eyes. "Wh-When?"

"Just now."

She turned into Thorne's chest again then drew back and looked up at him. "How long until she's… I mean, when the Final Comfort's performed, how much time…" She could not bring herself to finish the question.

Thorne drew her into the sanctuary of his embrace once more. "Not long, I'm afraid. Usually a few hours at most."

She sobbed harder.

For several moments, St. Jordan sat and stared at the fire. Thorne held Teska while she wept.

Eventually, she found some strength to stand on her own. She wiped her eyes with both hands. "Shit...oh shit," she said between snuffles.

"I'm terribly sorry, Miss Vaun. You have my deepest and most sincere condolences," St. Jordan said.

She nodded and rubbed her reddened nose. "It's my fault, you know," she confessed. "If I hadn't told her she was Nahoru'brexia— If I hadn't taken her away from her home—" She began to cry again, slower this time, her grief nearly exhausted.

"No," Thorne said. "This isn't your fault, Tes. You told me she wanted to see the world, to make the trip with you."

"But I should've told her no! I shouldn't have let her come along."

Thorne rubbed her back and repeated, "It's not your fault."

Teska stared into the fireplace. "I should never have let her go into those tunnels. She had no business down there."

"We didn't really have a choice," Thorne reminded her. "We had guards on our tail. We couldn't have left her behind to be captured." He hoped the logic of this would ease her suffering.

But logic meant nothing in the face of raw grief.

"She wasn't a fighter!" Teska shouted. Her red eyes were filled with sorrow, guilt and anger. "We should've—*I should've*—protected her. Made sure she was okay. She was my responsibility. I brought her into all this." She buried her face in her hands.

Tua'Ahtaki walked in. He sensed the emotion in the air like heat from a blacksmith's forge. He looked at Thorne, who motioned him aside and explained what had happened. The Nermernuh's dark eyes grew moist as he lowered his head.

"Can I—? Can I see her?" Teska asked St. Jordan.

He offered a sympathetic smile. "I'll see what I can do."

"Tes, that's risky," Thorne said. "Even if the medical ward isn't guarded—which it likely is, given the trouble we've stirred up—you'll be exposing yourself to—"

She whirled on him, fists clenched, daggers of ice shooting from her eyes. "*I'm going to see her!* I owe her that!" She struggled to suppress another sob. "I owe her," she said, voice weakening. "I-I *need* to be with her."

Thorne nodded, chastened. Tua hugged Teska, and she broke down again on his shoulder.

St. Jordan motioned for Thorne to follow him into the hallway. "It won't be easy getting her into the ward. I need to go and see if I can figure something out. It's possible"—he hesitated—"I may not be able to get her in."

"I understand. Just do the best you can." He patted St. Jordan's bony shoulder. "Thank you."

The old man gave a thin smile before limping away.

Behind Thorne, the soft weeping continued.

Teska, Tua and St. Jordan followed the physician down the ward's central hallway. Cubicles large enough for a bed, table and two chairs sat opposite one another the entire length of the ward. The sides and back walls were wood; a sliding curtain served for privacy. Some were open, revealing patients abed. Most were closed. Moans and whimpers floated on the sickly air, interspersed with the calming voices of physicians and assistants.

The Cartulian Order maintained eighteen such wards in Attagon. Most were refurbished pre-Cataclysm buildings of one or two floors. Three wards had been constructed in the mid-200s AE, making them the newest facilities, although they were nearly eight hundred years old.

Holes in the walls had been patched and repatched by stone or wood. Floors had been shorn up on multiple occasions. Every effort had been made to ensure a comfortable refuge for the sick and dying, but cracks still existed in the mortar. Leaden seals around windows still chipped away. Rain slipped through ancient shingles. The trio had climbed a flight of stairs, where the wind shrilled through fist-sized holes in the stonework.

Teska walked behind Tua, St. Jordan and the physician. Her feet and legs felt like kuzda jelly. She lifted them, set them down, lifted them, set them down—but felt only a quivering reluctance. The cloying air, heavy with suffering and herbal medicines, coated her lungs. Her mouth was dry. She already felt her eyes watering again.

Christopher St. Jordan and the physician talked quietly in familiar tones, the tap-tap-tap of his cane a rhythm she could focus on. He was one of the wealthier men in the city. His family had made their fortune generations before in textiles and dyes, and they counted Patriarchs, Sempects and Monarchs of the Church, as well as Witchfinders, Lawyers and Bishops among their clients.

St. Jordan had turned the family business over to his two sons several years ago following the accident that injured his leg. Since then, he had used his position and wealth to make Attagon a better place. His list of beneficences included orphanages and the repurposing of pre-Cataclysm buildings for housing.

Members of the Paracletian Order were prevalent as sticks in a bird's nest with the upcoming festival and the threat of the resistance. The three had arrived at the ward in St. Jordan's private carriage, and he had talked them past the guards at the main gate with eloquent ease. They bypassed the front doors, entering instead around the back. Even though thick coats and heavy hoods concealed them, Teska wondered if she would have to use her gift at any point.

"Here we are," the physician said. He pulled the curtain aside.

Teska hesitated. Tua laid a hand on her shoulder.

They had the wrong bay.

"Th-That's not Amelia," she said, her gaze pinned to the waxy figure beneath the blankets.

The physician's face was stoic but held a trace of sympathy. "I'm afraid it is, daughter."

St. Jordan smiled at Teska. "We'll wait back by the door. Take your time." The physician and St. Jordan retraced their steps.

Teska was not sure whether to go in or turn and leave. She immediately chastised herself for being selfish.

You've seen sick people before. You've seen dead people before. This isn't any different.

But it was, and she knew it. Legs still shaking, she stepped inside. She was grateful for Tua's resilient presence behind her. He drew the curtain to give them privacy.

She approached the bed and was glad for the chair as she eased down onto its worn and cushionless seat. Tua took up vigil beside her, jaw clenched as he stared down at their friend.

Looking at Amelia, Teska felt an icy river closing around her. She was conscious of everything and nothing at the same time.

Amelia's beautiful face had grayed, her cheeks and eyes sunken into the flesh. Beneath the bandages that swathed her head, her blonde hair had the color and consistency of forgotten straw in a dungeon. Her eyelids were closed. Teska saw no movement behind them.

She reached out and gingerly took Amelia's scrawny hand that lay above the covers. It reminded Teska of a dead chicken's foot, and she forced herself not to release it in disgust. She felt the wrist for a pulse but found none. Pressing a finger against Amelia's throat, she finally placed it. It was feeble and slow. Too slow.

"I'm sorry, Amelia," she said, trying to control her voice. "You didn't deserve this. All you wanted was to visit someplace new and learn how to use your gift. You wanted to be part of the Communion…" She wiped tears away with her free hand. "I don't know if you can hear me, but I want you to know you were a good friend." Her voice hitched, and she stopped to compose herself as tears slipped down her cheeks.

Tua did his best to cry without making a sound but was unsuccessful.

"I only wish I'd had the chance to know you longer. I felt— I felt like… we were sisters." She pressed her fingers against Amelia's neck once more, hoping against all hope to feel the pulse jump or become stronger. But it only continued its sluggish journey toward the inevitable. Teska lowered her head.

God, I still don't know if you're real, she said silently. *If you are, I think you're shitty for letting this happen to Amelia. She believed in you. Why didn't you do something to save her? Why can't you do something now to save her? I know I'm not good at praying, and I'm probably the last person who should be asking for favors. But couldn't you make her better? Heal her? Would that be so hard for you?*

Tua placed his hand back on her shoulder, and she began weeping again. She released Amelia's hand. "I hope that wherever you're going—that Paradise you talked about—that you'll be happy there. I hope you get to see your husband again." Her words trailed away. "I'm so sorry," she whispered. "Please forgive me." She leaned forward, elbows on her knees, and hid her face with her hands, as if she could make the world around her disappear forever.

After twenty minutes, Teska rubbed Amelia's hand and arm, leaned forward and gave her a tiny kiss on the forehead. It was like touching a lukewarm dumpling. She pulled away and hurried past Tua, fresh tears accompanying her toward the entrance. From the cubicle, she heard a haunting dirge rise and fall as Tua sang his ancestral goodbye.

Two hours later, shortly before noon, Amelia Sloan was reunited with her husband.

"He's asking for you," the young man told Thorne. He worked as a posel for the Church, delivering information and documents. He also secretly ran messages for the resistance.

"Dario?" Thorne asked. "You're sure?"

The young man nodded. "It was Physician Melnic who told me, sir."

"Where's Christopher?"

"I'm not sure, sir. After he returned Miss Vaun, I think he was headed to the mill."

Thorne scratched at his stubbly beard. "Are you doing anything for the Church right now?"

"No, sir. I'm done for the day."

"I need you to find Christopher. Tell him I need to get to Dario's ward."

The boy's eyes widened. "Are you sure, sir? I mean, the Church knows who Master Darien is. And if he's asking for you, they'll have guards everywhere."

Thorne nodded. "I know. That's why I need Christopher's help to get in. Now off you go. Time is of the essence."

As the posel hustled away, Thorne put his hands on the windowsill and stared out at the falling snow. A hot spoon stirred in his guts.

Thorne hurried between the bays. It had turned out to be a wretched day. First Amelia, now Darien. There was an old pre-Cataclysm saying—Thorne could not remember it just now. Something about when it rains…

He thrust his hands into the pockets of his coat to hide the trembling. The two men had thrown this plan together in less than an hour. Both knew how rickety it was. They had barely made it into the ward. St. Jordan's carriage had been stopped twice—once at the main gate and again as they passed the front of the building. Crusaders both times. The Fifth Order knew exactly who they had in the ward. More than that, they knew Dario Darien was the perfect bait.

St. Jordan had been able to bribe two of the guards inside, but they had only promised him half an hour. That was assuming they even kept the promise. A nice bribe plus a likely promotion for capturing two resistance leaders was too great a temptation to resist. But Thorne knew he *had* to be here, just as Teska had needed to be with Amelia.

Thorne looked from side to side as St. Jordan followed behind. Some cubicles had drawn curtains. How many Crusaders were hiding behind any one of them? How many constables or Witchfinders? Thorne quickened his pace and tried to calm the pounding of his heart.

Someone stepped into the hallway in front of Thorne. His heart leapt into his throat. Behind him, St. Jordan nearly tripped over his cane.

But it was only Physician Melnic, motioning them inside. St. Jordan breathed a sigh of relief.

Once behind the curtain, Melnic said, "I'll go keep the guards busy as long as possible. But you hurry. Only one way out; you need be on time."

"We will," St. Jordan assured him.

The little man slipped from the cubicle.

Thorne sat beside Darien's bed. He reached out and took the old man's hand as he offered it.

"Malachi," he said. His voice cracked, unable to sustain more than a few words at a time. "Thank you…for coming."

"You knew I would, my friend." Thorne stared down into the pruned face with its cap of wooly white hair. The skin stretched so tightly across his face that the contours of the skull could be traced. A milky substance covered one eye. The other blinked and squinted as if trying to focus. Darien attempted to smile, but the facial muscles did not cooperate.

Thorne swallowed hard. The spoon in his guts twisted like a serpent. Part of his stomach sent signals that it might soon disgorge its contents. Thorne swallowed again, hoping to keep it down.

At the same time, his heart was a lead plumb dropping through his chest. It ached just as it had when he had lost Merrick—his mentor's life pouring from the gash in his abdomen. The hot blood, the shattered shock in Merrick's eyes, watching as the old man's heart slowed and slowed until eventually…

Thorne swiped tears with his hand, just as Teska had done hours before in a place similar to this. "You know I'd brave the Twelve Planes of Hell for you."

Darien did a little better with his second attempt at a smile. "I know…you would. And I know—" He struggled for a deeper breath, but unable to catch one, gasped for several seconds. "I know…you're risking everything…to be here." He gestured weakly around the cramped bay with his free hand. "I…shouldn't have… called your name."

"Nonsense. Don't worry about it. Is there anything I can get you? Anything you need?"

The old man rolled his head against the pillow. "I wanted you to know that… it was an honor…serving you."

"The honor was mine," Thorne replied around the lump in his throat.

"We…had some good times, didn't we?"

"That we did. You were always there for me. I can't tell you how much I appreciate your loyalty and friendship." A tear rolled down beside his nose.

Darien looked at Thorne but his eyes seemed focused on something in the distance. "I sent Demerra…and the children…east."

"I know."

"Wh-When everything is over…and Deiparia finally has freedom and peace—" Another bout of gasping wracked his body.

Thorne squeezed his hand as if the pressure could aid his friend's breathing.

"—would you…check on them? See…that they're okay?"

Thorne nodded but did not know if Darien could see it. "Of course, I will."

Darien closed his eyes, lids fluttering. Perspiration stood out on his forehead. "They've…been through…so much."

"I-I give you my word," Thorne said, his voice breaking.

"Thank…you, my friend."

For the next few minutes, Darien said nothing. He lay with his eyes closed, his chest fighting to rise and fall.

St. Jordan stepped closer to Thorne and touched him gently on the shoulder. "Malachi…"

"Huh?" He looked up as if he had forgotten anyone else was around.

Reluctance and pity filled St. Jordan's voice. "It's time. We…we need to go. You have to get out of here."

Thorne nodded and looked back at Darien. The old clerk had opened his eyes but seemed focused on something far away. Thorne squeezed his hand, but there was no response. He squeezed again. Darien blinked and struggled to draw breath.

"Tell them…I love them."

"Dario, I—" As he spoke, the old man's chest settled. Thorne realized he was holding his own breath as he waited for his friend to breathe.

Watching.

Thorne's heart began to crack like an eggshell.

Waiting.

Darien's chest did not rise.

The plumb line broke.

Thorne squeezed the hand again and again. No response. He placed a trembling finger beneath Darien's nose and held it there while he watched the motionless chest.

A sob escaped his throat. "Oh, my friend," he said between tears.

St. Jordan still had his hand on Thorne's shoulder. He squeezed it in support. And to gently remind him they were running out of time.

Thorne swabbed his eyes and wiped his fingers on his sleeve. He touched Darien's eyelids and slowly lowered them, sealing the world out forever. "Goodbye," he whispered.

A minute passed. St. Jordan was about to say something when the curtain opened, and Physician Melnic's plump face appeared. "Time's up. You go, *now*."

Thorne stood mechanically. He placed Darien's hand back on the bed and stepped back. The crumbled pieces of his heart ached. Part of him wanted to stay. Part of him wanted to go. He felt soft pressure from St. Jordan's hand, and he slid the curtain aside.

Neither said anything as they followed Melnic downstairs to a side door. The physician cracked it and peered out into the gathering dusk. He waited. Thorne wondered which of the Twelve Heavens his friend had gone to.

"Go, now!" Melnic said, opening the door and stepping aside.

The winter wind rudely welcomed Thorne back to reality. As a wagon full of dirty bedclothes was searched by Crusaders at the front gate, Thorne and St. Jordan melted into the darkness of the trees at the edge of the ward. Both remained silent as they rode back through the emptying streets. The air was frigid, but Thorne's soul felt colder still.

31
CONCERN

MONDAY, DECEMBER 28, 999 AE

Klaus Lodaec and Tejharmal the Abomination burst into Strang's sanctum in the highest turret of the palace. Each of the Fathers claimed areas of the palace as their own. Within their sulfurous domains, they engaged in magical experiments of the blackest nature. Their rooms were gorged with shelves and arcane tomes, weights and scales, bottles of living and dead substances. Cages, chains with razored links and body parts hung from ceilings. Mortars and pestles, glass vials and sheaves of parchment covered every available surface. Sigils and glyphs adorned walls, floor and ceiling. The living remains of failed experiments—animal and human—mewed and blubbered and keened inside filthy cages. The air felt warm and soft, like fresh vomit, and reeked of a charnel house.

"What is the meaning of this intrusion?" Strang barked. His face twisted in a repulsive scowl.

"Undying One!" Lodaec gasped for breath. "We've just come from the vault—"

"Gone! Gone!" Tejharmal shrieked. He waved his furry arm in the air, the talons of his claw clicking together in agitation. "We are undone!"

"What about the vault?" Strang's expression verged on apprehension. He placed a small wooden box on the tabletop behind him.

"The Flame! Gone! Stolen!"

"*What!*" Strang roared.

Lodaec regained his breath. Sweat poured down his face from the furious rush up the stairs. Small insects dropped from his beard and scurried into the many dark places of the room. "We went to check. Kaige had a vision."

"The Flame is missing from the vault?" If Strang had actually been alive, the color would have drained from his face. He ground his teeth together, sunken eyes glinting like tempered steel. "How?" he demanded.

"Thieves! Thieves broke in!" Tejharmal's orbs were wider than usual and protruded from their sockets. Drool hung from the corners of his mouth.

"The lock was picked. Inside, we found our bones. Scattered, broken. Our animation spells raised them as we planned when the sword was removed from the altar. There were bloodstains on the floor and a large one smeared down a pillar. Tejharmal tasted it."

"Female!" he screeched, his mouth curling down. "Weeks old!"

A tiny hand with two missing fingers stretched through the bars of a nearby cage. Strang glowered in the hazy orange lamplight, snarled and kicked at it. The hand retracted swiftly.

"How was the vault discovered?" he asked. "We hid it behind a wall of rock."

"A crack in the wall—a crevice," Lodaec said, fiddling with his eye amulet. "Probably happened during an earth tremor. We found the doors open, the vault raided. There were four thieves, based on the prints I found."

Strang rubbed the side of his face. He turned away from Lodaec and Tejharmal, back to his workbench, but did not look at it. His gaze drifted up to the ceiling timbers. He put his scrawny arms behind his back and clasped his graying hands together. A faint drip-drip-drip, the moans of a suffering experiment and the tapping of Strang's foot were the only sounds.

Lodaec and Tejharmal waited.

Strang turned again to face them. "It is the resistance. They are responsible."

"The resistance! Of course, of course! The red sword!"

"Yes," Strang murmured, almost to himself. "Somehow they found their way into the tunnels."

"Do you think they were searching for the Flame?"

Strang shook his head, the bones in his neck creaking with the effort. "Of course not, Klaus. They have heard the rumors, the legends. But there is no way for them to know where the vault was."

"Found it! They did!" Saliva sprayed through the air.

"I know they found it!" Strang snapped. "It had to have been an accident. No one but us would know where to look. We were too cautious."

Lodaec raised an eyebrow. "So you believe the resistance accidentally stumbled upon the crevice? That they picked the lock and took the sword?"

Strang traced the outline of his nasal cavity. "Of course. How else could it have happened?"

"The Communion! Help from foul witches!"

"They *have* joined forces with the resistance."

"No, no," Strang said, waving a hand in the air. "We know the Communion is nearly broken. They haven't the power to scry through the barriers we erected. Perhaps they aided the resistance in locating the tunnels…" His voice, hoarse and cruel, trailed off. He was quiet for a moment. "No, they could not have discovered the vault."

"What do you wish to do, Undying One?"

Strang turned back to his table. He picked up a parchment, studied it and said over his shoulder, "Gather us in the Circle."

Lodaec and Tejharmal had informed their Death Brothers about the vault and the Flame. All of them had been arguing but ceased when Strang entered. Even Avhorus Godfury, with his near uncontainable outbursts, said nothing behind his barbed wire wrapping.

Strang took his place in front of his chair but remained standing. "The resistance is in possession of the Flame. The crude symbol left at the site of their attacks confirms this. Through an accident of sheer luck, four of them discovered our vault. They broke in and now hold the one thing that can destroy us, just as it did nearly a thousand years ago."

Phaeddark Deathlord, the second of the Fathers to be resurrected and second in command, raised his chin so his voice could be heard plainly from the hole in his throat. His lips quivered as he spoke, his mouth unable to open due to the thick stitches that held it closed. Each word vibrated the edges of the peeled opening in his throat, and a pearly substance oozed from it. "They have not released the power—*our power*—that is contained within. If they had, we would be aware of it."

"Doesss the Communion know how to accesssss it?" Oste'warg Braun asked, grinding his two sets of teeth.

"Doubtful!" Tejharmal interjected.

The crimson veil that hid Kaige Paleblight's skeletal face swayed as he said, "I agree. It is highly unlikely. My vision did not suggest such a thing."

"Still, we can't have that thing out in the open," Callodin Valhalla added. "We must get it back!"

Several of the Fathers nodded and voiced their agreement.

"And we shall." Strang sat down. His eyes glittered. "Send word through the Fifth Order. The Flame is to be procured at all costs. Instruct the familiars to increase their vigilance. A weapon such as the Flame will stand out. It cannot be carried publicly without attracting attention." He looked toward the window and the

Celestial Akropolis below. "*Someone* has seen it. I want to know who. Before the festival. We are also implementing the Freethinker Law, as of now."

"Then we have learned enough from those who are immune to the rank pins?" Jaccomus Veidt asked. His right eye lay like a slug against his cheek.

"We have," Strang replied. "All who have displayed immunity to the pins are to be executed immediately. Inform the compliance camps and ensure their obedience."

"I shall see to it," Valhalla said.

"What is the status of eluruum?" Strang asked.

Temias the Bonesorrow leaned forward, the veins of his skull palpitating. He smacked flabby lips and stared at his Death Brothers with globular eyes. "All goes well. Our army continues to grow, amassing at Last Chapel. Many of the realm's basest thieves, murderers, rapists and mercenaries are joining us."

"And the army? When will it be ready?"

Nem'kai the Masaga moved his misshapen head in what might have been a nod. "The reconnaissance and first advance, in a few months. It will take longer for the infantry since they are obstinate scum. We have already sent spies south and west to map the land and assess our enemy's capabilities."

"Excellent," Strang said. He stood, bones once again protesting. "Damn these bodies."

"Need new ones soon!" Godfury shouted, looking at Veidt's eyeball that crept lower down his face each week.

"First, the Flame," Strang said, "then new flesh."

32

SURPRISES

THURSDAY, DECEMBER 31, 999 AE

Susara was not happy. At the last minute, Thorne had instructed Hawkes and Warner to accompany her into the palace. She had protested but to no avail. "You'll need the help," Thorne had told her. "The Palace of the Heiromonarch is massive." The decision also provided her with protection.

They set out at six o'clock in the morning, just as the east teased a watery pink. The wind cut through their clothing as if they were naked. No one spoke. Hoods pulled down, they slipped like liquid shadows through the empty streets.

Ice layered the road leading up Outlook Mountain. Trees beckoned to the sky with empty limbs. As they climbed, the sunrise brightened. Snow flurries promised to join the festival later in the day.

Susara knew the quickest and easiest way into the palace was through the main gate, so they melded into the throng of servants heading to work. It was too early for the administrative personnel and functionaries to arrive. They would show up later, taking their places in rooms with blazing fireplaces that had been stoked by some of these same servants.

"Remember, once we get in," she said so only her two companions could hear, "we survey the place. We can go just about anywhere since people don't pay no attention to servants coming an' going. Just be sure you got something in your hands—a bundle of wood, a mop an' bucket, even a tray of empty cups. An' keep your explanations vague if asked what you're doing someplace."

"We gonna split up?" Warner asked.

"Initially, just to cover more ground. We'll arrange a meeting place, compare information, then get busy spreading the word. But we gotta be careful, gotta time things just so."

"Time things?" Hawkes asked.

Susara shot him a glance. "Yeah, we say something too soon, somebody gonna blab to the Fathers. We say something too late…" She did not need to finish. They all knew the consequences if they were not off the mountain before noon.

"What if we run into the Fathers?" Warner wondered aloud. "Will they know why we're there? Can they…*read minds?*"

Susara shrugged. "We don't know half a nothing about them. Just keep your heads down. Try not to look conspicuous. And pray."

The palace gate loomed into view. The trio said no more as they lumbered underneath the iron scrollwork, feet crunching through the snow and ice, past the half-frozen palace guards who paid them no mind.

Tua'Ahtaki had no idea how the old woman could even walk. Rebekkah Barlowe limped awkwardly on a twisted foot. Despite the heavy garments, her bent, scrawny form seemed more like a poor man's scarecrow than a formidable witch. But she did not complain. In fact, she had not spoken all morning. Her face was a mask of resigned determination. Two younger witches, Violet and Constance, helped her. They talked to each other in low whispers but said little to him or Elijah Corbyn.

Tua hauled the iron portcullis open, and they entered the icy mausoleum in Forest Hills Cemetery. Empty niches stared back at them. In the dimness, their breath blossomed like dying lilies.

He found the secret door ajar, just as they had left it two months ago.

Hard to believe it's been that long, Tua thought.

Putting his shoulder into the door, he shoved it open another few inches. Stone grated across stone, an explosion in the trapped silence. He stepped through onto the landing and led them into the frozen bowels of the earth.

"Light your torches," he said, producing a box of matches as they reached the room at the bottom of the stairs.

It was also just as they had left it. Tua looked at the table where he had put Amelia's injured body. He touched the dried bloodstains where her head had been and felt his eyes watering.

Such a beautiful life so brutally snuffed out. So rich with potential.

Turning away, he opened the wooden door on the other side of the room. The stale, frigid air that greeted him carried painful memories. This was one place he never imagined he would go again. He was struck by a sudden sense of suffocation and doom. He looked back, suddenly desperate to scurry up the stairs and into the rising sun. Instead, he took a deep breath, forced his anxiety down and entered the tunnel.

❖   ❖   ❖

For all her gruffness, Susara was right. They had almost unfettered access to the halls and rooms of the palace. By seven o'clock, Warner was carrying an ash bucket and small scoop from room to room on the second floor. He marveled at the architecture, the artwork and frescoes and all the gilded glory that surrounded the most powerful man in the Church.

Or who used to be the most powerful man in the Church—when we had an actual livin' Heiromonarch and not a simulucrum, Warner corrected himself.

After cleaning out a few fireplaces while assessing the second floor, he returned downstairs and met Susara at their prearranged location. It was a waiting room. They stood behind a floor-to-ceiling tapestry that hung away from the wall and was as wide as two horses.

"Where's Hawkes?" she asked.

"He ain't back yet?"

Susara raised one eyebrow. "You see him here? What'd you find?"

"Second floor's got plenty of rooms—offices, storage, some unused. I'd estimate around thirty or forty people, not includin' servants. What about you?"

Susara shook her head, her tight curls bouncing. "I couldn't get to the third floor. That's the Heiromonarch's chambers an' such. Got no idea how many people might be up there."

The waiting room door opened. Susara put a finger to her lips.

Footsteps crossed the polished floor, drawing closer.

Warner eased his short sword halfway out of its sheath. He did not know when she had pulled it out, but Susara held her dagger ready.

Hawkes appeared around the edge of the tapestry. A young woman followed him.

Susara snatched the girl by the hair and yanked her behind the tapestry. The dagger flew to her throat. She held her free hand against the woman's mouth.

"No, no! *Wait!*" Hawkes exclaimed in a hushed voice.

"What the hells you think you doing?" Susara snapped.

The girl trembled, eyes full of fear.

"It's okay," Hawkes said. "She's okay. Just— Just let her go, Susara. She's not going to hurt us."

"You let me be the judge a' that."

The woman, no more than twenty years old, raised trembling hands to show she was no threat.

"Report," Susara ordered Hawkes.

He hesitated, glancing between Susara and the woman. "Lots of room on this floor," he finally said. "Banquet halls. Meeting rooms. The kitchens. Did you know they have *three* of them?"

"Never mind that. How many people?" she asked.

"Thirty, maybe forty."

"What's *this* all about?" Warner asked, tilting his head toward the captive.

Hawkes frowned. "Let her go, Susara. I give you my word; she's not going to do anything to us."

"Don't have to do anything *to* us. She can scream, though."

"Her name's Grace. She's a servant here." Hawkes sighed. "And she told me something."

"Yeah? Like what?" The dagger remained against Grace's throat.

Hawkes pointed at the floor. "There's…there's kids here. Downstairs."

Susara and Warner exchanged glances. Warner knew that his friend's head injury would never fully heal, but what he did not know was if it was already worsening. This was no time for hallucinations.

Grace attempted to nod against the cold steel.

"There're kids down below?" Susara whispered in Grace's ear while glaring at Hawkes. "You make any sound other than 'yes' or 'no,' I'll kill you."

Grace nodded again, tears beginning to roll down her cheeks.

Susara eased the pressure from Grace's mouth but kept her hand in place.

"Yes, yes," Grace whispered.

"Explain," Susara said. She moved her hand down to the woman's shoulder and held her tight, relaxing the blade only an inch.

Hawkes smiled. "Go ahead, Grace, tell them what you told me."

Grace nodded again. "There are kids downstairs. Below the cellars. The Fathers, they keep 'em in a big room, all asleep."

"What for?" Susara demanded.

"I don't know, your ladyship. I-I saw them just once, when I went for something down there. There's a big door at the end of the cellar. It was open, so I-I went in. That's where I saw the kids."

"Don't call me 'your ladyship.' Why haven't you reported this to the authorities?" Susara asked.

Grace's eyes went wide. "Your ladyship, I'd be killed. In a most gruesome, horrible way! The Fathers say—well, their servants, anyway, since we don't ever see 'em—that if anything leaves the palace, no matter if it's a crust of bread or even a whisper, they come get you. I got no reason to doubt that."

"And how do we know you ain't a spy for them red bastards?"

"Oh no, your ladyship! Not me! I hate them! They—they got my daughter down there." Fresh tears rolled down her face.

"I told you I don't have no title." Susara thought for a moment. The deep lines in her square face made her look like a bulldog. "We stick to the plan," she said, eyeing Hawkes and Warner with an unchallengeable frown. "Quietly alert people to flee the palace. Don't linger to answer no questions. Get in an' out. Then meet back here an' we'll see about them kids."

Hawkes and Warner nodded, their faces somber.

"What about Grace?" Hawkes asked.

"She'll stay right here, with me."

Tua navigated them down the side passage marked *CEMETERY* and into the main tunnel. The cold air burned their lungs. They passed the crack in the wall behind which lay the final resting place of the Crimson Fathers. Tua did not look at it.

Behind him, Violet and Constance all but carried Rebekkah Barlowe. Corbyn brought up the rear. Even though everyone but the old woman carried a torch, the tunnels seemed darker, as if the very stones were furious at their trespass.

Still maintaining the illusion of servants, Hawkes and Warner slipped into rooms and chambers and informed the men and women they encountered that they needed to leave the palace as soon as possible.

"The Crimson Fathers are enraged," they repeated in spooked whispers, "and looking for anyone to vent their fury upon. Nobody knows why. But we've been told to say that if you can get out of the palace for a little while, it's for your own good." Curious looks and unanswered questions followed them.

They did not wait to see who responded. There was no time. Anyone who chose to remain here today would have to take their chances. Most responded without hesitation and scampered through the corridors like frightened mice. Others clustered in small groups, whispering and waiting for confirmation.

It was past eight in the morning when Hawkes and Warner returned to the tapestry.

"Show us," Susara ordered Grace. They slipped from the waiting room, and the timid blonde servant led them toward the back of the palace.

Rebekkah Barlowe's party moved into a tall cavern with more of the phosphorescent lichen on the walls.

"Rest here a moment," Tua said before walking the perimeter of the cavern. He checked the metal signage bolted at the mouth of each of the five tunnels and found the one marked *PALACE*.

Violet and Constance sat on a boulder with Barlowe in between them. All three shivered despite their bulky garments. Corbyn stood with his hands on his hips, staring around the cavern. He had remarked on the network of tunnels ever since they entered, awed by their scope and troubled by how many other secrets the Church might be keeping from the people.

"Sir, how much farther is it?" Violet asked.

Tua shook his head. "I do not know. We did not explore any of these tunnels." He pointed to a sloping hole to one side of the cavern. "We crawled out of there and went toward the cemetery."

Barlowe coughed long and hard, the effort shaking her body. She sounded phlegmy, and Tua knew this air was bad for her. He checked the small timepiece that Thorne had given him. It had already taken them over two hours to get to this point, and he did not know how much farther they had to go.

Factoring in the time just to get here, he thought, *means we will be cutting things close. Too close.*

After five minutes, he roused them and set off into the new tunnel.

Susara, Hawkes and Warner followed Grace through a kitchen ripe with the smell of yeast. Tureens hung above crackling fires, and fresh dough sat on flour-dusted kneading boards.

Before they reached the second kitchen, Grace stopped at a blue wooden door. Hawkes opened it, and they descended wide stone stairs, the air chilly and filled with the potent aroma of wines and liquor. Tapped barrels sat one after the other, forming long lines between which the four hurried. Wine racks occupied several adjoining chambers.

"There," Grace said, shivering and pointing to the end of the cellar. As they moved closer, the air took on a peculiar smell—like too many strong spices thrown together. The hairs on their arms stood up. Some of the hair on their heads did the same.

Susara wrinkled her nose. "What's that smell?"

"I know not, your ladyship. It comes from back there. Nobody's allowed beyond here."

Warner tested the door and found it locked.

"Key?" Susara pressed.

Grace shrugged her thin shoulders. "I don't know who might have a key."

"Are you shitting us?" Susara asked. She stared into Grace's scared green eyes. "There aren't any kids down there. Admit it."

"I swear to you, your ladyship—"

"An' stop calling me that! I'm no lady. I actually make my own way in the world."

Grace dropped her gaze. "I swear on my life—and on my daughter's life."

Susara looked at Hawkes and Warner. "Either of you pick it?"

Both shook their heads.

"I swear to the Church," she groused, pushing past them. "You two are about as useful as a eunuch in a whorehouse."

"Hey, we used to be deputies in the Paracletian Order," Warner replied. "They didn't teach us breakin' and enterin'."

Tua'Ahtaki had never been prone to discouragement. He tried to see the possibilities in every situation. But what lay before him tested that resolve.

"What're we gonna do now?" Corbyn said over Tua's shoulder, the defeat evident in his tone.

Tua lifted his torch higher as he surveyed the pile of rubble in the collapsed tunnel ahead.

With the door unlocked, Warner led them down a short torch-lit corridor. The smell intensified, and their scalps tingled as they neared another door. They looked through the barred window.

"By the Church," Susara whispered into the door's ancient wood.

On the other side was a large chamber. Tables overflowing with glass bottles, urns, cups, buckets, racks and boxes ran along the sides. The shadows of the vaulted ceiling remained undisturbed by the torches and lanterns that burned throughout the room. Another closed door lay sixty yards distant.

In the center of the chamber stood a cylindrical marble obelisk at least ten feet tall. Arranged around it were two dozen wooden tables on raised legs, like petals on an unholy flower. Each held the prone form of a child. Covering the children were crimson cloths emblazoned with glyphs and golden arcane script. Each child wore a diadem of shimmering metal, and a series of chains linked each table to the carved stone in the middle.

Susara, Hawkes, Warner and Grace were too busy to hear the chamber door open. They worked frantically, unhooking the chains from the tables and tossing the woolen blankets and diadems aside. Once these things were done, the children groaned, stretched lethargically and forced their eyes open. They looked around, some in confusion, others in fear.

Everyone smelled the stench first, like a rotten egg in a closet. It replaced the pungency of spices and chemicals. Several children screamed.

The adults spun around.

One of the Crimson Fathers stood in the doorway.

"You've gotta be kidding me," Hawkes said.

"*Halt!* Stop what you are doing!" The Father's voice boomed across the chamber. "Do not move!"

Warner glanced at Susara and Grace. "Get these kids loose. We'll handle that." His mind tried to choke back an *I hope* but was unsuccessful. He and Hawkes drew their short swords.

The Father strode purposefully across the room. Dressed in a red robe slit up the sides, he had dark breeches underneath. A sword hung across his chest. A second likewise at his back, its handle facing the opposite direction.

The head sat like a mound of lard atop the shoulders. The eyes were stretched at the corners, as if invisible twine pulled them toward the ears. The wide, thin mouth contained a few teeth of varying sizes. A hump rested beneath the robe on the left shoulder.

"What the hells *are* you?" Warner asked in revulsion as he witnessed his first Crimson Father up close.

The mouth curled in a disgusting parody of a grin. The air grew putrid as he moved nearer. "I am Nem'Kai the Masaga," he said, "Eighth of the Fathers. And what your death looks like."

"You sure smell like death," Warner replied. He motioned for Hawkes to flank the Father.

At six-and-a-half feet tall, Nem'Kai moved with fluid grace. He seemed unconcerned as Hawkes edged around him. In fact, he waited until Hawkes was almost behind him before he did something unexpected. With a red-gloved hand, he undid the buttons that covered the hump on his shoulder and pulled the cloth down.

From Warner's perspective, it was a lump much like Nem'Kai's head, only smaller. Blue veins lay beneath the jellied surface.

Hawkes gasped. His eyes went wide.

He stared into the misshapen face of the lump. Two baleful eyes with pale irises glared back at him while slitted nostrils quivered with each breath. The cleft mouth drooled and champed, revealing diseased gums and scattered, jagged teeth. It glared at Hawkes with fury and anticipation.

Nem'Kai began to shrug his left shoulder, leaning sideways and wiggling his arm. A loud crack followed. Nem'Kai grimaced, shrugged again and straightened up. Bone shifted against bone as the shoulder dislocated. Nem'Kai's left arm hung backward.

The Father drew the sword in front. The reversed arm drew the one in back. Warner watched in stunned silence as one of Nem's eyes went milky. Behind, Hawkes saw the same thing happen to one of Kai's orbs.

Both swords sliced through the air. Warner parried. But if he had been a second slower, he would have lost his other eye. And half of his head. Hawkes was not so lucky. Blood ran from the gash in his upper arm.

"Your companion will die beneath Kai's blade," the twisted face said to Warner, "while I end your wretched existence!" On Nem's back, Kai gnashed his teeth and keened eagerly.

In spite of the number of congregants, Teska moved around the city with relative ease. Congregants streamed along the streets, heading toward the Cathedral of the Heiromonarch. Laughter filled the blustery air. The excitement was tangible.

She had been going from house to house where her brexia sisters were hidden, checking on them and ensuring they were prepared for what was soon to come. She went about her business swiftly and cautiously, alert to any members of the Paracletian Order.

As she crossed a crowded intersection, a Crusader came toward her. She stopped instinctively but then forced herself to continue walking.

Don't attract attention!

She set her jaw and mentally prepared to use her gift if necessary.

A dozen yards before the Crusader reached her, he staggered. Righting himself, he tried to walk but stumbled again. He looked at Teska, who watched in fascination as his eyes turned black. The Crusader opened his mouth and released a shrill, agonized scream before collapsing into the muddy street. A crowd gathered as the body began to smolder. A pungent, spicy odor spread on the wind. Teska stared. The Crusader's flesh bubbled and oozed like hot wax. Acrid purple smoke steamed upward, carried off with the swirling snow. In a matter of minutes, only a charred husk remained that was part skeleton, part cancerous blob leaking from the chain mail armor and clothing.

It felt like they had been fighting for an hour. Warner barely parried another stroke. Blood ran down his arm from several cuts Nem had landed. He knew

Hawkes was barely holding his own as well. But it was not enough. Whatever else this Nem'Kai was, a skilled swordsman sat high on the list. Warner wiped sweat from his forehead as the Father's slashing blade forced him back yet again.

He had never seen anything like it before. Kai fought as skillfully from the back as Nem did from the front. There was no way to flank it. The creature lunged forward and back. It sidestepped, leapt and parried as if it were two separate entities. Just watching it move made Warner queasy.

Kai's blade bit deep. Hawkes screamed.

The floor was slick with blood. Warner slipped. As he caught himself, Nem's sword cut him again. He groaned, holding his bloody side. Hawkes yelled in pain.

We've gotta get outta here!

Warner began to panic. His attacks became sloppy, leaving him open to counterstrikes. Nem obliged, hitting him twice more—in the leg, on the arm.

Gettin' tired…weak…

"Tycho!" he yelled.

"I'm still here!"

Steel grated against steel. Grunts filled the air. Children screamed.

"Get outta here! Make for the door!"

Nem never stopped grinning. Spittle dripped between his crooked teeth. Kai's keening assumed a near sensual quality as it anticipated the kill.

"I'm not leaving you!"

"Just go, damn it! One of us has to survive!"

Hawkes hesitated and Kai squealed. Its sword arced down, nearly severing Hawkes's left arm. Blood spurted onto the cold flagstones. Hawkes collapsed. The crimson-robed figure slid back toward Hawkes to deliver the killing blow.

Warner saw a blur out of the corner of his eye. He risked a glance.

Susara raced toward Nem'Kai's side, her teeth clenched and lips drawn back. Without a sound, she launched herself through the air, striking the Father in the ribs with all her momentum. She wrapped her arms around its waist in a tackle and drove the thing to the ground.

Susara and Nem'Kai rolled over and over. The Father came out on top. Nem thrust his sword into Susara's side.

Her eyes bulged. Blood sprayed from her mouth.

Nem licked the drops that hit his face and grinned. He shoved the blade deeper. Susara screamed. The point ripped out her other side just below her ribcage. She convulsed, gasping.

Warner noticed that Kai's eye had returned to normal. He screamed and ran toward Susara. As he closed in, the eye became milky again as the twins prepared to share their unique vision.

Kai's shrill voice crescendoed just as Warner drove his sword through the Father's back. Nem'Kai screamed and raised up from Susara. Warner yanked the sword free and brought it down with all his might. The blade cleaved Kai's globby form. Blood and foul-smelling fluid spurted from the wound. Nem'Kai bellowed in pain.

The rotated arm twitched, dropping the sword. Warner planted his weapon in Nem's skull for good measure. The Father convulsed and fell off Susara's body without another sound.

Panting, his limbs quivering, Warner spit on Nem'Kai. "Fuck you!" He staggered back to Hawkes.

"You didn't listen," he said in gasping breaths. "You damn redheaded idiot!"

Hawkes offered a weak smile. "Wasn't going to leave you, Jester. You should know that. How…how bad is it?"

This time Warner grinned. "Mine or yours?" he asked as he assessed his friend's injuries. Hawkes had at least a dozen cuts. The worst by far was the shoulder. The arm hung limp, the gash deep and raw like a slice taken from an apple. Warner hoped Hawkes would be able to keep the arm.

But I ain't no physician.

"That door," Hawkes gestured weakly toward the portal far across the chamber. "Maybe…a way out of here?"

Warner finished binding the wounds as best he could with cloth cut from the Father's robe. The corpse stank even worse now that it was dead. He wrapped bandages around his own arms as he walked toward the door. The spicy odor reasserted itself. His scalp tingled again.

Grabbing the metal ring, Warner tugged the door open.

It was not just his scalp. Every inch of his skin tingled. He stared into the room beyond.

"Well?" Hawkes asked, his voice tiny in the vaulted chamber.

Warner did not answer. Hawkes managed to climb to his feet, his arm dangling from a makeshift sling. He kept looking back at the main door. If anyone else came in, they were done for.

The freed children clung to Grace, terror etched across their faces.

"C'mon, Sol. What is it?"

Warner swallowed hard. He was slowly shaking his head. "Aw, no. No!"

He stared into a chamber at least twice as large. Children lay on wooden beds in long rows, stretching back into the darkness. To his right, stairs led up to a balcony that ran the length of the chamber, which held even more occupied beds. Hundreds of them.

Maybe thousands.

33
COLLAPSE

THURSDAY, DECEMBER 31, 999 AE

Thorne eased the hayloft window open a few more inches but still not enough to be noticed. As if anyone cared. They streamed toward the cathedral, children skipping and cavorting, adults laughing and reveling in the day of festivities and the countdown to a new millennium.

Funny, Thorne thought, *just a few months ago, most of these people were petrified of what the future held.*

He had to hand it to the Fifth Order and the Church. Somehow, they had turned fear and anxiety into a carefree celebration.

As he watched through the flurrying snow, he applied a coat of oil to the Flame's blade. In the chaos that neared, he needed to be seen. In the stable below, a massive charger waited for him.

After breakfast, he and Teska had kissed and held each other, trying to ignore the possibility that this could be the last time they saw one another. He had watched her leave, trying to memorize as much about her as he could. Just in case.

She had gone to make sure all the brexia and Nahoru'brexia in her assigned section of the city were prepared. Thorne had spent the morning doing the same with the resistance. The leaders had reviewed every detail over and over until there was nothing left to do but disperse, take their places and wait.

He finished oiling the blade, slid it into the sheath and watched the Cathedral through the window.

"Look," Tua said, nodding at his torch. He held it near the pile of rubble, and the flame flickered.

"An air current!" Corbyn said with a relieved smile. "Means this can't be too thick."

"It is also good news because it means no one has used this passage in a while. Nor are they likely to."

Both men planted their torches among the rubble and began removing rocks. Violet and Constance sat with Barlowe in between them. The old woman seemed to be withering away before their very eyes.

Tua and Corbyn worked quickly but carefully. They could not risk another cave-in. As they built a new pile of stones from the old, the current grew stronger.

"What are we going to do?" Grace asked Warner for the third time. She was surrounded by two dozen children, all of them under the age of twelve. They clung to one another, the little ones crying while the older ones tried to calm and reassure them. Grace did her best to maneuver them away from the bodies of Susara and Nem'Kai.

"We've got to get them out, Sol," Hawkes said.

Anxiety built within Warner like a furious bull thundering in his chest. He had no idea what to do about the children. They did not have time to release them all. But they could not just leave them here to be buried alive when the palace fell. He turned to Grace.

"What's the closest exit from here?"

She thought for a moment. "The main doors."

Warner shook his head. "No good, it's too far. Isn't there anythin' closer?"

"Does this place have a back door?" Hawkes asked, his face pale.

Grace's eyes brightened. "Upstairs, through the third kitchen! There's a hallway that leads to the delivery entrance at the back."

"What time is it?" Hawkes asked.

"Gotta be at least nine," Warner replied. "Grace, can you and the kids help us?"

"What do you need us to do?"

Warner looked toward the far door. "We're gonna free those kids and get the hells out of here."

Teska returned to the apartment she shared with Thorne. He was not there, so she went into a small side room and drew a curtain across the doorway. Lighting several candles, she knelt on the cold floorboards, tucked her elbows to her sides and extended her arms, palms up. Softly, she began to intone the words that would grant her access to Maiden Mallumo, the Witch of Darkness.

She did not have to wait long. The light in the room assumed a nauseous green tint, causing the candles to appear like decaying flesh rather than tallow. The smell of burning wicks was replaced by a musky, reptilian odor. What felt like an invisible hand pressed against her head and shoulders while the air around her constricted, pinning her in place. She heard a voice inside her skull. It was sultry, like languid fire, a forbidden affair wherein two lovers were united not by love or passion, but serpentine coils.

Speak, Teska Vaun. The Maiden's words slid through Teska's mind.

"Blessed are you, Mother of Lunacies. Thank you for honoring me with your presence. We're almost ready."

Rebekkah Barlowe is not yet in place. When she is ready, we will begin.

"She's not in…it's been over three hours now. They should be on their way out!"

Daughter of the Moon. Relax your spirit. Trust us.

"B-But what if they—" She collected her thoughts. "What if they don't make it out?" Her voice had all the strength of a broom straw.

Things shall be as they are meant to be. We do not control the future.

The pressure against her grew heavier, tighter—like she was being squeezed by an invisible fist.

Do not forget our bargain, the Maiden said. *Bring us the Flame. In the event that Malachi Thorne does not honor his bargain with us.*

Teska would have nodded, but she could not move. "H-He will."

For his sake—and for yours—he better.

Tua'Ahtaki and Elijah Corbyn were exhausted and covered in dirt. Both wanted to rest but knew that was impossible. The timepiece showed nearly ten o'clock. They had widened the gap between the rock pile and tunnel wall, their fingers bloody from the effort. The air current pulled at their torches.

Tua crept through the gap and motioned for the women to follow. Corbyn handed each a torch, silently praying they were close to their destination. And that they would be able to get out in time.

Thirty minutes from the site of the cave-in, they reached their goal.

The tunnel stopped at a set of stone stairs that led up into the darkness. Although his limbs ached, Tua jogged to the top. He returned a moment later, announcing that there was another safe room above.

"This is it, then," Corbyn said, unable to hide the relief in his voice. "What happens now?"

Rebekkah Barlowe spoke for the first time. "Ye ken let me lay right there." Her voice was brittle but resolute.

Tua respected the old woman's journey and her commitment to her sisters. "Are you sure, Grandmother? This floor is cold and—"

"Whole damn place is cold," she snapped. "Jes' help me lay down."

Violet and Constance assisted her. Rebekkah spread her arms out in a cruciform position and put her palms flat against the floor. She released a long, gentle breath. A faint smile played at the corners of her mouth like the promise of a distant dawn.

"Bless you, Sister," Constance said.

"May the Three-Who-Are-One receive you, and may Hecate remember you for this sacrifice," Violet added. They watched Barlowe reverently for a moment before stepping close to the men.

"We must go," Constance whispered.

"That's it?" Corbyn asked in surprise. "We just leave her laying there? How's that supposed to help?"

Violet smiled. "We'll explain on the way out."

Tua checked the timepiece. His stomach felt like iron. "We— We cannot go back. There is not enough time."

"Th-Then what'll we do?" Constance cried in alarm.

"We will do the only thing we can. We have to risk going up into the palace."

Rebekkah Barlowe listened as they climbed the steps behind her. Then she listened to the silence and thought about all the friends and family she would soon see again.

Even with the children's help, Warner knew they were not going to be able to free all of them. He looked around the vast chamber and shook his head.

We haven't even started on those up there, he thought as he glanced at the balcony. He felt a lump in this throat. His wounds bled, but he had no time to staunch them. He yanked more chains and diadems free, tossed more blankets aside, knowing some of these faces would never see the sun again.

Never play outside again. Never grow up. Never fall in love.

He cursed the Fathers and the Fifth Order as he kept working.

Grace instructed the older children to keep the smaller ones close. When the time came, they all had to run as fast as they could.

On tables throughout the chamber, children awoke to find themselves in a torchlit world of strange smells, sobbing youngsters and three frantic adults.

At eleven o'clock in the morning, Thorne watched the high-ranking Church officials arrive at the cathedral in their fancy carriages, resplendent in their robes and uniforms of office. They moved through the throng of congregants like peacocks on parade.

Something at the edge of Thorne's vision caught his attention.

A hundred yards distant, a Crusader collapsed at his post.

Thorne heard an agonizing wail of pain and thought he saw smoke rising before the wind snatched it away. The Crusader didn't move.

What the hells?

Tua, Corbyn, Violet and Constance slipped from the secret door into a storage cellar. They climbed another flight of steps to a landing. A bucket of sand had several torches sticking out of it. Tua extinguished his alongside the others and faced a stone door. He grasped the metal handle and pushed.

The door did not move.

He tried again. Nothing.

With Corbyn's help, it scraped against jamb and floor. A current of warm air welcomed them, escorting rays of brighter light. Tua eased the door open a little farther and peeked out.

The room was ostentatious, verging on gaudy. Twin glass windows with silken drapes looked down upon Attagon. The walls were adorned with mounted animal heads, painted landscapes and rich tapestries. A golden candelabra on a heavy chain hung from the middle of the ceiling. Plush cushions rested on gilded chairs and lounging seats. Two suits of ancient plate armor flanked the wooden double doors.

"Wow," Corbyn said. His mouth hung open.

Tua moved to the doors without a sound. Opening one, he looked into a quiet, wood-paneled hallway.

"Come on," he said. "We cannot be far from the main doors."

The elite and wealthy were already seated in the cathedral.

Thorne saw two more Crusaders drop. The members of the Paracletian Order were becoming agitated. Thorne watched them look around in confusion. They threw cloaks over the remains of the Crusaders, smothering the purple smoke that curled from the bodies.

A wagon pulled up across the road. Several men bundled the Crusaders in the cloaks and hoisted them into the back of the wagon. When the canvas tarp was drawn back, Thorne saw at least half a dozen more corpses inside.

Hawkes felt faint. He slumped against a table while the child on it awoke. He wiped sweat from his forehead and realized his hand was trembling. His arm ached like a bitch, and gray spots had begun to dance before his eyes. But he said nothing to Warner. There were still too many children to free. He moved to the next table.

Tua, Corbyn and the two brexia ran out the front doors of the palace. The gravel drive was empty of horses or carriages. The road winding down the mountain, likewise. Snow fell harder, and the air bit into them with its frozen teeth.

Teska was not sure how it was going to happen. No one in the Communion was. Nothing like this had ever been attempted before. It was exhilarating and terrifying all at once.

She felt herself growing tired—as if she had used her gift too many times without rest. Her fingertips tingled. Then something inside her *changed*. It happened quickly, and she had no time to react. It was as if someone opened a vein and allowed her blood to run out. Except it was not blood she was losing. It was her magic, her power. She weakened and fell over on the floor. The resistance member assigned to protect her watched with concern but not surprise. He had been briefed about the fatigue Teska would experience. He put a pillow under her head and covered her with a blanket.

Across Attagon, every sister in the Enodia Communion experienced the same thing. They freely offered their power. Maiden Mallumo collected it, shaped it and fed it to Rebekkah Barlowe.

The old woman's body pulsated with energy. Tendrils of jagged emerald light leapt from her prostrate form. She opened herself to receive all of the magical power being funneled into her. It coursed through her body like mercury on fire, throbbing and prickling, building up like floodwaters behind a dam. She threw her mouth open. Green light burst from her body, splitting her skin. She quivered and convulsed but never took her palms from the tunnel floor. From the ground. From the roots of the mountain itself.

Tua, Corbyn, Violet and Constance were one quarter of the way down the mountain when the first tremor struck, as if some great giant was beginning to awaken from slumber.

Across from the Cathedral of the Heiromonarch, Thorne descended into the stable and mounted his horse.

Hawkes, Warner and Grace stopped and looked around. They had released a little over half of the children in the chamber. Dust sifted from the darkness of the ceiling. They looked at each other, the grief plain on their faces.

They were out of time.

"Go, go, go!" Warner shouted.

He herded a wave of children ahead of him and motioned for the group that followed. He had put Grace in front since she knew the way out. He and Hawkes rode the churning, crying, frenzied mass of small bodies—yelling for them to keep moving, hurry up, hold on to someone, don't stop.

They raced back through the cellar and up the stairs.

A second tremor hit, stronger than the first. Warner had to brace himself against a wall. Children were knocked off their feet. Dirt and dust rained down. There was a distant groaning, like the earth stretching. From somewhere in the palace came the sound of breaking glass and grinding stone.

Halfway down the mountain, Tua, Corbyn and the two brexia were thrown to the ground. It shuddered beneath them. Dead tree limbs dropped into the snow. When the tremor passed, they helped each other up.

"Run!" Tua ordered.

❖ ❖ ❖

"The children, Undying One! The children are gone! And our Death Brother, Nem'Kai the Masaga, is dead!" Temias the Bonesorrow shrieked as he met Vaelok Strang and the other Fathers on the grand staircase.

"What madness is this!" Strang shouted. "What is happening?"

Bits of the ceiling dropped around them. Dust fell like rain. The second tremor sent several of the Fathers crashing against the wall.

"Magic!" Avorhus Godfury yelled. "Magic built up! The Communion!"

"Where are the children?" Strang snatched the Bonesorrow by the robes, hauled him close to his empty nasal cavity and glared into the expanding, pulpy eyes. *"Where?"*

"I-I do not know, Undying One! Some are still in the chamber below. But many others are missing."

Strang snarled, seething. He thrust Temias aside.

"Find them! We must have them back!" Tejharmal the Abomination shouted, flailing his arms to keep his balance.

"We mussst ssstrike back!" Oste'warg Braun hissed. "We are under attack!"

Callodin Valhalla gripped the banniser. "How is this possible? Who is behind this?"

"The children! The children! We need them!"

"Destroy our enemies!" Klaus Lodaec bellowed. "Vengeance for our Death Brother!"

Strang hurried down the stairs, the rest of the Fathers trailing behind. He whirled around and grabbed Temias by the shoulders. "How many children remain?" he demanded.

"L-Less than half, Undying One."

A third tremor sent them all to the floor. The tiles cracked, shards catapulting into the air. Artwork fell from the walls. Fractures raced up and around columns. Chunks of masonry vibrated loose. The grinding of stone against stone grew louder, stronger, deeper.

Strang struggled to his feet. "Phaeddark, Temias, Kaige, Callodin—join me. The rest of you, cast a protection sphere around the children. We *must* keep them alive if we are to have Crusaders!"

"But what of Nem'Kai? And the Communion?" Jaccomus Veidt asked. "Surely we—"

"Not now!" Strang shrieked. "Protect the children!"

A fourth tremor brought with it the resounding crash of walls collapsing. The palace bucked like a young foal.

"What do you wish of us?" Phaeddark Deathlord gurgled through his throat.

Hatred blazed in Strang's deep-set eyes, icy and evil. "Form the pentacle. While our Death Brothers secure the children, we shall attempt to secure all of us."

Outside the cathedral, congregants picked themselves off the snowy ground following the second tremor. Screams filled the air. Witchfinders, constables and deputies attempted to quell the panic, but there were too many people. As they had streamed into the magnificent building a little over an hour before, now they stampeded out.

Thorne opened the stable door. He climbed into the saddle and drew the Flame from the sheath across his back. The horse was jittery, but he managed to keep it in check. He steered toward the door, but before he exited, he struck a match across his saddle horn. He touched it to the edge of the Flame. There was a whoosh of air, and flames raced up the metal. Holding the blazing weapon aloft, he spurred the horse toward the cathedral.

Warner shoved children out the door, but they just kept coming. He looked at the long line snaking its way up the shuddering mountainside. Boulders tumbled down the slopes. Trees splintered and fell, sliding and gathering momentum.

The entire mountain reverberated with ear-splitting thunder.

Behind him, Warner heard the palace coming apart. He ducked back inside and tried to force the children to go faster. Hawkes stumbled past him, eyes wide, his complexion a ghastly alabaster.

And still the children kept coming.

Ceiling beams snapped, filling rooms with dust and debris. Vaulting stones crumbled, weight redistributed, and vast sections of the structure plunged into the foundations and down the mountain.

Through the blowing dust, Warner thought he could see the final few children. He tried his best to smile and motioned for them to hurry.

They were right beside him when the floor disintegrated, and they plummeted into the earth.

Thorne charged through the throng of people. The sword's fire blazed brighter as the wind fed the flames. The ground pitched violently in the throes of the third tremor. He had to redirect his horse several times to avoid gaping chasms that opened along the ground.

The stained-glass window on the northern end of the cathedral shattered in a hundred million shards that, for a brief second, hung in the air like painted snowflakes. Several of the cathedral bells broke from their headstocks, smashing through stone and beam and facade in a waterfall of masonry.

People screamed and prayed and wept, assuming the new millennium was, indeed, the end of the world. Others stood, transfixed, eyes riveted on the side of Outlook Mountain.

Crying children brought Warner out of darkness. He winced as he tried to move. He was not dead but sure as hells felt like it. He opened his eye. Along with three small children, he was lying on a slab of masonry overhanging the ruinous gulf of what had once been the back half of the palace. He coughed dust from his lungs and sat up.

The ledge groaned. Small stones and debris rattled down into the swirling, smoky dust.

The children clung to each other, whimpering.

Around them, the ground continued to tremble and heave.

They had minutes left. If that.

Rebekkah Barlowe breathed her last. Tons of stone buried her as the full magical might of the Enodia Communion poured into the soil and rock. Maiden Mallumo exerted her mystical influence over the mountain, sheathing it in a translucent jade light that would, from that day on, allot it the name Witchfire Mountain.

Attagon shook and rattled as the earth vibrated. Waves crested across the River Tense, flooding the streets of the business district. Buildings burnt as oil lanterns and torches fell among combustible materials. Animals fled. People raced through the streets, beseeching the Church for aid and mercy.

And outside the cathedral, Malachi Thorne rose in his stirrups, held the Flame high and screamed over the cacophonous roar of the mountain, "Death to the Crimson Fathers! Death to the Fifth Order! Rise up, Attagon! This is the hour of your freedom! Stand with us and shape a bold, new world!"

High above, the Palace of the Heiromonarch shuddered one last time. Its stones surrendered to the call of gravity. With a deafening smash, it plunged down the mountain, pulverizing everything in its path.

When the avalanche settled, a two-story mound of rubble abutted the western edge of the city.

34
LOSSES

THURSDAY, DECEMBER 31, 999 AE

No one moved.

Speechless, they stared at the talus pile of debris beyond the Paracletian Order offices. The echoes died away, and the dust dispersed on the wind. The mountain bore a massive scar down its eastern slope.

Before the shock could wear off, and before he lost the initiative, Thorne spurred his horse through the crowd, shouting, "Long live the resistance! Freedom for all!" He held the burning blade aloft. The wind bit his ears and nose.

It worked! By all that's holy, it worked!

He could barely contain his elation. The blood raced in his veins, and his heart swelled with victory.

"Long live the resistance!" someone yelled.

Thorne grinned wider and whooped at the snowy sky. Now that he was out in front of the crowd, he wheeled his horse around. He looked them over. Thousands of faces stared back. He waved the sword, the flames crackling.

"Citizens of Attagon and congregants of Deiparia!" he bellowed. The wind caught his voice and carried it over the crowd. "Today is the day of our freedom! The Crimson Fathers are defeated! It's time for the Fifth Order to fall! The resistance fights for *you*, and for a realm free of control and deception!"

Shouts of acclamation resounded. Fists pumped in the air.

"This"—he waved at the Paracletian Order campus and the tower of rubble behind him—"is the work of the resistance and the Enodia Communion! We joined forces to liberate Deiparia! But our fight is not over! We need your help!"

More cheers.

Thorne saw Witchfinders, constables and deputies shoving their way toward him.

"This is very important!" he shouted. His deep voice flowed well among the buildings. "Capture—*do not kill*—the Crusaders! They are somehow tied to your children! Do *not* harm them!"

"Lies!" a Witchfinder yelled.

"This man is a known heretic and traitor," another added. "Restrain him!"

The authorities continued to push through the congregants. Thorne did not want to fight them. They were just like he was, once. But he also could not let himself be captured. He was about to turn his horse when he saw the crowd move.

It began small, like a ripple. But it spread quickly. Congregants grabbed the Witchfinders, constables and deputies and held them. As more Churchmen appeared and attempted to reach Thorne, they were also restrained.

They're doing it! he thought. *By God, they're rising up!*

Chants of "FREEDOM!" began, picked up and shared by more and more voices. From his vantage point, Thorne saw some of the resistance members moving among the crowd, encouraging and stoking the people's fervor. He could not help laughing as a resistance member with tears in his eyes gave him a thumbs-up.

"Friends!" Thorne yelled louder so he could be heard over the rising tide of emotion. "Don't injure the Churchmen! Don't bloody your hands or your conscience!"

More and more people arrived to swell the mass that shouted and whooped before him.

"Tomorrow begins a new millennium! A new day dawns, where all people will be free to live as they desire. The resistance demands the dissolution of the Fifth Order! We will no longer take orders from them!"

"NO MORE, NO MORE!" the people shouted.

"Down with the Fifth Order!"

"Freedom for Deiparia!"

"Give us back our children!"

"No more Crusaders!"

"This is the end of the world! We're all going to die!"

"Tear down the compliance camps!"

Thorne rose in his stirrups. "Friends! Congregants! We have but struck the first blow! Much hard work lies ahead of us! The resistance will do everything possible to help—"

A woman screamed, then another. Like the wave of support a moment before, a different wave broke over the people. More screams, gaping mouths, pointing fingers, all directed toward Thorne.

No, not at him. *Behind* him.

He turned, expecting to find a contingent from the Paracletian Order ready to surround him. Instead, what he saw froze his blood.

Jagged forks of purple lightning shot up from the palace rubble. At first, there were only a few scattered here and there. But they grew in number and intensity, flickering higher. A tremor passed through the ground. Loose masonry toppled from the pile.

Thorne's horse began pawing the ground. A second, stronger tremor brought with it a far-off rumbling and grinding. The purple light quivered. Lightning raced across the talus pile.

Thorne's heart no longer swelled. It turned cold as a corpse. Disbelief and the bitterness of despair stunned him.

The rumbling continued. As everyone watched, massive chunks of stone encased in purple light floated upward, as if unseen hands were lifting them from the earth. More and more pieces arose, each rotating slowly, until the air seemed like a mirror image of the ground.

The purple light intensified. Debris shifted and fell.

Something pushed on it from underneath, then busted out, flinging rubble in every direction. The levitating wreckage rocketed into the sky. From the center of the rubble, a globe of purple light arose.

Thorne's mouth fell open. The crowd shouted and cried. Panic seized them as the floating stones began to rain from the sky. Screams of fear and agony filled the air. The heavier blocks crushed people like bugs. The crowd fled, trampling one another to escape the glowing sphere that held the Crimson Fathers.

Thorne's heart shattered. He counted seven of them.

"Sol! Sol! Can you hear me?" Hawkes shouted. His voice was like crystal in the frigid air after the deafening collapse of the palace.

"Down here!" Warner yelled.

A moment later, Hawkes appeared at the edge of the crater. The relief on his face was written large. "Shit, man, I thought I'd lost you."

"You gotta get these kids!"

Terrified, dirty faces stared up at him. Loose rock crumbled all around the hole. They were hunkered down on a tilted chunk of stone—about six feet below the rim—but there was no way they could climb out. There was no rope, either.

"Can you lift them up?" Hawkes asked. He lay on the edge and reached down toward them with his right arm.

Warner was worried about his friend. Hawkes's blanched face was streaked with sweat, and his hair lay plastered to his scalp. His skin was the color of old fireplace ashes.

Something tugged at Warner's sleeve.

A dust-streaked little boy with wide brown eyes looked up at him. "Are we gonna die?" he asked in a tiny voice. Warner saw the lad searching his face for a sign of hope.

He smiled. "No way, kid. My buddy's gonna help get us outta here."

The ledge shifted a little more. Warner squatted down so he was eye level with the children. The ledge groaned again.

"Now listen," he said, trying to keep his voice firm but gentle. "What're your names?"

"Joseph," the boy at his side said. "That's Micah, an' she's Samantha."

"Great. Now, I need all of you to do somethin' very brave. I'm goin' to lift you up one at a time. You grab my friend's hand, and he'll pull you to safety. We gotta get off this rock and get you back to your parents. I'll bet you've been missin' them, huh? Who wants to go first?"

The children looked at each other and at Warner. The ledge shifted again, the rocks scraping and cracking. More dirt fell from the sides.

"C'mon, kids, time to go!"

Without waiting, Warner picked up Micah and thrust him toward Hawkes. The boy wiggled, his short arms flailing. Hawkes latched onto his wrist and hauled him up. Warner was troubled by the intense strain on his friend's face. *He can't keep goin' much longer.*

"Samantha," he said, beckoning for her.

She shook her head. Tears spilled from the corners of her eyes.

Instead, he hoisted Joseph toward the rim, and Hawkes managed to lift him out.

The ledge swayed beneath them. Warner grabbed Samantha and flung himself against the side of the crater, trying to minimize the weight on the stone. It tilted and began sliding away from the wall.

"Tycho!"

Warner stood on his tip toes, holding Samantha up. She continued to cry as Hawkes once again threw himself down, reached into the abyss and pulled the little girl up by the arm.

The ledge gave a final shudder. The sides of the crater shed dirt and stone. A low rumbling rose from deep in the ground. It grew in magnitude. The mountainside trembled in the aftershock.

Warner leapt just before the ledge collapsed. His hands clawed for the edge but found only crumbling soil.

A hand locked around his wrist.

Hawkes lay on the edge, perilously close to sliding over himself. His breath came in ragged gasps. He shook like a leaf in a storm. Sweat poured down his face and arms.

Hawkes must have known what Warner was thinking, could probably read it on his face. In his condition, there was no way Hawkes could pull him to safety. Warner weighed too much.

"Hang…on," Hawkes said through clenched teeth.

Grimacing in pain, Hawkes pulled his injured left arm out of the sling. Tears ran from his eyes as he groaned through the agony. He was white as the fresh snow.

"Tycho, no! You can't—"

With supreme effort Hawkes grabbed Warner's wrist with both hands. He panted like a dog, his body convulsing with every breath. He strained to pull Warner up.

Warner had always been the shorter but stockier of the two. Hawkes was tall and lean, an acrobat during his childhood among the traveling carnivals. He pulled again but had no leverage. Even with several of the older children now holding onto his legs, trying to anchor him, he could not do it.

"You're gonna…have to climb up!"

"Tycho, I can't! The strain on your arm—"

"Just do it!" he shouted, and immediately regretted the extra exertion. Spots exploded across his vision. He clenched his teeth and fought against the blackness that pulled at him.

Warner knew he had no choice. He reached higher, grabbed at the elbow, trying to ignore his friend's scream. They had shed their heavy coats in the warm chamber below while releasing the children. There had been no time to put them back on. The sweat on Hawkes's bare arms caused Warner's hand to slip off like a greased pig. The sudden shift in weight and balance caused his other hand to slide down.

"NO!" Hawkes bellowed as he attempted to get a better grasp. Sweat ran into his eyes. A white-hot dagger of pain drove up into his shoulder. *"No!"*

Inch by inch, Warner's hand slid from Hawkes's sweaty, trembling clutch. He tried to find a foothold on the soft wall but only succeeded in losing his grip even more.

"Sol, no!"

Warner saw his friend laying on the edge, arms dangling. He was screaming something, but the wind rushing past Warner's ears drowned it out. He smiled as he saw Joseph, Micah and Samantha standing beside Hawkes.

Warner plunged, screaming, into the clouds of rising dust.

Hawkes heard his friend's scream dwindle and then abruptly end. He buried his face in the dirt and wept.

Vaelok Strang tilted his head back and looked down with malevolence on the pathetic mass. They screamed and shoved, responding only to the primitive instinct to preserve their miserable lives. They were insects. He scoffed as he pointed a bony hand down toward the chaos.

Purple lightning shot from his fingertip. It struck a man in the crowd at random. His body curled like a dying spider, consumed by indigo flames.

Beside him, Phaeddark Deathlord, Kaige Paleblight, Avorhus Godfury, Oste'warg Braun, Tejharmal the Abomination, and Temias the Bonesorrow floated in the air, glaring down upon the frenzied mob. They also dispensed death with lightning and purple fire. The stench of crisping flesh and the screams of the terrified and dying swirled with the wind.

Contorted, blackened bodies littered the street. The Fathers floated slowly away from the rubble, toward the cathedral, pursuing the crowd. They halted when they saw Thorne and the Flame.

We've failed! I underestimated their power! And now we're all going to pay for it, Thorne thought.

Their one chance had managed to destroy only a few of the Fathers. Eugenia Lusk had been right all along.

Suddenly, Thorne felt very small. Inconsequential. Hope fractured, disintegrated.

He cursed his arrogance and the Fathers. The crowd, so enthusiastic and enthralled only moments before, now scrambled for safety and cowered in fear.

He was alone.

The Crimson Fathers levitated closer. They did not walk through the air. They stood still, their forms gliding like hawks on the wind.

A fierce current tainted by the acrid stench of charred flesh whipped around Thorne, blowing snow in every direction. Behind him, the empty street seemed to darken and grow colder.

Or was it just the numbness of defeat and the inevitability of death settling upon him?

"Malachi!"

He turned in the saddle.

Armed members of the resistance walked toward him, their faces set in somber determination. There had to be several hundred of them filling the street. They stopped a few yards behind his horse. At the head of the pack were Bartholomew Fowler, Jon Cardwell, Michael Osman, Paul Keene and other resistance leaders. Most carried swords and axes. Some had pikes or bows and arrows. A few carried pitchforks and clubs.

"What're you doing?" Thorne asked, his voice caught between hope and despair. "Get out of here! They'll kill you all!"

"No way," Cardwell said, his mouth set in a firm line.

"We started this thing together," Fowler added. "We finish it together—one way or another."

Beneath his helmet, Paul Keene narrowed his gray eyes. "They might kill us all. But we'll take some of the bastards with us before they do."

Thorne's expression softened. He smiled, grateful to know that he would not die alone.

Overhead, the Fathers gloated. Vile hatred disfigured their faces even more. Purple light pulsated around each of them. The one in front, wispy gray hair and beard fluttering, pointed at Thorne.

"Take the Flame," it growled, "and kill every living thing here."

The resistance fighters looked around as the light in the street dimmed. It had an ashen quality to it, like seeing through smoke. They fidgeted but set their jaws and gripped their weapons tighter.

The Father with the skeletal, noseless head bellowed, "We shall shred your souls. They will hang in eternity, and we shall delight in flaying them bit by bit. You cannot stand against us. We are your masters."

The purple light flared around them.

Thorne felt a wave of— *What?* Energy? Power? Magic? It washed over him, causing he air to feel grimy and gritty.

"Ready yourselves!" Thorne yelled over his shoulder. "There's more of us than there are of them!"

The sky darkened. The clouds assumed a repellent, dingy hue.

Michael Osman stepped beside Thorne's horse and looked up. "Can we win this?"

Without taking his eyes from the Fathers, Thorne shook his head. He tried to keep the defeat out of his voice but failed. "Truthfully? No, I don't think we can. I'm sure they can pick us off one by one from up there. We can't fight power like that—"

"Of course, you can't," a voice said from behind.

Turning once again, Thorne's mouth dropped open. It was becoming a habit today.

"But *we* can."

At the far end of the street, behind the last of the resistance fighters, three female figures hovered in the air. The one in the middle was ancient, with cracked, blackened skin. To one side was a beautiful young woman, whose face was covered by veils. To the other side was a plump, matronly figure in a gray smock.

"Who the hells?" Osman asked.

A grin crept to the corners of Thorne's mouth, and his eyes shone. "Looks like our back-up. Say hello to the Three Witches of the Enodia Communion! I think our odds of survival just improved a whole lot."

35
BATTLEGROUND

THURSDAY, DECEMBER 31, 999 AE

Barbed tendrils of purple light crackled and flickered from each Father. Thorne glanced around as he heard running feet.

Crusaders in helmets and purple capes with broad swords drawn—and members of the Paracletian Order in wine-colored leather armor and black cloaks—filled the street in front of him. They blocked any possibility of retreat. They poured from alleyways along the street, boxing in the resistance, but made no move to engage.

"What're they doing?" Osman asked.

"Waiting for the signal to attack," Thorne replied. "The Fathers aren't going to come down here. One touch from this blade will destroy them for good."

"Obliterate them," Strang shouted. "Now!"

Angry lightning erupted from their fingertips, striking the mystical glowing shields the Three Witches raised just in time. It fizzed and arced around the shields. The Three-Who-Are-One made rhythmic gestures with their free hands. Jade-colored darts of energy shot back at the Fathers.

Crusaders and Churchmen yelled and charged into the resistance.

Metal sung as it clattered and slashed. Wheeling his mount around, Thorne rode to meet two Crusaders. Their broadswords grated against the Flame, birthing sparks. When he returned for another pass, the Crusaders sliced the horse out from under him.

Thorne toppled from the saddle. He landed hard but maintained his grip on the Flame. The Crusaders closed in. Behind them, he saw members of the resistance. A few were holding their own against Witchfinders or constables. Others were being driven back by Crusaders. Bodies lay in the street.

The jade energy could not penetrate the purple auras around each Father. It buffeted them and forced them to break ranks. But no damage had been delivered.

Still gliding on the air, the Fathers drifted apart. They encircled Maiden, Mother and Matriarch like rings around a planet. The Three-Who-Are-One stood back-to-back in a triangular formation.

Maiden Mallumo spoke ancient words and motioned at the palace debris. Large chunks of rock rose into the air. Another motion, and they crashed into the Fathers' shields. Mother Depresja also wove esoteric patterns in the air, and columns of flame erupted from the cracks in the earth, striking the Fathers.

Matriarch Trahnen waved blackened arms, protecting herself from multiple attacks with one hand while sending serpentine tendrils of energy at her opponents with the other.

While some of the Fathers maintained shields, others launched counterattacks. Purple flame struck the seething mass in the street, obliterating swaths of resistance, Churchmen and Fifth Order alike.

Slowly, the Crimson Fathers pushed in toward the Three Witches. The women fought hard but were no match for the varied attacks that came at them from every direction. They were weak before this confrontation began. Indigo light began to pierce their faltering shields.

Given the circumstances, Thorne counted himself extremely lucky. A bolt of energy had blistered the ground between him and his two attackers. He used the momentary reprieve to jump to his feet.

The two Crusaders came at him again. He knew he could not defeat both. But as he parried and thrust, he once again noticed his arm felt lighter. It did not seem as if he were holding a weapon at all. He had no time to analyze the peculiarity. All his focus was on his two adversaries.

Members of the resistance clustered against the front of a building. They tried to fight, but their better-armed, better-protected opponents gave no quarter.

Overhead, Oste'warg Braun paused in his assault upon the Three. He gestured, clenched his fist and cast an open palm toward the building. The structure quivered, and the front collapsed into the street, burying the freedom fighters. Braun gloated, his two sets of teeth shining.

Thorne could tell his opponents were getting frustrated. He had managed to stay just out of the reach of their blades. Of course, he had failed to land any meaningful blows, either. Their chain mail was nicked and broken in a few places, but there was no blood.

Although the sword felt light as a quill in his hand, Thorne grew winded. He heard screaming and something that sounded like a building falling. Dust billowed up, but he was unable to see what had happened through the two armies clashing in the street.

Suddenly, one of the two Crusaders fell in front of Thorne. Tua stood behind, sword in one hand, a large rock in the other. Dirt and blood streaked his face. The Crusader rose to his elbows, but Tua whacked him in the helmet with the rock. The giant fell back on the ground.

With Tua's help, Thorne managed to get the second Crusader down. Tua brained him with the rock as well.

"Thank you!" Thorne yelled as they both turned to reenter the melee.

Tua grunted an acknowledgement.

"Watch out!" a resistance member yelled.

Thorne grabbed Tua and yanked him aside just as a crevice split the street where he had been standing.

Tua looked at it and back at Thorne. "My thanks," he said, staring at the widening gap.

More bodies filled the street. Purple fire continued to fall from the sky. Buildings burned with a foul, pestilential odor. Coruscating ribbons of energy webbed the sky.

Thorne and Tua fought back-to-back. Thorne recognized some of the men who stood against him. They were Witchfinders and constables he had worked with, with whom he had broken bread and shared drinks by the fire. He wondered if his expression mirrored the confusion and trepidation he saw on their faces.

The resistance began to waver. Most still fought. A few had surrendered and were clapped in irons. Those that tried to flee down the alleys met sharp, silver death.

Tua slipped in a pool of blood. He tried to regain his balance but rolled his ankle on a piece of stone. He pitched to the ground, cursing.

Thorne reached down to help him up. Before Tua could grab his hand, a Crusader appeared out of the smoke and dust on Thorne's flank.

The giant had lost his sword. Instead, he carried a thick club. He swung it with both hands and slammed it into Thorne's back, knocking spittle from his mouth. He staggered forward, spine and shoulders screaming. Raising the Flame, he turned. But not in time.

The club struck his chest. Thorne was sure that he heard something crack. He left his feet and sailed backward through the air. The Flame spiraled from his grasp.

The Crimson Fathers and the Three Witches paused as the Flame clattered against debris and came to rest near the mouth of an alley. Strang's face broke into a greedy smile. The Three-Who-Are-One looked at the blade with eager possessiveness.

Matriarch Trahnen renewed her attacks. Maiden Mallumo and Mother Depresja joined her. Their spells shimmered in the smoke and flurrying snow. But the green of their magic continued to dim against the glowing purple thaumaturgy of the Fathers.

Thorne forced himself to sit up, grimacing as he held his chest. Pain flared through his torso. It was all he could do to keep from falling over. The Crusader walked toward him, club swinging.

Tua lay defenseless at the feet of two deputies, their swords pointed at his chest.

Bartholomew Fowler still fought, brandishing a pitchfork with skill and ease. Jon Cardwell lay dead. Michael Osman, too. Thorne gritted his teeth. He saw no sign of Paul Keene. A quick survey of the street found two more resistance leaders lifeless among the rubble and putrid fires.

Thorne was about to stand and meet his attacker with a chunk of stone in his hands when the Flame rose into the air.

Minh Van shook his head. "This is all wrong, ma'am, if you don't mind me saying such."

Teska groaned. "I do mind. Shut up and get me to Malachi."

He continued to bear Teska's weight as he navigated through the streets. He was a haberdasher by trade and only marginally proficient with a weapon. Thorne had assigned him the responsibility of guarding Teska during and after the Communion's spell had been cast. He had been briefed on what would happen to Teska in the aftermath. What the middle-aged man had not anticipated was her awakening so quickly—or that she would demand to be taken to Thorne.

He had tried to talk her out of the idea. "It isn't safe," he had told her. "You're too weak. Malachi told me to stay *here* with you. You need to rest."

She paid no attention to anything he said. In fact, the more he tried to reason with her, the angrier she became. When Minh first met Teska, she had short black hair. But over the past few weeks, it had grown to cover her neck, and she had removed the last of the walnut tree bark and pickled leeches she used for hair dye. Now it was her natural vermilion. So he understood her stubbornness. And her temper.

"Damn it, Minh! Take me to him—or I'll crawl across this city by myself!"

"M-Malachi will kill me."

"I'll do *worse* than kill you if you don't move your ass!"

Minh figured he would be able to weather Malachi's wrath if it came to that. But Teska was another matter. She was Nahoru'brexia. It was not worth the risk of being cursed or turned into a bat or something…unsavory.

So now here he was, nearly carrying her through muddy alleys and frightened crowds. Her hair hung in sweaty strands, yet her skin was freezing and blanched. Minh had thought about warning her of the risk of being out in the cold with wet hair but decided against it. It was probably the smartest thing he had done all day.

The sounds of battle reached them. Men screamed and cursed and died. Metal shrieked and clanged. A fetid aroma, like soured milk and burnt hair, mixed with smoke on the wind. The sky was a scintillating display of purple and green light. Mostly purple.

"Keep going," she instructed Minh when he slowed down.

"Ma'am, you don't want to get too close—"

"Minh!" she yelled and went limp against him like a stunned eel.

Grabbing her beneath the arms, he dragged her to the mouth of the alley and propped her against the wall. He looked out into the street. Bodies littered the ground. Wide, steaming fissures gashed the earth. Fires raged. Overhead, the witches were losing. On the ground, the resistance was shrinking.

Minh felt his stomach drop. Panic gripped him like a vise. He knew he should help. He should pick up a weapon, defend his colleagues, do *something*. But he could not move. He trembled. His feet felt like blocks of ice.

Teska opened her eyes and saw the carnage in front of her. Churchmen swarmed around resistance members, knocking them to the ground, restraining them. And she saw Malachi. He struggled to get to his feet. A Crusader with a club closed on him.

Without warning, a stabbing pain ripped through her chest. It felt like someone had run a spear all the way through her body. Her stomach cramped, nearly doubling her over. She cried out in torment.

Then she saw shooting stars in the sky. *Green* shooting stars.

Except they were not shooting stars.

Matriarch Trahnen, Mother Depresja, and Maiden Mallumo plummeted out of the sky, tattered ribbons of jade energy trailing behind them like shredded kites. Teska felt them diminishing, dwindling, dying. They crashed to the ground on the next street over. At that moment, the last vestige of strength fled Teska's body. She collapsed among the rubble.

Something called to Teska. Several voices said the same thing over top of each other. She could not make out the words. A part of her felt like she knew them from somewhere.

Behind the voices, a coldness lurked. It promised her something. The coldness would save her life, make her whole, give her power. She could live forever. Once more, the promises of rest and protection came. Everything she ever wanted was within reach. All she had to do was take it. She heard. She understood.

Forcing her eyes open, Teska scanned the debris-littered street. She pushed herself onto her hands and knees, then crawled slowly through the rubble and bodies. Unsure of where she was going, she let the voices guide her.

She found what she sought—found her life, her wholeness, her salvation. Sitting on her knees, she reached down and took the wire-wrapped grip in her hand. She exhaled and opened her mind.

It was like being struck by lightning except without the agony. Instead, strength and energy surged through her body. She raised the Flame over her head with one hand.

Crusaders and Churchmen continued to fight what remained of the resistance. The cries of the suffering and moans of the dying surrounded her. Besieged, Thorne had no weapon other than a rock. Tua was in trouble.

"NO!" she yelled and jumped to her feet. Her hazel eyes blazed with newfound fury. She swung the Flame down in front of her as hard as she could, the point striking the ground.

A wave of scarlet light exploded from the blade. It pushed outward, a single gigantic ripple that raced away from her in every direction. As it struck Crusaders and Churchmen, their flesh blackened and disintegrated, leaving behind only skeletons that crumpled to the ground. As the light wave washed against the buildings, it dissipated into nothingness.

The remaining members of the resistance stood dumbfounded.

The voices caressed Teska's mind with promises. The coldness opened its arms to her.

"Yes! Yes!" Avorhus Godfury shrieked. The Fathers descended toward the battleground.

"At last," Vaelok Strang exclaimed, "after so many agonizing centuries!"

Power coursed through Teska's veins. She had never felt anything like it. The Maiden's magic was parlor tricks compared to this.

She grinned.

Something colder than a thousand winters paralyzed Thorne as he saw her face. "Oh God, Tes— Wh-What've you *done*?"

The Crimson Fathers touched the earth. The purple auras disappeared. They stood in a semicircle in front of Teska. Strang smiled and rubbed bony hands together in triumph.

"We have our receptacle," Kaige Paleblight said from behind his veil.

"Perfect!" Godfury screamed. "Perfect!"

Temias the Bonesorrow licked his flabby lips. His boiled eyes nearly glazed with lustful greed.

"Nothing can stand before us now," Strang said. He stepped forward and extended his hand to her.

Teska saw the Crimson Fathers arrayed in front of her. They were talking, but she could not hear them. She heard only the icy voices. They penetrated her mind, sifted through her memories, scoffed at her dreams. They drank in her fears and feasted on her pain.

And they showed her things.

Familiar and unfamiliar lands.

Treasure.

Mountains in the middle of the sea.

A black void.

Decay.

Stars aligning.

An army on the move.

Dominion.

Children on tables.

A citadel among the precipices.

Obeisance before her.

Wrath.

Floating on the wind.

Eternal life.

Then Teska's soul peeled apart. Her mind collapsed. The voices and the coldness found sanctuary within her. They were now *her* voices, *her* coldness. She wanted to protect and nurture them, to see them reach their fullest potential.

Through red eyes, she saw the world as it really was. It was filled with magic. The scintillating colors never remained the same. Magic twisted and flowed, turning and spinning, never still. Waves of it coursed through the earth beneath her feet. It radiated from the Fathers. The whole world was made of magic. Pure, untainted, waiting to be channeled and used.

A movement at the corner of her eye caught her attention. Teska turned. A member of the resistance shouted something and brandished a sword. He charged toward the Fathers. Teska watched him move through the world. The magic warped away from him. It did not want to be corrupted by such baseness, such *flesh*. With every footstep, the eddies of magic in the ground fled.

He was a blight. A pestilence. His very existence was an affront, an assault against magic.

Teska jerked her head in the man's direction. He flew into the air, across the street, and slammed into a building.

As everyone watched, the man's high-pitched shrieks silenced as something unseen pressed him harder and harder against the stone. His bones snapped. Blood spewed from his ears, nose and mouth. Another second, and his ribs caved in. His skull burst like an egg. The body slid down the front of the building, leaving behind a viscous, bloody smear.

Teska looked at the Fathers. All of them grinned.

I am Vaelok Strang, one voice said when her gaze fell on the noseless one with the silver braided beard. *First of the Fathers. Welcome. We have waited an eternity for you.*

She looked at each of the Fathers in turn and a different voice introduced himself. But there were more voices in her mind than creatures in front of her.

Our bodies have been destroyed, Callodin Valhalla whispered. *I am no more, except for my power that was stored in the Flame and which now resides in you.*

The same is true of me, Nem'Kai the Masaga said.

The voices of Jaccomus Veidt, Maggard Blackscar, and Klaus Loedac all said the same. They had not had time to transmigrate into new bodies. They were dead, gone forever. Only their power, stored in the sword, remained.

Strang nodded and gestured around the street. Teska saw more congregants—more flesh that would corrupt and taint her magic. She thrust her arms in front of her and spoke words she did not know, but which came as easily as her own thoughts.

The remaining resistance members felt an invisible force sweep them into the air, pinning them against buildings. Their screams vanished, replaced by snapping bones. One by one, they were ground into the facades the way someone would extinguish a tabák.

"Excellent, Teska Vaun!" Strang shouted.

She turned her red eyes upon him. He was the Undying One, the leader.

But she was now something *more*.

"Teska Vaun is dead," she said with joyous finality. "You will address me as *the Crimson Mother*."

"Stay down!" Tua whispered.

Thorne lay on his side behind a pile of rubble. Pressed against his back, Tua had both arms wrapped around Thorne's torso. Tua was smaller, but Thorne struggled to break his friend's grip.

"Stop it!" Tua said to Thorne's shoulder blade. "If you get up, we are dead."

"But Tes! I've got to—"

Tua clamped a hand over Thorne's mouth. As he did, he felt Thorne wiggling from his grasp.

"For God's sake, man, *be silent!* They are not paying any attention to us. Do not do anything to change that."

Thorne growled through Tua's fingers. "I can't— I can't just lay here! I've got to help her!" His body trembled with adrenaline, fear and fatigue.

"We *will* help her. I promise you. But we cannot do that now. Not with them here."

Both men had seen the Three Witches fall. They had witnessed Teska annihilate the Crusaders and barely managed to hide in time. They clung to their hiding spot as their allies had been crushed to death before their eyes. By luck or fate, they had escaped notice in the furor.

Tua removed his hand.

"What's *wrong* with her?" Thorne asked in a desperate, agonized whisper. He was filled with an aching hollowness. Like when Merrick and Darien died—yet it was different. Stronger, more intense. There was grief and denial but also something else. Something grave. A vehement sense of separation. Someone precious, whom he could not live without, was slipping from him. And he was powerless to stop it.

"I am not sure," Tua replied, "but I have a nasty idea."

"Tell me."

He sighed. "From what we have learned about the Flame and the Crimson Fathers—from the resistance and Teska—I believe she has somehow *absorbed* the magic in that sword. One of the Fathers said something about a 'receptacle.' I pray I am wrong, but…"

Thorne nodded. "But your gut tells you otherwise."

Tua did not reply.

They heard the leader praising Teska, and then her voice, menacing and hard, "Teska Vaun is dead. You will address me as *the Crimson Mother*."

Thorne stiffened and tried to raise his head. Tua tightened his hold. "No no no," he said to Thorne's back again.

"She's not dead!" Thorne said through clenched teeth. "She's not!"

"I know. But shut up or you will get us killed!"

The Father with the hairy, clawed appendage turned. "Listen! Did you hear something?"

Save for the crackling of the fires, the street had grown silent as a cemetery. Heat still rose from the crevices. Snow swirled through the smoke.

The two men remained motionless.

"If they come over here," Thorne whispered, "let me go. I'm not going to die on my back."

Tua nodded. "We are in agreement. My sword is nearby. I do not wish to be crushed like a bug. Or taken by the Fathers."

Braun broke the silence. "It wasss nothing. Jussst falling ssstonesss."

Even though Tua still held him, Thorne shifted positions. He peered through a gap in the rubble.

Teska stood before the Fathers, still holding the Flame.

Swing, Tes! Kill them! Thorne almost shouted it out loud but caught himself. *All she needs to do is step forward and she can end them forever! Why doesn't she use the sword?*

Red curls framed the beautiful face—now savaged by an expression of supreme arrogance. It shocked Thorne. He had never seen her so callous, so imperious. So *twisted*. She stood with a regal air, as if performing a role in a traveling show.

But her eyes…

Baleful red light shone from her eyes. Supernatural. Primitive.

Demonic.

She tossed the Flame on the ground. "Form the circle," she ordered.

The Fathers exchanged glances but obeyed without protest.

"You know what must be done," she told them.

The Fathers began to chant. Teska made invisible signs in the air as she stared at the sword. The Fathers pointed their palms toward it. Teska raised her hands, then brought them down as if she were smoothing a quilt. Purple and red light shimmered on the crimson blade. There was a loud snap, like an icy tree branch breaking, and the light disappeared.

Teska reached down and lifted the heavy weapon with one hand. As she held it in front of her, the blade began to flake away. Rust-colored bits of ash joined the swirling snow. In less than a minute, the massive blade had disintegrated. She tossed the grip and hilt into a crevice.

"Now there is nothing to fear," she said, her voice frigid and haughty. "We are supreme. Deiparia is ours."

What must have been laughter from the Fathers, but sounded to Thorne like millstones grinding together, rose from the circle. Thorne's stomach convulsed. He thought he might vomit.

"HAIL THE CRIMSON MOTHER!" Phaeddark Deathlord gurgled. They all repeated it.

A tear slid through the grime on Thorne's cheek. It took all his resolve to stay hidden and silent. Later, he would be thankful for Tua's levelheadedness. But now he ached with despair.

Teska Vaun—the Crimson Mother—surveyed the carnage in the street. As her gaze drifted over his hiding place, Thorne thought he saw a flicker in her eyes, a waning of the redness.

Or maybe it was just what he wanted to see.

36
MILLENNIUM

FRIDAY, JANUARY 1, 1000 AE

The first day of the new millennium dawned bright and cold on Attagon. No clouds marred the blue-streaked sky that looked as if it had been painted on glass. Streamers of smoke rose across the city. Even though this was a Feast Day—and a unique one, at that—there were no festivities in the streets. Troubadours and minstrels had no songs to sing. Thespians left their stages empty. There were no cavorting acrobats to thrill the children—only a solemn, haunting pall where life should have thrived.

In the wake of the previous day's chaos, the Church had issued a decree. Posels had tromped through the muddy slush, nailing it to posts and walls. Anxious, frightened faces watched through shutters and around doors. When the messengers had moved on, congregants spilled into the streets to read the proclamation.

> THE RESISTANCE IS CRUSHED BUT DANGER REMAINS.
>
> ANYONE WITH INFORMATION ON THE RESISTANCE OR THE ENODIA COMMUNION IS ORDERED TO REPORT TO ANY MEMBER OF THE PARACLETIAN ORDER.
>
> REWARDS WILL BE GIVEN FOR INFORMATION THAT LEADS TO A CAPTURE.
>
> HOUSE-TO-HOUSE SEARCHES ARE UNDERWAY. ANYONE CAUGHT HARBORING HERETICS OR TRAITORS WILL BE EXECUTED IMMEDIATELY AND ALL PROPERTIES AND POSSESSIONS FORFEITED TO THE CHURCH.

> THE HEIROMONARCH HAS BEEN MURDERED
> BY THE RESISTANCE AND THE COMMUNION.
> A THREE-DAY PERIOD OF MOURNING
> BEGINS TOMORROW AT NOON.
>
> THE CHURCH IS GOD.

On the south side of Attagon, the palace rubble lay like a shattered dream. Only two of the Paracletian Order buildings had been damaged. Everything else from them to the foot of the mountain was obliterated. It would take months to pick through the debris. The death toll could not even be estimated at this point.

No one had found the bodies of the Three Witches. It was evident where they had landed from the scorched ground. But they had simply vanished. Whether they were alive or dead, no one knew.

The sisters of the Enodia Communion awoke from their fatigue-induced sleep to the news of what had transpired. They cowered behind bolted doors, as emptied of magic as a dry well. The younger ones would recover quicker than their elders. But all were still vulnerable.

Crusaders and Witchfinders hammered on doors throughout the city, often forcing themselves in and searching every nook and niche. They missed not an attic or cellar, loft or stable, business or home. By the end of the first day of the new millennium, Attagon's dungeons swelled with congregants. The Paracletian Order marching people down the street while mounted Crusaders looked on became a common sight.

❖ ❖ ❖

Only two resistance leaders remained—Thorne and Christopher St. Jordan. Along with Tua, they huddled together at Winpeskah Lake. They had already moved twice this morning as search parties had drawn too close. They sat shivering in a small building that had once been used for storage. They chanced no fire.

"What happens now?" St. Jordan asked, rubbing his hands together before stuffing them in the pockets of his heavy coat. His sixty-six years could be weighed by the heaviness in his voice.

Thorne looked around the cramped shack. There was little to see, just a few more chairs, some blocks of stone and a wheelbarrow. Sunlight filtered through weather-beaten boards, and the sky watched them through large holes in the roof.

For the last twenty-four hours, Thorne had functioned in a benumbed haze. The gnawing guilt and grief refused to give him a moment's respite. There was so much to process, and his brain just kept shutting down. Or returning to one thing.

Her eyes.

His stomach hurt. Whether from lack of food or yesterday's horrors, he was not sure. His heart kept a solitary vigil in his hollow chest. He stared at his hands, wondering why he could not see all the blood that was on them.

"Malachi?"

St. Jordan's voice tunneled into his consciousness. He looked at the haggard old man.

"What do we do now?"

Thorne shook his head and stared at the muddy floor.

"There are two paths before us, as I see it," Tua said, his tone measured and gentle. "The first is to disappear. Go into hiding. Make new lives for ourselves somewhere else. Maybe back in my homeland. The second would be to continue the fight against the Fathers and the Fifth Order."

Thorne looked up at him, brow creasing. *"Continue the fight?"* he repeated in disbelief. "There is no more fight! We lost! It's over."

"That is one way of looking at it," Tua replied.

"Just shut up."

St. Jordan cleared his throat. "Actually, Malachi, the resistance is not crushed. We still have all those who were guarding the witches. They weren't there. They aren't dead."

Thorne ran a hand through his hair and sighed. "They might as well be."

"Why do you say that?"

Thorne stared at the elderly man. "Minh Van. We assigned him to protect Teska, for the simple fact that he can't fight. Most of those who were given that detail can't—"

St. Jordan shook his head. "That's not true. A good many of them are quite capable of handling themselves."

Thorne snorted. "There aren't enough of them. And we have no more leaders. Besides us."

"Others will rise to positions of leadership," St. Jordan said.

"Not enough. And not before the Fifth Order can solidify its hold over everything." Thorne sighed again. "By the time it takes to ascertain who the best leaders would be and train them sufficiently, there won't be anybody left. The compliance camps will be overflowing."

Tua folded his arms. "My people had a saying. Every member of the tribe carries the whole of the tribe here"—he pointed to his forehead—"and here." He pointed to his heart. "So even a single person can carry the idea of freedom forward," Tua said.

"But one man can't fight the Church, can they?" Thorne barked.

Tua's eyes were a flinty gray, and he fixed them hard on Thorne. "*You* did."

"Yeah—and look what it got us. Who knows how many are dead? The resistance shattered. Hawkes and Warner—" He caught himself before the lump in his throat could escape. "And Teska…" Tears filled his eyes.

"Yes, all that is true," St. Jordan said. "But you are forgetting, Malachi—the resistance was *not* Attagon. There are an untold number of congregants throughout the realm who will join and resist. The Fifth Order may have broken the resistance *here*, but they have not crushed the *idea* of freedom. If anything, after yesterday's events, I believe it will only grow stronger."

Tua nodded. "I agree."

St. Jordan shivered again.

"Did you— Did you see her eyes?" Thorne asked in a small, wooden voice.

Both men nodded.

"Why did she do that? She knew she wasn't strong enough."

St. Jordan put a hand on Thorne's arm. "She wanted to help—probably *needed* to help. From what I've come to know of her, when she sets her mind to something…"

The ghost of a smile touched Thorne's mouth but disappeared. "Do you think she's… Do you think I'll…" He could not figure out what to say, much less how to say it, so he shook his head and lapsed into silence. Tears slipped down his cheeks.

St. Jordan squeezed his arm. "I do not believe she is dead."

"And I believe you *can* get her back," Tua added.

"Why do you say that?" Thorne asked, pawing tears from his face.

Tua stroked one of his braids. "Because I do not think she can maintain control of such power for long. I believe it has taken her over. The *essence*, I suppose, of the Fathers dwells within her. They will want that back, I would assume."

"Would giving that back to them…hurt her?"

"I do not know. I am not an expert in these matters."

"Do you think she's like Thurl was?"

Tua shrugged. "As I said, I do not know. I suspect there may be similarities." Then he quickly added, "But that does not mean she will—"

"What? That she'll kill herself? Like Thurl did?" Thorne asked. Hopelessness colored his words.

Tua shook his head. "No, of course not. But deep in my spirit, I feel that the only way she survives all of this is with you by her side."

Thorne felt he knew what Teska would be thinking.

If there's anything left of her in there to think.

Stop it! Stop thinking that way!

He knew that if even the tiniest fragment of her remained, she would be furious as a stirred-up hornet's nest. She would lash out and try to regain control. He had no doubt she would try and fight the dark power.

But how long can she do that? What will the Fathers do to her? And even if she is still fighting, how could I help her?

He was staring at the space between his boots when they heard footsteps outside. Tua was behind the door with his dagger out before Thorne even registered his movement. He knew he should draw his own weapon but was beyond caring. He was so tired of fighting.

The footsteps halted outside the door. The handle rattled.

One set of footsteps moved slowly around the shed, stopping occasionally at a crack, the sunbeams temporarily eclipsed. A second set remained at the door.

"Malachi?" a familiar voice whispered. "You in there?"

The footsteps returned to the front. "I can't see enough to tell if there's anyone inside," the second voice, also familiar, said.

Thorne nodded at Tua, who slid the bar off the door. He opened it. Hawkes and Warner stood there, grinning.

"Hey, Boss!" Warner exclaimed. "I told Tycho this is where you'd be!"

The sun crept toward the horizon as Thorne learned what had happened to his friends.

Immediately after the palace came down, Warner had fallen into the pit left behind. His descent was interrupted when he slammed into what he described as a "dome-like thing made of purple light." It was solid enough to support his weight and slowed his fall enough so he could slide down the curvature of the dome. Through its semitransparent surface, he saw rows of children on tables. The Fathers had cast a spell to protect the remainder of the children, which explained the Crusaders still about.

After thinking that he had lost Warner, Hawkes rejoined Grace. They led the children around the side of the mountain, taking shelter wherever they could during the aftershocks. They descended the north face and straggled back into Attagon late last night. They had missed everything that happened during the battle, although that was the only thing people talked about when they came back into town.

Hawkes had no intention of surrendering the children to the Paracletian Order—just like his compliance camp friend Oliver Wycroft had once done. He and Grace had secured the children in a warm stable, where they could rest. Hawkes had left to find Thorne and instructed Grace to round up anyone she trusted to help get the children back to their homes. That was the last he had seen of them.

The outcome of yesterday's battle devastated Hawkes and Warner. They apologized for not being there to help fight.

Thorne was glad to have them back. It assuaged a tiny portion of his pain and lifted his spirit somewhat. He was proud of them for saving so many children. At least something good had come from this.

But the Crimson Fathers—and the Crimson Mother—reigned supreme. They still had children across the realm to keep their Crusaders going. And Thorne felt it would not be long before the rescued children were retaken and enslaved all over again. The Fifth Order was stronger than ever. They no longer needed to keep up the pretense of a Heiromonarch. And if the rumors that they had heard were true, an army was assembling at Last Chapel. Reports smuggled out of that city told of Crusaders and members of the Paracletian Order training companies of cutthroats and mercenaries.

Across Deiparia, the first day of the new millennium went on like the first day of any new year. There were celebrations in homes and feasts in villages. Congregants made promises about the things they would do better in the coming year. Wine and ale and beer flowed. Farmers tended to their livestock. Stories of ages past were retold around fireplaces. It would be several days before they received news of the collapse of the palace, the Heiromonarch's death and the subsequent assumption of power by the Crimson Fathers.

Life would go on as before—except with fewer children. The Fifth Order would continue to take them as necessary, abandoning the ruse of educating or blessing them, and relocate them to special centers. The Crusaders who had fallen at the Battle of Witchfire Mountain, as it came to be known, were soon replaced. Parents who attempted to rescue their children found themselves serving sentences in cold, miserable jail cells. This fueled clandestine support of the resistance.

In compliance camps around the realm, inmates dug graves for those who had been slaughtered when the Freethinker Law went into effect. Some said as many as three thousand people had been executed. Others claimed the number was much higher.

Matthias Hart and his daughters had made it back to Three Waters, where he served as the top resistance leader in the city. His family had gone into hiding.

High in the Great Appian Mountains, in the village of Brookhaven, Lillia Pittman and her children had settled in for the winter. Her youngest had taken ill just before they were to leave, forcing a change in plans. She still held out hope that her husband was alive and looked forward to their reunion when winter was over.

Demerra, Cassidy and Cassandra Gray had reached their cousin's house near the eastern coast. It would be weeks before they learned of Dario's death.

Attagon mourned and buried its dead as bodies were discovered beneath the palace rubble. More snow hindered excavation efforts, and it would not be until the middle of April that the final corpse would be laid to rest. Repairs commenced almost immediately on the cathedral and other damaged buildings, providing more employment and boosting the economy.

Eluruum would be made public on the first day of February. The Fifth Order and the Church promised to expand the borders of Deiparia so that congregants could "spread out, enjoy full and fruitful lives and share in the reward of the righteous." Soon, the Church promised, the Tex'ahn lands would be open for colonization and commerce. Of course, the idea of new land meant new opportunities for merchants and artisans, as well as those who thrived on the underbelly of society.

For three days after the Battle of Witchfire Mountain, the Crimson Fathers and the Crimson Mother sequestered themselves in the cathedral. No one saw them, save for two overlooked laborers, who were clearing out one of the crypts. Their sworn-on-the-Testament, eyewitness stories of conjured demons, blood sacrifices and someone called "The Soulstealer," made for wild gossip and raging speculation. It also kept the two in free drinks until more salacious news came around.

On Monday, January 4th, the Fathers and the Mother departed Attagon. They would journey to Three Waters, to their citadel in the headlands of the Appian Mountains, before joining their army in Last Chapel. No one saw them leave. No one knew how they traveled. One day, they were in the cathedral, and the next, it was empty save for the workmen allowed to enter.

Malachi Thorne, Tycho Hawkes, Solomon Warner, Tua'Ahtaki and Christopher St. Jordan hid, tended to their wounds—although the one to Thorne's heart refused succor—and tried to piece together what would happen next.

37

MOBILIZATION

WEDNESDAY, JANUARY 13, 1000 AE

The Crimson Fathers and Crimson Mother reached their citadel on Monday, January 11th. They lost no time in preparing for the transference of their power. Their sorcerous arts and eldritch rituals had been completed earlier that day, and the surviving Fathers now held all their current magic, plus that which they had lost when they were killed centuries ago.

The magic of the five deceased Fathers, however, could not be claimed by the survivors. It was decided that the Crimson Mother would continue to retain that power. She now had power equivalent to five of the seven existing Fathers. Following the transference ritual, they gathered in the great hall of their citadel.

A dozen purple-robed acolytes with intricate tattooed scalps stood around the room, heads bowed, awaiting any command from their masters. The voluminous robes kept them warm against the bitter cold that poured in through the high-arched windows. The Fathers and the Mother ignored it.

Vaelok Strang stood with his hands clasped behind his back. His head was lowered against his chest, causing his unbraided silver beard to look like a spider web against his robe. He turned from the window and joined the others at a long mahogany table. He sat in the head chair.

"What is the status of the army?" he asked Temias the Bonesorrow.

"The army is doing well, Undying One. We will be able to dispatch our reconnaissance teams by the end of February. The first advance will be ready at the beginning of March. Rann estimates the infantry will set out on the first of May."

"Have we word from our scouts and spies?"

Temias nodded, his mucus-like eyes never moving. "We do. Over the past few weeks, the redvalks they took with them have returned. They report a land more than capable of fulfilling our desires—rich in timber and ores. There are scattered villages, whose only protection are the militias they are able to raise. Our army will obliterate them. Cities such as Dallastown will prove more challenging, but only because of their size. They have minimal defenses and no armies."

"Excellent," Strang said, resting his elbows on the table and steepling his pallid fingers.

"What are the projected losses among our troops?" the Crimson Mother asked.

"Irrelevant! Unimportant!" Avhorus Godfury exclaimed. His tongue flicked across the barbed wire below his mouth.

Strang nodded. "Avhorus is correct. The army is expendable. They are to fight and conquer and die when necessary. Those who survive will be rewarded."

"What is that reward?" she asked.

Since arriving, Teska had donned a brilliant crimson dress, split up the sides. It had long sleeves with embroidered cuffs and a black metal cincture around the waist. The hem brushed against her black boots. A carmine corset encircled her torso and was arrayed with a multitude of thimble-length spikes. Her curly red hair cascaded over her shoulders.

Temias looked at her. "The spoils, of course. They may take whatever they wish and do whatever they wish with those we subjugate. Such is the nature of warfare."

"If you like, I can guide you to Dallastown. I have been there before," she said.

"An offer we shall embrace," Phaeddark Deathlord replied.

Strang lay his hands on the tabletop. "Yes, you have witnessed much that will be of benefit to our plans. I look forward to hearing what you have to say."

"It will be my pleasure," she purred. She looked down at her body. "At least this little bitch will be good for something."

"Let us prepare ourselves, Death Brothers—and Sister. In a fortnight, we depart for Last Chapel. Kaige, see to the preparation of our secondary bodies. We lost our primaries when the palace fell. We must have new ones before we leave. We do not wish to be like Maggard Blackscar. Unprepared."

"As you command, Undying One."

"What of your Death Brothers who perished in Attagon?" the Mother asked. "Did they not have bodies prepared for such an eventuality?"

Deathlord offered her a regal nod. "They did, Queen Mother. However, the destruction of the palace also resulted in the destruction of the secondary bodies. When our brothers expired, their host forms had already been extinguished."

"But Nem'Kai the Masaga died before the palace fell," she said.

Strang nodded. "That is true. But even if he was able to transmigrate to his primary replacement body, it would have been destroyed beneath the palace." He rose and returned to the window. The wind blew his beard and clothing as he stared into the west.

Nothing could stop them now. The Flame no longer held any threat. None in the realm could dare stand against them. Their powers were at their peak. Soon, the land to the southwest would become theirs.

Centuries ago, the Heiromonarch had used and discarded them, fearful of their combined power. He betrayed them. Now there was no Heiromonarch—nor anyone else—who could stand in their way. Soon the whole world would see what they could do. Their power was absolute, their dominion unchallengeable.

Among the Enodia Communion, some speculated that the Three Witches still lived. But no one knew for certain. In their absence, the Nahoru'brexia stepped forward and assumed leadership of the witch cult. This did not go without conflict or controversy. A key point of contention was Teska Vaun.

After hearing of her defection to the Crimson Fathers, the elderly brexia demanded her exile from the sisterhood. The Nahoru'brexia refused to treat one of their own in such a manner. Nor did the older witches want to surrender their control to the younger ones. And so, the seeds for civil war were sown.

Several young women among the Nahoru'brexia vied for power and leadership. Their discord presented the older witches with an opportunity for a coup. For fifty-seven days, between January and April, the Communion was rent asunder by dissention, distrust and accusation.

On Tuesday, March 30th, a council of seven Nahoru'brexia—who vowed to aid Teska Vaun however they could—claimed complete authority over the Enodia Communion. But not all the old wounds were forgiven.

Malachi Thorne traveled north toward Knox. Due to the weather, the journey took an extra two days. He rode inside an enclosed wagon that Christopher St. Jordan had procured for them. Warner rode his horse behind the wagon with the other mounts tied to it. Hawkes and Tua sat on the driver's bench, exchanging stories.

They headed north for two reasons. The first was because they could no longer risk staying in Attagon. Thorne knew that if they were captured, he would never see Teska again.

The second reason was because he *needed* to find her. She would be with the Crimson Fathers—at least that was what he hoped. That meant either Last Chapel or Three Waters. At Knox, he could position himself to push on if the path lay farther north. If it led west, then Knox was closer to Last Chapel.

The Crimson Fathers had raised an army. Rumors filled the taverns and were carried along by pilgrims and merchants. The army was mobilizing in Last Chapel, which indicated to Thorne that his path lay in that direction. He did not know when or if the Fathers would be there. But before long someone would see them. Word of their plans would become public. He and his companions intended to lay low in Knox and wait.

After several days of uncertainty, and nights besieged by sorrow and guilt, Thorne knew what he had to do.

He had left St. Jordan in charge of what remained of the resistance in Attagon. The old man was correct. There were still people in the city—maybe even more now—who could continue the fight. It would take time to reorganize enough to make a difference, but they could at least get back on their feet. Thorne did not envy them. The streets crawled with members of the Paracletian Order and Crusaders. Meeting together would be ten times harder now.

But his own future was just as dangerous.

He would find Teska, and he would do whatever was necessary to bring her back. He did not understand magic, certainly had no aptitude for it and had no idea how he would rescue her from the very heart of evil itself.

Some of the members of the resistance had volunteered to come with him, but Thorne had turned them down.

"You're needed here," he had told them. "You can accomplish more here than spending time on the road."

He appreciated their enthusiasm and willingness to take such risks for him. But the greater risks lay in the streets and taverns and alleys of Attagon. He might be going to save Teska, but they were fighting for freedom. And as they had discovered again and again, the price for freedom was paid in blood.

Save Teska, Thorne thought. *That's what I want to do. But—*

The unfinished thought was a patch of mold in his mind. No matter what he did, he was unable to remove it. And like mold, it spread slowly, methodically, darkening his thoughts with greater frequency. He tried to change his mindset, to see possibilities and hold to hope. Yet he found the despair waiting for him when he closed his eyes at night. It joined him in the morning before he even climbed from his bedroll.

I want to save Teska—but what if I can't? What if she's lost forever?

Then the worst thought of all barreled in with relentless force and callous indifference to his feelings. It threatened to shatter his soul. It hurt his head just thinking it.

What if the only way to save her…is to kill her?

The first time it poisoned his mind, he had almost vomited. So horrifying and unthinkable was the notion. It haunted his every moment. He knew that Hawkes and Warner and Tua were also thinking it. They had to be. He hoped they would not bring it up. He did not know if he could talk about it without losing his mind.

When he sat watch late at night, and only the sound of snoring punctuated the falling snow, he stared into the sky and remembered a dream he once had. A red-haired woman had put her head on his shoulder and drifted off to sleep. She trusted him enough to be defenseless in a world that was falling apart. In that dream, he knew he would do whatever it took to keep her safe.

He would not stop until he found Teska, even if he had to fight every single solider in the Fathers' army. Then it would be *their* turn.

"I love you, Tes," he said to the bright stars, and whispered a prayer for her safety and her soul.

ACKNOWLEDGMENTS

To Vern and Joni Firestone at BHC Press: my thanks for your support and the excellent work you do. It's an honor and privilege to be part of such a fantastic publishing house.

To Tori Ladd: there aren't enough adjectives to describe what an amazing job she did as my editor. Not only did she suffer through my (many!) punctuation mistakes, she offered insights and suggestions that improved the story. The encouragement I found through her notes was most appreciated.

To the band Queensrÿche: for the song "Take Hold of the Flame," which was played many times to help shape the story and set the mood.

To my wife, Felicia: your constant encouragement and confidence in me means more to me than you know. I couldn't do this writing or this life without you.

To you, the reader: thank you so much for your support of *The Crimson Fathers*. I hope you enjoy this installment of the saga even more. Whether I met you at a signing, through social media or friends, I'm grateful to you and honored that you've taken time out of your busy lives to be a part of this story.

ABOUT THE AUTHOR

J. Todd Kingrea is the author of the Deiparian Saga, which includes *The Witchfinder*, *The Crimson Fathers*, and *Bane of the Witch* (slated for a 2024 release). An ordained pastor, he lives with his wife in Tennessee with their dogs, plenty of 80s metal, and an ever-expanding movie collection.

CPSIA information can be obtained
at www.ICGtesting.com
Printed in the USA
LVHW110447251022
731487LV00023B/896/J